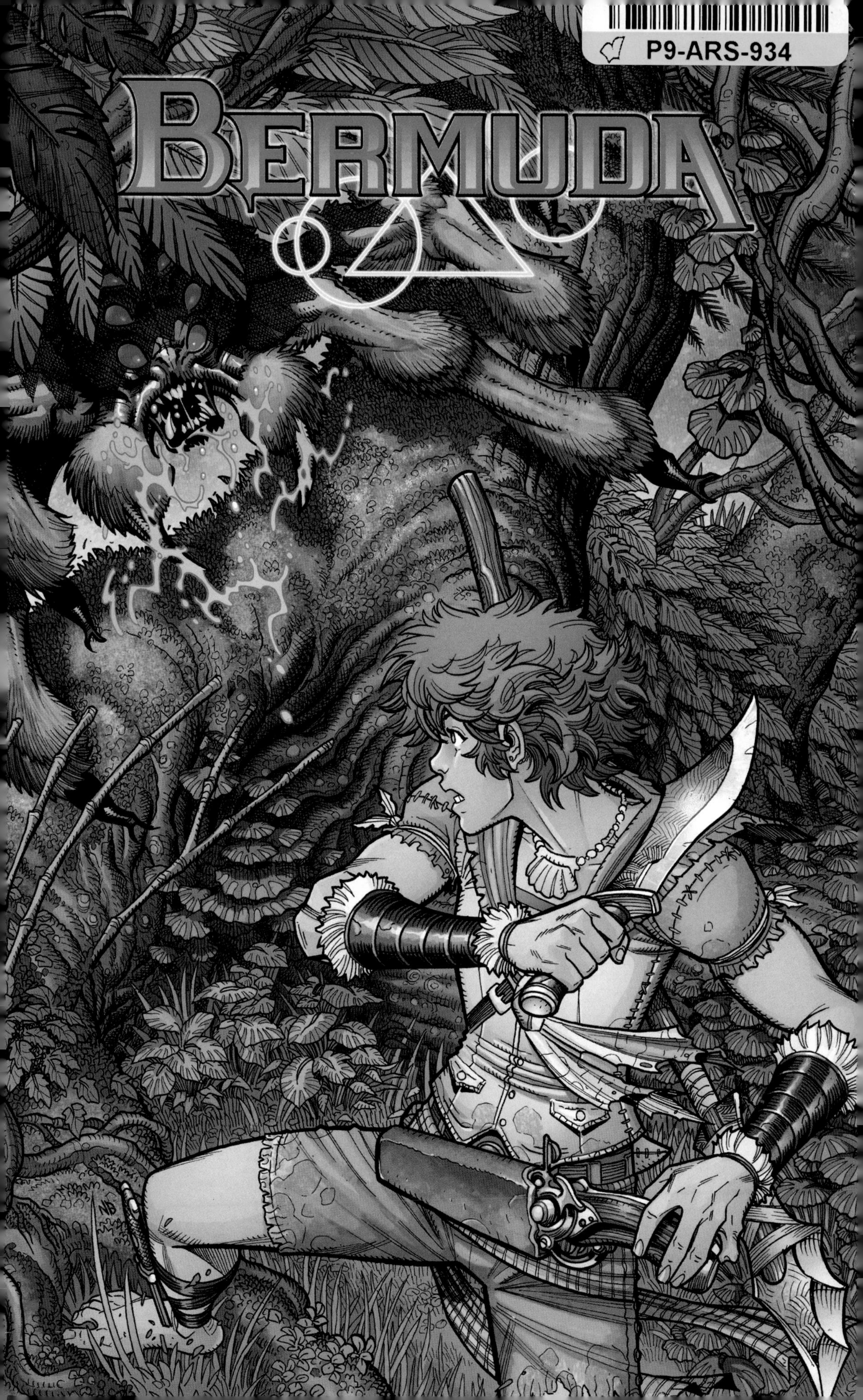
BERMUDA

IDW

Facebook: **facebook.com/idwpublishing**
Twitter: **@idwpublishing**
YouTube: **youtube.com/idwpublishing**
Instagram: **@idwpublishing**

ISBN: 978-1-68405-733-7   25 24 23 22   1 2 3 4

Cover Art by
Nick Bradshaw

Proofreader
Scott Tipton

Editor
Scott Dunbier

Collection Design by
Nathan Widick

Nachie Marsham, Publisher
Blake Kobashigawa, VP of Sales
Tara McCrillis, VP Publishing Operations
John Barber, Editor-in-Chief
Mark Doyle, Editorial Director, Originals
Erika Turner, Executive Editor
Scott Dunbier, Director, Special Projects
Lauren LePera, Managing Editor
Joe Hughes, Director, Talent Relations
Anna Morrow, Sr. Marketing Director
Alexandra Hargett, Book & Mass Market Sales Director
Keith Davidsen, Director, Marketing & PR
Topher Alford, Sr Digital Marketing Manager
Shauna Monteforte, Sr. Director of Manufacturing Operations
Jamie Miller, Sr. Operations Manager
Nathan Widick, Sr. Art Director, Head of Design
Neil Uyetake, Sr. Art Director, Design & Production
Shawn Lee, Art Director, Design & Production
Jack Rivera, Art Director, Marketing

Ted Adams and Robbie Robbins, IDW Founders

SCRIPT AND LETTERS BY
John Layman

ART AND MAIN COVERS BY
Nick Bradshaw

COLORS BY
Len O'Grady

Introduction

Here's the problem with working with an artist like Nick Bradshaw: the guy can draw anything, so you want him to draw everything. That was the biggest obstacle when I got the opportunity to create a book with him. What kind of book would we do? You know Nick is gonna knock it out of the park drawing monsters, so maybe we do a monster book. But… but… but… He'd also be great drawing creatures, lizards and bugs. Or pirates! Or crazy science fiction-y super tech! Or samurais!

You don't want to get locked into just one thing for the duration of an entire story, not when you have a guy who is just so amazing at drawing so many things. The solution, then, was to find a way so Nick could draw everything.

And thus, BERMUDA was born. The comic, that is.

It would be set on an island, a magical land untouched by time, so all those things I wanted Nick to draw could exist in the same place at the same time. And to get there, you'd have to cross through a door, a door in that mysterious region of the Atlantic where so many souls have gone inexplicably missing, a place that has long fascinated and intrigued me (and–admit it—you too!) …the "Bermuda Triangle."

Of course, we'd need a character to act as our guide to introduce us to this strange and amazing new world. Somebody tough, raised in this place, that would know the ropes and be able to survive its many dangers, cut from the same action-adventure cloth as Tarzan or Kamandi. The star of the book would be a feisty, fearless teen, with a great big generous heart beating beneath an attitude-filled exterior.

And thus, Bermuda was born. The character, that is.

Within these pages is Bermuda's first adventure, and an introduction to her home, the jungle island of Trangle. We only had four issues to pack this world with as much as we could, and thanks to my creative partners—Nick working his magic alongside colorist Len O'Grady and editor Scott Dunbier—we succeeded beyond my wildest dreams.

As much as I wanted to squeeze in everything, though, I couldn't find a place for the samurais. But, ya know… that's what sequels are for.

Welcome, friends, welcome to Trangle, the island that has a little bit of everything. We're happy you've come for a visit and hope you enjoy it as much we have!

John Layman
September 2021

To James and Paul and Jack, who inspired this book.
And then Nick and Len and Scott, partners in making it happen.

—JL

Bravery, strength, adventure, precociousness, love. These are all qualities I've been blessed to experience from a Grandmother who raised me, a Mother who loved me and my Partner Danica who grows with me every day. I'm surrounded by people who inspired so many little pieces (that is, if I've done my job right) you'll find in Bermuda.

—NB

For Tara, who stuck with me.

—LO

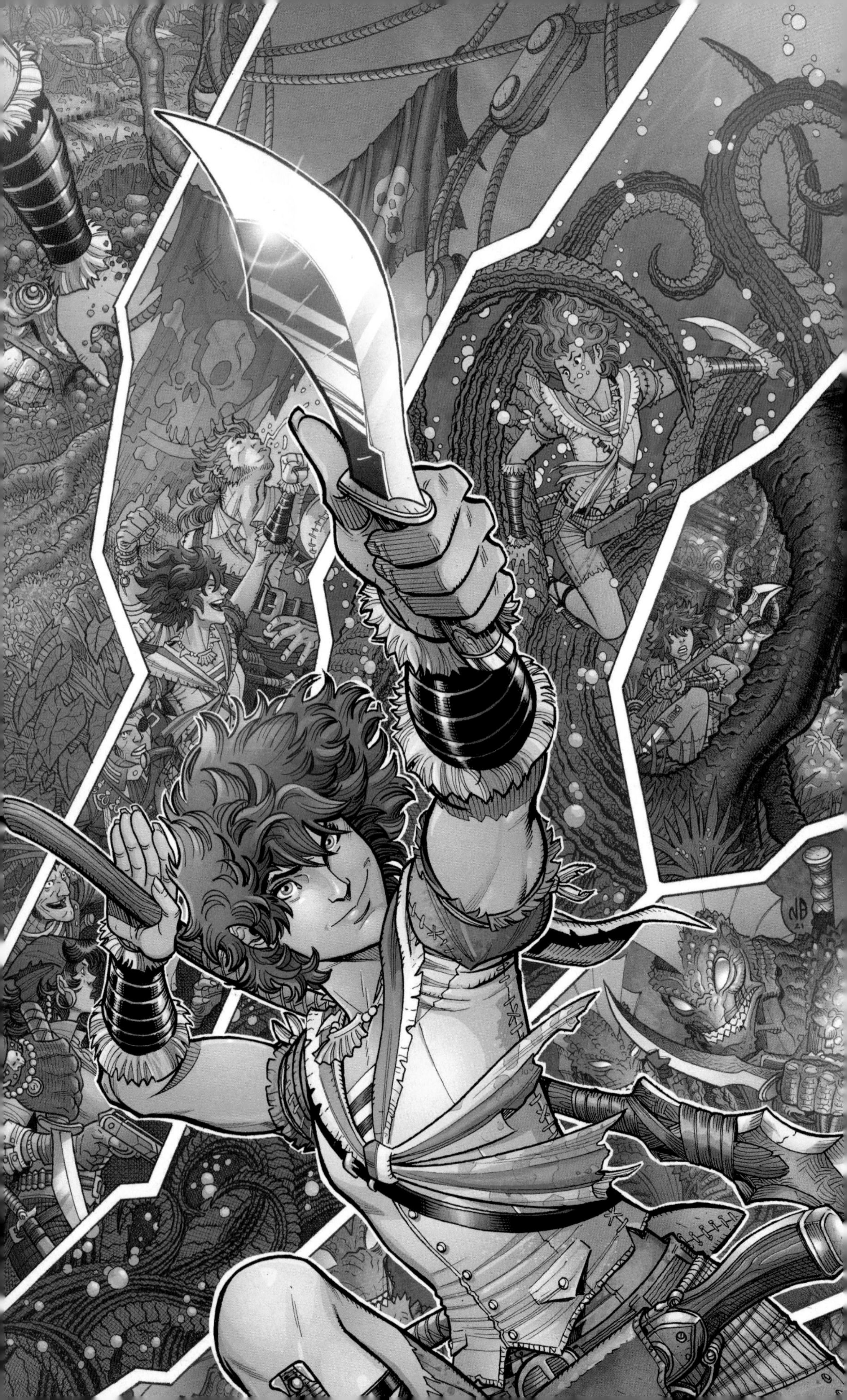

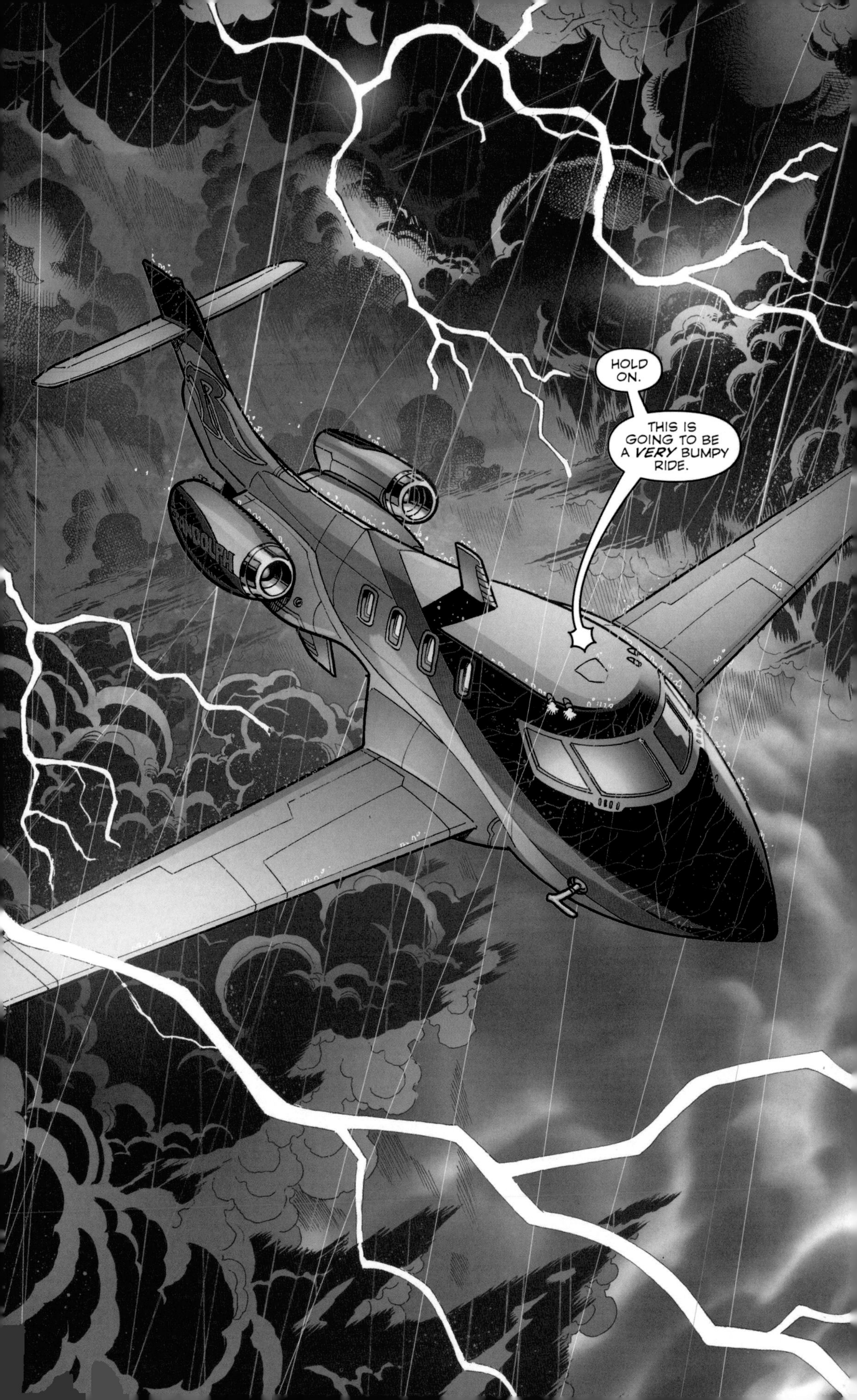
HOLD ON.
THIS IS GOING TO BE A *VERY* BUMPY RIDE.

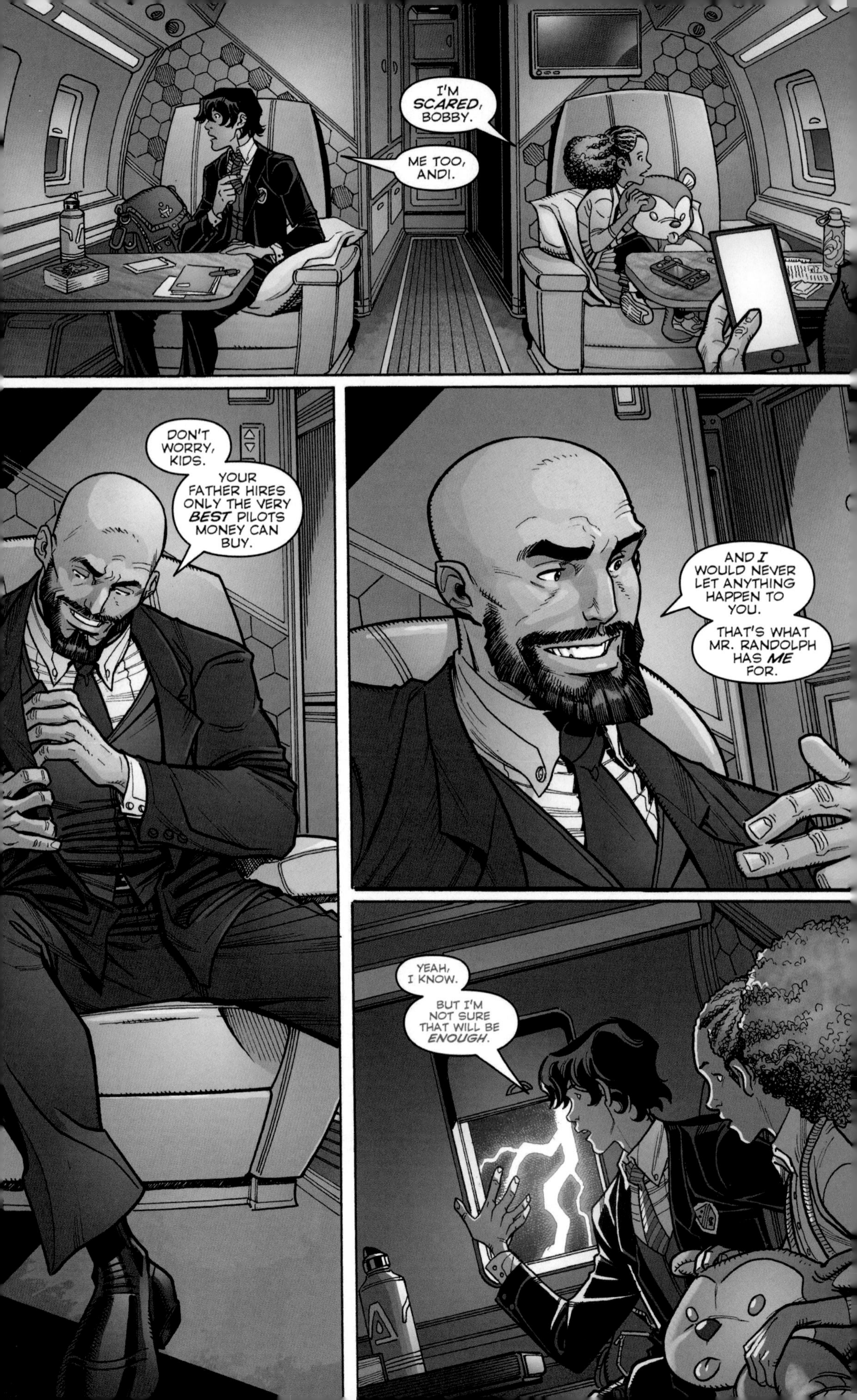
I'M SCARED, BOBBY.
ME TOO, ANDI.
DON'T WORRY, KIDS.
YOUR FATHER HIRES ONLY THE VERY BEST PILOTS MONEY CAN BUY.
AND I WOULD NEVER LET ANYTHING HAPPEN TO YOU.
THAT'S WHAT MR. RANDOLPH HAS ME FOR.
YEAH, I KNOW.
BUT I'M NOT SURE THAT WILL BE ENOUGH.

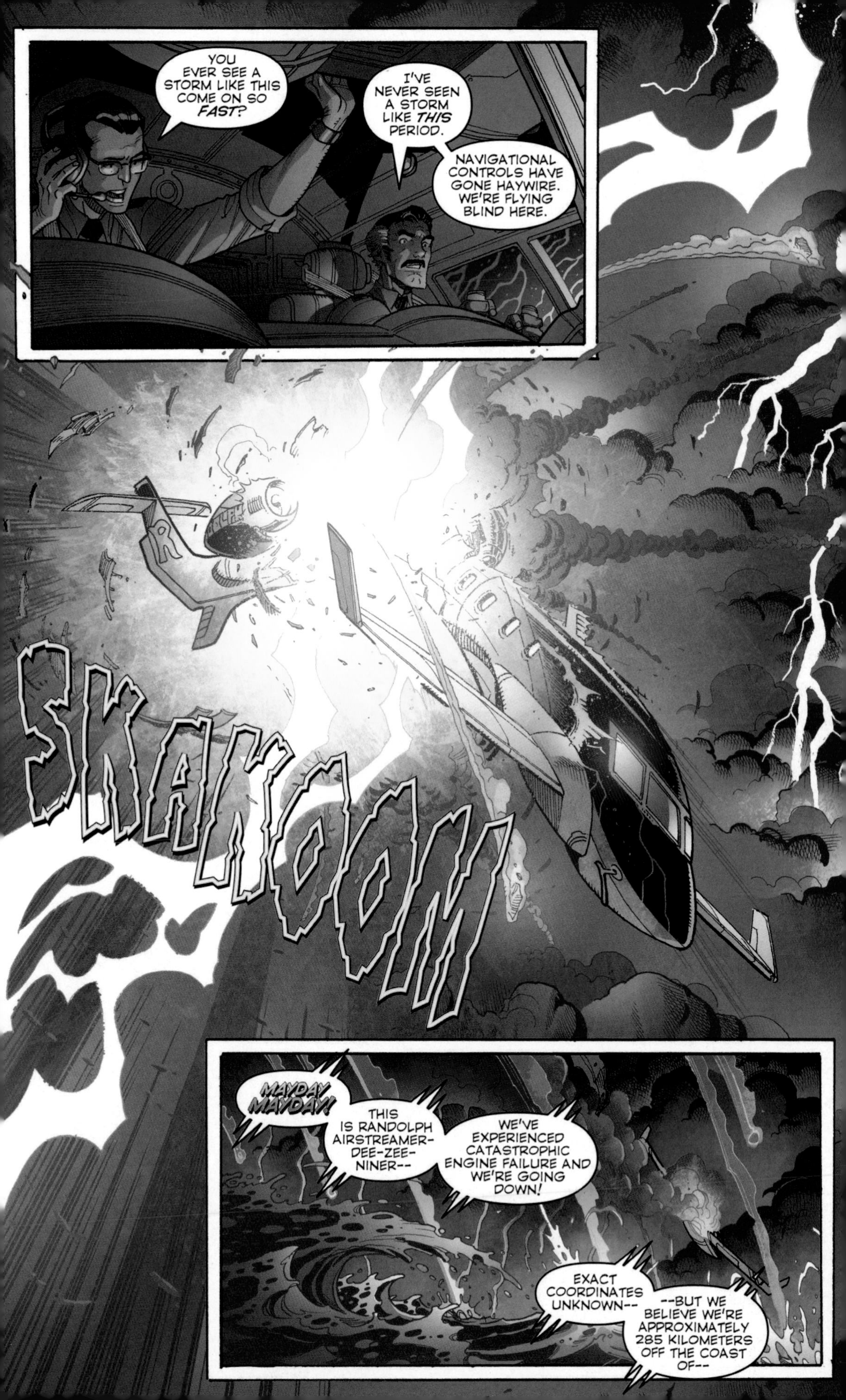

YOU EVER SEE A STORM LIKE THIS COME ON SO *FAST*?
I'VE NEVER SEEN A STORM LIKE *THIS* PERIOD.
NAVIGATIONAL CONTROLS HAVE GONE HAYWIRE. WE'RE FLYING BLIND HERE.
SKAROOM
MAYDAY MAYDAY!
THIS IS RANDOLPH AIRSTREAMER-DEE-ZEE-NINER--
WE'VE EXPERIENCED CATASTROPHIC ENGINE FAILURE AND WE'RE GOING DOWN!
EXACT COORDINATES UNKNOWN--
--BUT WE BELIEVE WE'RE APPROXIMATELY 285 KILOMETERS OFF THE COAST OF--

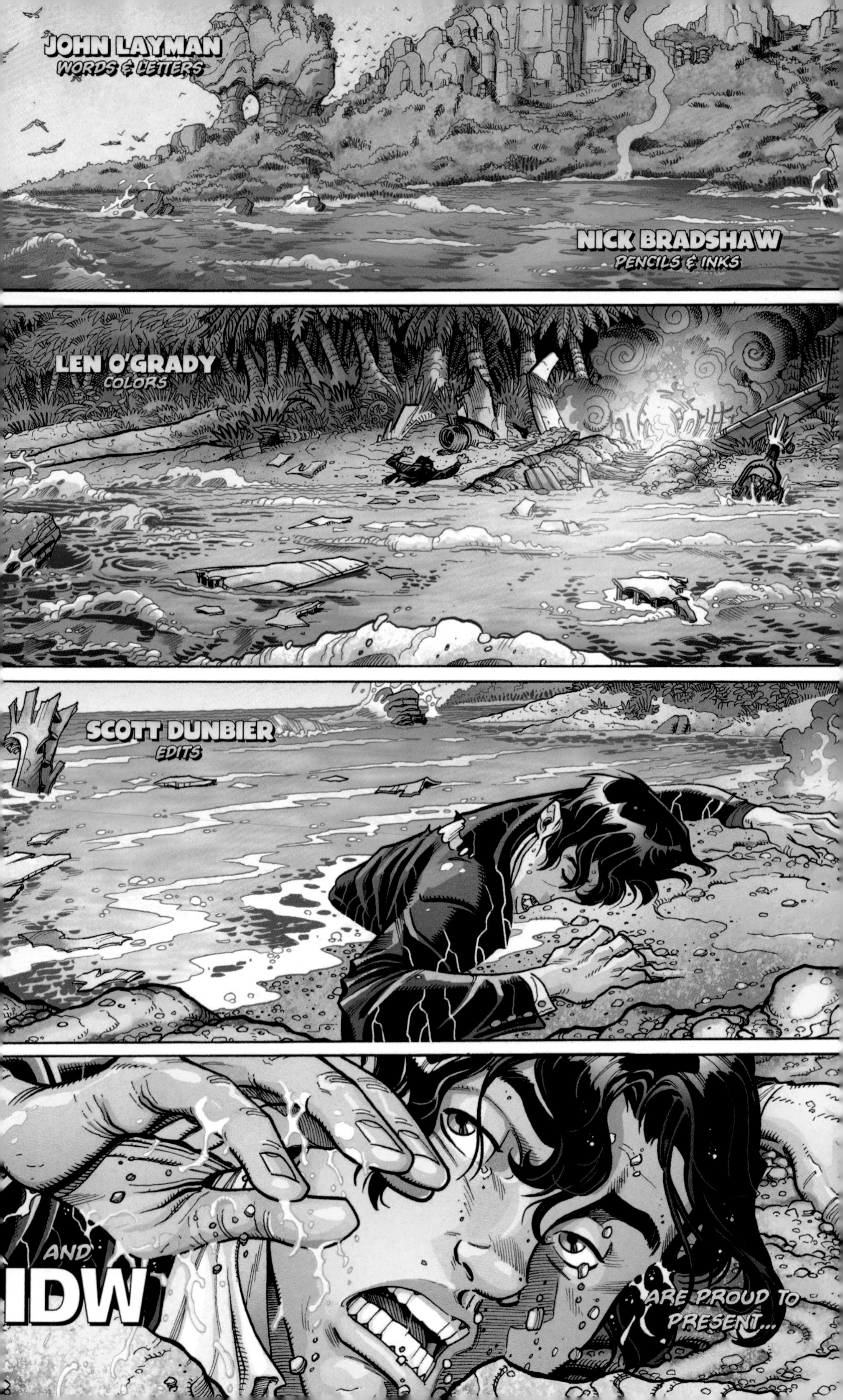

JOHN LAYMAN
WORDS & LETTERS
NICK BRADSHAW
PENCILS & INKS
LEN O'GRADY
COLORS
SCOTT DUNBIER
EDITS
AND
IDW
ARE PROUD TO PRESENT...

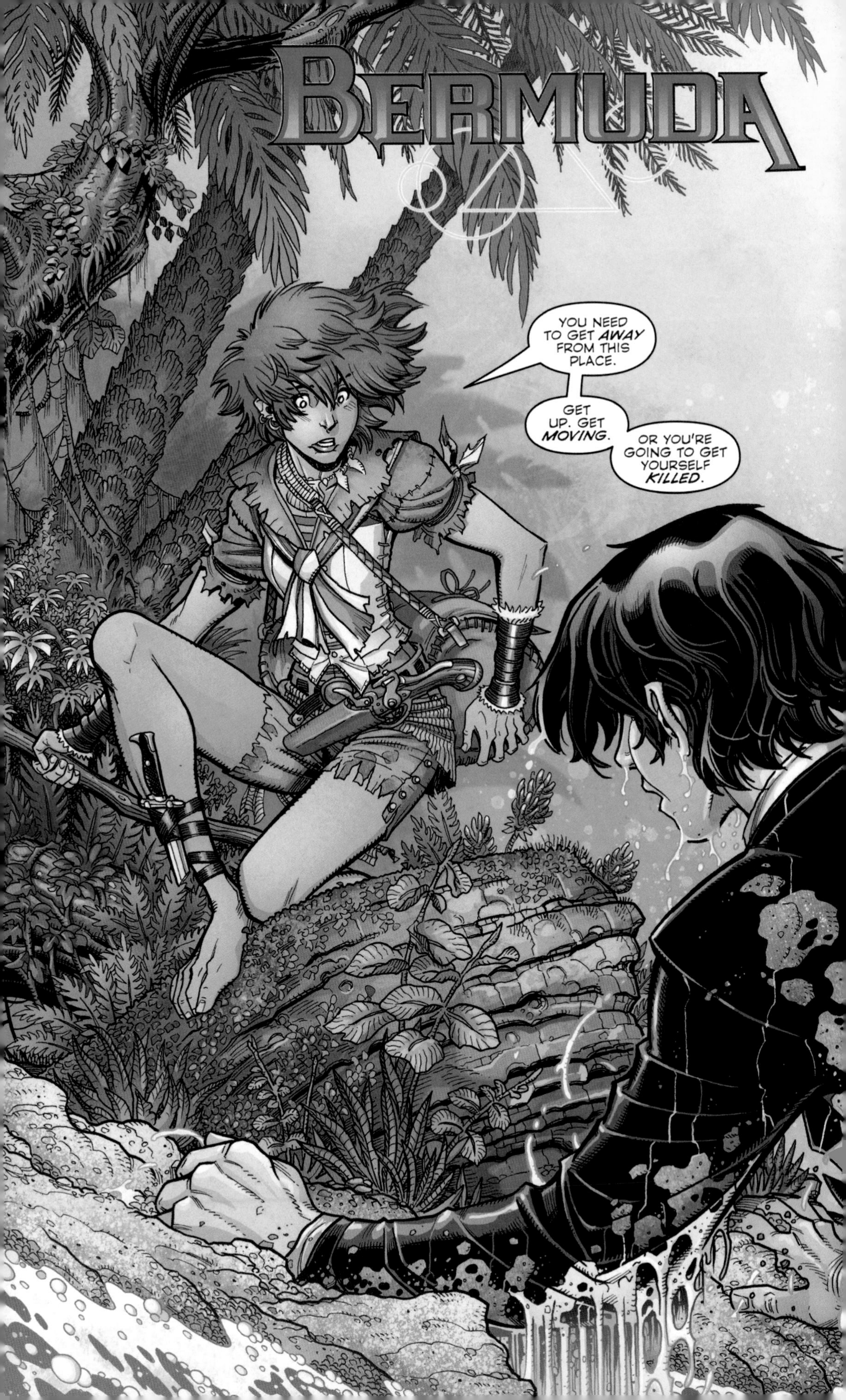
BERMUDA
YOU NEED TO GET AWAY FROM THIS PLACE.
GET UP. GET MOVING.
OR YOU'RE GOING TO GET YOURSELF KILLED.

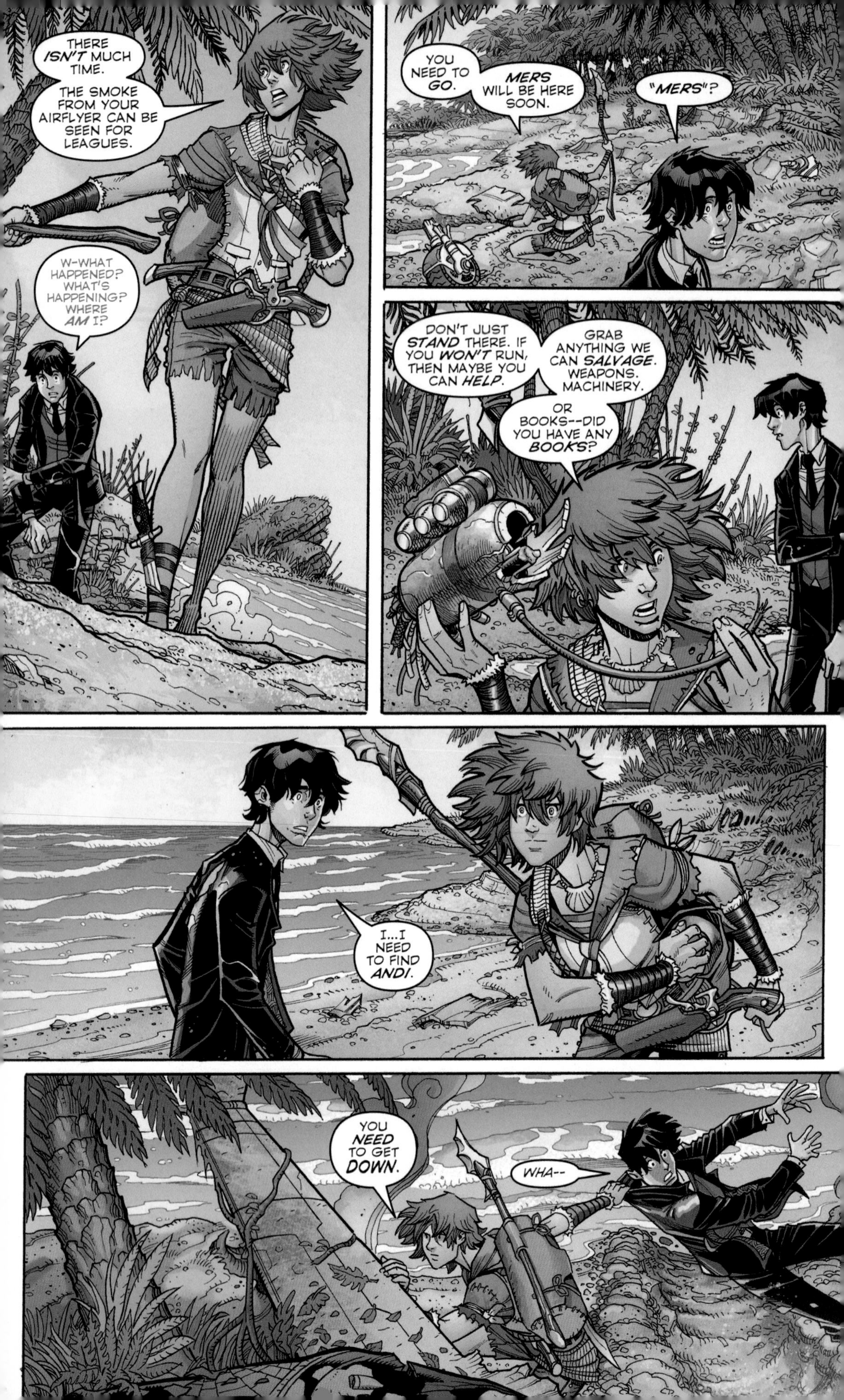
THERE ISN'T MUCH TIME.
THE SMOKE FROM YOUR AIRFLYER CAN BE SEEN FOR LEAGUES.
W-WHAT HAPPENED? WHAT'S HAPPENING? WHERE AM I?
YOU NEED TO GO.
MERS WILL BE HERE SOON.
"MERS"?
DON'T JUST STAND THERE. IF YOU WON'T RUN, THEN MAYBE YOU CAN HELP.
GRAB ANYTHING WE CAN SALVAGE. WEAPONS. MACHINERY.
OR BOOKS--DID YOU HAVE ANY BOOKS?
I...I NEED TO FIND ANDI.
YOU NEED TO GET DOWN.
WHA--

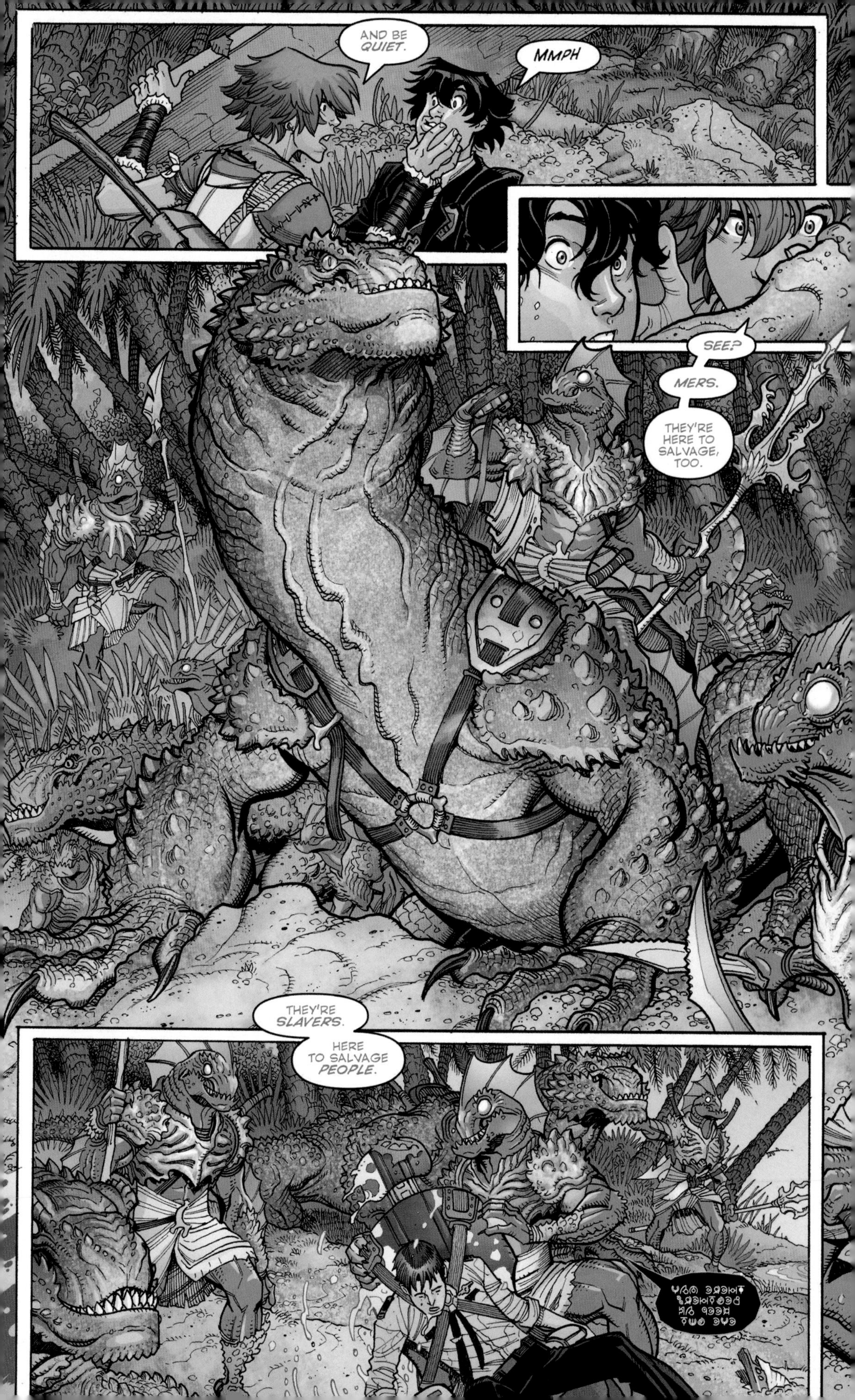
AND BE QUIET.
MMPH
SEE?
MERS.
THEY'RE HERE TO SALVAGE, TOO.
THEY'RE SLAVERS.
HERE TO SALVAGE PEOPLE.

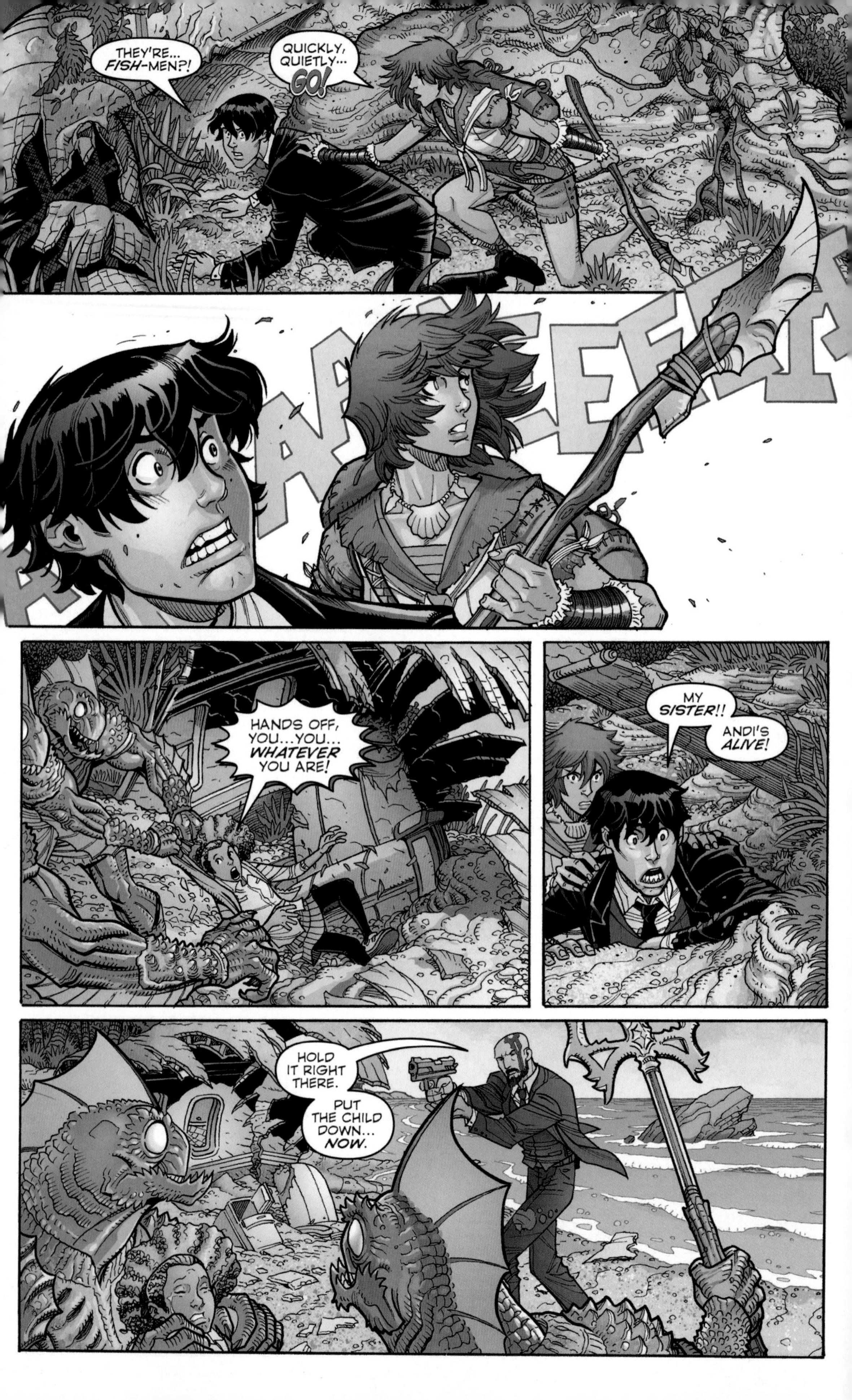

THEY'RE... FISH-MEN?!
QUICKLY, QUIETLY... GO!
HANDS OFF, YOU...YOU... WHATEVER YOU ARE!
MY SISTER!!
ANDI'S ALIVE!
HOLD IT RIGHT THERE.
PUT THE CHILD DOWN... NOW.

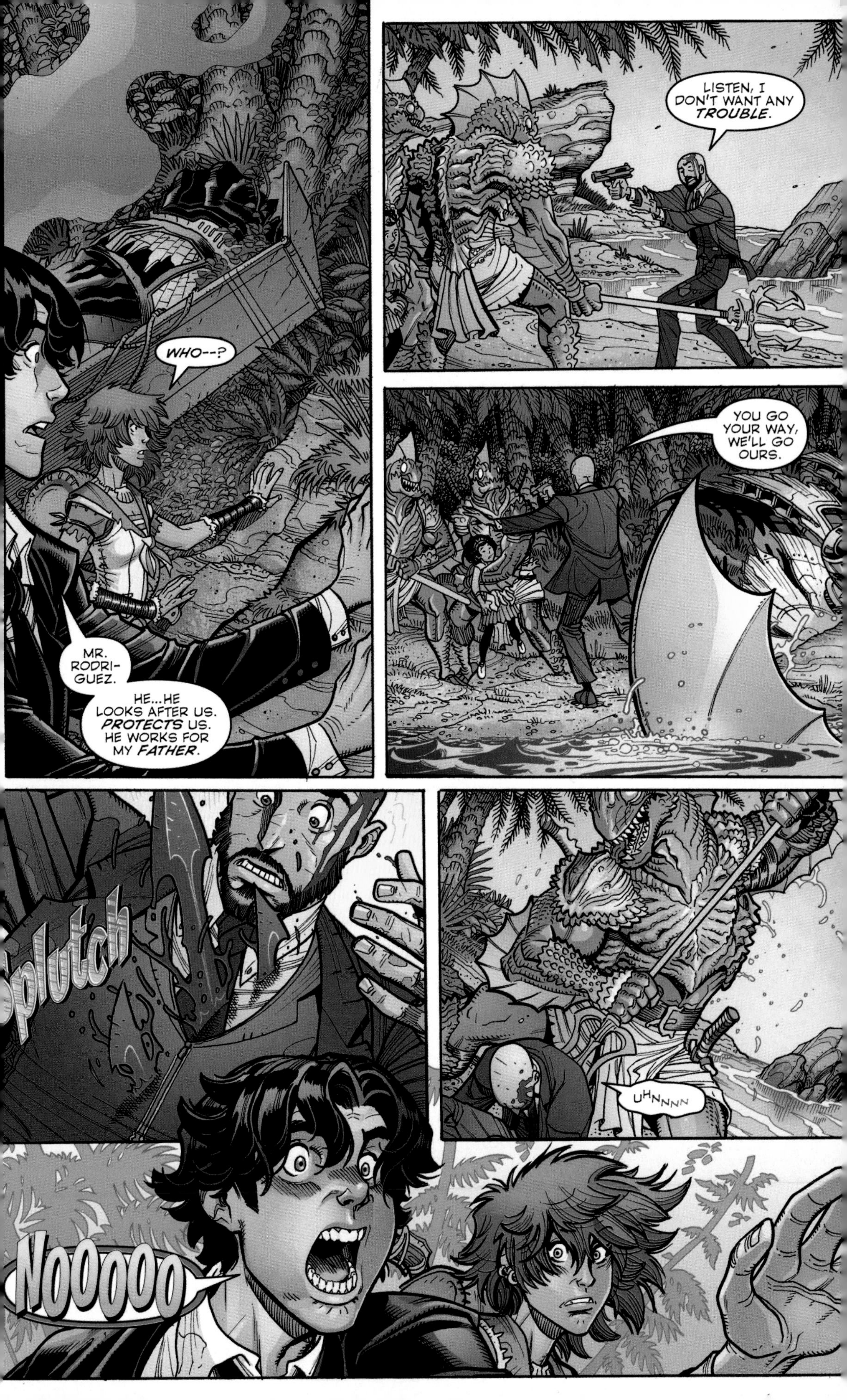
WHO--?
MR. RODRIGUEZ.
HE...HE LOOKS AFTER US. PROTECTS US. HE WORKS FOR MY FATHER.
LISTEN, I DON'T WANT ANY TROUBLE.
YOU GO YOUR WAY, WE'LL GO OURS.
SPLUTCH
UHNNNN
NOOOOO

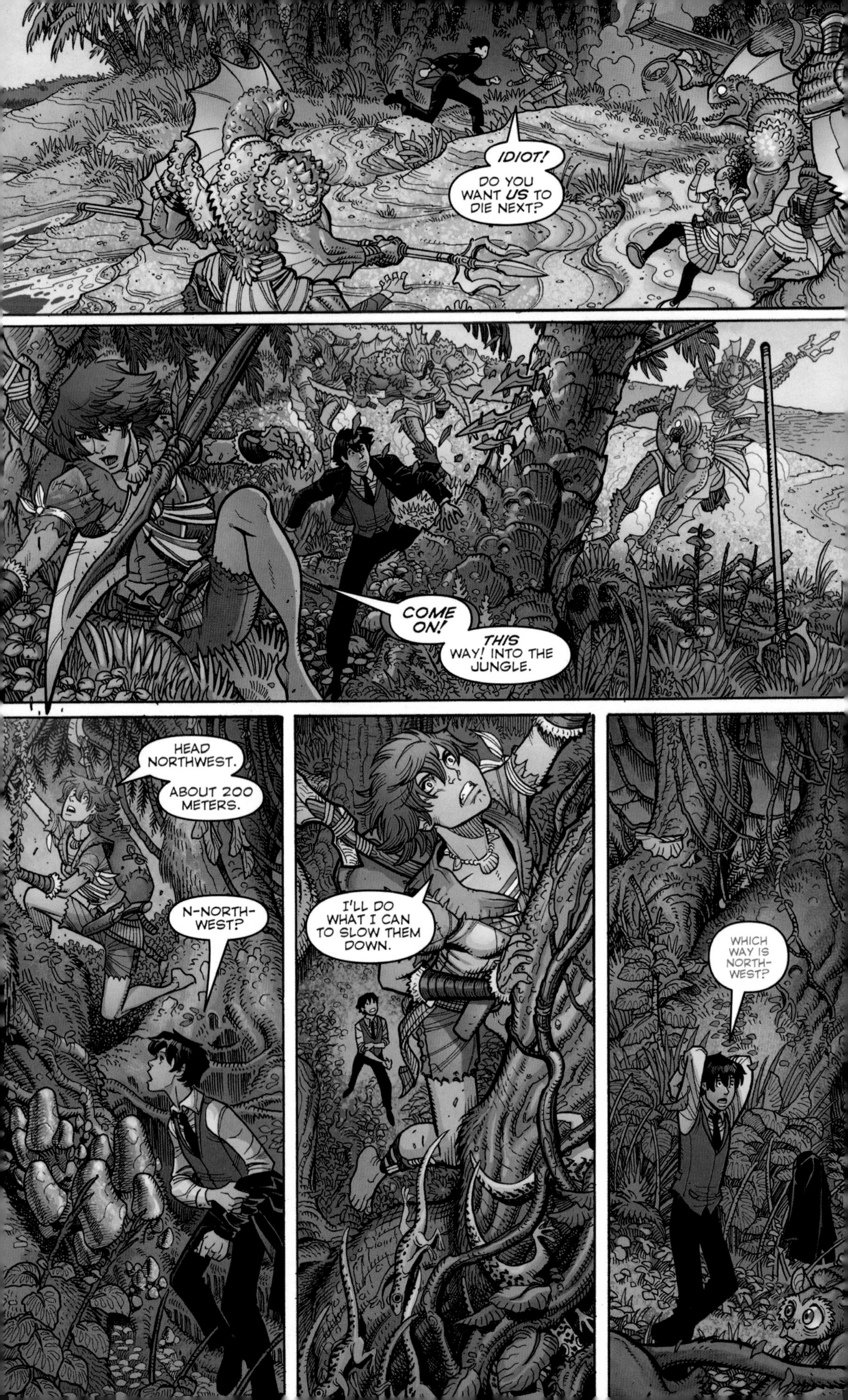
IDIOT! DO YOU WANT US TO DIE NEXT?
COME ON!
THIS WAY! INTO THE JUNGLE.
HEAD NORTHWEST.
ABOUT 200 METERS.
N-NORTH-WEST?
I'LL DO WHAT I CAN TO SLOW THEM DOWN.
WHICH WAY IS NORTH-WEST?

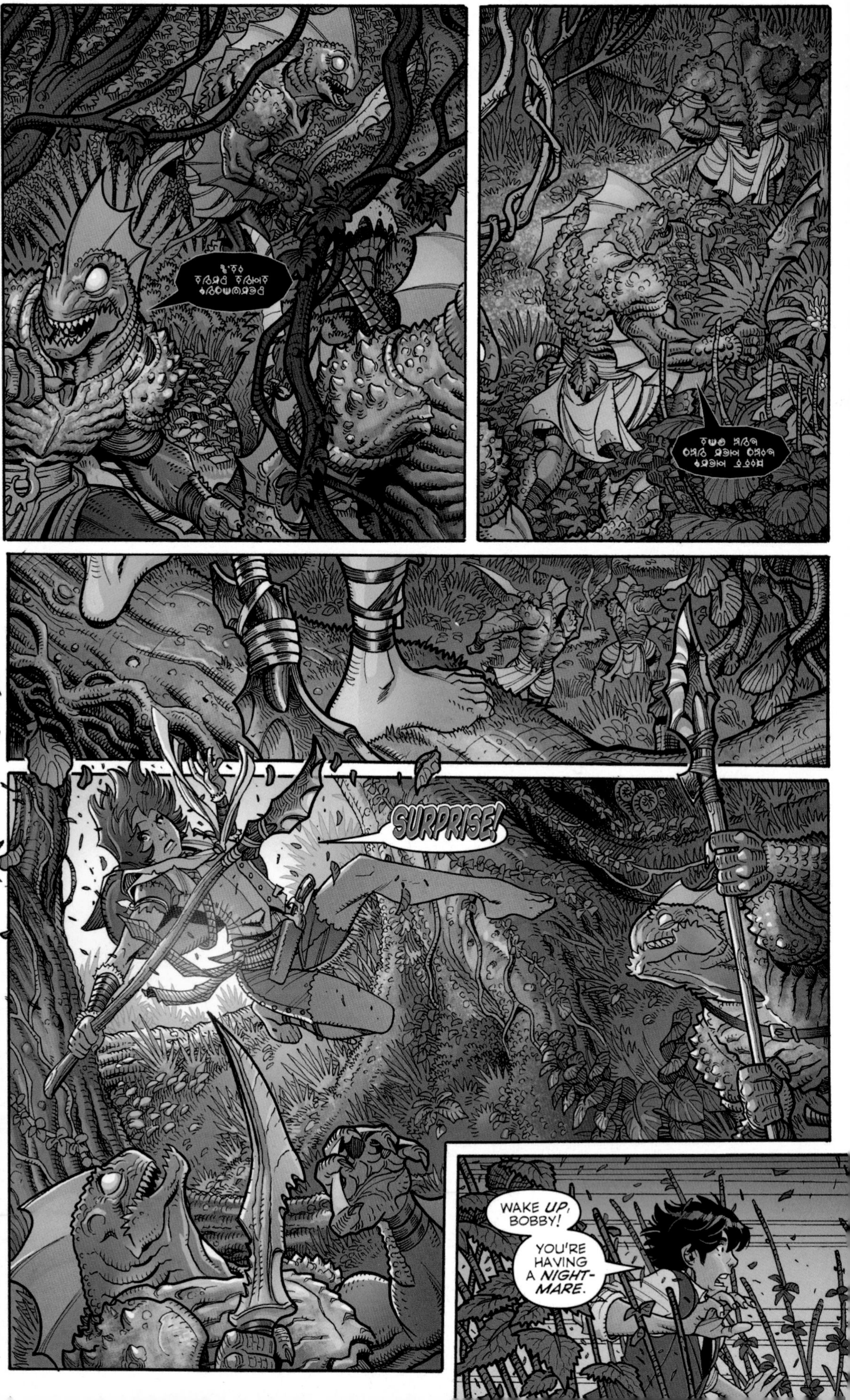
SURPRISE!
WAKE UP, BOBBY!
YOU'RE HAVING A NIGHT-MARE.

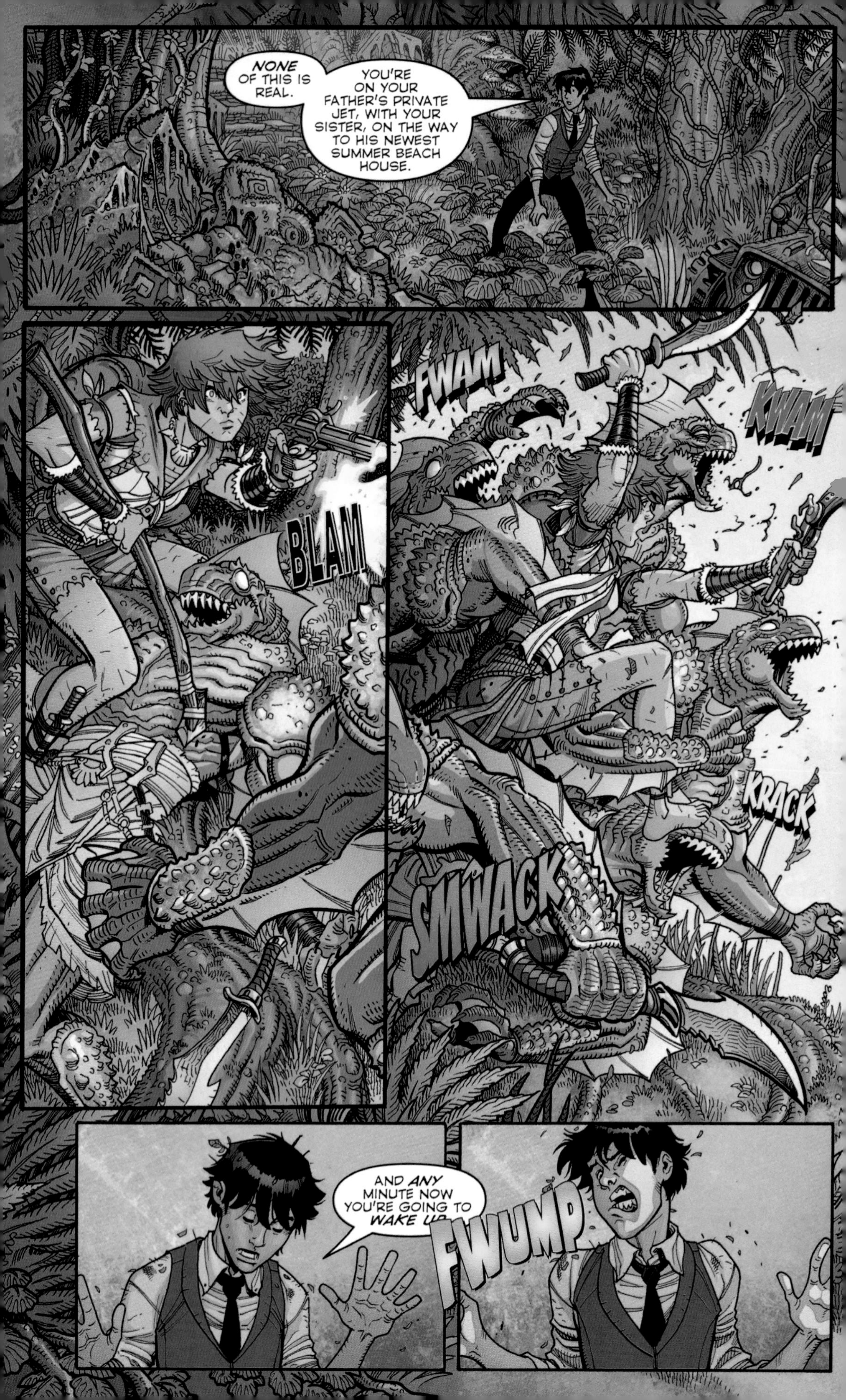
NONE OF THIS IS REAL.
YOU'RE ON YOUR FATHER'S PRIVATE JET, WITH YOUR SISTER, ON THE WAY TO HIS NEWEST SUMMER BEACH HOUSE.
BLAM
FWAM
KWAM
KRACK
SMWACK
AND *ANY* MINUTE NOW YOU'RE GOING TO *WAKE UP*
FWUMP

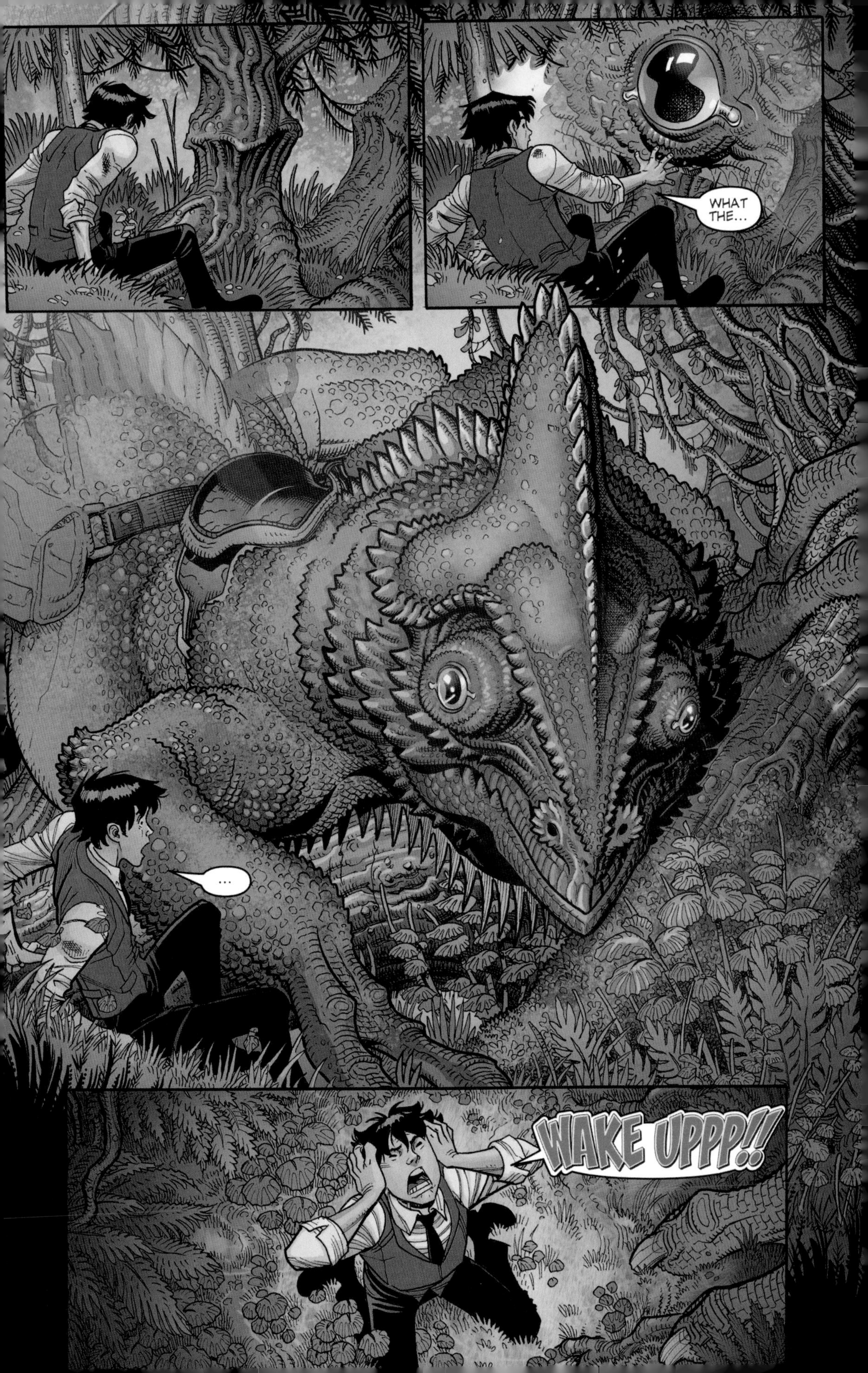
WHAT THE...
...
WAKE UPPP!!

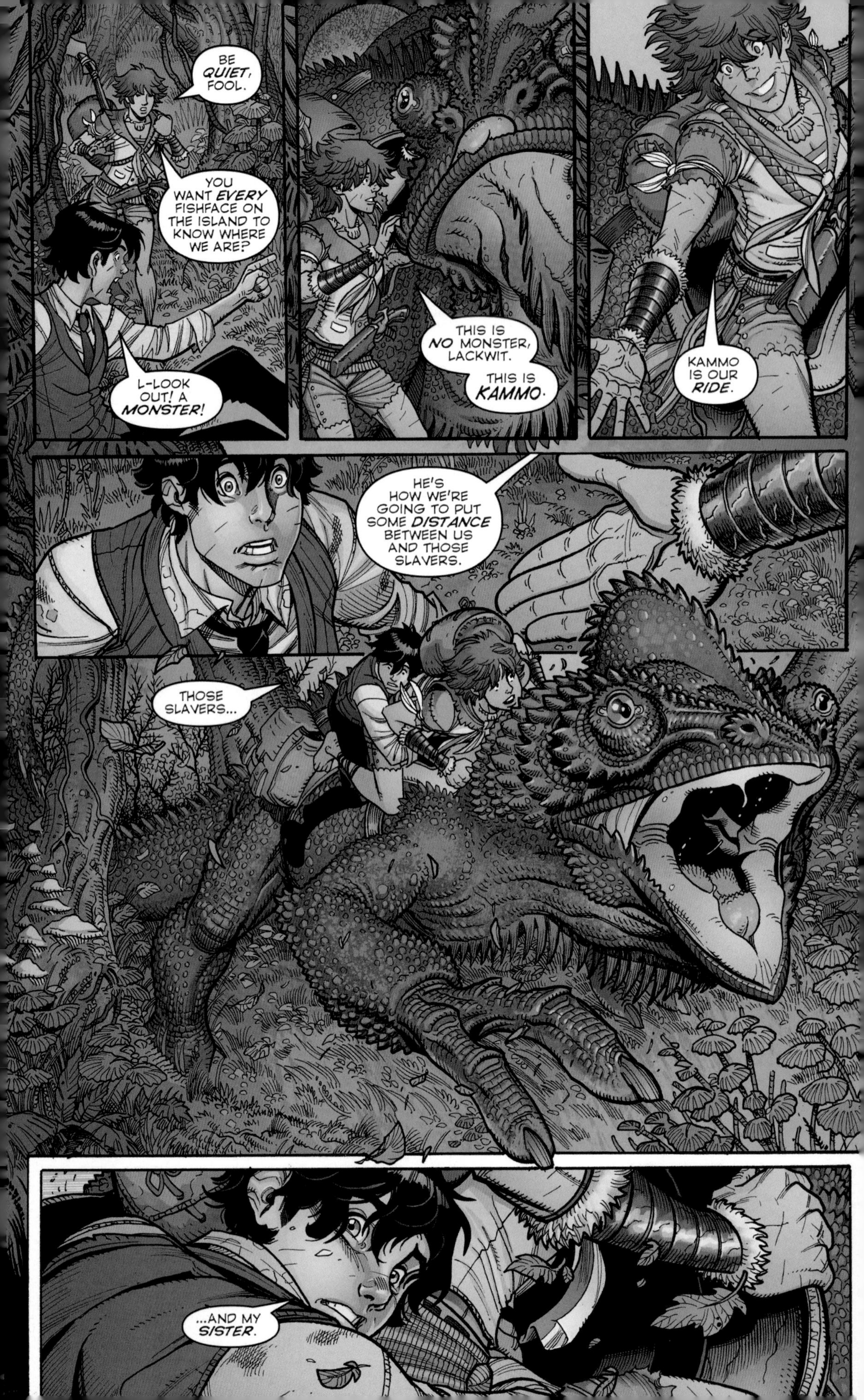
BE QUIET, FOOL.
YOU WANT EVERY FISHFACE ON THE ISLAND TO KNOW WHERE WE ARE?
L-LOOK OUT! A MONSTER!
THIS IS NO MONSTER, LACKWIT.
THIS IS KAMMO.
KAMMO IS OUR RIDE.
HE'S HOW WE'RE GOING TO PUT SOME DISTANCE BETWEEN US AND THOSE SLAVERS.
THOSE SLAVERS...
...AND MY SISTER.

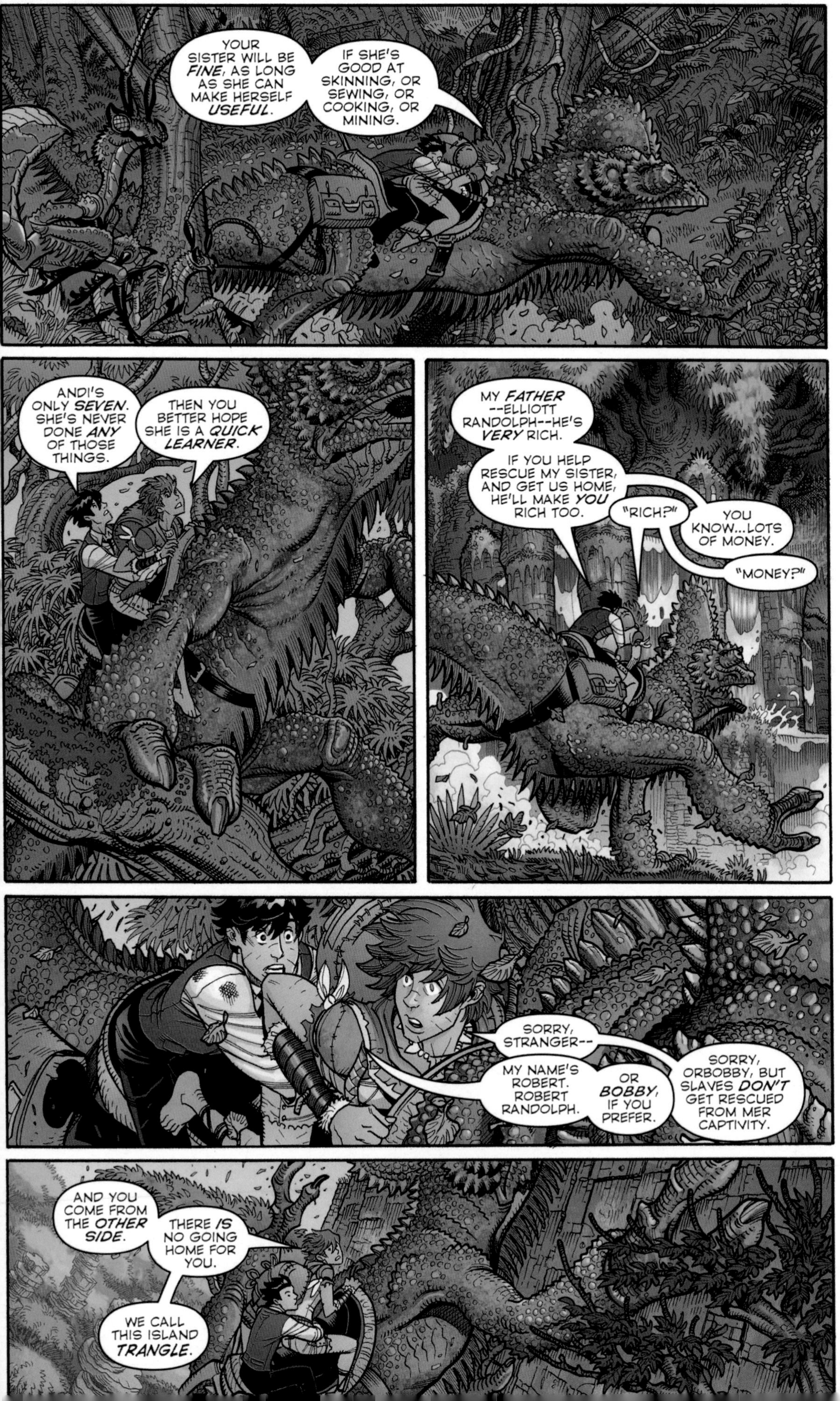
YOUR SISTER WILL BE *FINE*, AS LONG AS SHE CAN MAKE HERSELF *USEFUL*.
IF SHE'S GOOD AT SKINNING, OR SEWING, OR COOKING, OR MINING.
ANDI'S ONLY *SEVEN*. SHE'S NEVER DONE *ANY* OF THOSE THINGS.
THEN YOU BETTER HOPE SHE IS A *QUICK LEARNER*.
MY *FATHER* --ELLIOTT RANDOLPH--HE'S *VERY* RICH.
IF YOU HELP RESCUE MY SISTER, AND GET US HOME, HE'LL MAKE *YOU* RICH TOO.
"RICH?"
YOU KNOW...LOTS OF MONEY.
"MONEY?"
SORRY, STRANGER--
MY NAME'S ROBERT. ROBERT RANDOLPH.
OR *BOBBY*, IF YOU PREFER.
SORRY, ORBOBBY, BUT SLAVES *DON'T* GET RESCUED FROM MER CAPTIVITY.
AND YOU COME FROM THE *OTHER SIDE*.
THERE *IS* NO GOING HOME FOR YOU.
WE CALL THIS ISLAND *TRANGLE*.

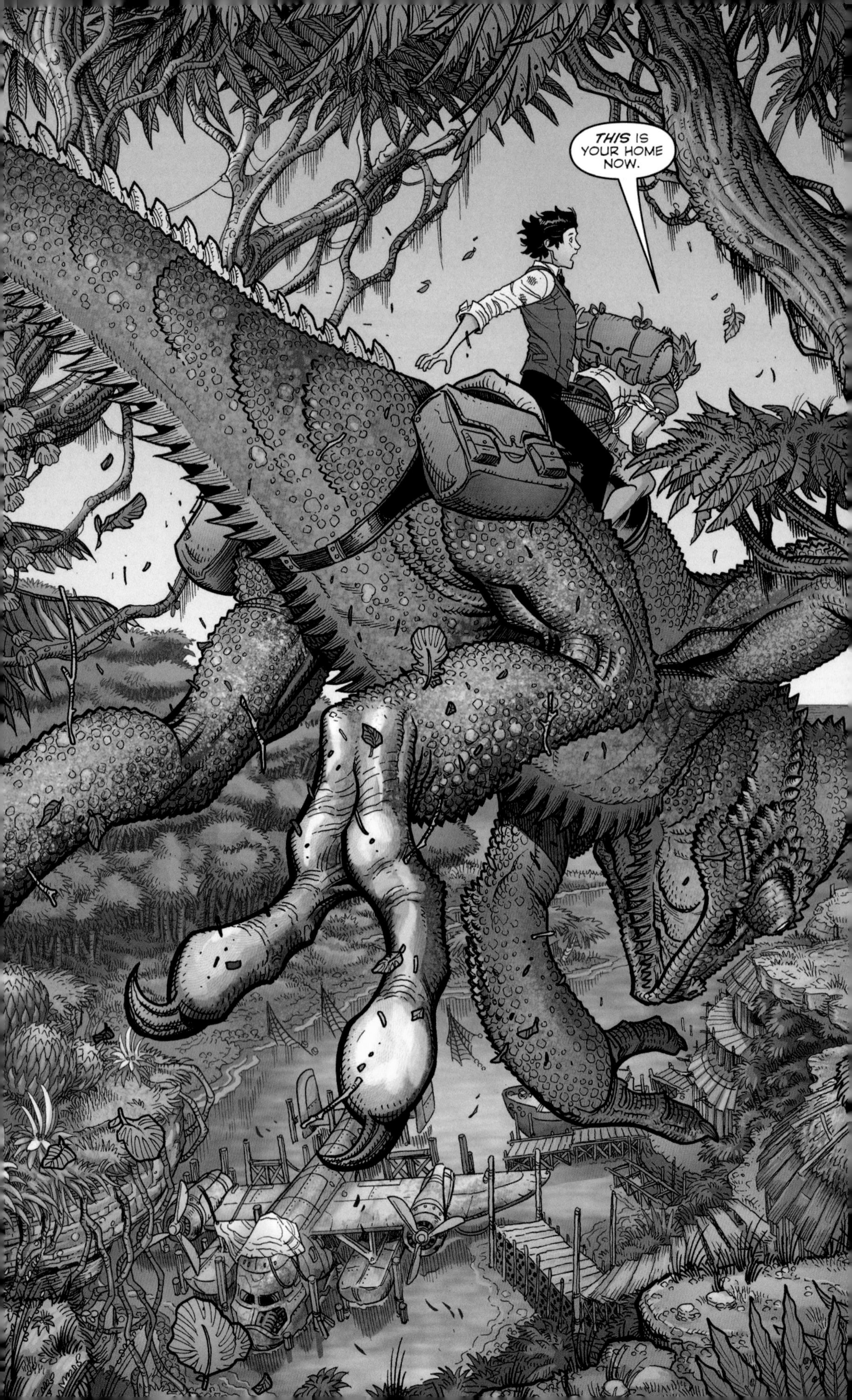
THIS IS YOUR HOME NOW.

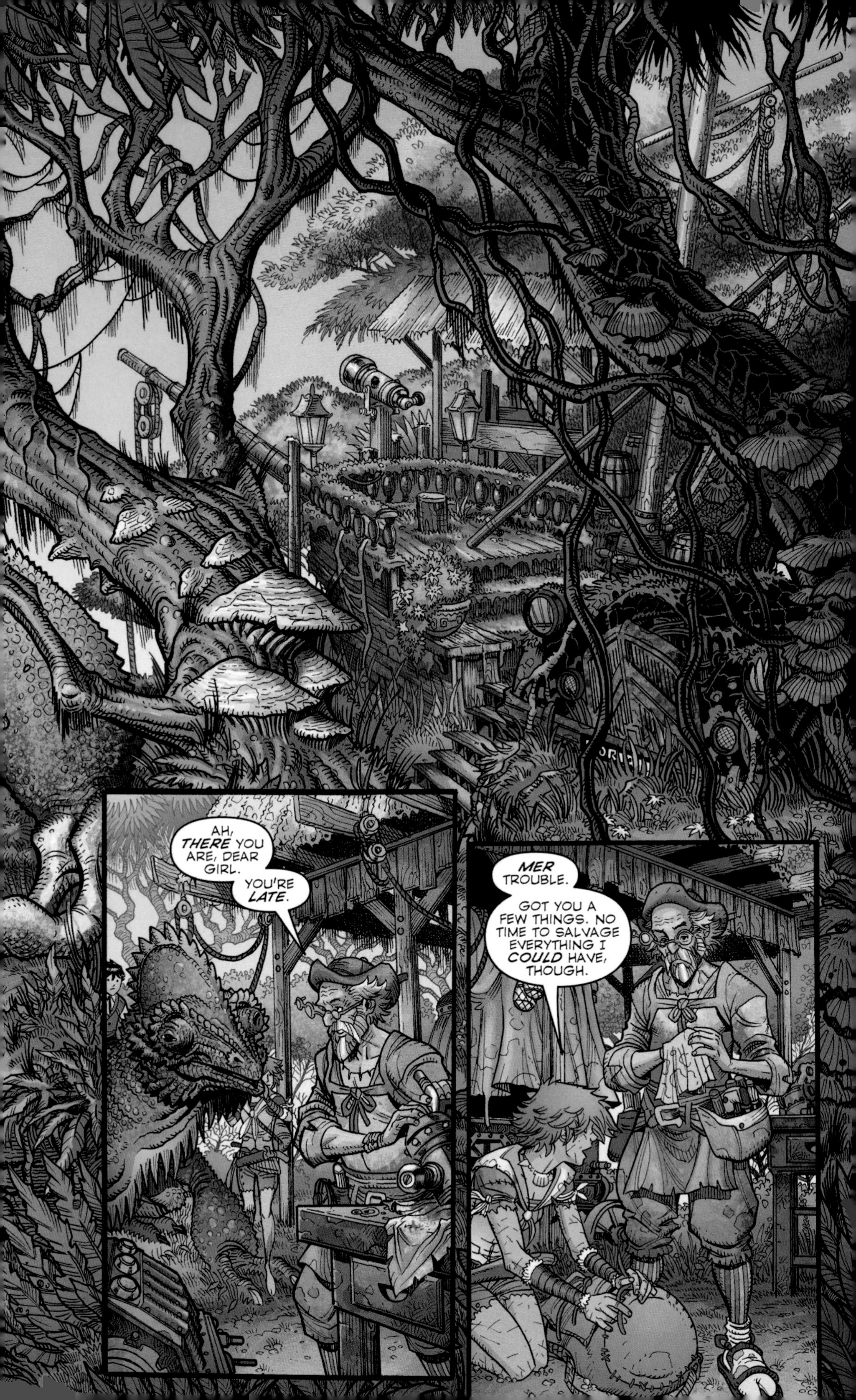
AH, THERE YOU ARE, DEAR GIRL.
YOU'RE LATE.
MER TROUBLE.
GOT YOU A FEW THINGS. NO TIME TO SALVAGE EVERYTHING I COULD HAVE, THOUGH.

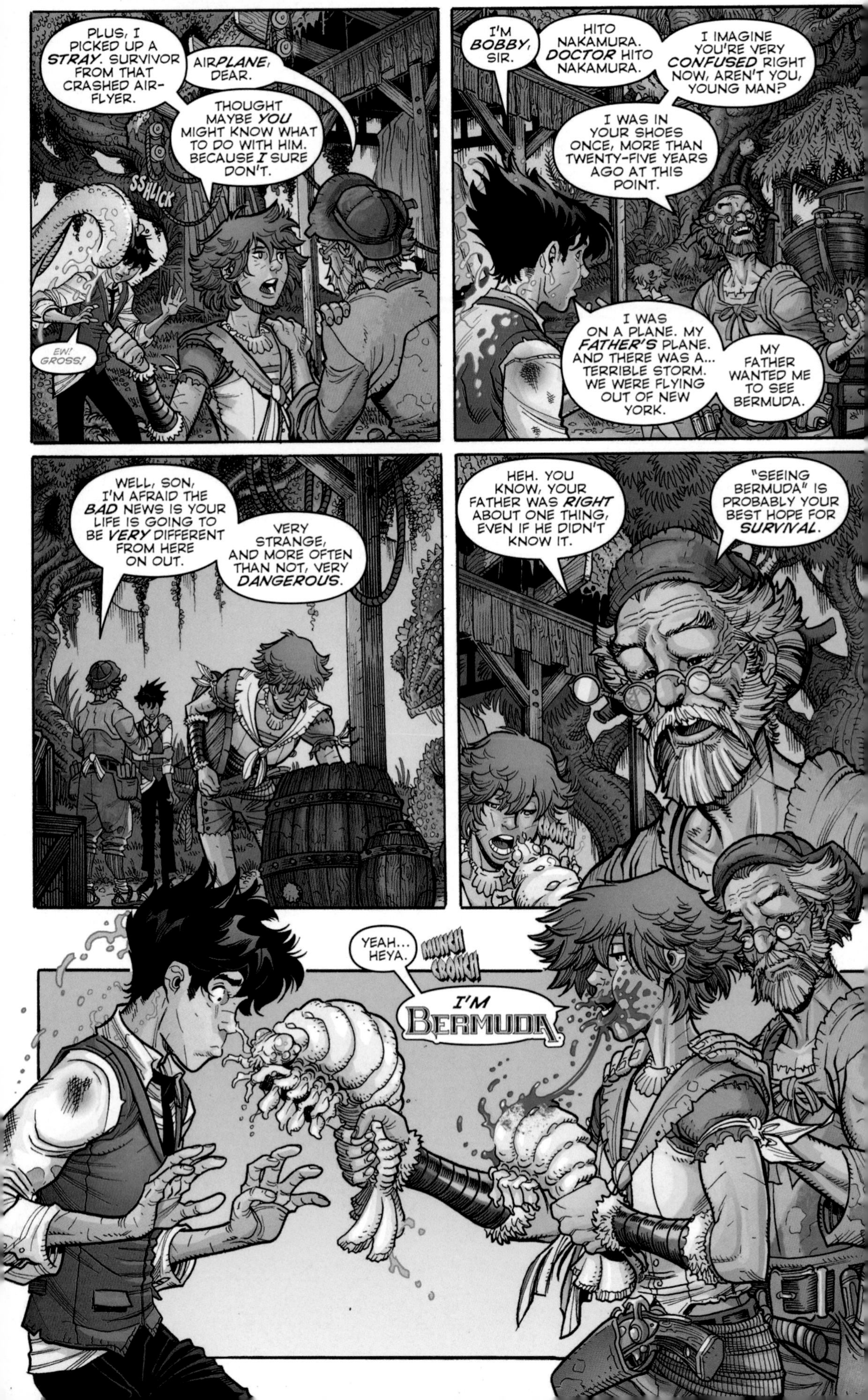
PLUS, I PICKED UP A STRAY. SURVIVOR FROM THAT CRASHED AIR-FLYER.
AIRPLANE, DEAR.
THOUGHT MAYBE YOU MIGHT KNOW WHAT TO DO WITH HIM. BECAUSE I SURE DON'T.
SSHLICK
EW! GROSS!
I'M BOBBY, SIR.
HITO NAKAMURA. DOCTOR HITO NAKAMURA.
I IMAGINE YOU'RE VERY CONFUSED RIGHT NOW, AREN'T YOU, YOUNG MAN?
I WAS IN YOUR SHOES ONCE, MORE THAN TWENTY-FIVE YEARS AGO AT THIS POINT.
I WAS ON A PLANE. MY FATHER'S PLANE. AND THERE WAS A... TERRIBLE STORM. WE WERE FLYING OUT OF NEW YORK.
MY FATHER WANTED ME TO SEE BERMUDA.
WELL, SON, I'M AFRAID THE BAD NEWS IS YOUR LIFE IS GOING TO BE VERY DIFFERENT FROM HERE ON OUT.
VERY STRANGE, AND MORE OFTEN THAN NOT, VERY DANGEROUS.
HEH. YOU KNOW, YOUR FATHER WAS RIGHT ABOUT ONE THING, EVEN IF HE DIDN'T KNOW IT.
"SEEING BERMUDA" IS PROBABLY YOUR BEST HOPE FOR SURVIVAL.
CRONCH
YEAH... HEYA.
MUNCH CRONCH
I'M BERMUDA

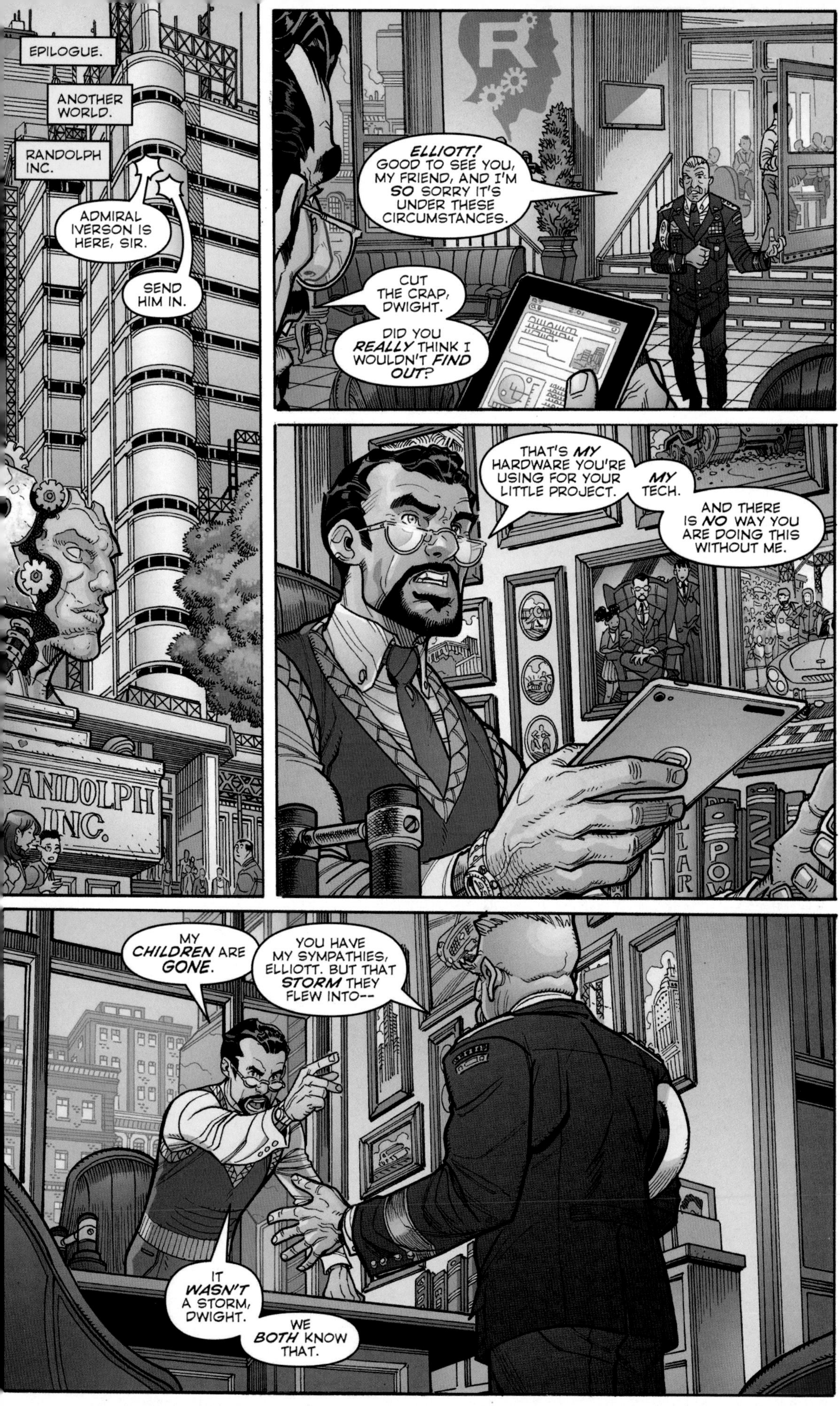
EPILOGUE.
ANOTHER WORLD.
RANDOLPH INC.
ADMIRAL IVERSON IS HERE, SIR.
SEND HIM IN.
RANDOLPH INC.
ELLIOTT! GOOD TO SEE YOU, MY FRIEND, AND I'M SO SORRY IT'S UNDER THESE CIRCUMSTANCES.
CUT THE CRAP, DWIGHT.
DID YOU REALLY THINK I WOULDN'T FIND OUT?
THAT'S MY HARDWARE YOU'RE USING FOR YOUR LITTLE PROJECT.
MY TECH.
AND THERE IS NO WAY YOU ARE DOING THIS WITHOUT ME.
MY CHILDREN ARE GONE.
YOU HAVE MY SYMPATHIES, ELLIOTT. BUT THAT STORM THEY FLEW INTO--
IT WASN'T A STORM, DWIGHT.
WE BOTH KNOW THAT.

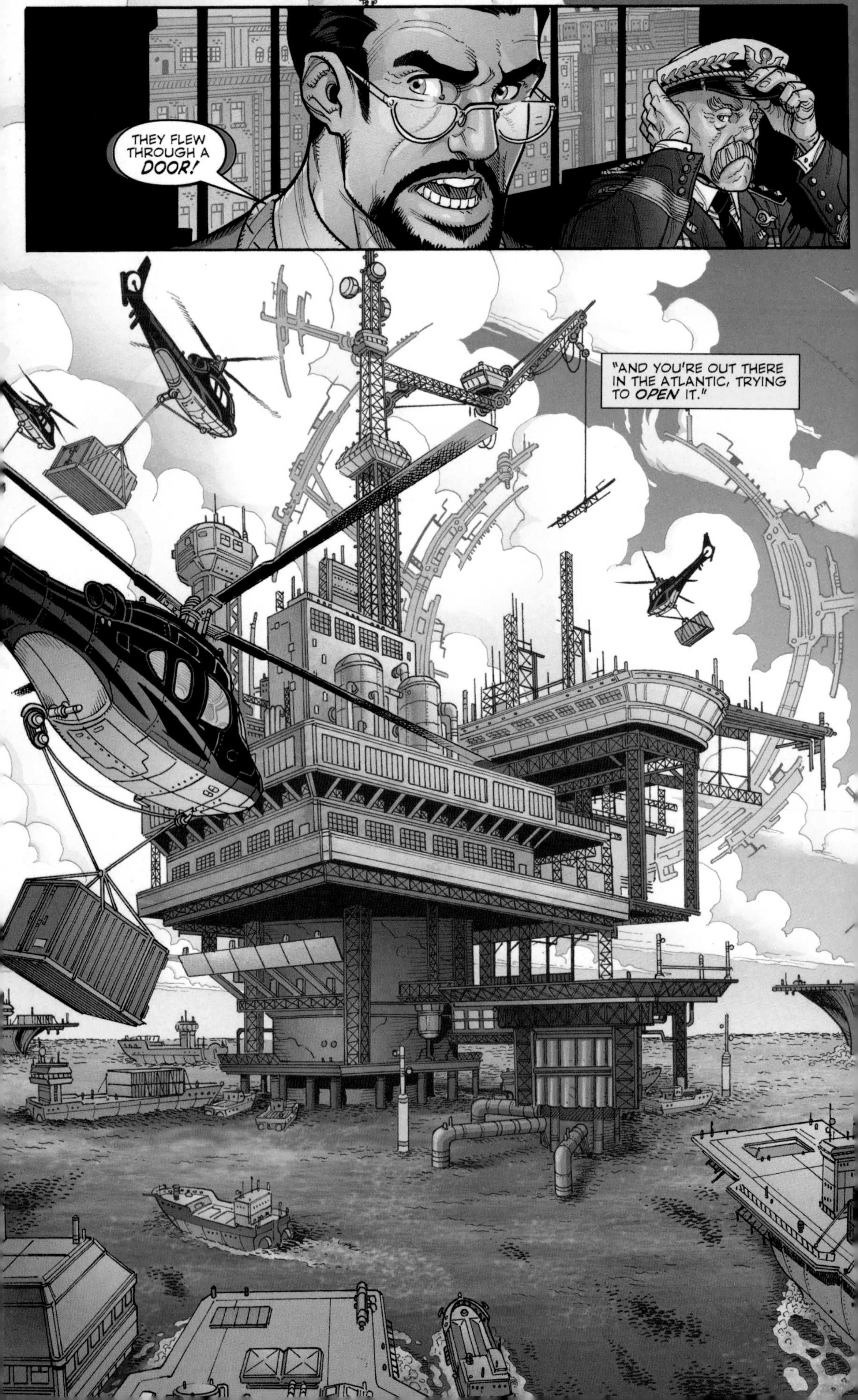
THEY FLEW THROUGH A DOOR!
"AND YOU'RE OUT THERE IN THE ATLANTIC, TRYING TO OPEN IT."

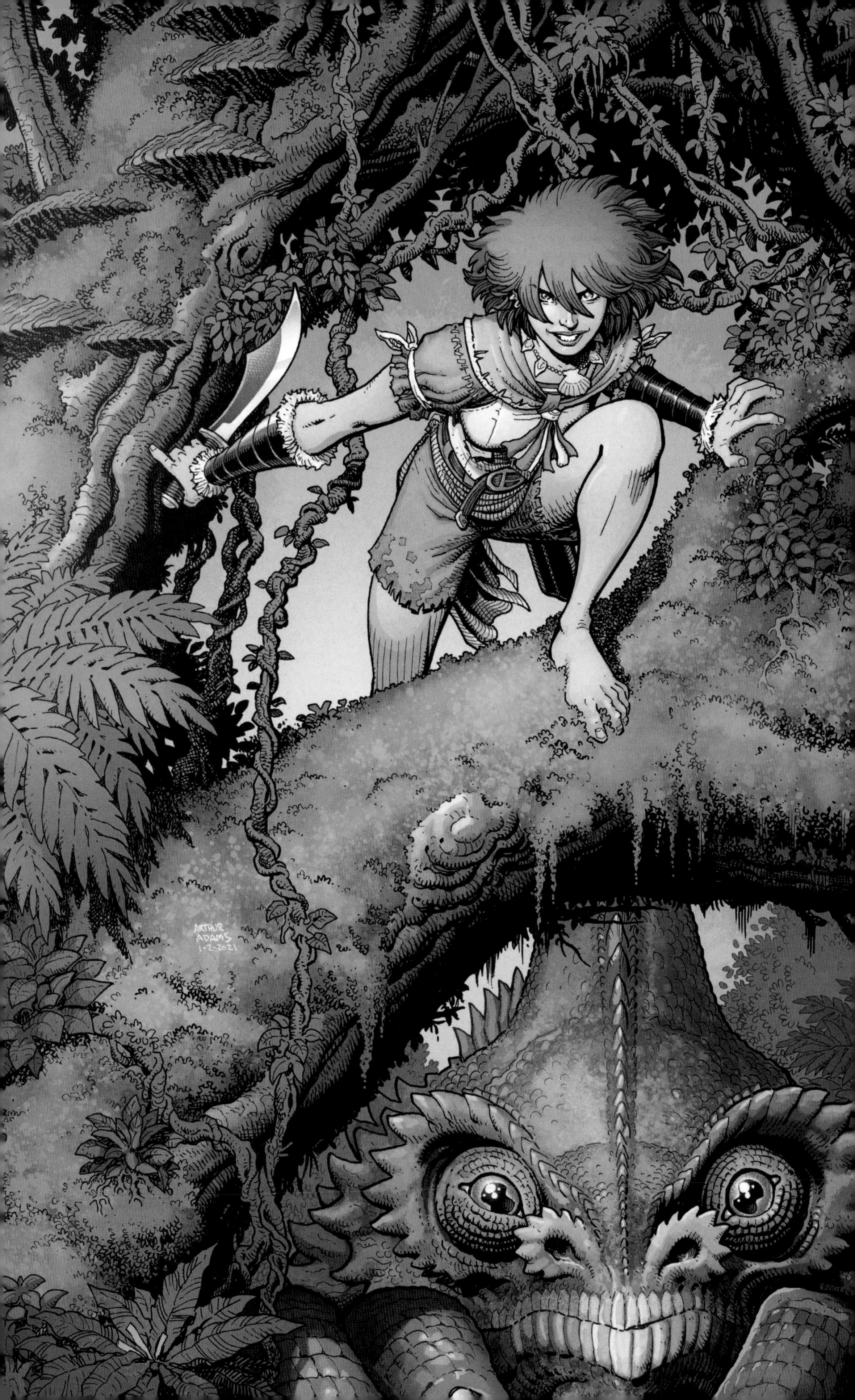
ARTHUR
ADAMS
1-2-2021

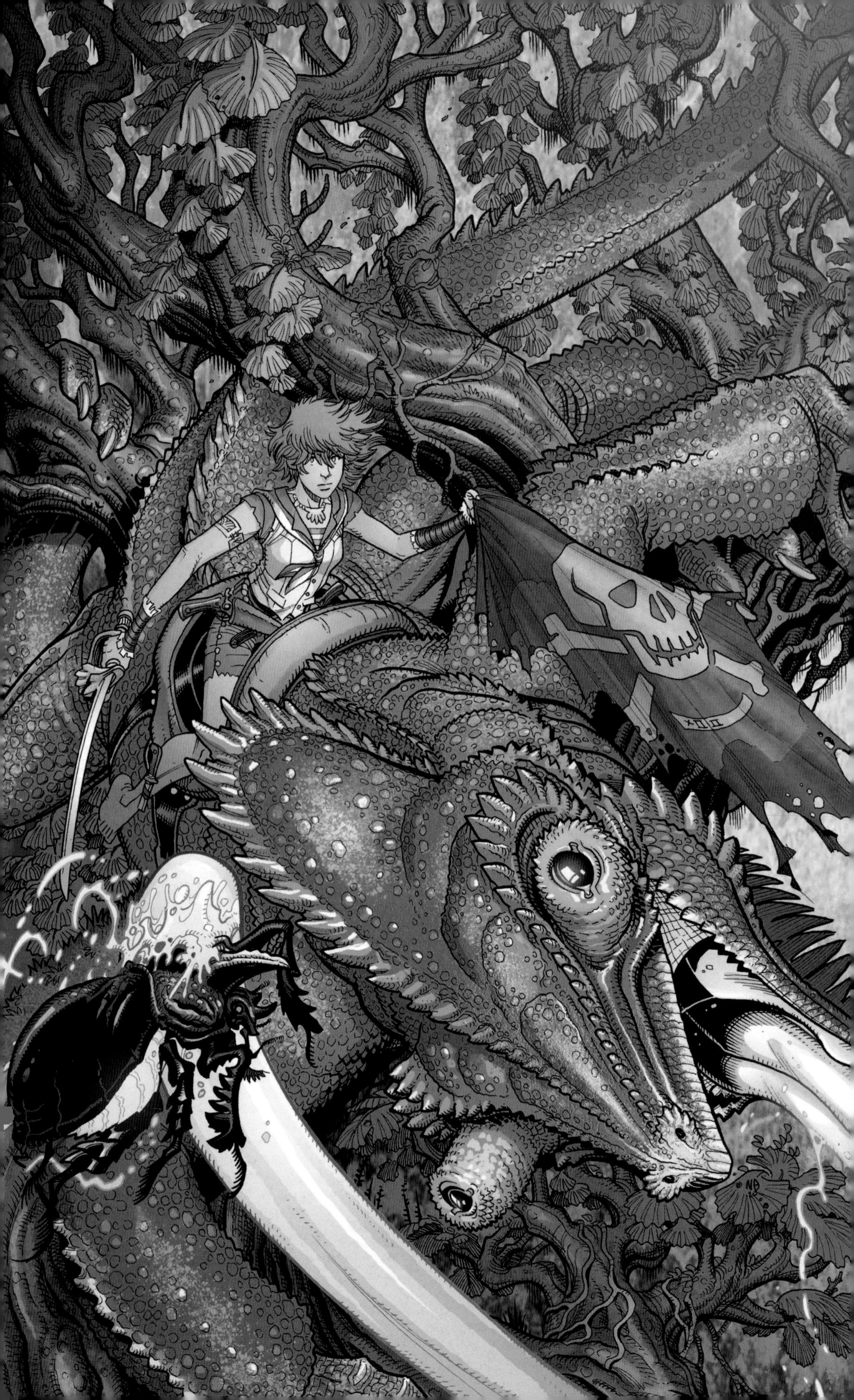

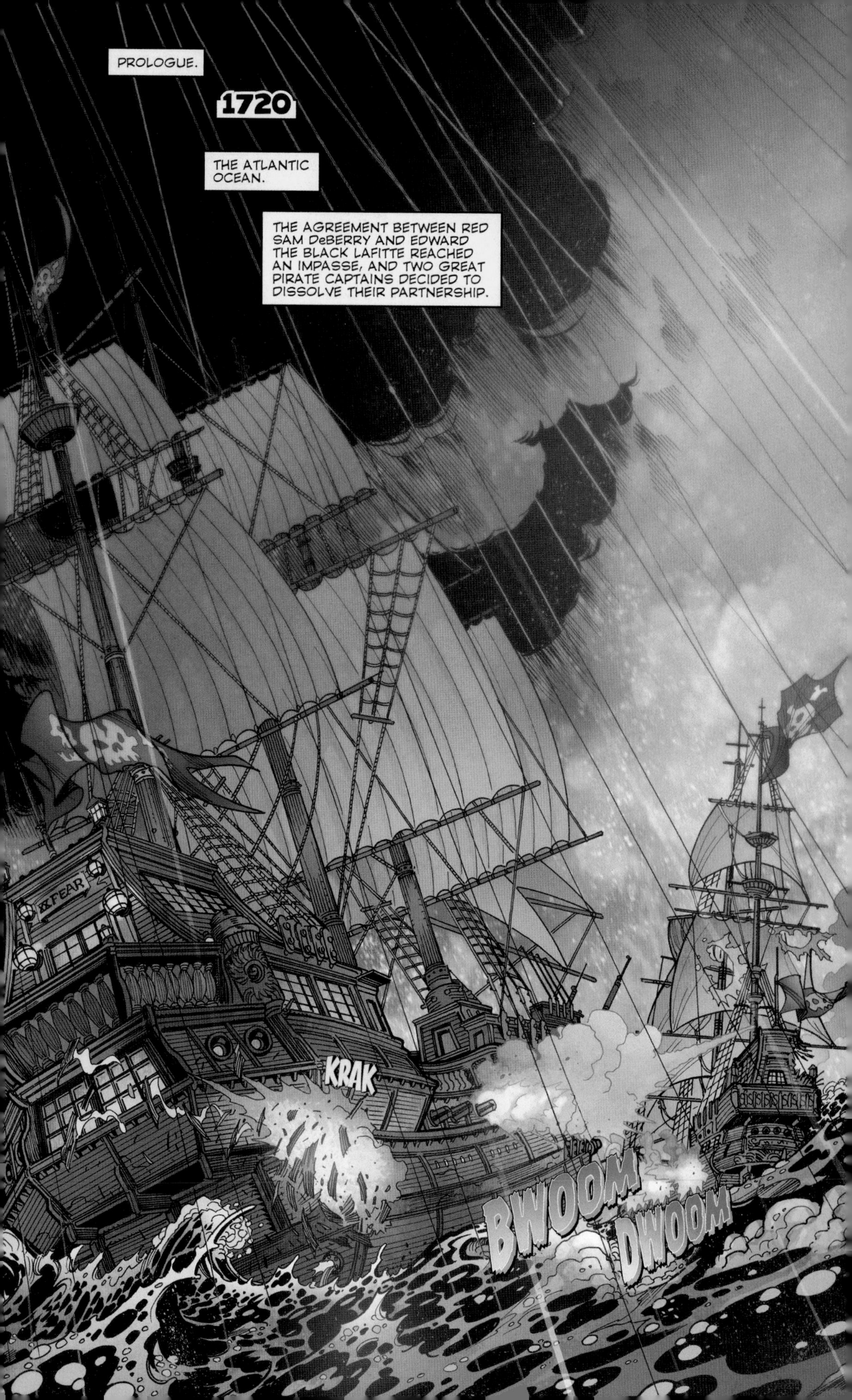
PROLOGUE.
1720
THE ATLANTIC OCEAN.
THE AGREEMENT BETWEEN RED SAM DeBERRY AND EDWARD THE BLACK LAFITTE REACHED AN IMPASSE, AND TWO GREAT PIRATE CAPTAINS DECIDED TO DISSOLVE THEIR PARTNERSHIP.
FEAR
KRAK
BWOOM
DWOOM

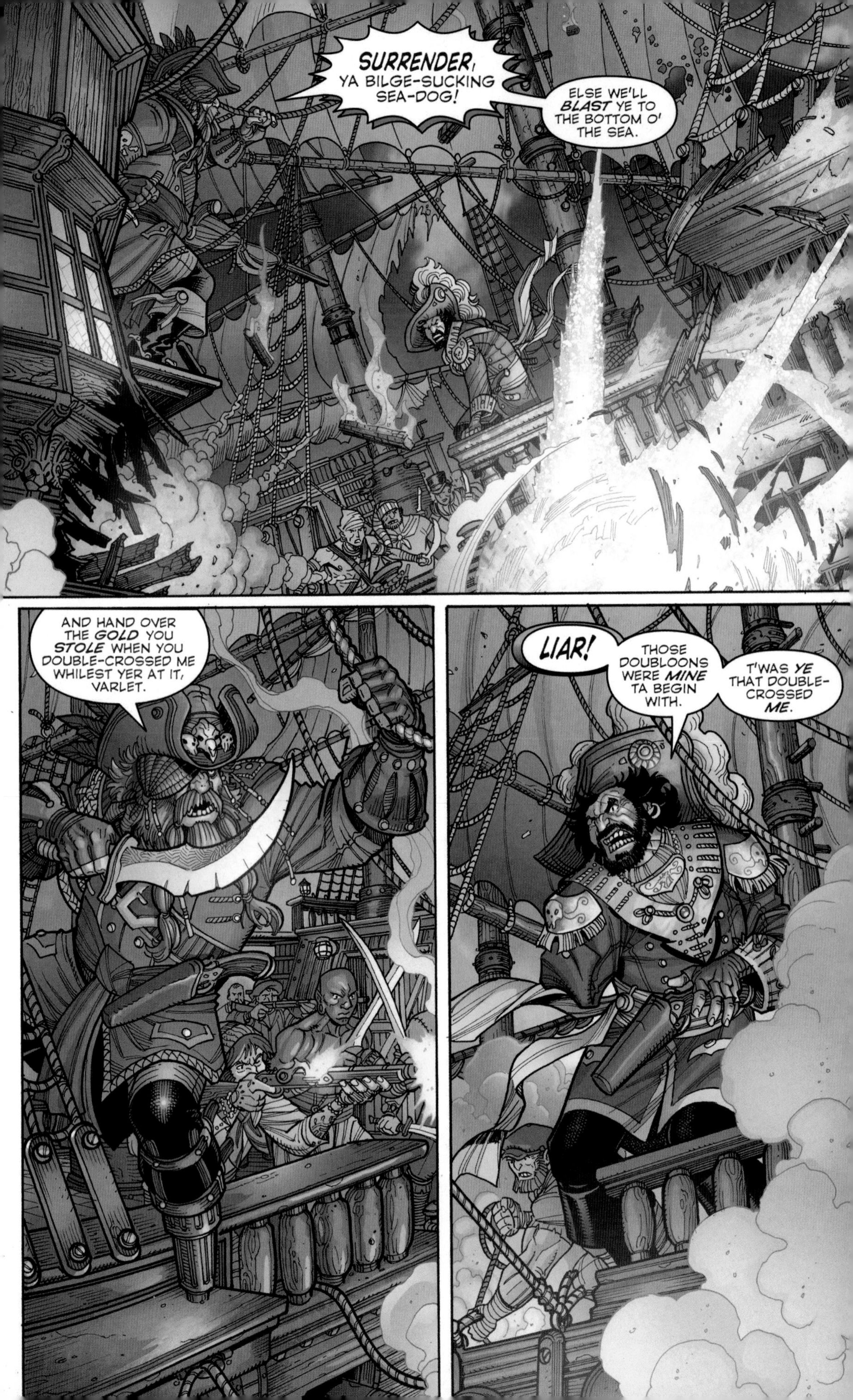
SURRENDER, YA BILGE-SUCKING SEA-DOG!
ELSE WE'LL BLAST YE TO THE BOTTOM O' THE SEA.
AND HAND OVER THE GOLD YOU STOLE WHEN YOU DOUBLE-CROSSED ME WHILEST YER AT IT, VARLET.
LIAR!
THOSE DOUBLOONS WERE MINE TA BEGIN WITH.
T'WAS YE THAT DOUBLE-CROSSED ME.

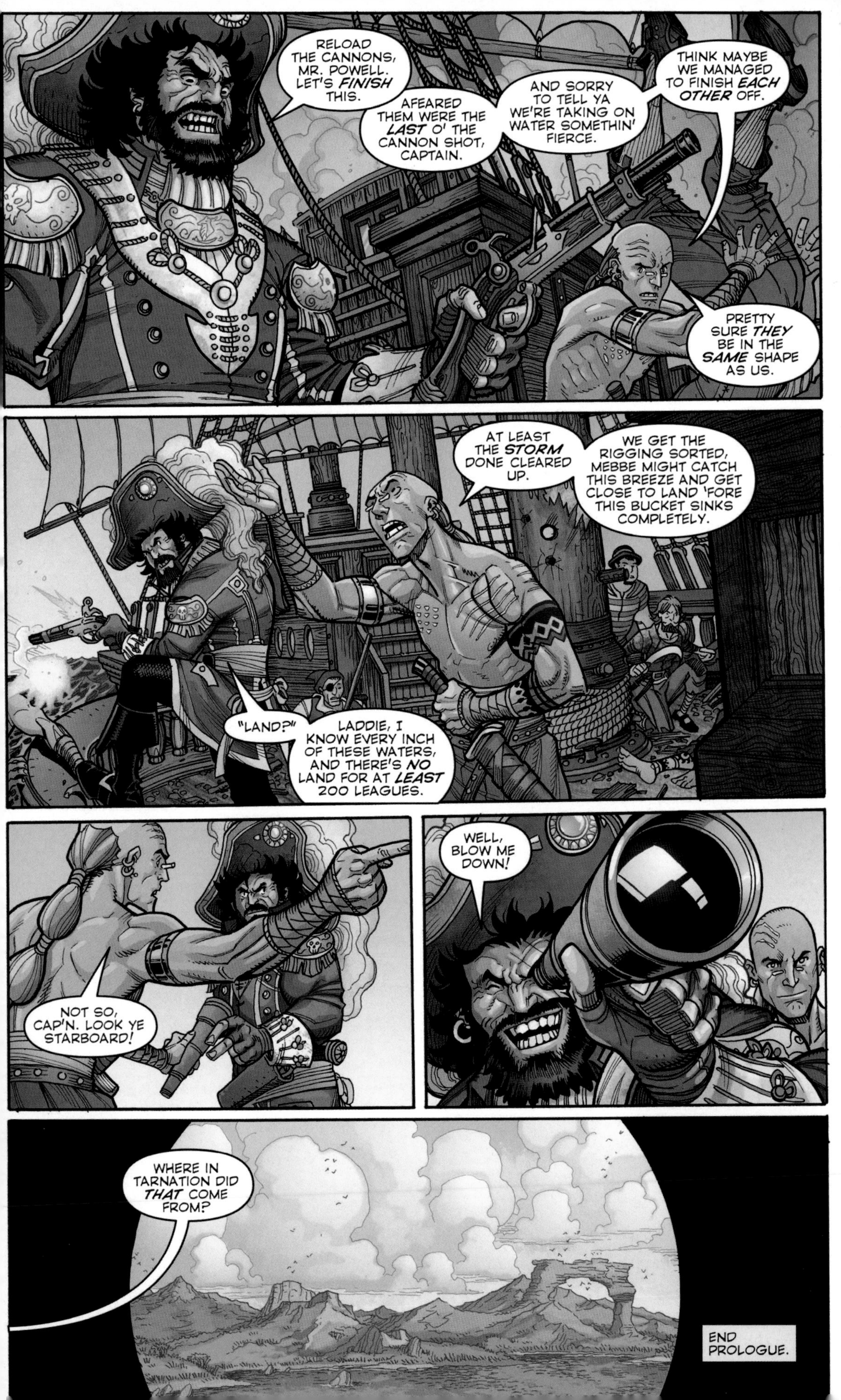
RELOAD THE CANNONS, MR. POWELL. LET'S FINISH THIS.
AFEARED THEM WERE THE LAST O' THE CANNON SHOT, CAPTAIN.
AND SORRY TO TELL YA WE'RE TAKING ON WATER SOMETHIN' FIERCE.
THINK MAYBE WE MANAGED TO FINISH EACH OTHER OFF.
PRETTY SURE THEY BE IN THE SAME SHAPE AS US.
AT LEAST THE STORM DONE CLEARED UP.
WE GET THE RIGGING SORTED, MEBBE MIGHT CATCH THIS BREEZE AND GET CLOSE TO LAND 'FORE THIS BUCKET SINKS COMPLETELY.
"LAND?"
LADDIE, I KNOW EVERY INCH OF THESE WATERS, AND THERE'S NO LAND FOR AT LEAST 200 LEAGUES.
NOT SO, CAP'N. LOOK YE STARBOARD!
WELL, BLOW ME DOWN!
WHERE IN TARNATION DID THAT COME FROM?
END PROLOGUE.

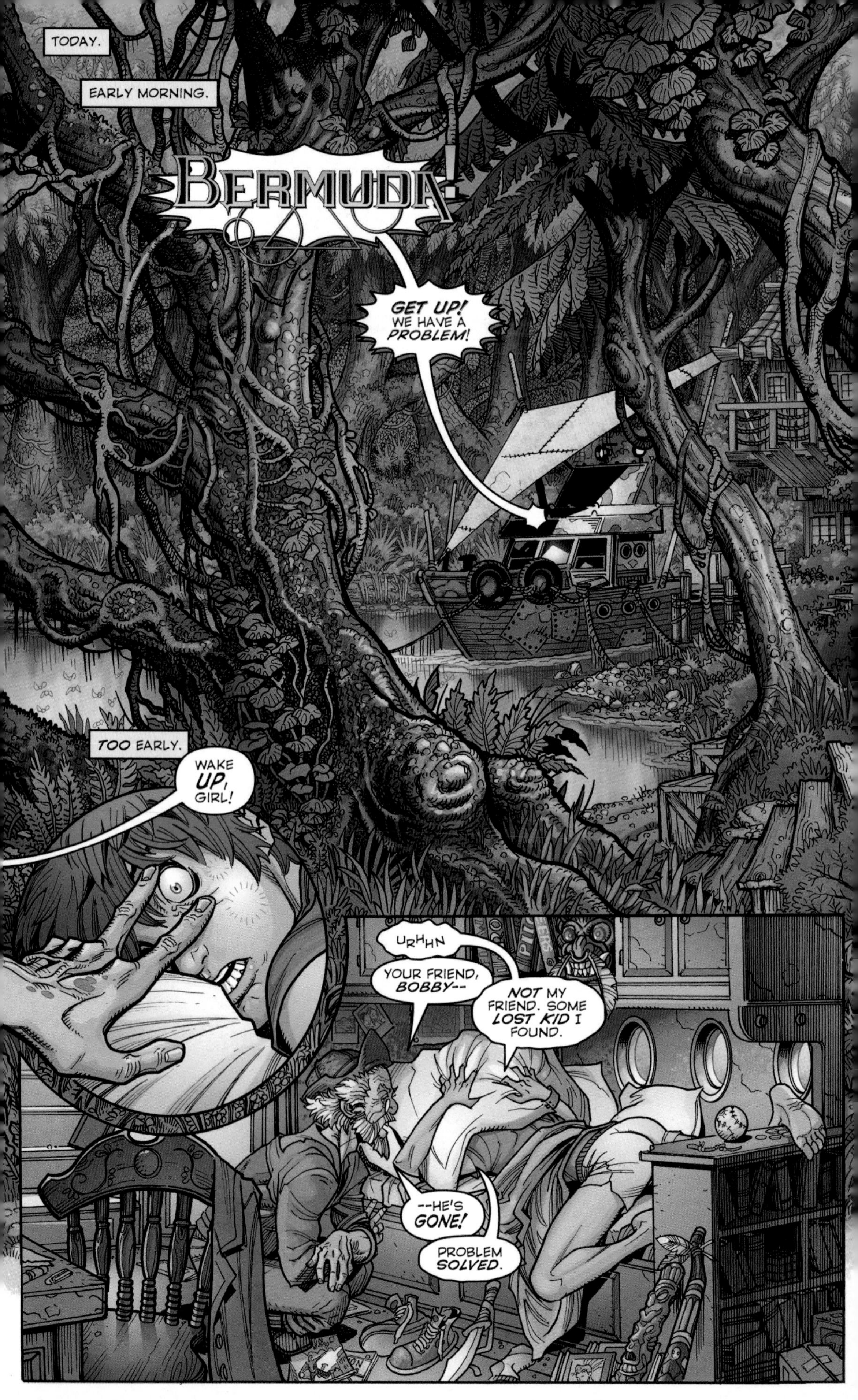
TODAY.
EARLY MORNING.
BERMUDA!
GET UP! WE HAVE A PROBLEM!
TOO EARLY.
WAKE UP, GIRL!
URHHN
YOUR FRIEND, BOBBY--
NOT MY FRIEND. SOME LOST KID I FOUND.
--HE'S GONE!
PROBLEM SOLVED.

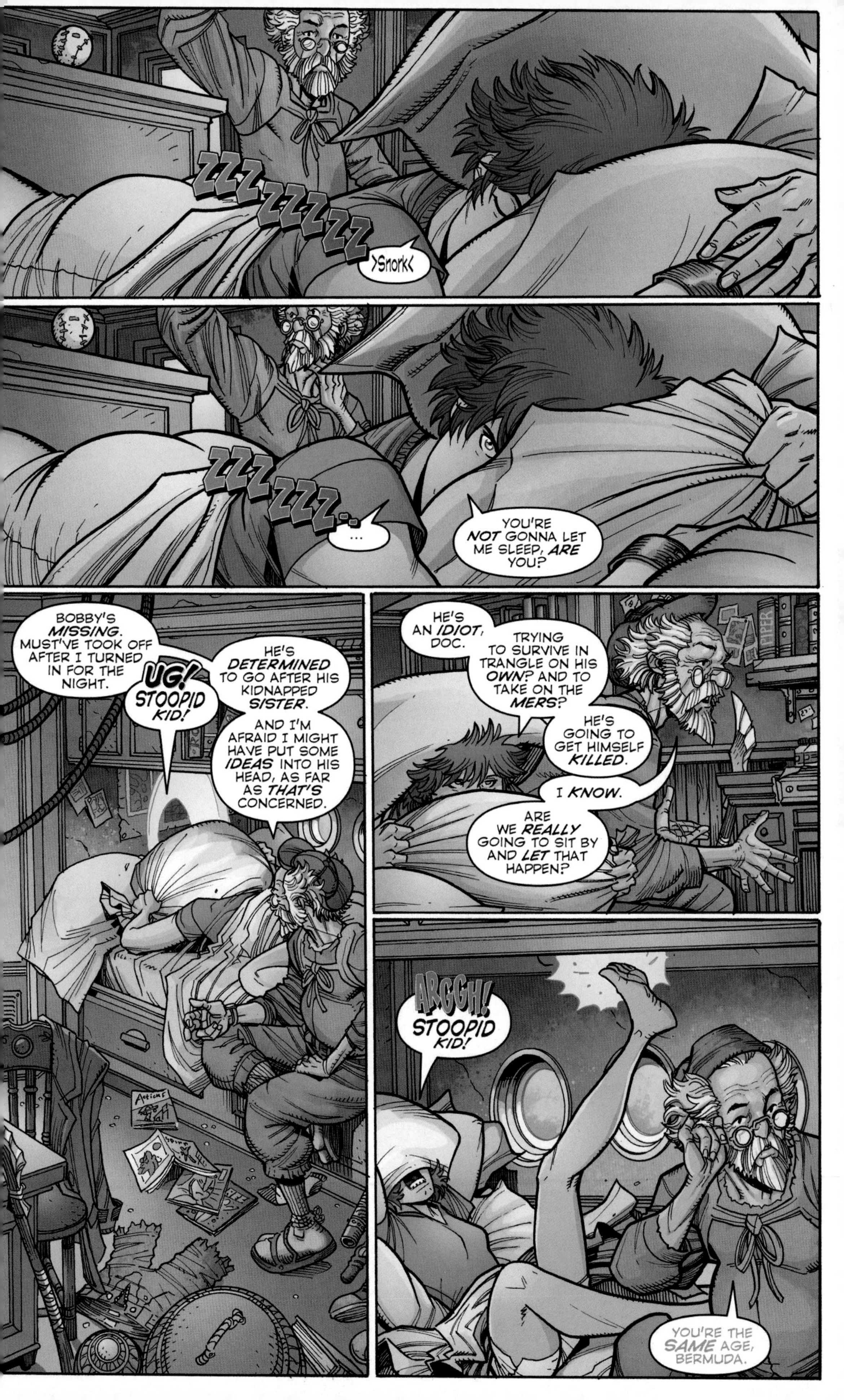
ZZZZZZZZZ
>Snork<
ZZZZZZ..
...
YOU'RE NOT GONNA LET ME SLEEP, ARE YOU?
BOBBY'S MISSING. MUST'VE TOOK OFF AFTER I TURNED IN FOR THE NIGHT.
UG! STOOPID KID!
HE'S DETERMINED TO GO AFTER HIS KIDNAPPED SISTER.
AND I'M AFRAID I MIGHT HAVE PUT SOME IDEAS INTO HIS HEAD, AS FAR AS THAT'S CONCERNED.
HE'S AN IDIOT, DOC.
TRYING TO SURVIVE IN TRANGLE ON HIS OWN? AND TO TAKE ON THE MERS?
HE'S GOING TO GET HIMSELF KILLED.
I KNOW.
ARE WE REALLY GOING TO SIT BY AND LET THAT HAPPEN?
ARGGH! STOOPID KID!
YOU'RE THE SAME AGE, BERMUDA.

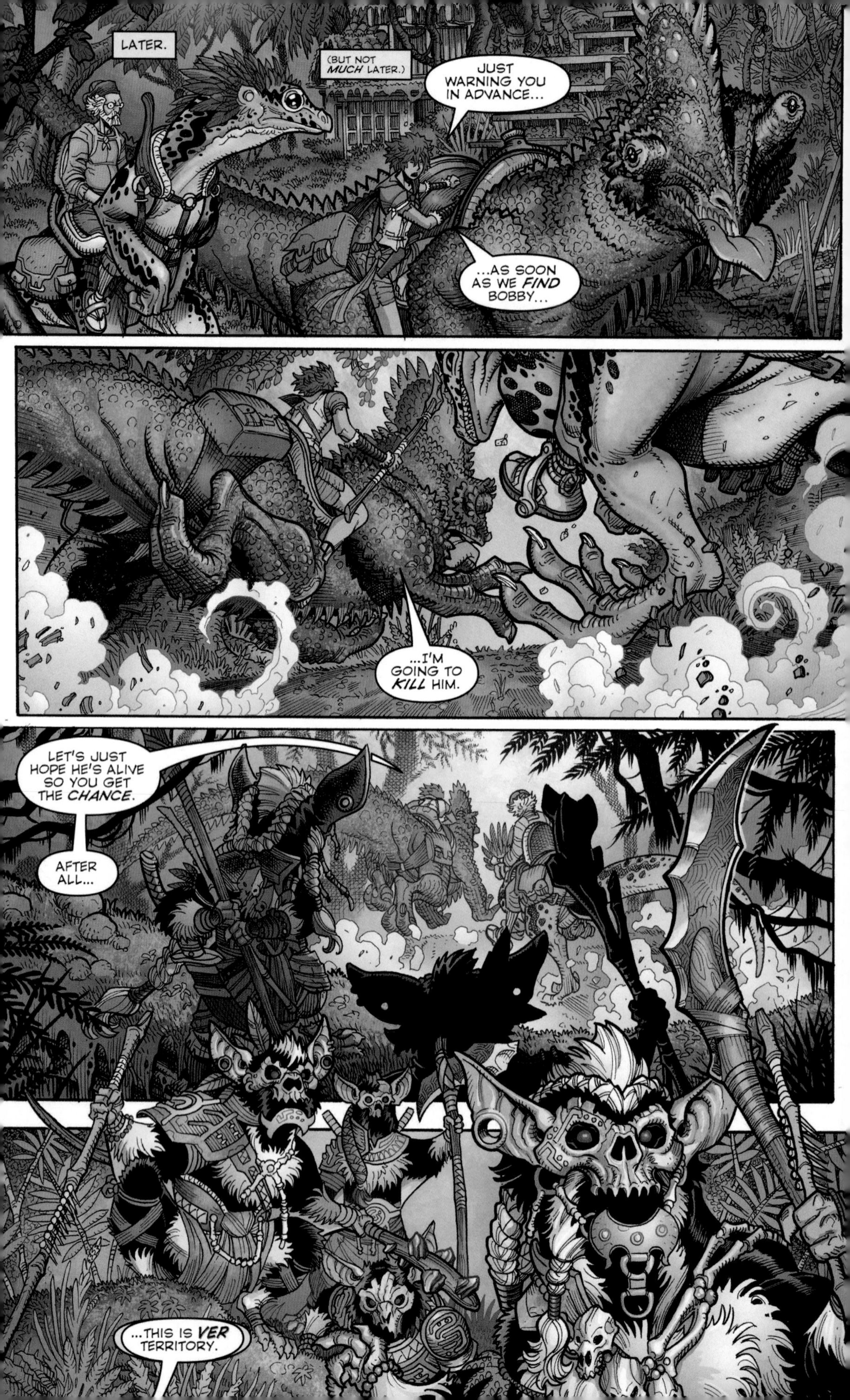
LATER.
(BUT NOT MUCH LATER.)
JUST WARNING YOU IN ADVANCE...
...AS SOON AS WE FIND BOBBY...
...I'M GOING TO KILL HIM.
LET'S JUST HOPE HE'S ALIVE SO YOU GET THE CHANCE.
AFTER ALL...
...THIS IS VER TERRITORY.

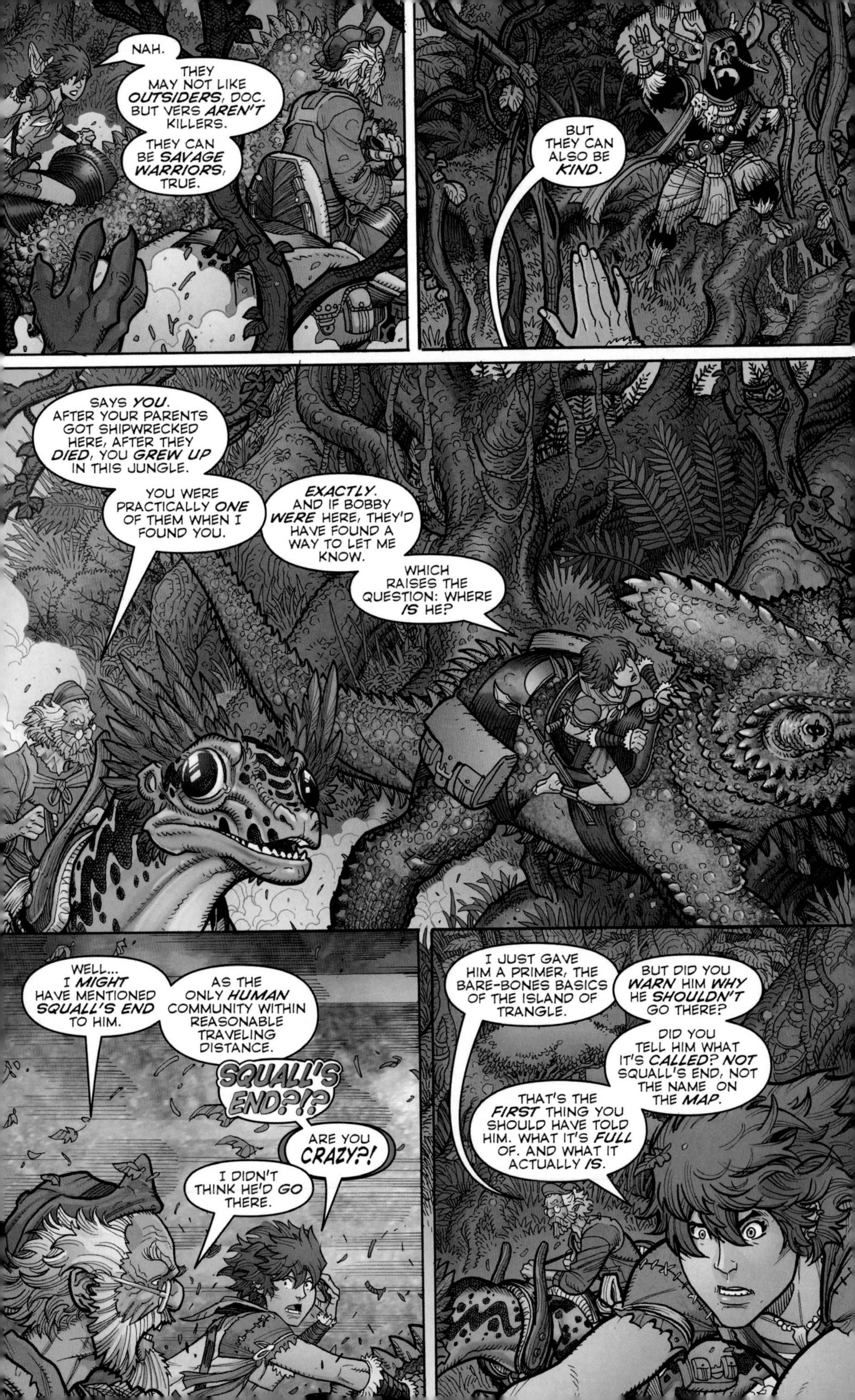
NAH.
THEY MAY NOT LIKE OUTSIDERS, DOC. BUT VERS AREN'T KILLERS.
THEY CAN BE SAVAGE WARRIORS, TRUE.
BUT THEY CAN ALSO BE KIND.
SAYS YOU. AFTER YOUR PARENTS GOT SHIPWRECKED HERE, AFTER THEY DIED, YOU GREW UP IN THIS JUNGLE.
YOU WERE PRACTICALLY ONE OF THEM WHEN I FOUND YOU.
EXACTLY. AND IF BOBBY WERE HERE, THEY'D HAVE FOUND A WAY TO LET ME KNOW.
WHICH RAISES THE QUESTION: WHERE IS HE?
WELL... I MIGHT HAVE MENTIONED SQUALL'S END TO HIM.
AS THE ONLY HUMAN COMMUNITY WITHIN REASONABLE TRAVELING DISTANCE.
SQUALL'S END?!?
ARE YOU CRAZY?!
I DIDN'T THINK HE'D GO THERE.
I JUST GAVE HIM A PRIMER, THE BARE-BONES BASICS OF THE ISLAND OF TRANGLE.
BUT DID YOU WARN HIM WHY HE SHOULDN'T GO THERE?
DID YOU TELL HIM WHAT IT'S CALLED? NOT SQUALL'S END, NOT THE NAME ON THE MAP.
THAT'S THE FIRST THING YOU SHOULD HAVE TOLD HIM. WHAT IT'S FULL OF. AND WHAT IT ACTUALLY IS.

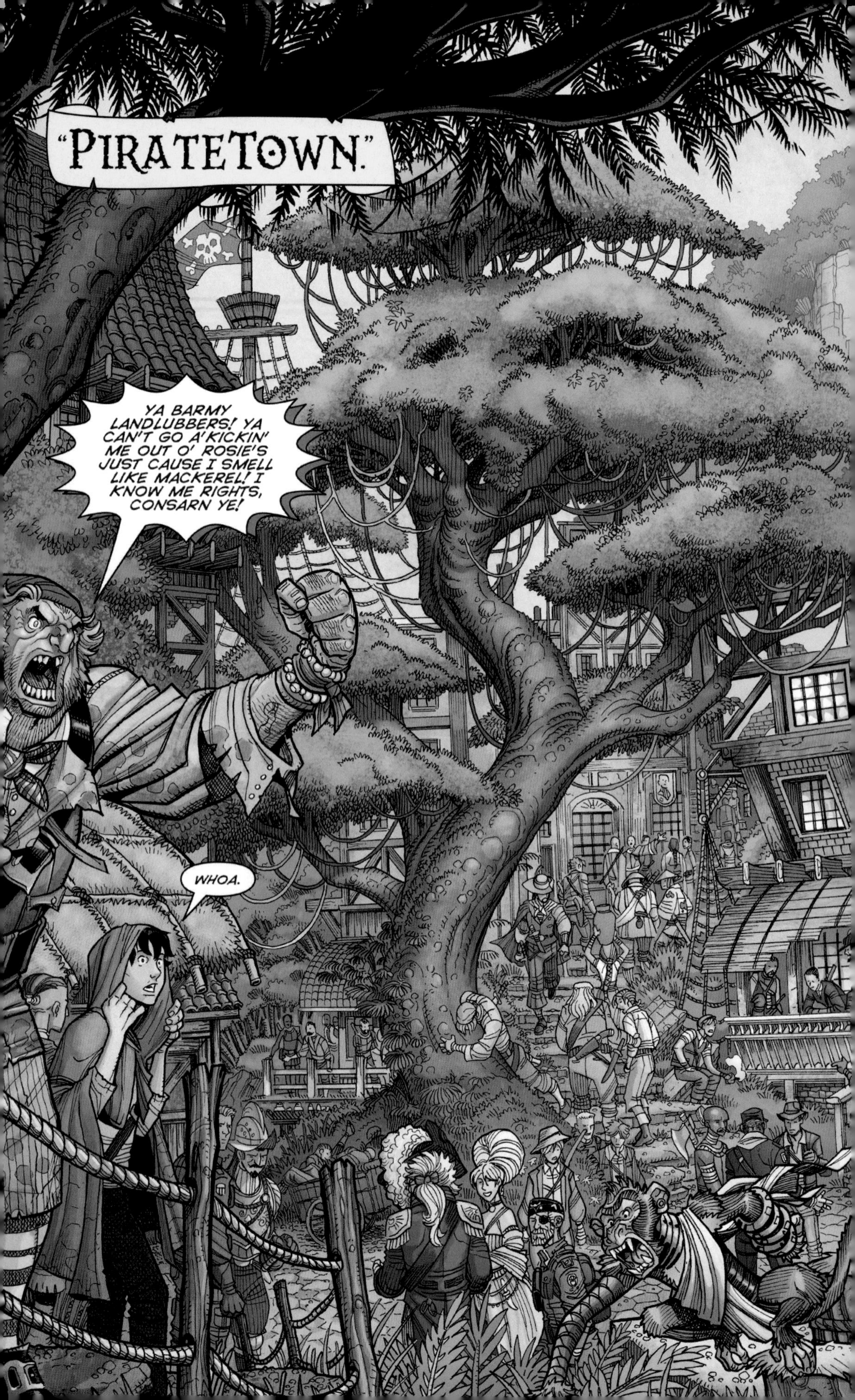
"PIRATETOWN."
YA BARMY LANDLUBBERS! YA CAN'T GO A'KICKIN' ME OUT O' ROSIE'S JUST CAUSE I SMELL LIKE MACKEREL! I KNOW ME RIGHTS, CONSARN YE!
WHOA.

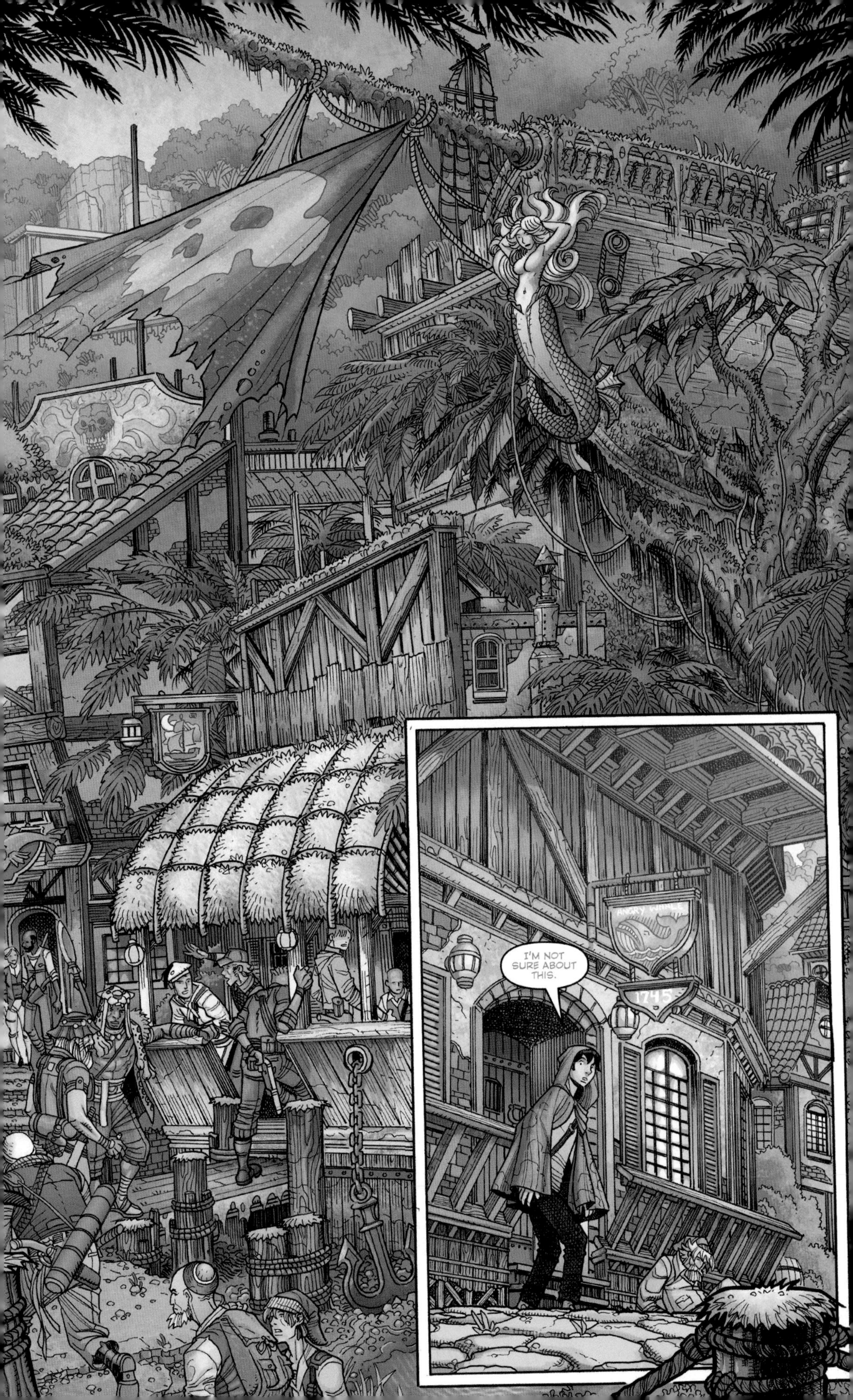
ANGRY WHALE
1745
I'M NOT SURE ABOUT THIS.

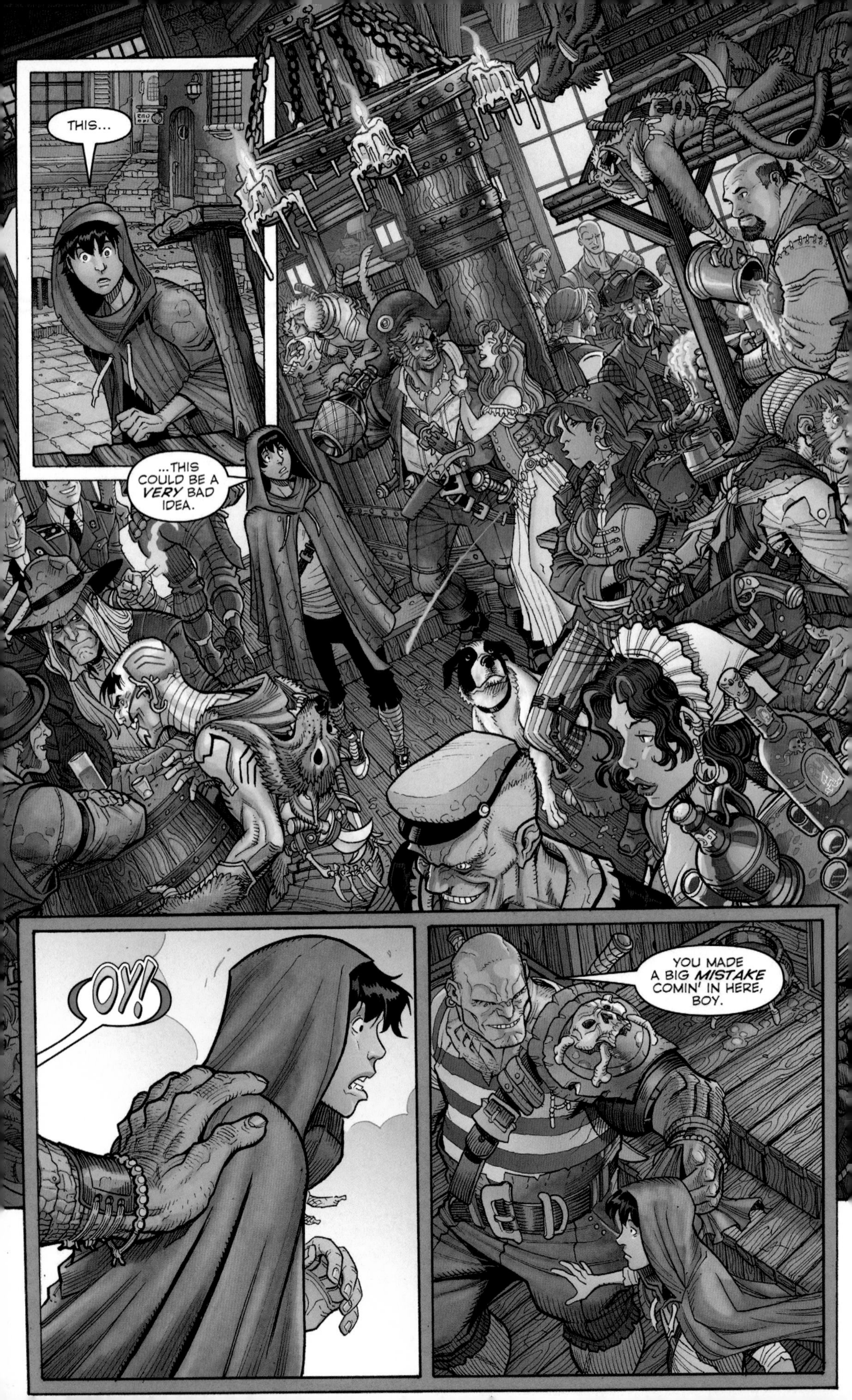

THIS...
...THIS COULD BE A *VERY* BAD IDEA.
OY!
YOU MADE A BIG *MISTAKE* COMIN' IN HERE, BOY.

LAST DeBERRY BOY THAT WANDERED IN HERE *LEFT* STUFFED IN AN EMPTY RUM BARREL.

IN *MULTIPLE* RUM BARRELS, IF'N YOU CATCH ME MEANING.

DeBERRY? YOU *SLOW* IN THE HEAD, KID? YOU'RE IN THE *WRONG* CREW.

THIS HERE ESTABLISHMENT IS A *LAFITTE* BAR. BEEN FOR GENERATIONS NOW, KEEPIN' WITH THE *OLD WAYS*--

--EVER SINCE OL' BLACK EDWARD LAFITTE AND *HIS* CREW FIRST WASHED UP HERE, AND SETTLED IN.

NO... I-I'M NOT PART OF *ANY* CREW.

I'M HERE ON MY *OWN.* I'VE GOT A *JOB* I WANT TO TALK TO YOU ABOUT.

AH, WELL, *THAT'S* A DIFFERENT KETTLE OF FISH ALTOGETHER.

YOU HEAR *THAT,* DRAKE?

STRAPPING YOUNG LADDIE HERE SAYS HE'S HERE ABOUT A *JOB.*

IZZAT SO?

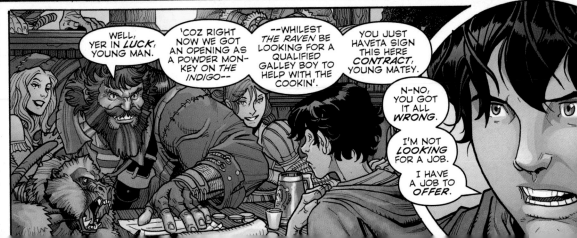

WELL, YER IN *LUCK,* YOUNG MAN.

'COZ RIGHT NOW WE GOT AN OPENING AS A POWDER MON-KEY ON *THE INDIGO*--

--WHILEST *THE RAVEN* BE LOOKING FOR A QUALIFIED GALLEY BOY TO HELP WITH THE COOKIN'.

YOU JUST HAVETA SIGN THIS HERE *CONTRACT,* YOUNG MATEY.

N-NO, YOU GOT IT ALL *WRONG.*

I'M NOT *LOOKING* FOR A JOB.

I HAVE A JOB TO *OFFER.*

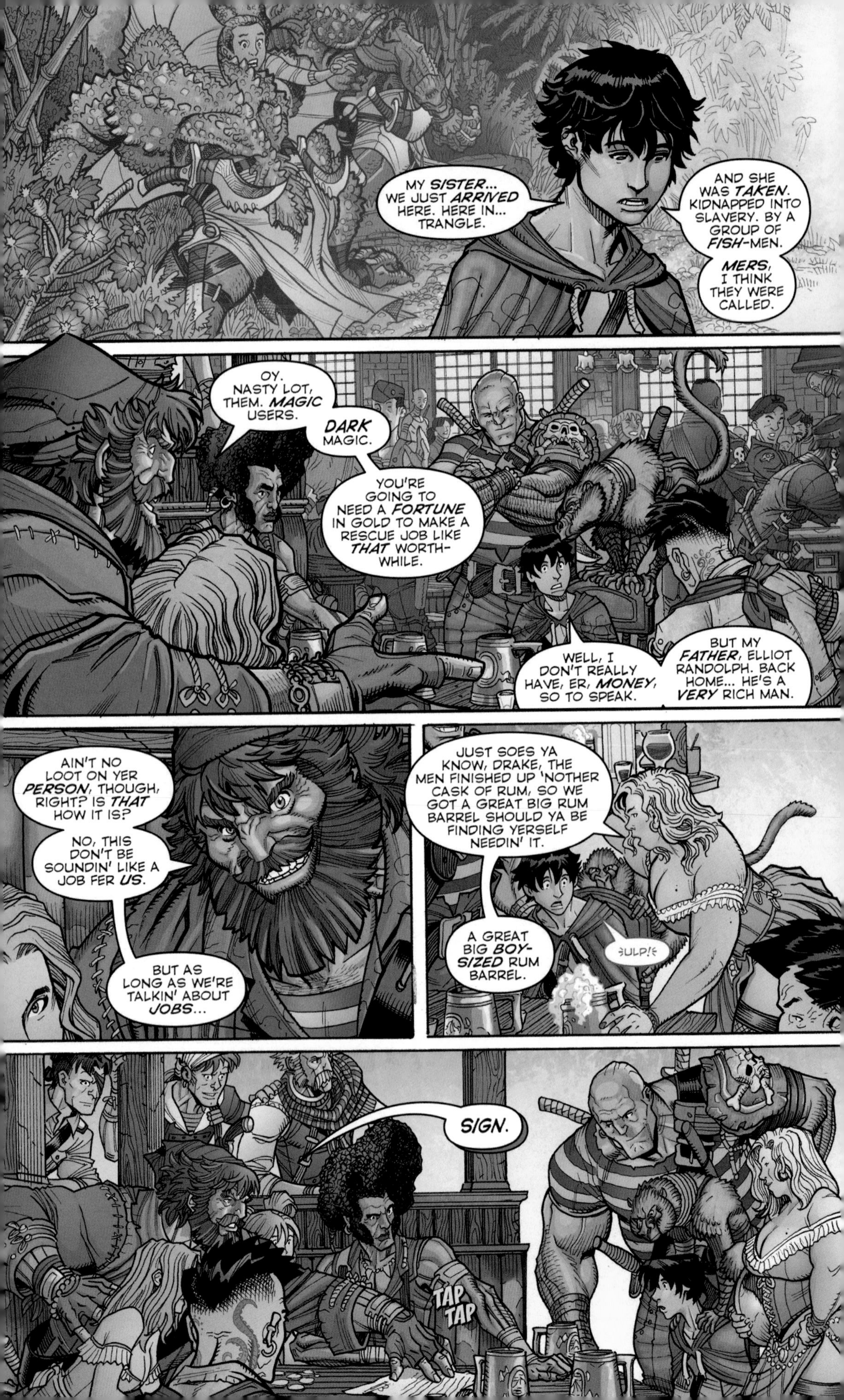
MY SISTER... WE JUST ARRIVED HERE. HERE IN... TRANGLE.
AND SHE WAS TAKEN. KIDNAPPED INTO SLAVERY. BY A GROUP OF FISH-MEN.
MERS, I THINK THEY WERE CALLED.
OY. NASTY LOT, THEM. MAGIC USERS.
DARK MAGIC.
YOU'RE GOING TO NEED A FORTUNE IN GOLD TO MAKE A RESCUE JOB LIKE THAT WORTH-WHILE.
WELL, I DON'T REALLY HAVE, ER, MONEY, SO TO SPEAK.
BUT MY FATHER, ELLIOT RANDOLPH. BACK HOME... HE'S A VERY RICH MAN.
AIN'T NO LOOT ON YER PERSON, THOUGH, RIGHT? IS THAT HOW IT IS?
NO, THIS DON'T BE SOUNDIN' LIKE A JOB FER US.
BUT AS LONG AS WE'RE TALKIN' ABOUT JOBS...
JUST SOES YA KNOW, DRAKE, THE MEN FINISHED UP 'NOTHER CASK OF RUM, SO WE GOT A GREAT BIG RUM BARREL SHOULD YA BE FINDING YERSELF NEEDIN' IT.
A GREAT BIG BOY-SIZED RUM BARREL.
ULP!
SIGN.
TAP TAP

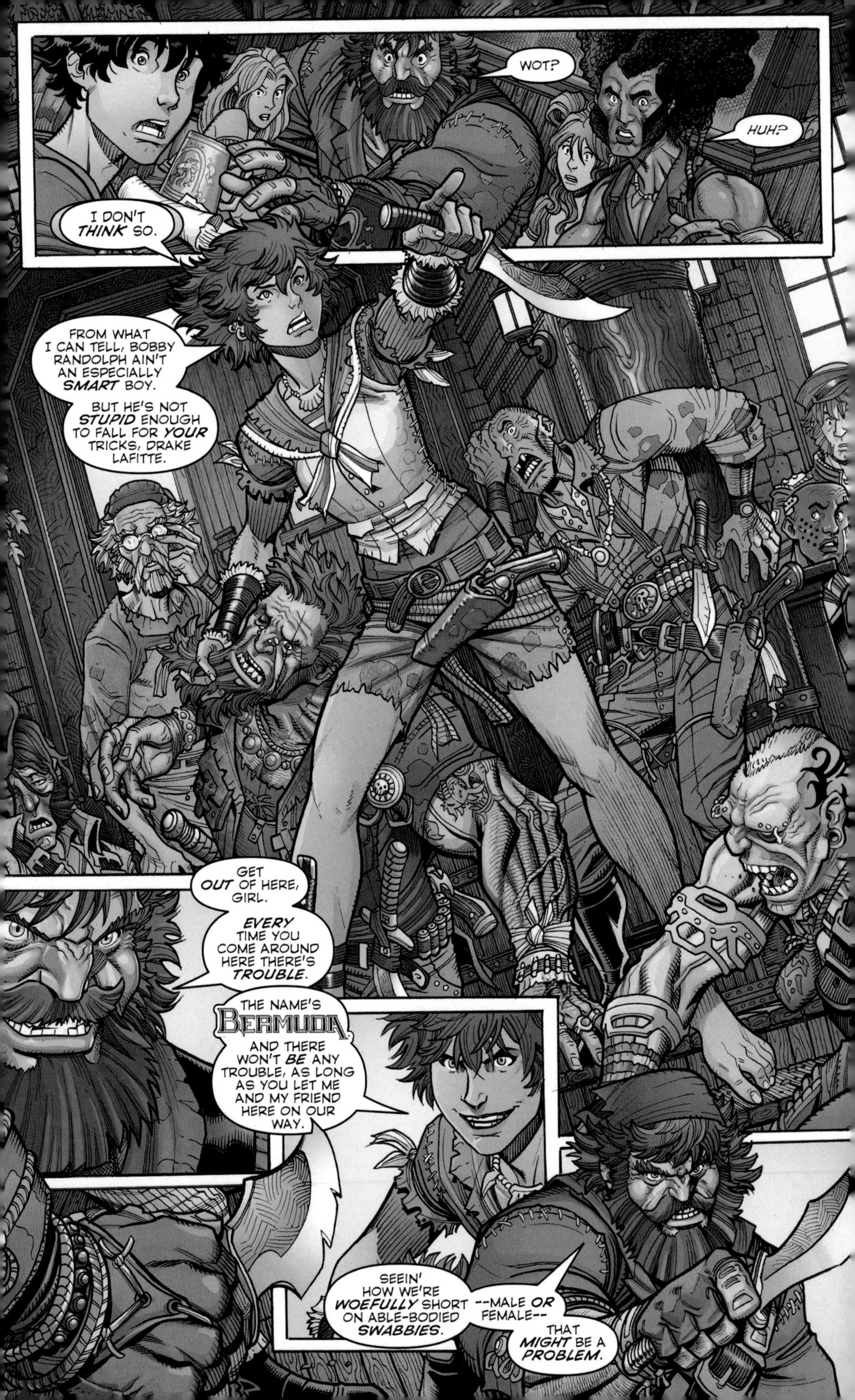
WOT?
HUH?
I DON'T THINK SO.
FROM WHAT I CAN TELL, BOBBY RANDOLPH AIN'T AN ESPECIALLY SMART BOY.
BUT HE'S NOT STUPID ENOUGH TO FALL FOR YOUR TRICKS, DRAKE LAFITTE.
GET OUT OF HERE, GIRL.
EVERY TIME YOU COME AROUND HERE THERE'S TROUBLE.
THE NAME'S BERMUDA AND THERE WON'T BE ANY TROUBLE, AS LONG AS YOU LET ME AND MY FRIEND HERE ON OUR WAY.
SEEIN' HOW WE'RE WOEFULLY SHORT ON ABLE-BODIED SWABBIES.
--MALE OR FEMALE--
THAT MIGHT BE A PROBLEM.

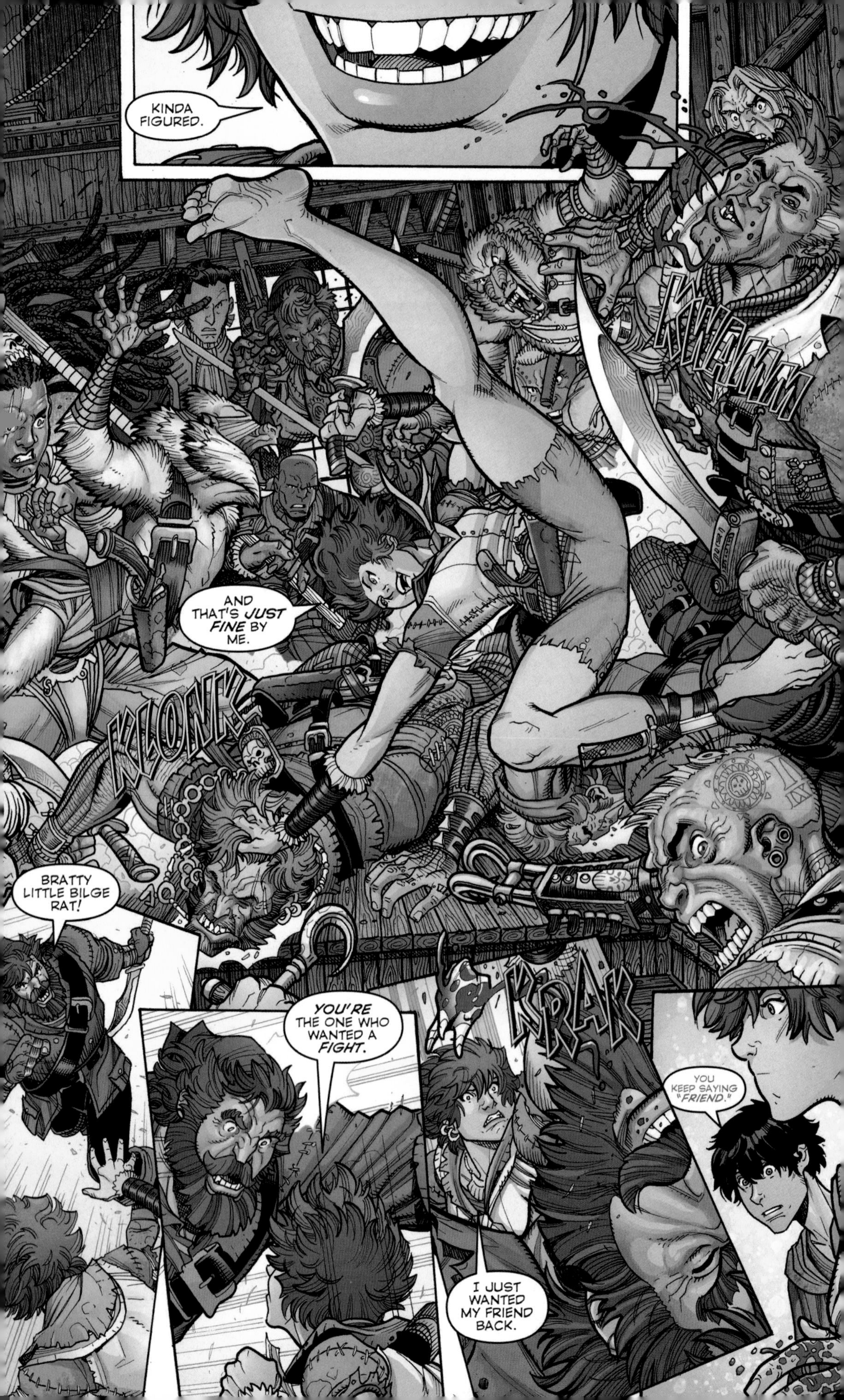
KINDA FIGURED.
KWAMM
AND THAT'S JUST FINE BY ME.
KLONK
BRATTY LITTLE BILGE RAT!
KRAK
YOU'RE THE ONE WHO WANTED A FIGHT.
I JUST WANTED MY FRIEND BACK.
YOU KEEP SAYING "FRIEND."

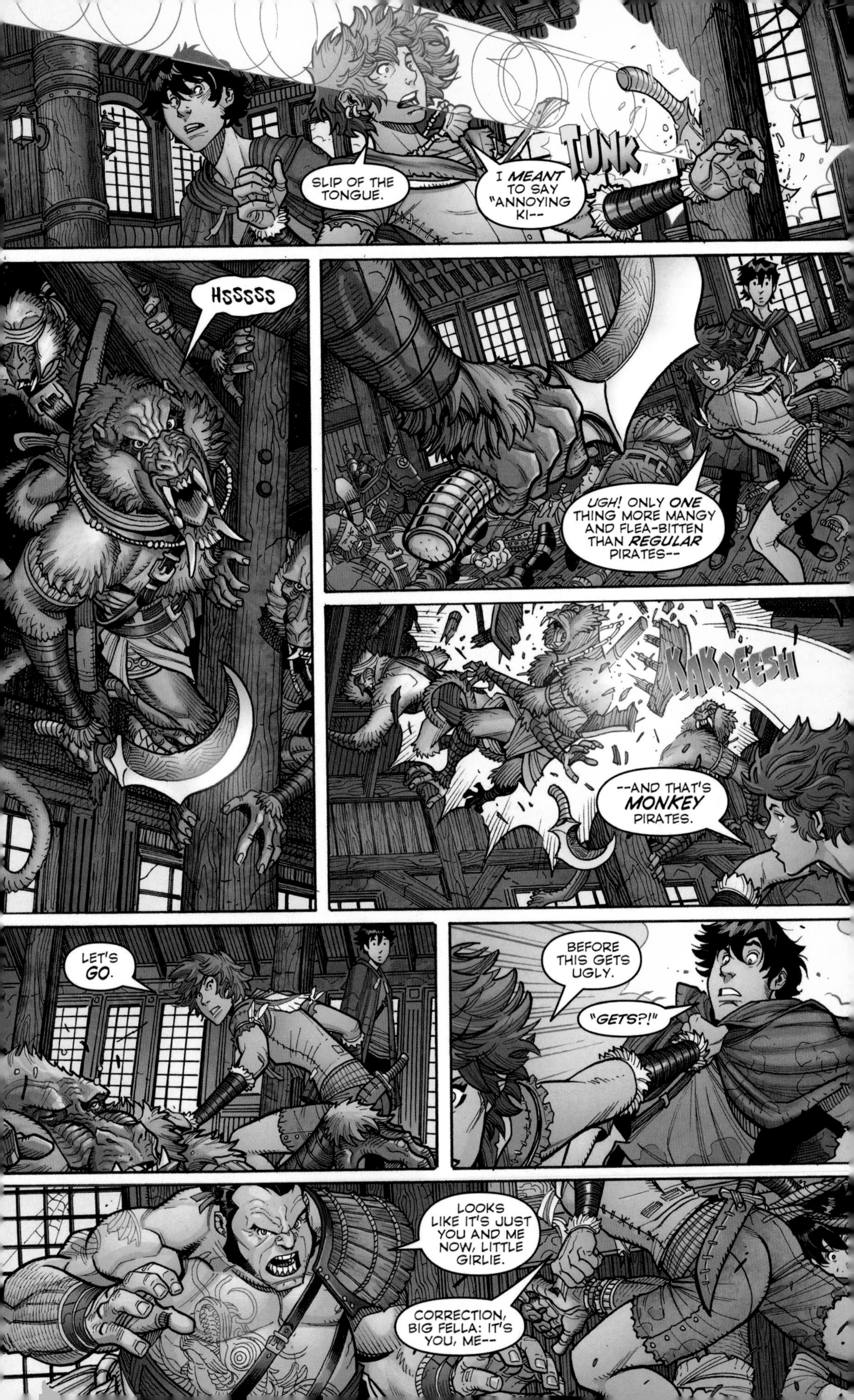
SLIP OF THE TONGUE.
I MEANT TO SAY "ANNOYING KI--
TUNK
HSSSSS
UGH! ONLY ONE THING MORE MANGY AND FLEA-BITTEN THAN REGULAR PIRATES--
KAKREESH
--AND THAT'S MONKEY PIRATES.
LET'S GO.
BEFORE THIS GETS UGLY.
"GETS?!"
LOOKS LIKE IT'S JUST YOU AND ME NOW, LITTLE GIRLIE.
CORRECTION, BIG FELLA: IT'S YOU, ME--

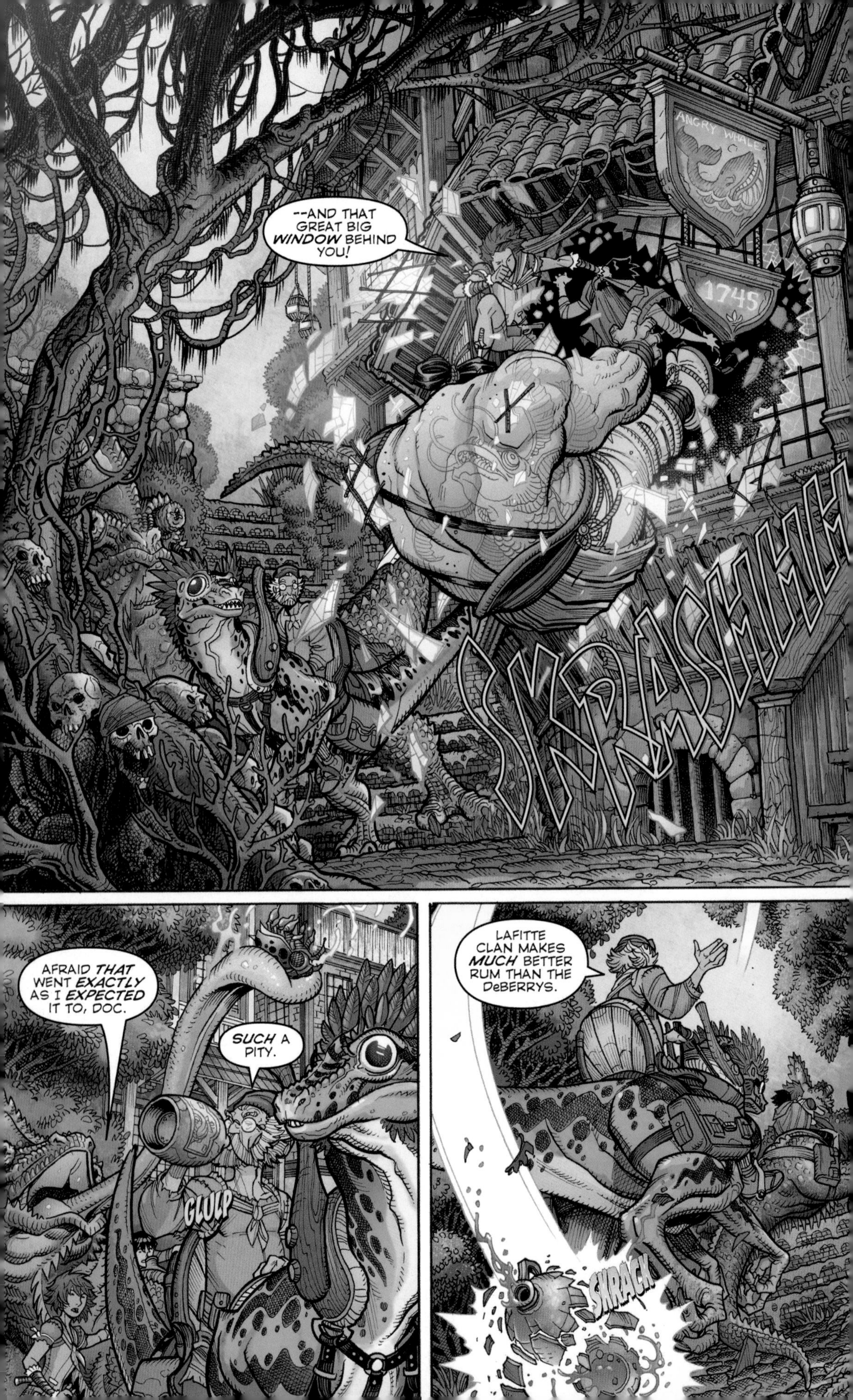
ANGRY WHALE
1745
--AND THAT GREAT BIG WINDOW BEHIND YOU!
AFRAID THAT WENT EXACTLY AS I EXPECTED IT TO, DOC.
SUCH A PITY.
GLULP
LAFITTE CLAN MAKES MUCH BETTER RUM THAN THE DeBERRYS.
SHRACK

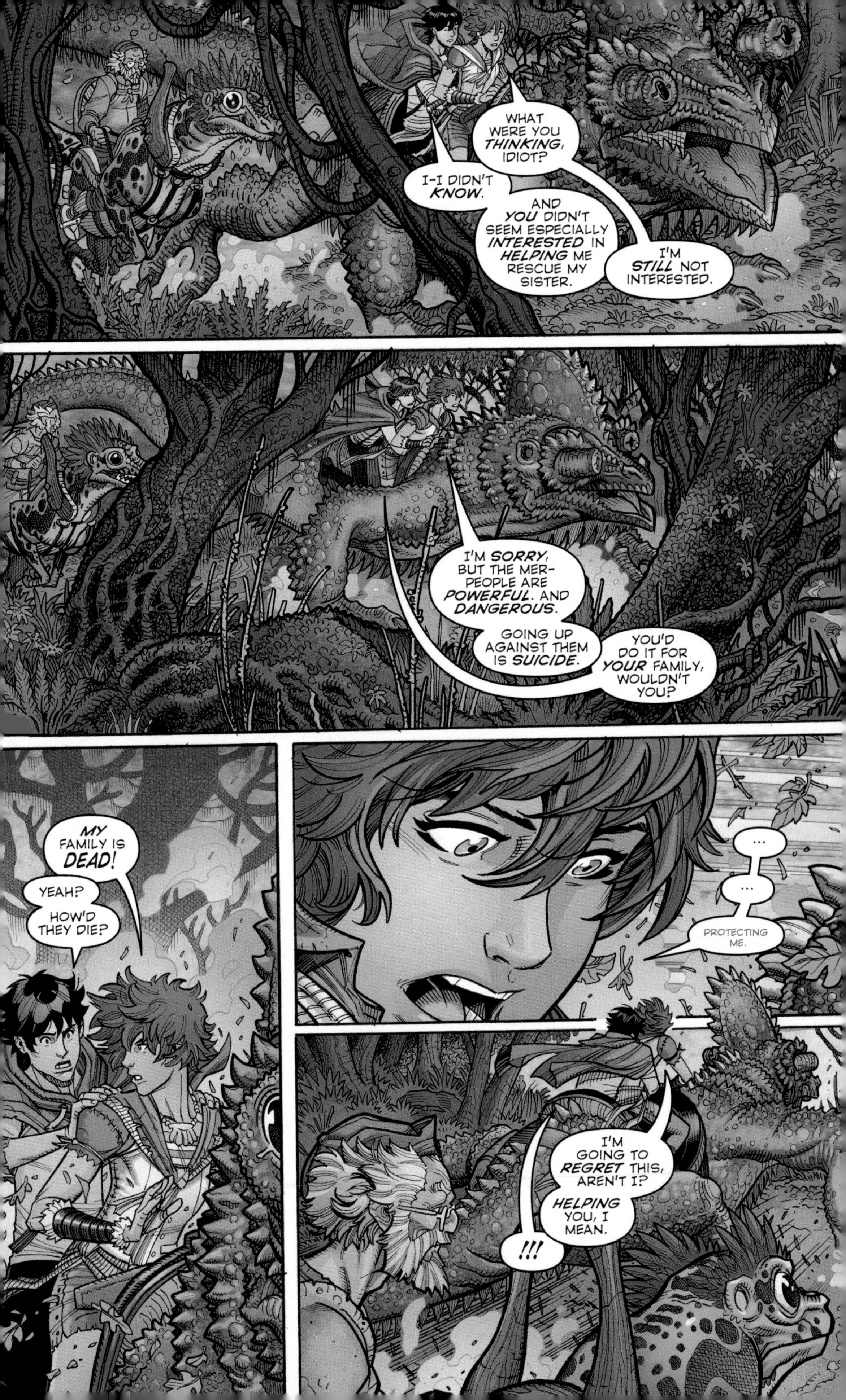
WHAT WERE YOU THINKING, IDIOT?
I-I DIDN'T KNOW.
AND YOU DIDN'T SEEM ESPECIALLY INTERESTED IN HELPING ME RESCUE MY SISTER.
I'M STILL NOT INTERESTED.
I'M SORRY, BUT THE MER-PEOPLE ARE POWERFUL. AND DANGEROUS.
GOING UP AGAINST THEM IS SUICIDE.
YOU'D DO IT FOR YOUR FAMILY, WOULDN'T YOU?
MY FAMILY IS DEAD!
YEAH? HOW'D THEY DIE?
...
...
PROTECTING ME.
I'M GOING TO REGRET THIS, AREN'T I?
HELPING YOU, I MEAN.
!!!

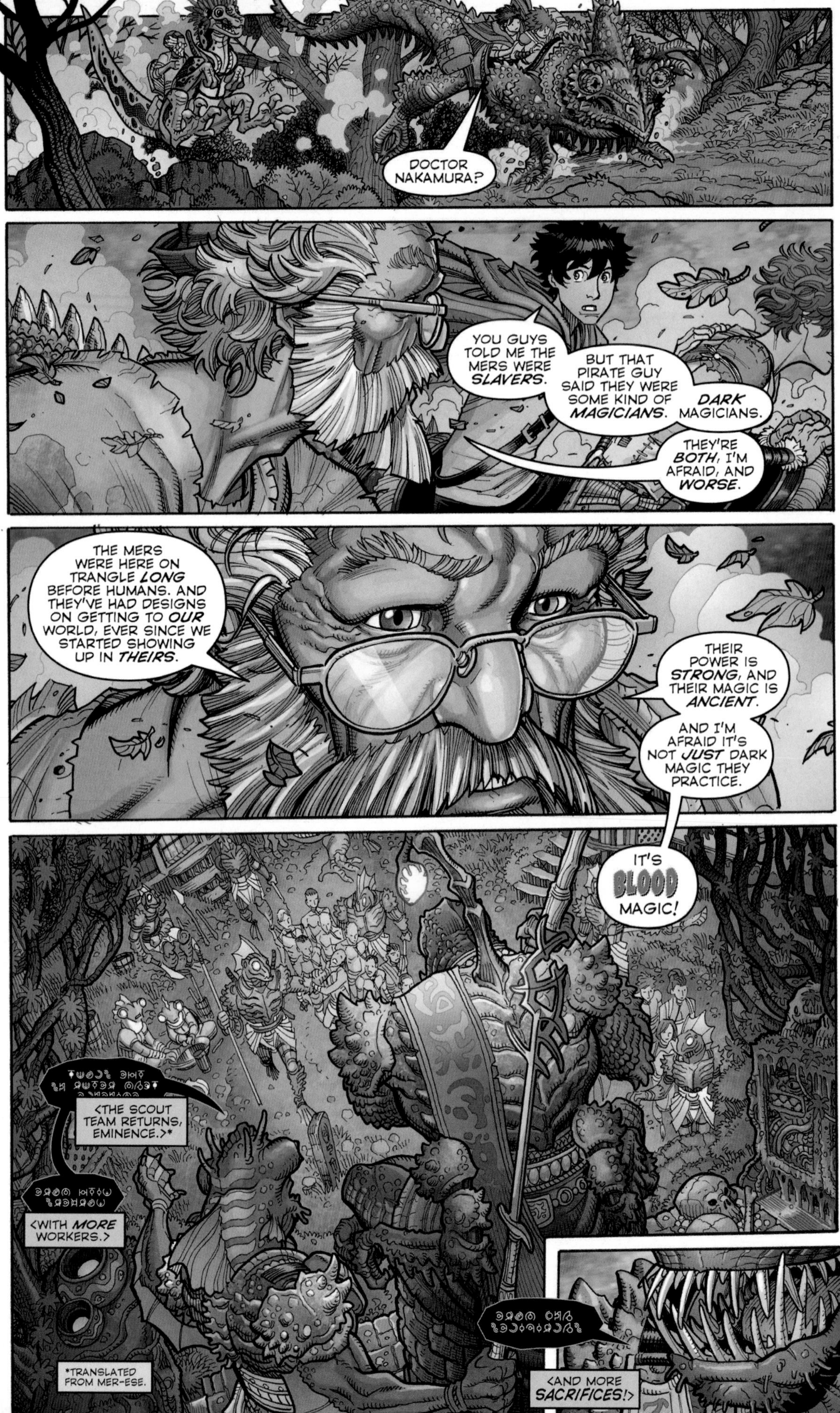
DOCTOR NAKAMURA?
YOU GUYS TOLD ME THE MERS WERE SLAVERS.
BUT THAT PIRATE GUY SAID THEY WERE SOME KIND OF MAGICIANS. DARK MAGICIANS.
THEY'RE BOTH, I'M AFRAID, AND WORSE.
THE MERS WERE HERE ON TRANGLE LONG BEFORE HUMANS. AND THEY'VE HAD DESIGNS ON GETTING TO OUR WORLD, EVER SINCE WE STARTED SHOWING UP IN THEIRS.
THEIR POWER IS STRONG, AND THEIR MAGIC IS ANCIENT.
AND I'M AFRAID IT'S NOT JUST DARK MAGIC THEY PRACTICE.
IT'S BLOOD MAGIC!
<THE SCOUT TEAM RETURNS, EMINENCE.>*
<WITH MORE WORKERS.>
*TRANSLATED FROM MER-ESE.
<AND MORE SACRIFICES!>

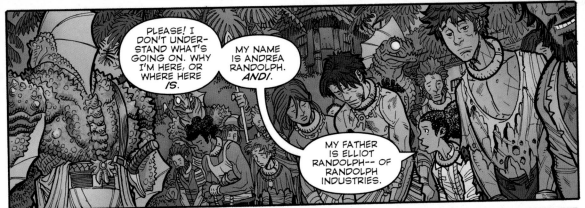

PLEASE! I DON'T UNDERSTAND WHAT'S GOING ON. WHY I'M HERE, OR WHERE HERE *IS.*

MY NAME IS ANDREA RANDOLPH. *ANDI.*

MY FATHER IS ELLIOT RANDOLPH-- OF RANDOLPH INDUSTRIES.

<HER.>

<I... *SENSE* SOMETHING.>

<BRING HER TO THE *SCRYING POOL.*>

WHAT'S HE *SAYING?*

PLEASE! WHAT'S *HAPPENING?*

OWW!

SCRIPP

P-PLEASE...

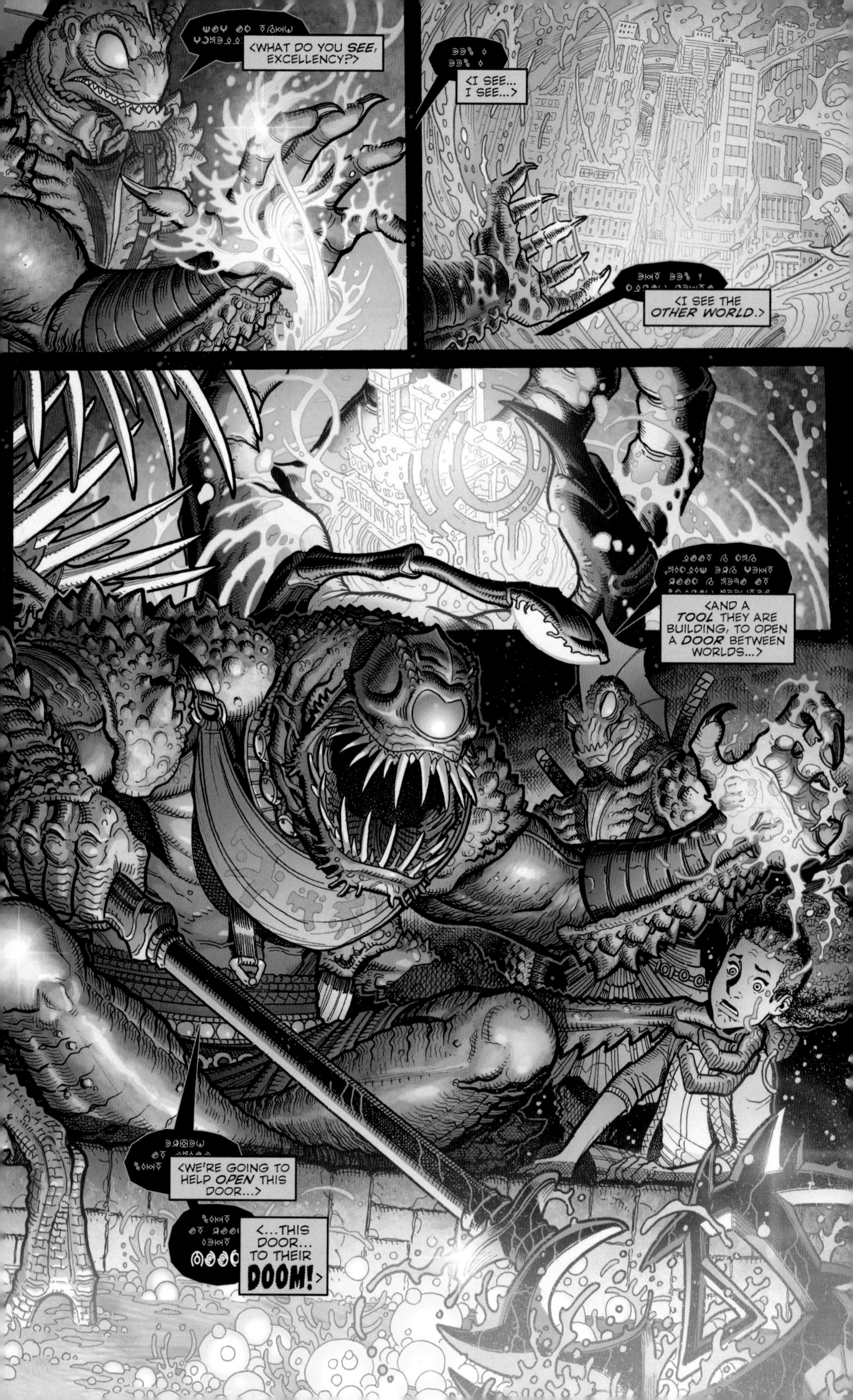
<WHAT DO YOU SEE, EXCELLENCY?>
<I SEE... I SEE...>
<I SEE THE OTHER WORLD.>
<AND A TOOL THEY ARE BUILDING, TO OPEN A DOOR BETWEEN WORLDS...>
<WE'RE GOING TO HELP OPEN THIS DOOR...>
<...THIS DOOR... TO THEIR DOOM!>

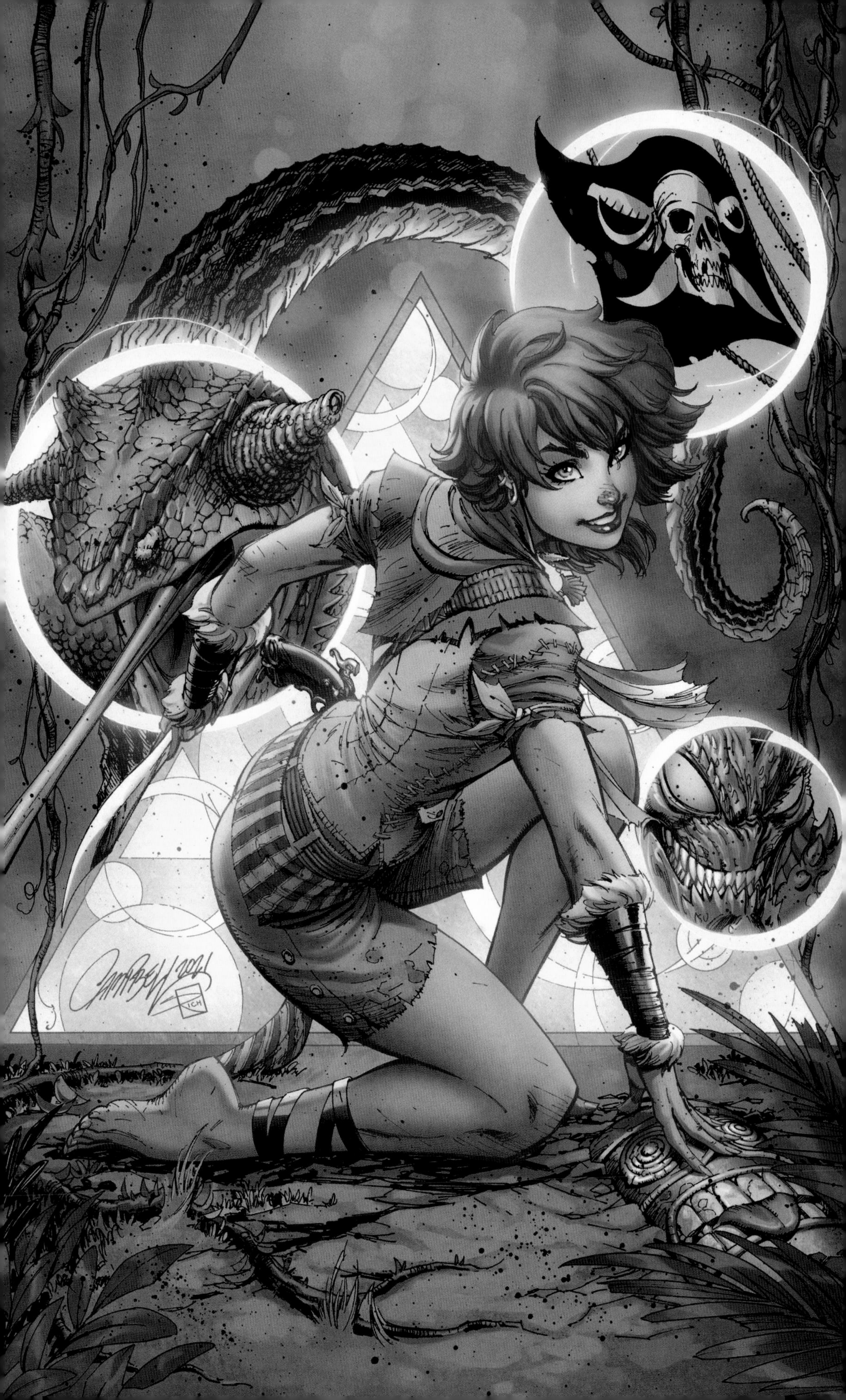

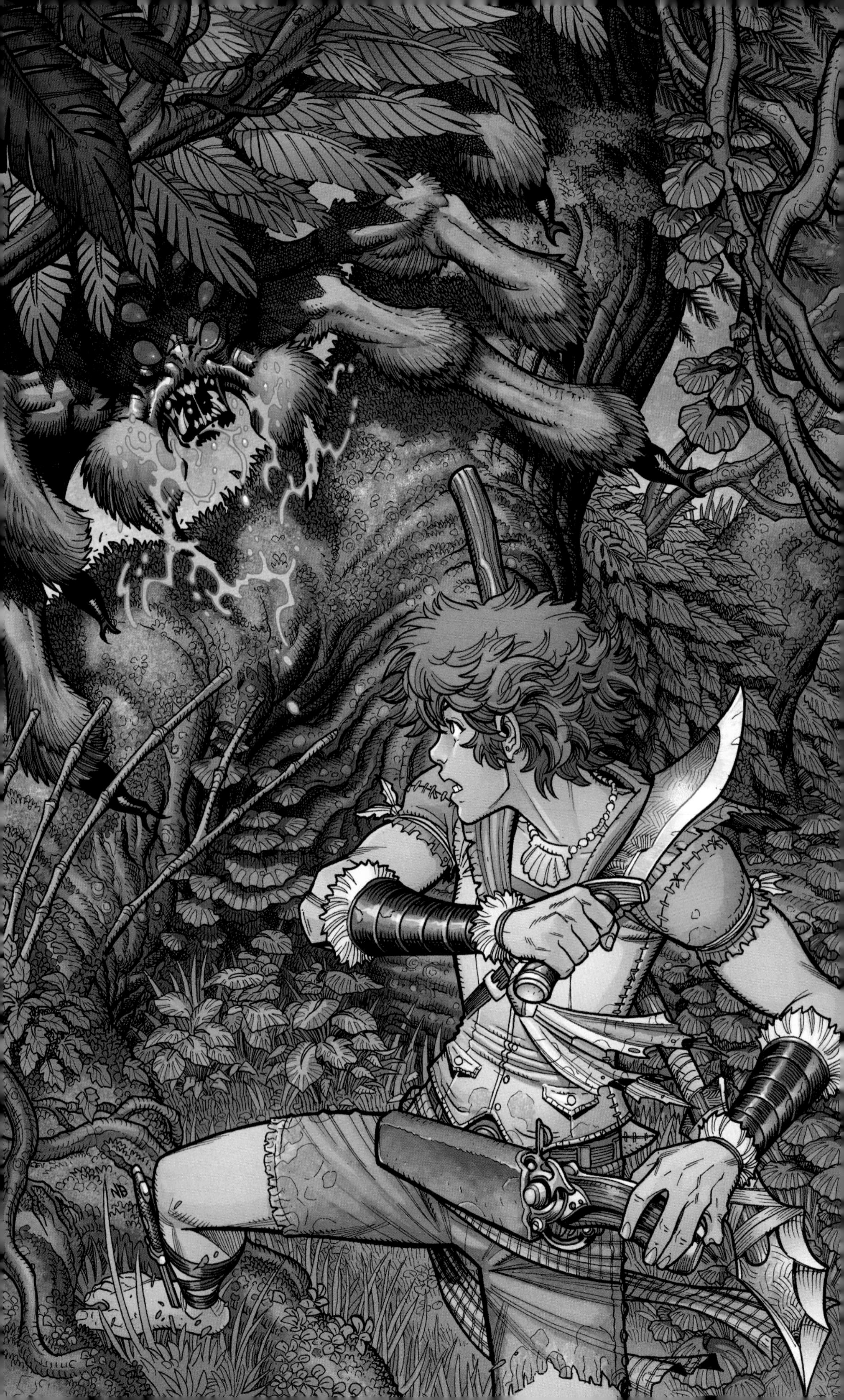

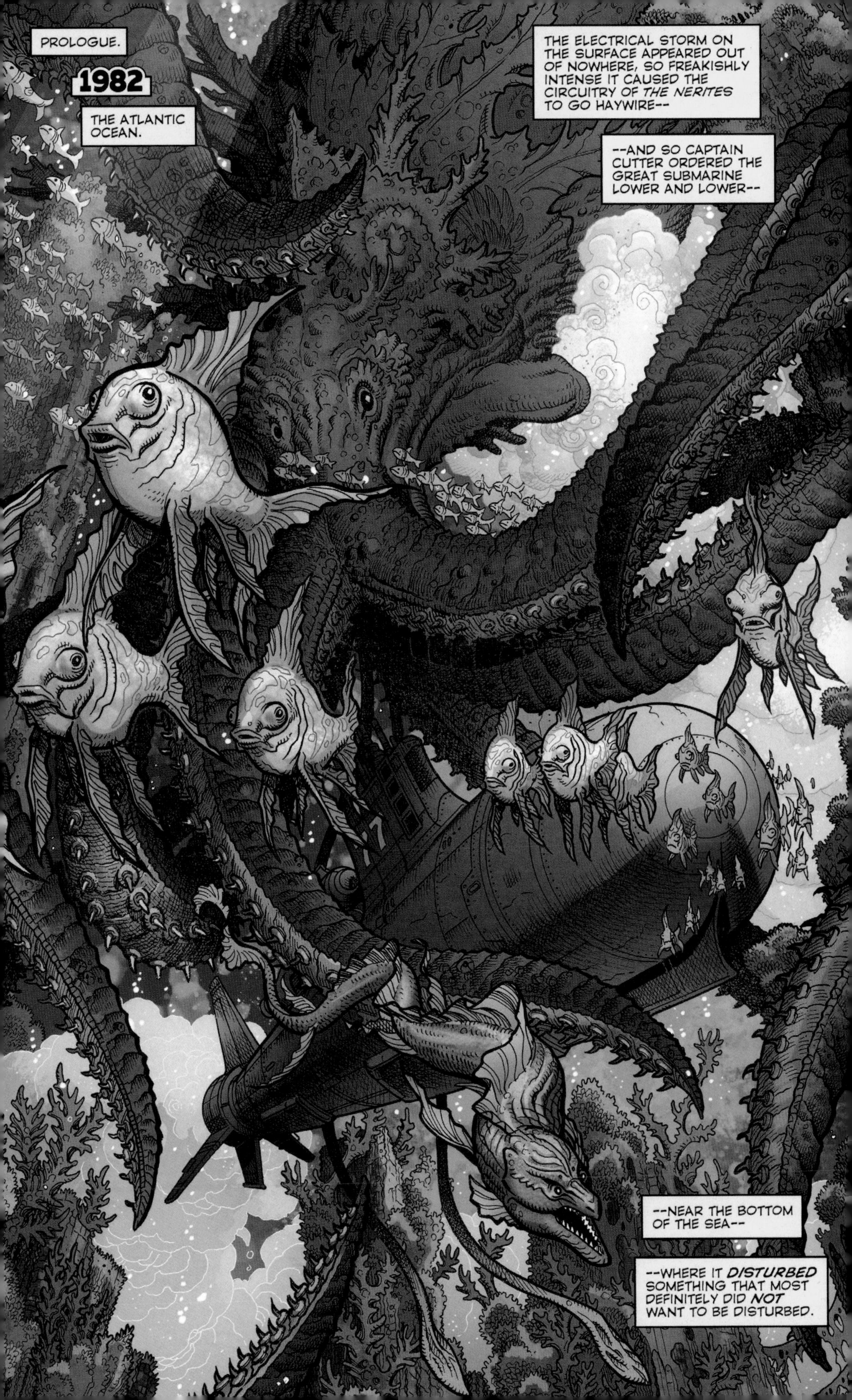
PROLOGUE.
1982
THE ATLANTIC OCEAN.
THE ELECTRICAL STORM ON THE SURFACE APPEARED OUT OF NOWHERE, SO FREAKISHLY INTENSE IT CAUSED THE CIRCUITRY OF *THE NERITES* TO GO HAYWIRE--
--AND SO CAPTAIN CUTTER ORDERED THE GREAT SUBMARINE LOWER AND LOWER--
--NEAR THE BOTTOM OF THE SEA--
--WHERE IT ***DISTURBED*** SOMETHING THAT MOST DEFINITELY DID ***NOT*** WANT TO BE DISTURBED.

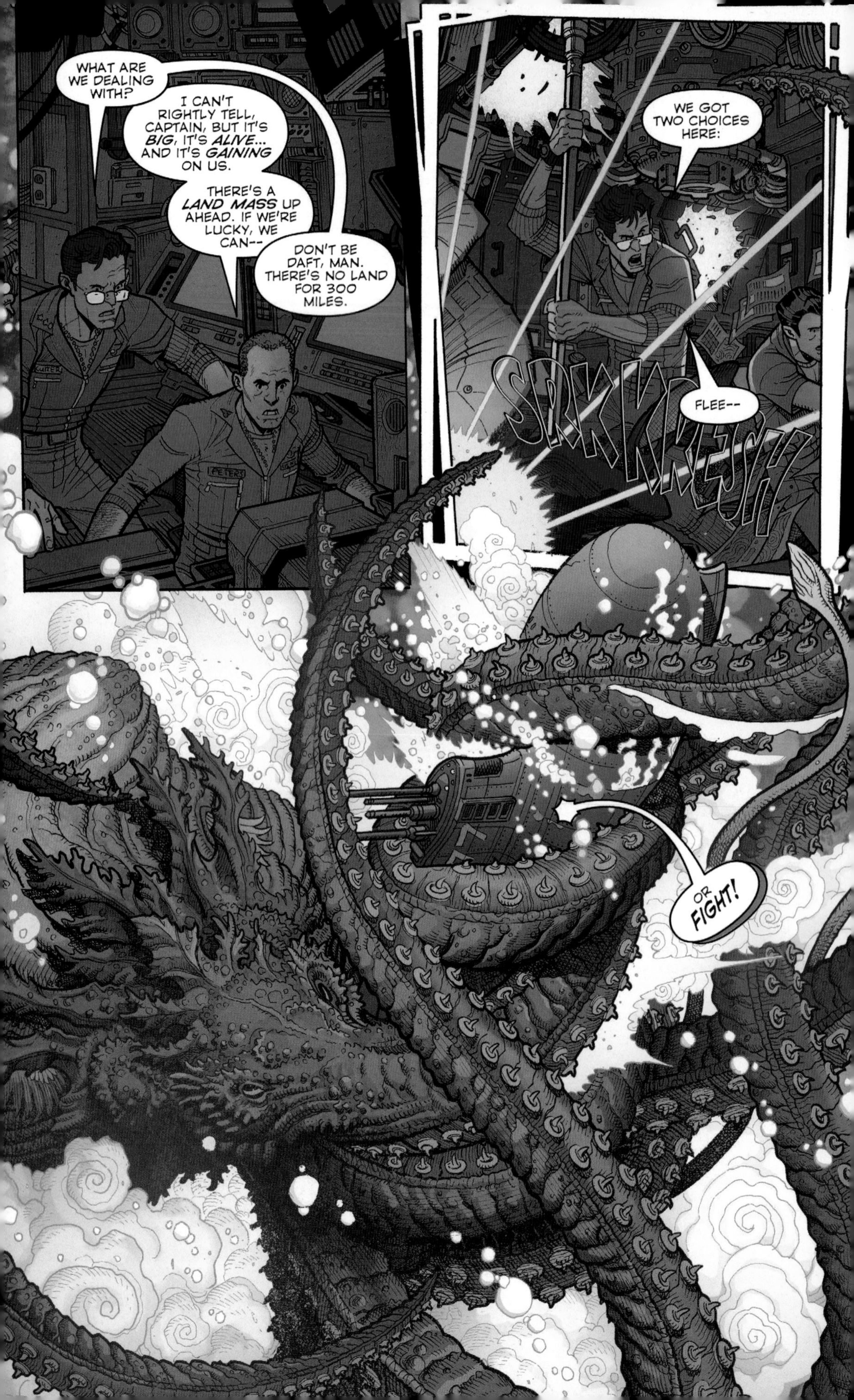
WHAT ARE WE DEALING WITH?
I CAN'T RIGHTLY TELL, CAPTAIN, BUT IT'S *BIG*, IT'S *ALIVE*... AND IT'S *GAINING* ON US.
THERE'S A *LAND MASS* UP AHEAD. IF WE'RE LUCKY, WE CAN--
DON'T BE DAFT, MAN. THERE'S NO LAND FOR 300 MILES.
WE GOT TWO CHOICES HERE:
FLEE--
SRKKRESH
OR *FIGHT!*

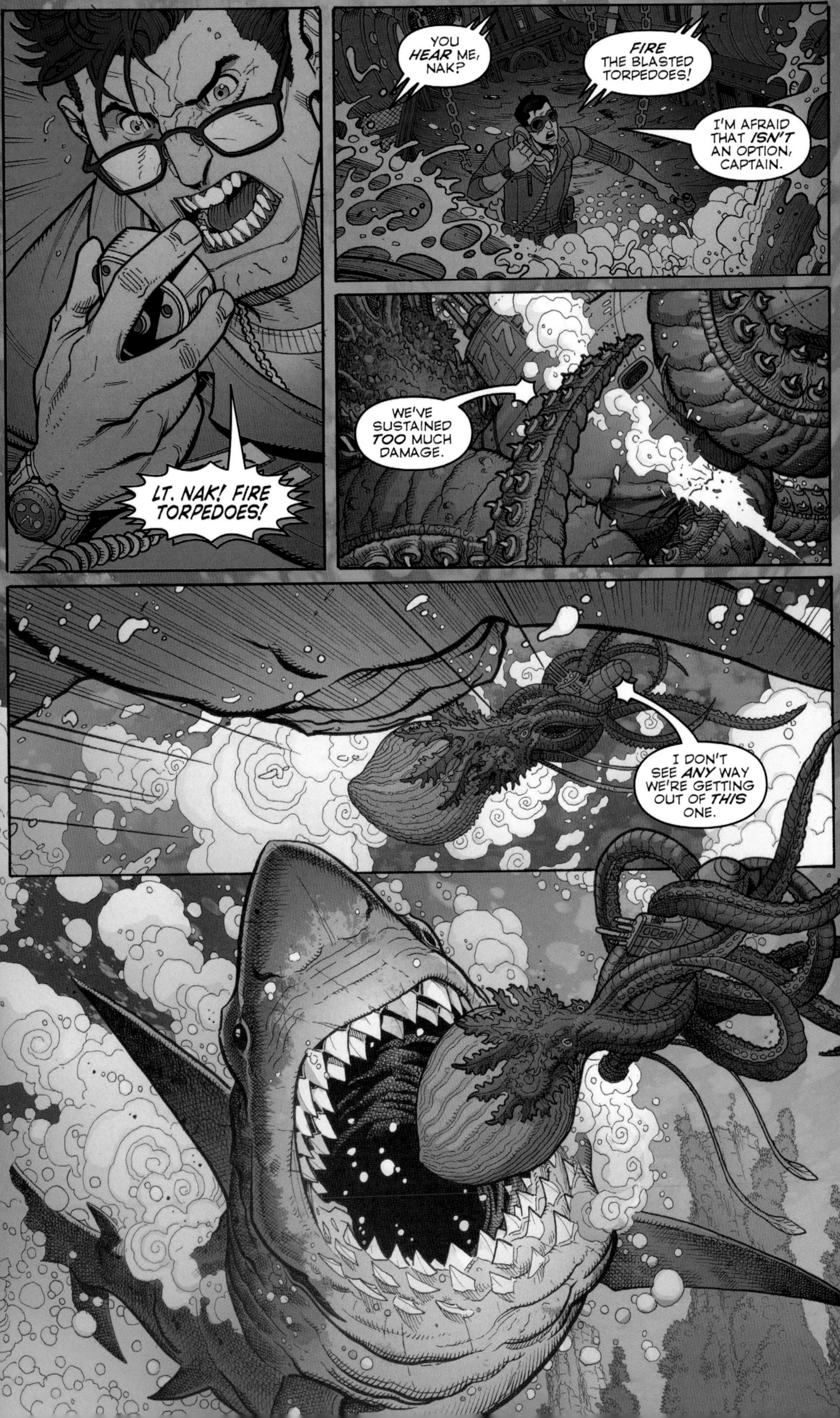
LT. NAK! FIRE TORPEDOES!
YOU HEAR ME, NAK?
FIRE THE BLASTED TORPEDOES!
I'M AFRAID THAT ISN'T AN OPTION, CAPTAIN.
WE'VE SUSTAINED TOO MUCH DAMAGE.
I DON'T SEE ANY WAY WE'RE GETTING OUT OF THIS ONE.

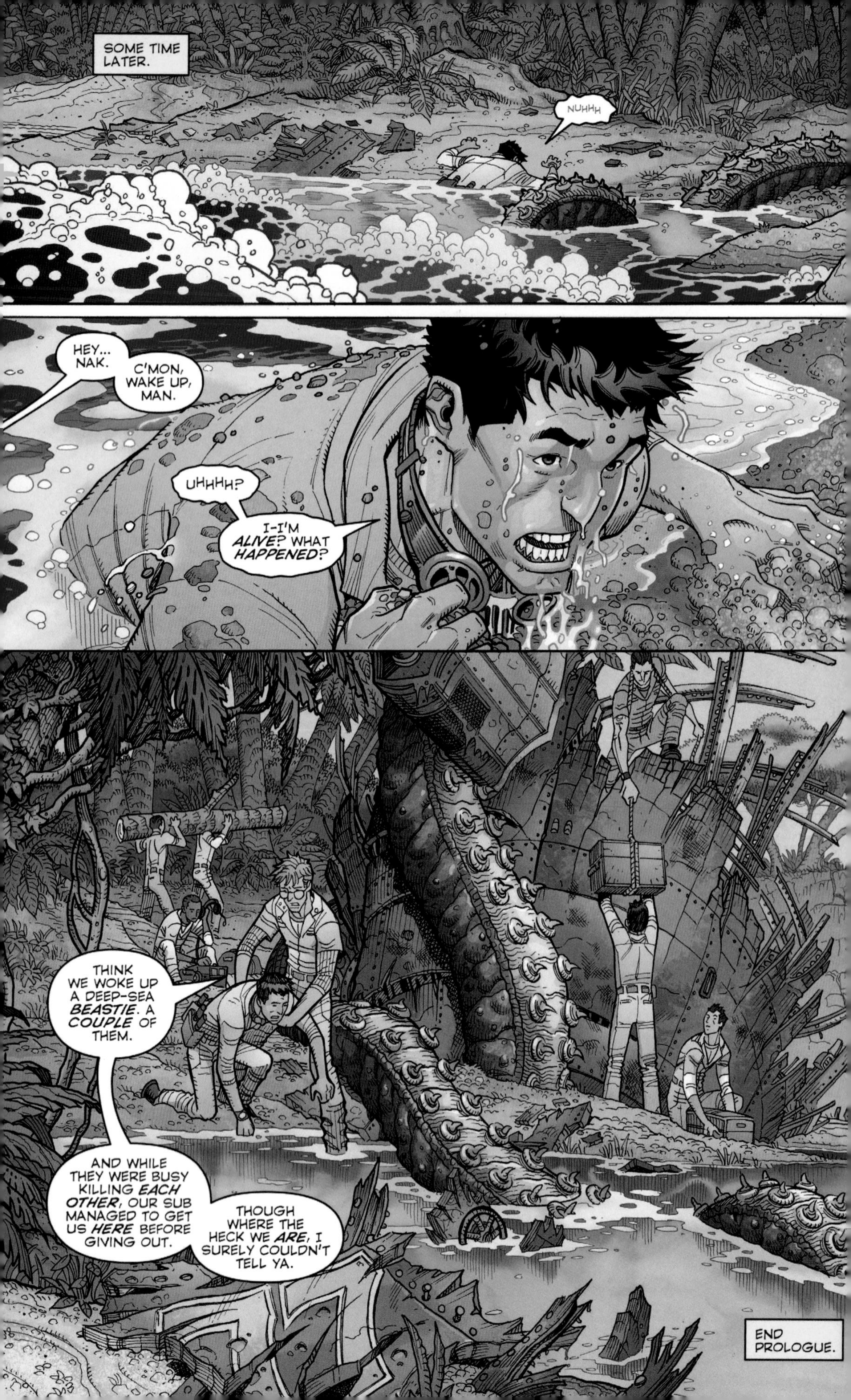
SOME TIME LATER.
NUHHH
HEY... NAK.
C'MON, WAKE UP, MAN.
UHHHH?
I-I'M ALIVE? WHAT HAPPENED?
THINK WE WOKE UP A DEEP-SEA BEASTIE. A COUPLE OF THEM.
AND WHILE THEY WERE BUSY KILLING EACH OTHER, OUR SUB MANAGED TO GET US HERE BEFORE GIVING OUT.
THOUGH WHERE THE HECK WE ARE, I SURELY COULDN'T TELL YA.
END PROLOGUE.

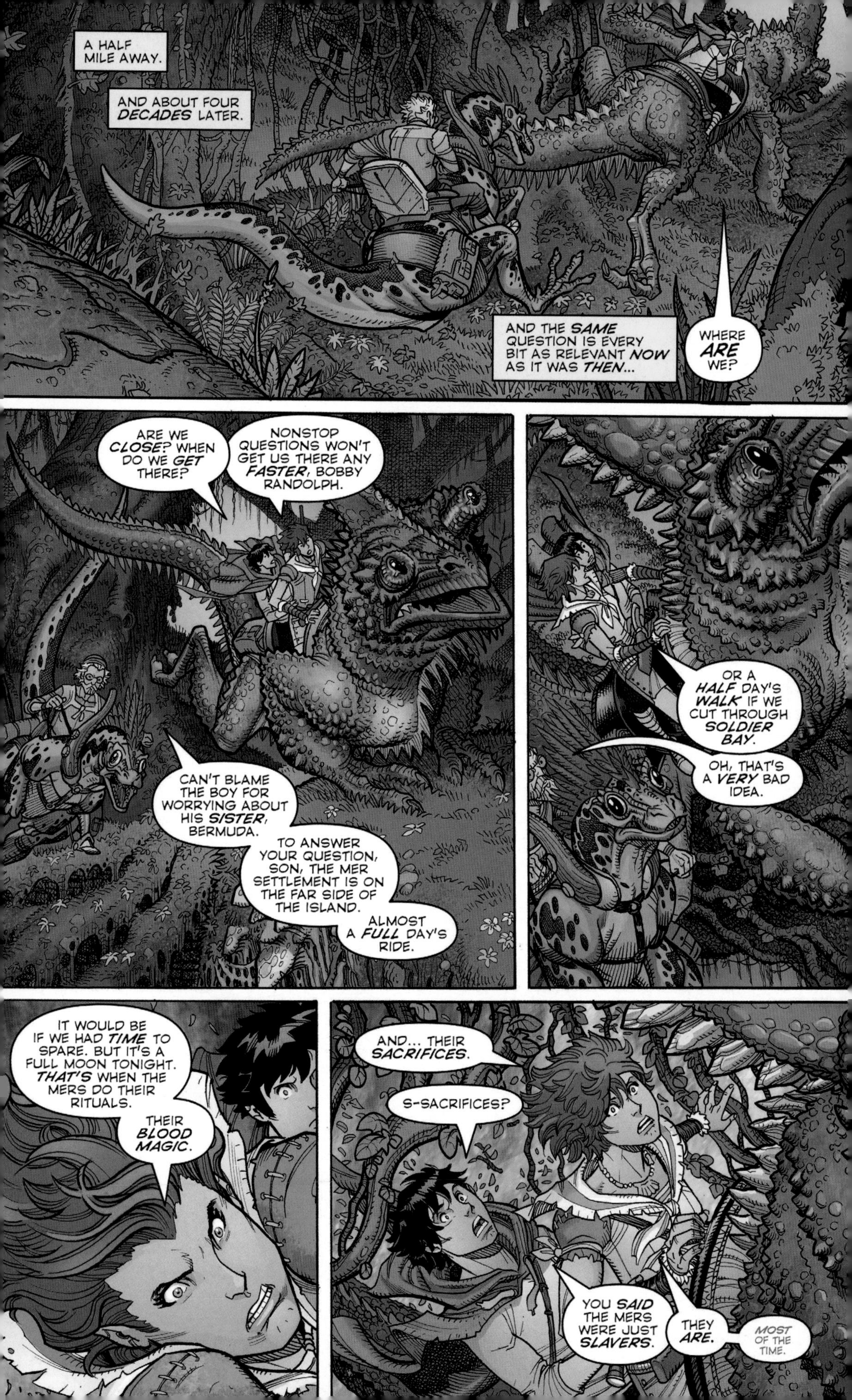
A HALF MILE AWAY.
AND ABOUT FOUR DECADES LATER.
AND THE SAME QUESTION IS EVERY BIT AS RELEVANT NOW AS IT WAS THEN...
WHERE ARE WE?
ARE WE CLOSE? WHEN DO WE GET THERE?
NONSTOP QUESTIONS WON'T GET US THERE ANY FASTER, BOBBY RANDOLPH.
CAN'T BLAME THE BOY FOR WORRYING ABOUT HIS SISTER, BERMUDA.
TO ANSWER YOUR QUESTION, SON, THE MER SETTLEMENT IS ON THE FAR SIDE OF THE ISLAND.
ALMOST A FULL DAY'S RIDE.
OR A HALF DAY'S WALK IF WE CUT THROUGH SOLDIER BAY.
OH, THAT'S A VERY BAD IDEA.
IT WOULD BE IF WE HAD TIME TO SPARE. BUT IT'S A FULL MOON TONIGHT. THAT'S WHEN THE MERS DO THEIR RITUALS.
THEIR BLOOD MAGIC.
AND... THEIR SACRIFICES.
S-SACRIFICES?
YOU SAID THE MERS WERE JUST SLAVERS.
THEY ARE.
MOST OF THE TIME.

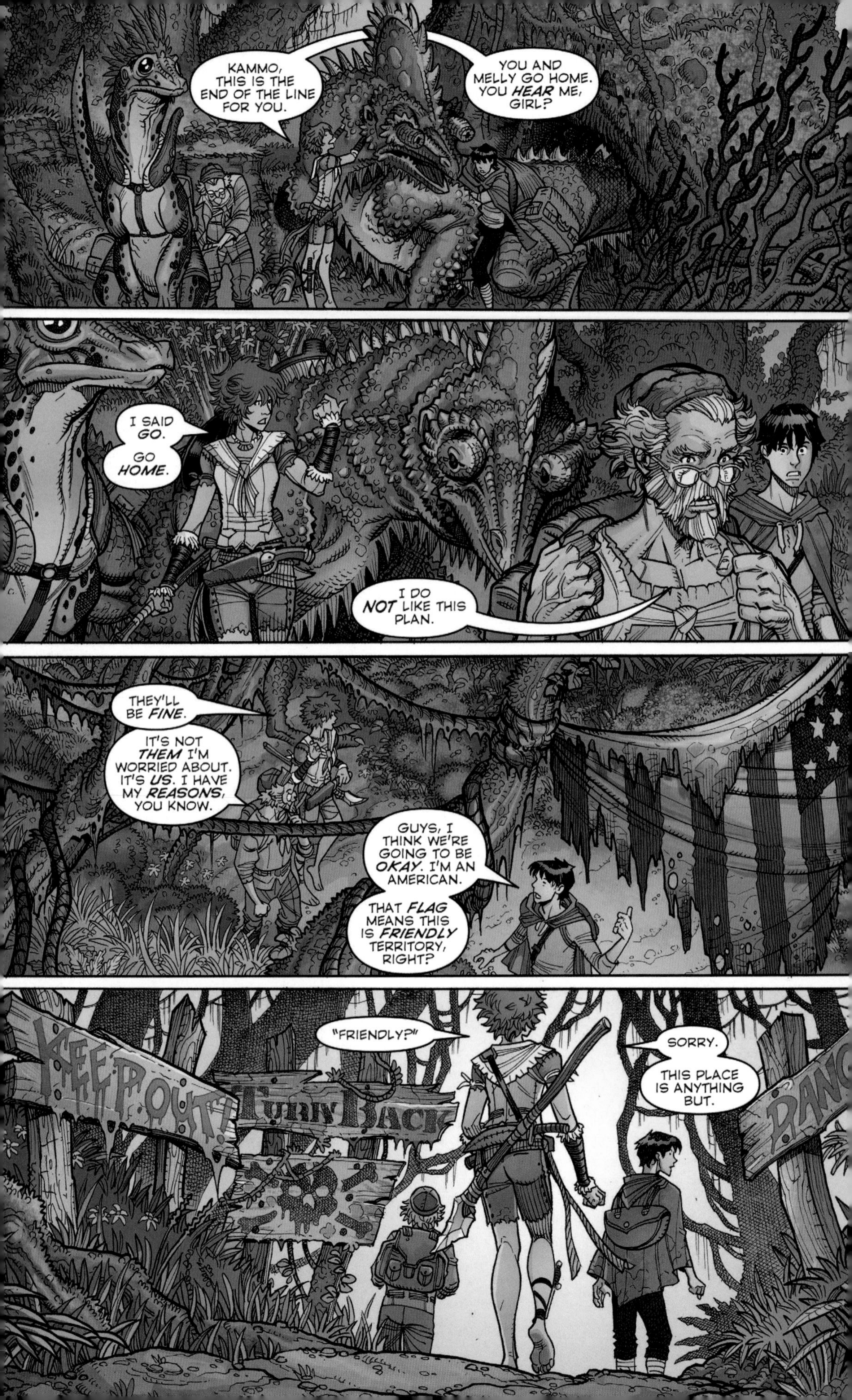
KAMMO, THIS IS THE END OF THE LINE FOR YOU.
YOU AND MELLY GO HOME. YOU *HEAR* ME, GIRL?
I SAID *GO*.
GO *HOME*.
I DO *NOT* LIKE THIS PLAN.
THEY'LL BE *FINE*.
IT'S NOT *THEM* I'M WORRIED ABOUT. IT'S *US*. I HAVE MY *REASONS*, YOU KNOW.
GUYS, I THINK WE'RE GOING TO BE *OKAY*. I'M AN AMERICAN.
THAT *FLAG* MEANS THIS IS *FRIENDLY* TERRITORY, RIGHT?
KEEP OUT!
TURN BACK
"FRIENDLY?"
SORRY.
THIS PLACE IS ANYTHING BUT.

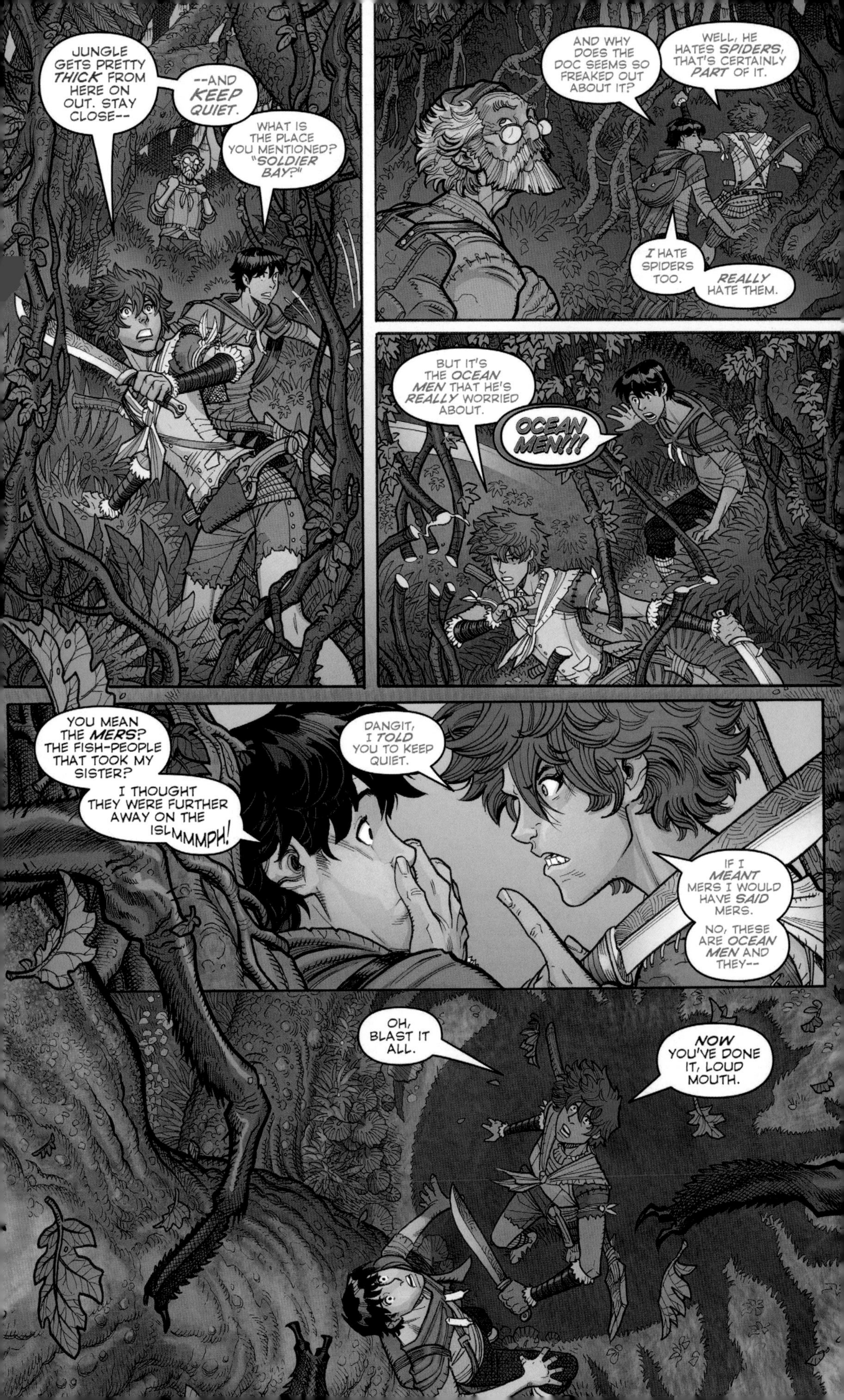

JUNGLE GETS PRETTY THICK FROM HERE ON OUT. STAY CLOSE--
--AND KEEP QUIET.
WHAT IS THE PLACE YOU MENTIONED? "SOLDIER BAY?"
AND WHY DOES THE DOC SEEMS SO FREAKED OUT ABOUT IT?
WELL, HE HATES SPIDERS, THAT'S CERTAINLY PART OF IT.
I HATE SPIDERS TOO.
REALLY HATE THEM.
BUT IT'S THE OCEAN MEN THAT HE'S REALLY WORRIED ABOUT.
OCEAN MEN!!!
YOU MEAN THE MERS? THE FISH-PEOPLE THAT TOOK MY SISTER?
I THOUGHT THEY WERE FURTHER AWAY ON THE ISLMMMPH!
DANGIT, I TOLD YOU TO KEEP QUIET.
IF I MEANT MERS I WOULD HAVE SAID MERS.
NO, THESE ARE OCEAN MEN AND THEY--
OH, BLAST IT ALL.
NOW YOU'VE DONE IT, LOUD MOUTH.

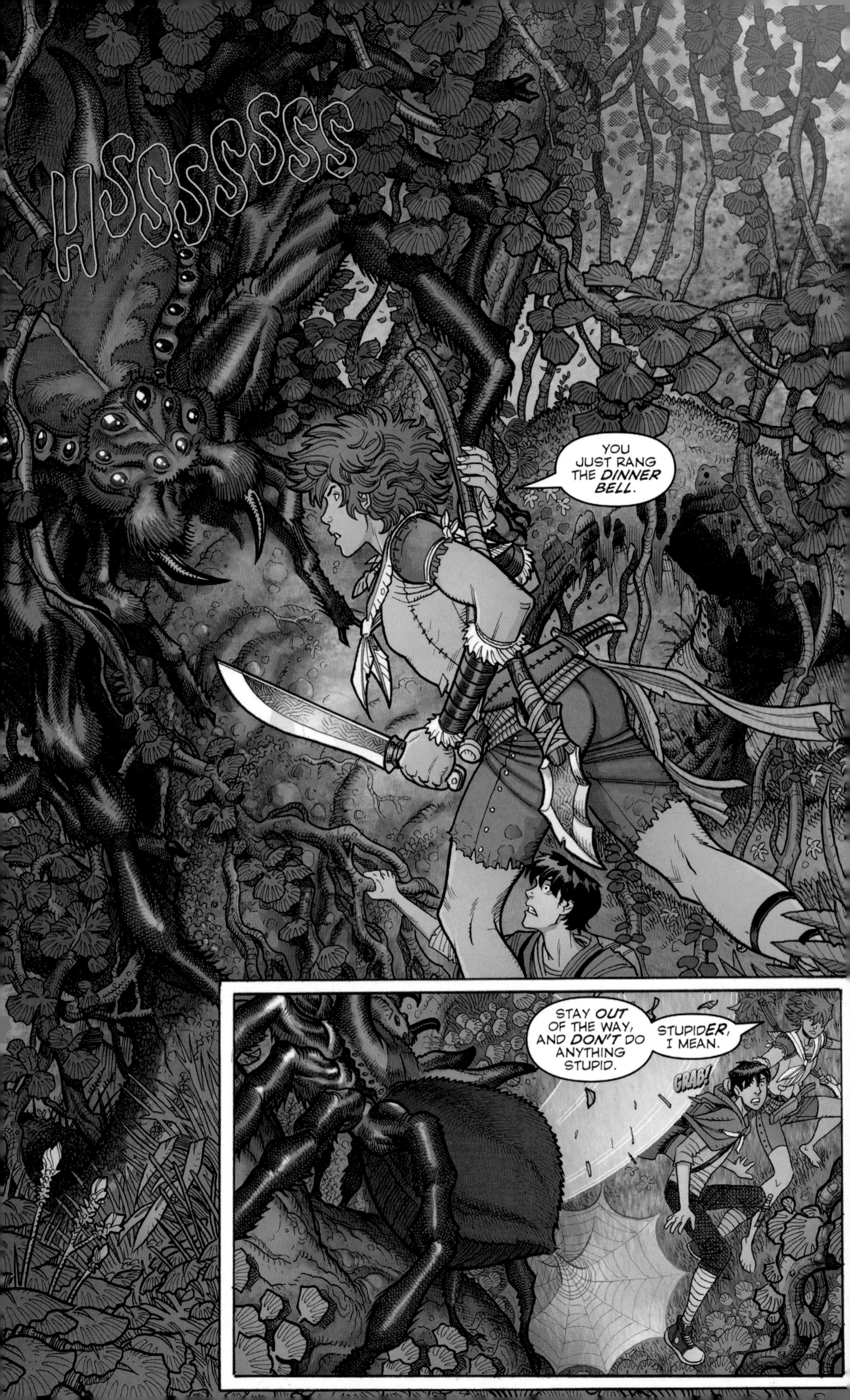
HSSSSSSS
YOU JUST RANG THE DINNER BELL.
STAY OUT OF THE WAY, AND DON'T DO ANYTHING STUPID.
STUPIDER, I MEAN.
GRAB!

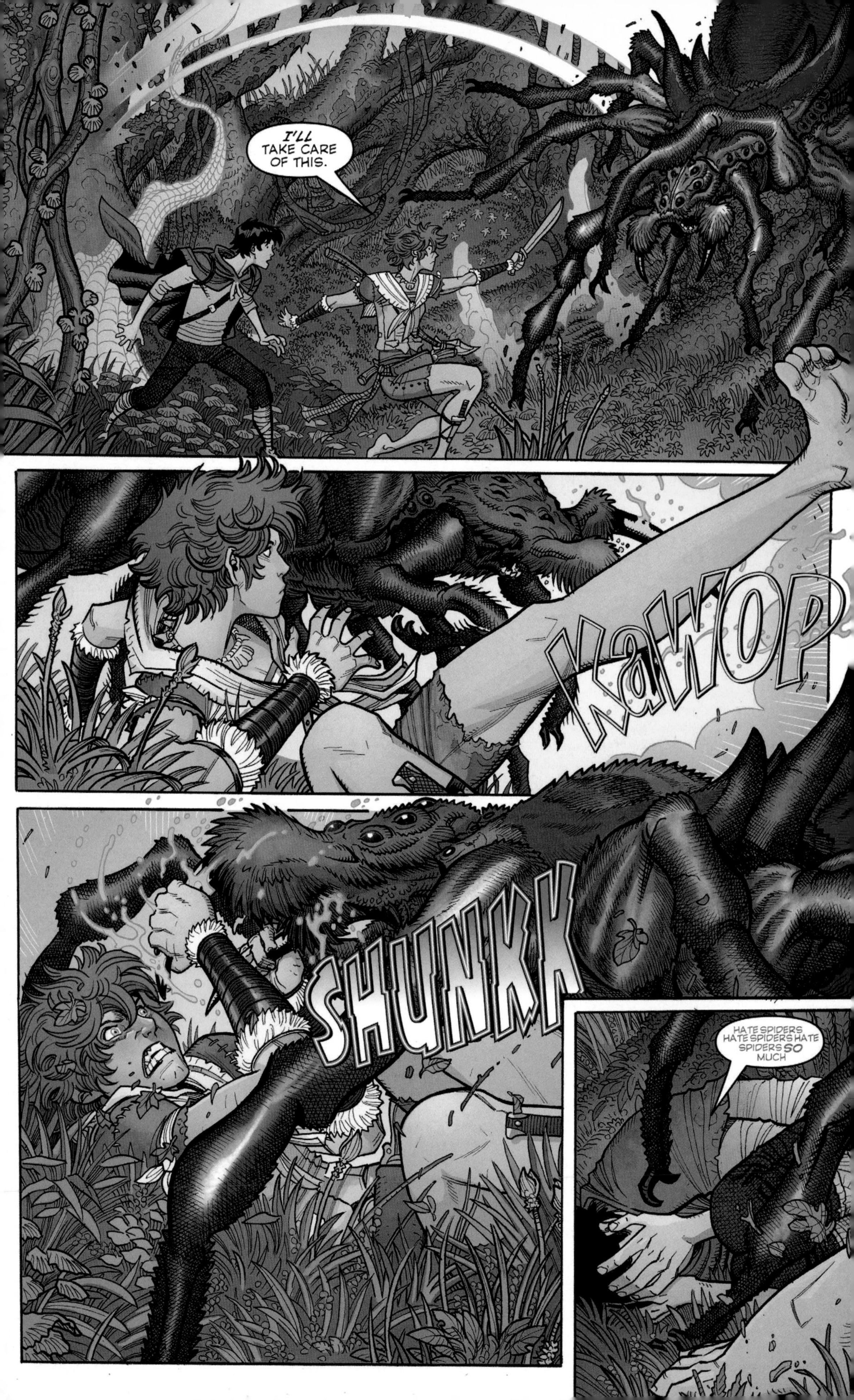
I'LL TAKE CARE OF THIS.
KAWOP
SHUNKK
HATE SPIDERS HATE SPIDERS HATE SPIDERS SO MUCH

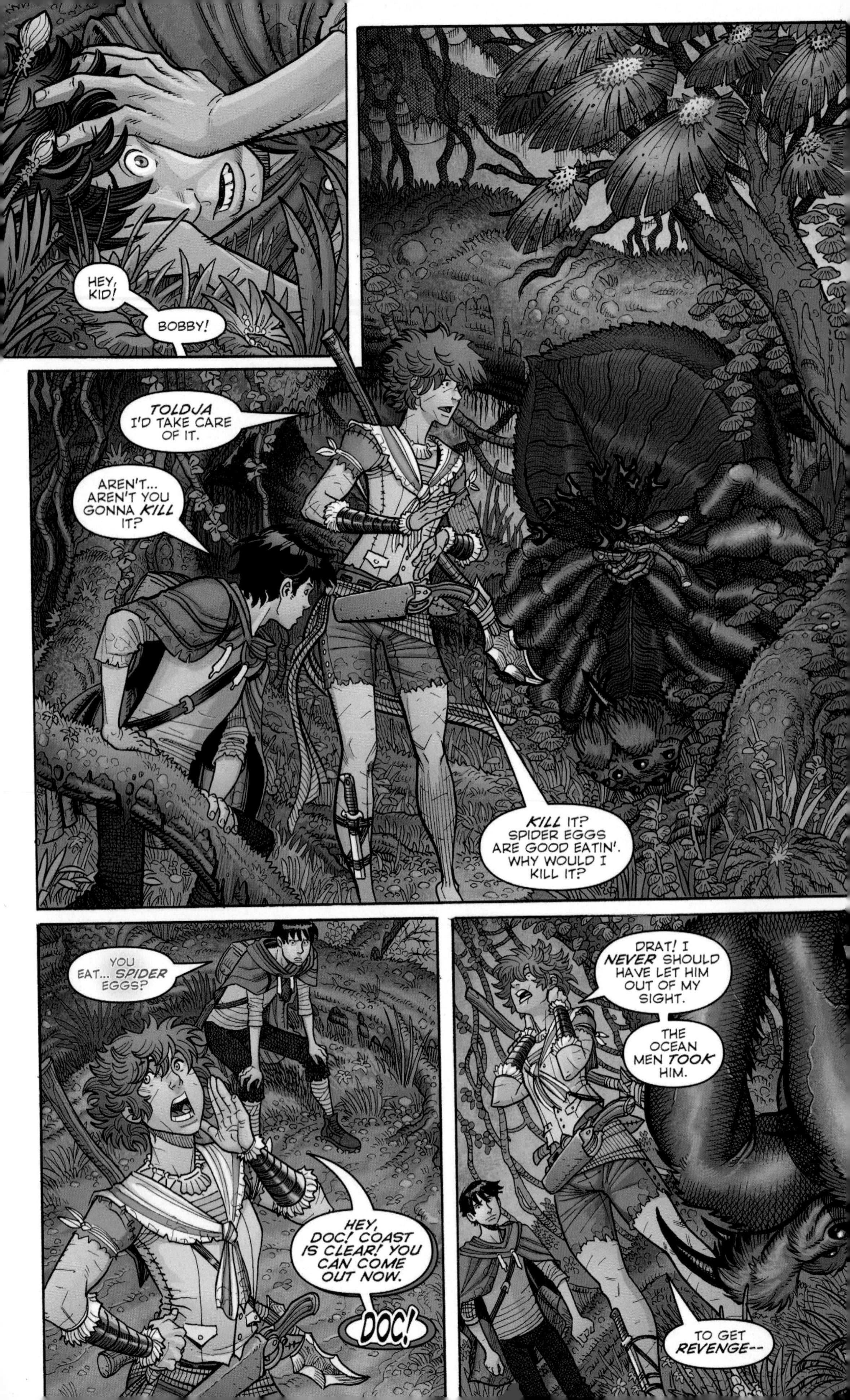
HEY, KID!
BOBBY!
TOLDJA I'D TAKE CARE OF IT.
AREN'T... AREN'T YOU GONNA KILL IT?
KILL IT? SPIDER EGGS ARE GOOD EATIN'. WHY WOULD I KILL IT?
YOU EAT... SPIDER EGGS?
HEY, DOC! COAST IS CLEAR! YOU CAN COME OUT NOW.
DOC!
DRAT! I NEVER SHOULD HAVE LET HIM OUT OF MY SIGHT.
THE OCEAN MEN TOOK HIM.
TO GET REVENGE--

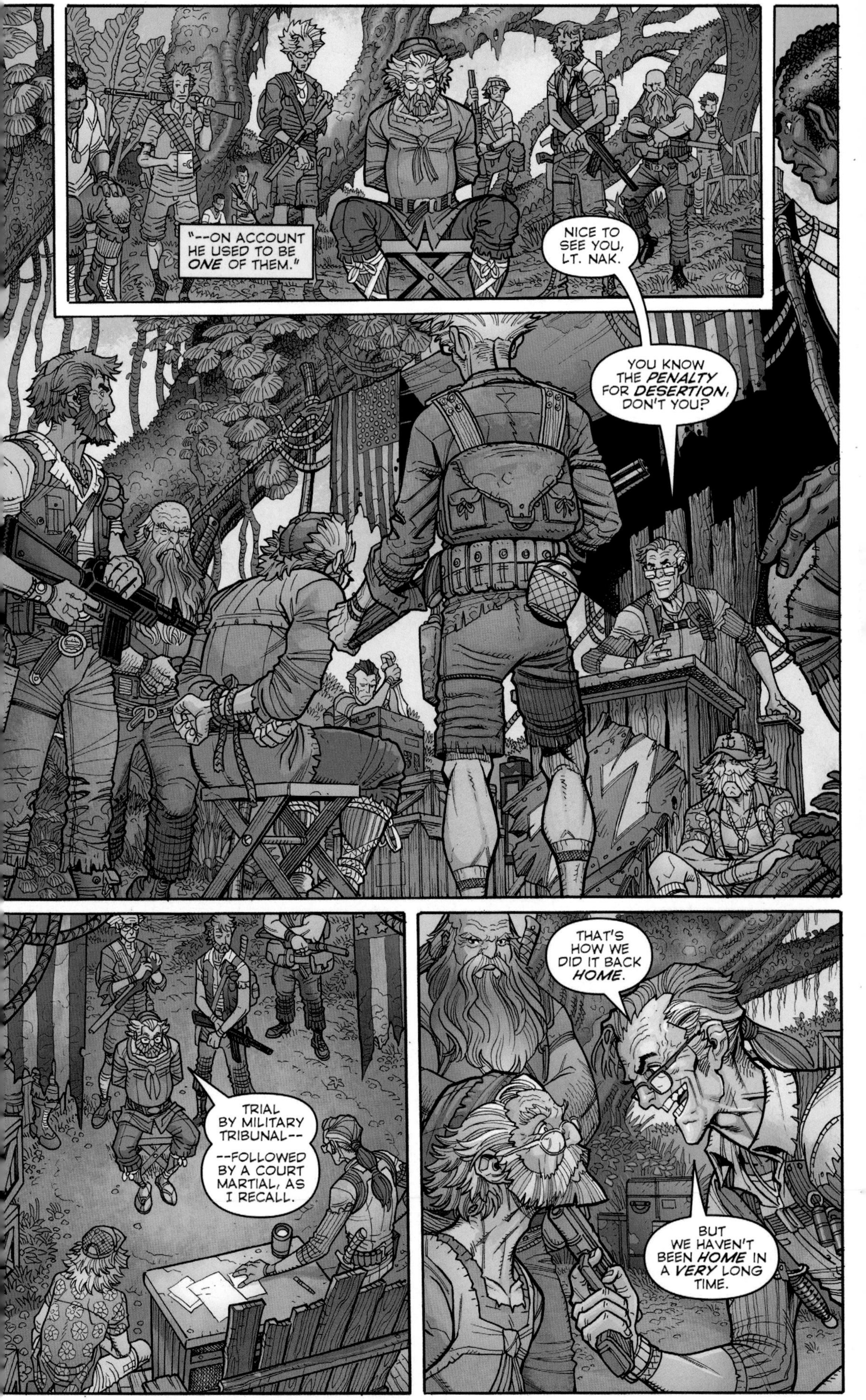

"--ON ACCOUNT HE USED TO BE *ONE* OF THEM."
NICE TO SEE YOU, LT. NAK.
YOU KNOW THE *PENALTY* FOR *DESERTION*, DON'T YOU?
TRIAL BY MILITARY TRIBUNAL--
--FOLLOWED BY A COURT MARTIAL, AS I RECALL.
THAT'S HOW WE DID IT BACK *HOME*.
BUT WE HAVEN'T BEEN *HOME* IN A *VERY* LONG TIME.

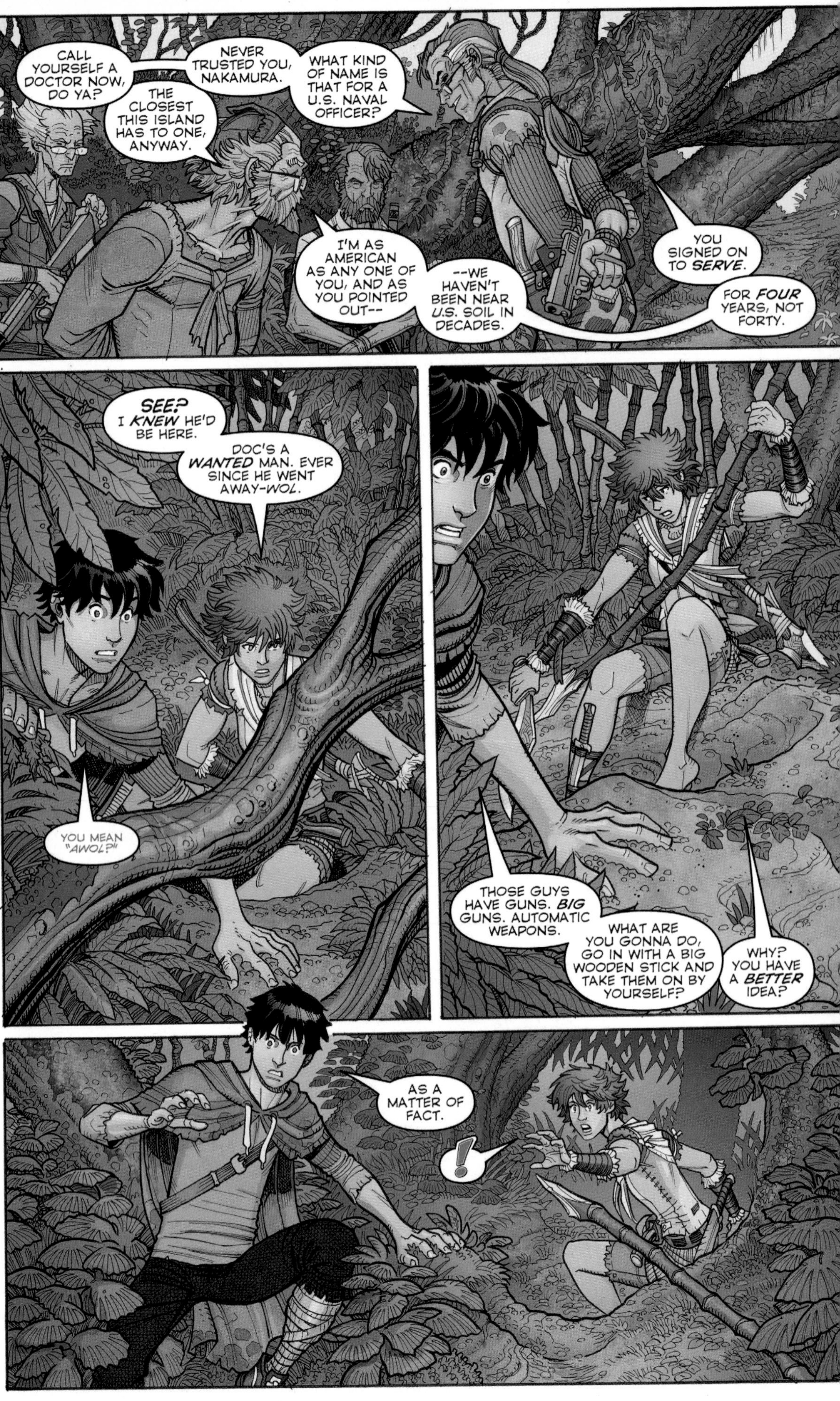
CALL YOURSELF A DOCTOR NOW, DO YA?
NEVER TRUSTED YOU, NAKAMURA.
WHAT KIND OF NAME IS THAT FOR A U.S. NAVAL OFFICER?
THE CLOSEST THIS ISLAND HAS TO ONE, ANYWAY.
I'M AS AMERICAN AS ANY ONE OF YOU, AND AS YOU POINTED OUT--
--WE HAVEN'T BEEN NEAR U.S. SOIL IN DECADES.
YOU SIGNED ON TO SERVE.
FOR FOUR YEARS, NOT FORTY.
SEE? I KNEW HE'D BE HERE.
DOC'S A WANTED MAN. EVER SINCE HE WENT AWAY-WOL.
YOU MEAN "AWOL?"
THOSE GUYS HAVE GUNS. BIG GUNS. AUTOMATIC WEAPONS.
WHAT ARE YOU GONNA DO, GO IN WITH A BIG WOODEN STICK AND TAKE THEM ON BY YOURSELF?
WHY? YOU HAVE A BETTER IDEA?
AS A MATTER OF FACT.
!

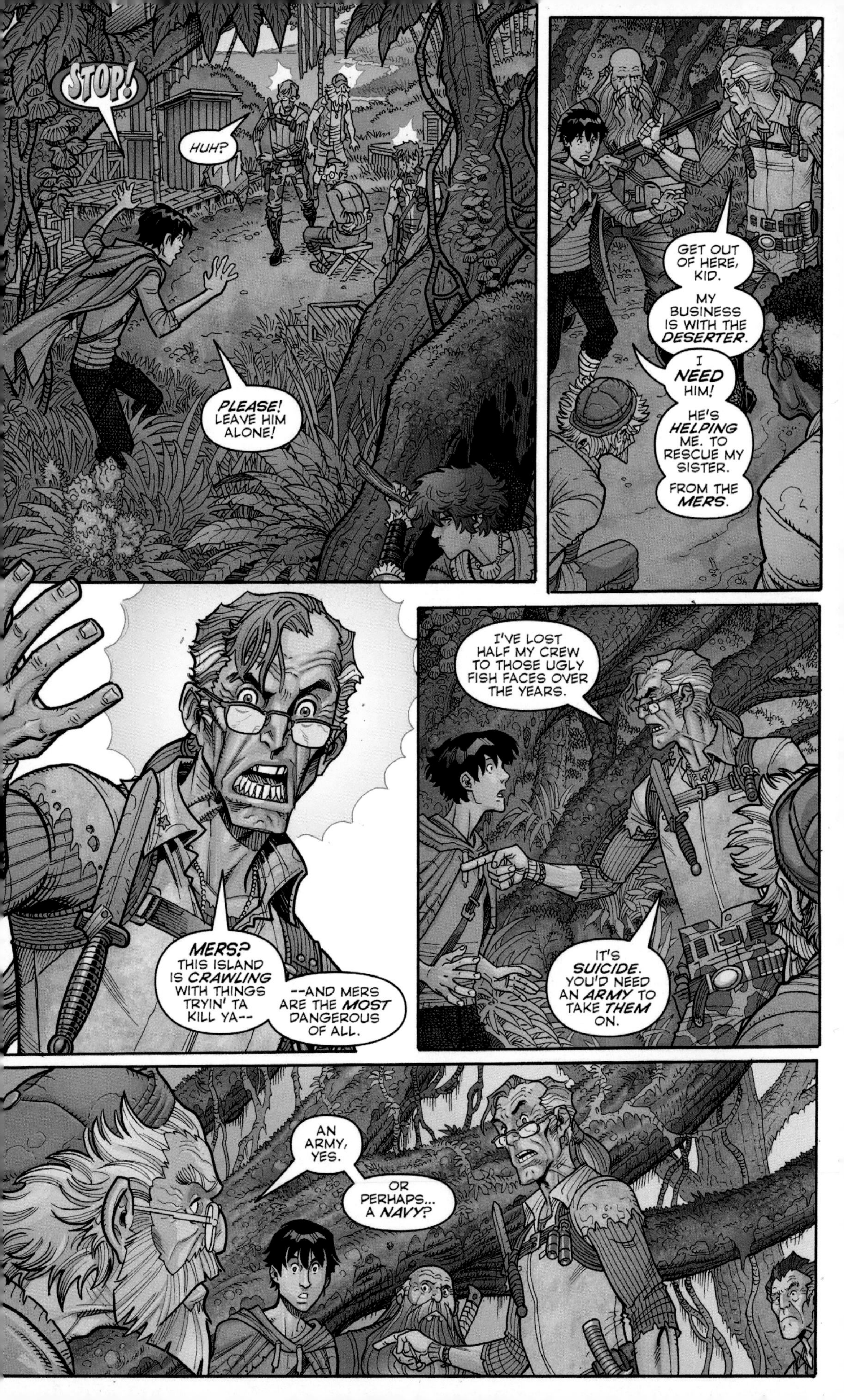
STOP!
HUH?
PLEASE! LEAVE HIM ALONE!
GET OUT OF HERE, KID.
MY BUSINESS IS WITH THE DESERTER.
I NEED HIM!
HE'S HELPING ME. TO RESCUE MY SISTER.
FROM THE MERS.
MERS? THIS ISLAND IS CRAWLING WITH THINGS TRYIN' TA KILL YA--
--AND MERS ARE THE MOST DANGEROUS OF ALL.
I'VE LOST HALF MY CREW TO THOSE UGLY FISH FACES OVER THE YEARS.
IT'S SUICIDE. YOU'D NEED AN ARMY TO TAKE THEM ON.
AN ARMY, YES.
OR PERHAPS... A NAVY?

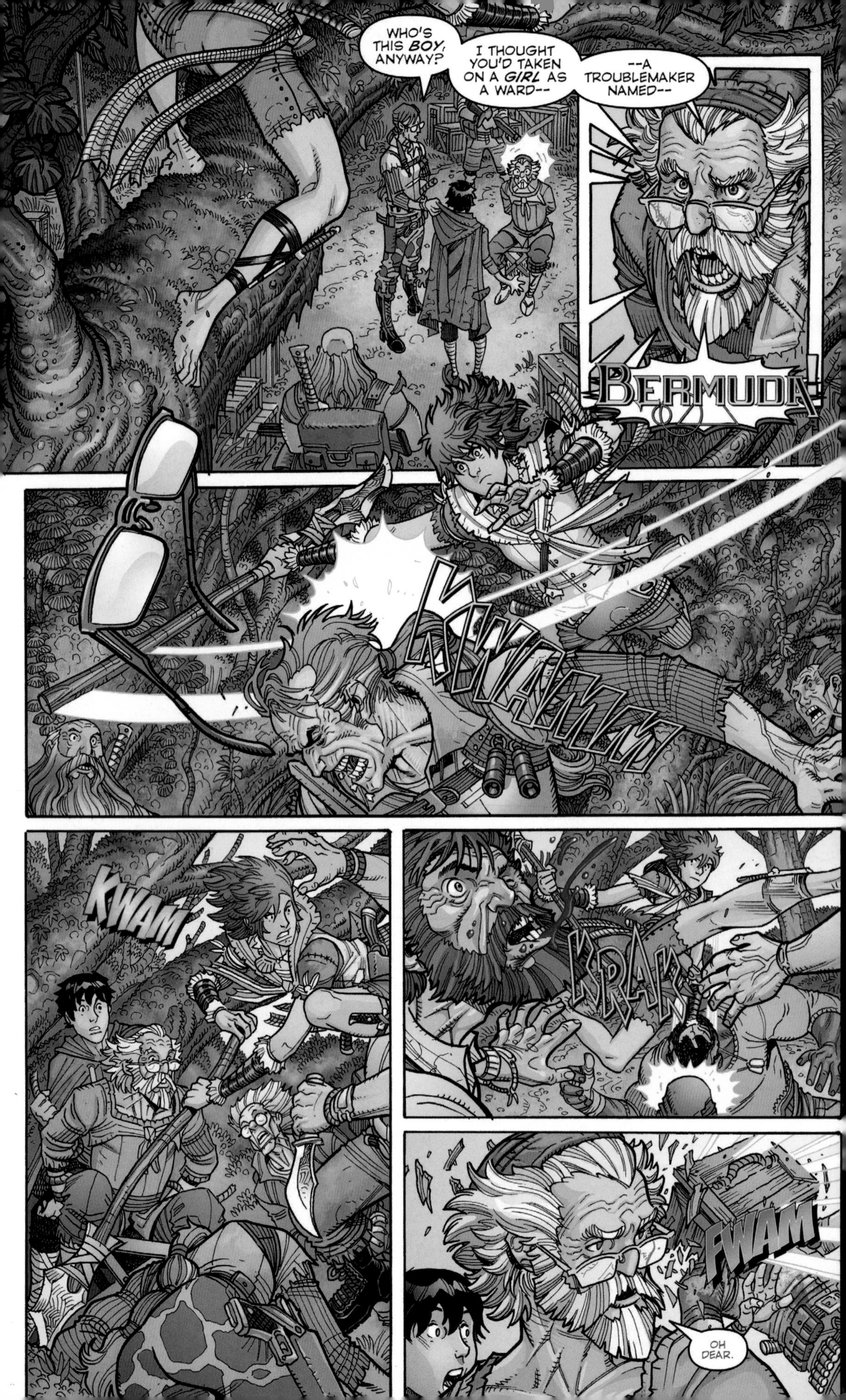
WHO'S THIS BOY, ANYWAY?
I THOUGHT YOU'D TAKEN ON A GIRL AS A WARD--
--A TROUBLEMAKER NAMED--
BERMUDA!
KWAM
KRAK
FWAM
OH DEAR.

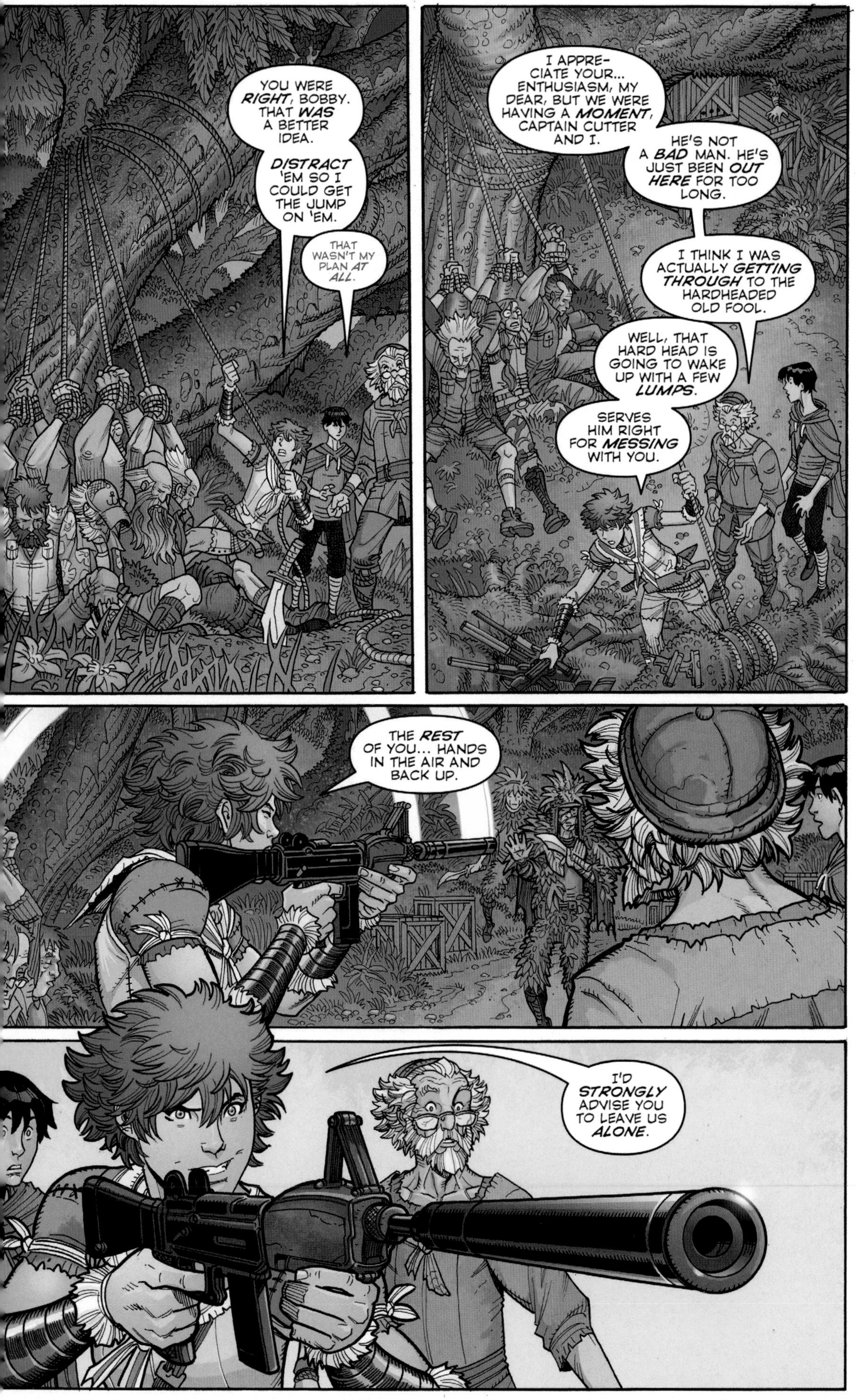
YOU WERE RIGHT, BOBBY. THAT WAS A BETTER IDEA.
DISTRACT 'EM SO I COULD GET THE JUMP ON 'EM.
THAT WASN'T MY PLAN AT ALL.
I APPRECIATE YOUR... ENTHUSIASM, MY DEAR, BUT WE WERE HAVING A MOMENT, CAPTAIN CUTTER AND I.
HE'S NOT A BAD MAN. HE'S JUST BEEN OUT HERE FOR TOO LONG.
I THINK I WAS ACTUALLY GETTING THROUGH TO THE HARDHEADED OLD FOOL.
WELL, THAT HARD HEAD IS GOING TO WAKE UP WITH A FEW LUMPS.
SERVES HIM RIGHT FOR MESSING WITH YOU.
THE REST OF YOU... HANDS IN THE AIR AND BACK UP.
I'D STRONGLY ADVISE YOU TO LEAVE US ALONE.

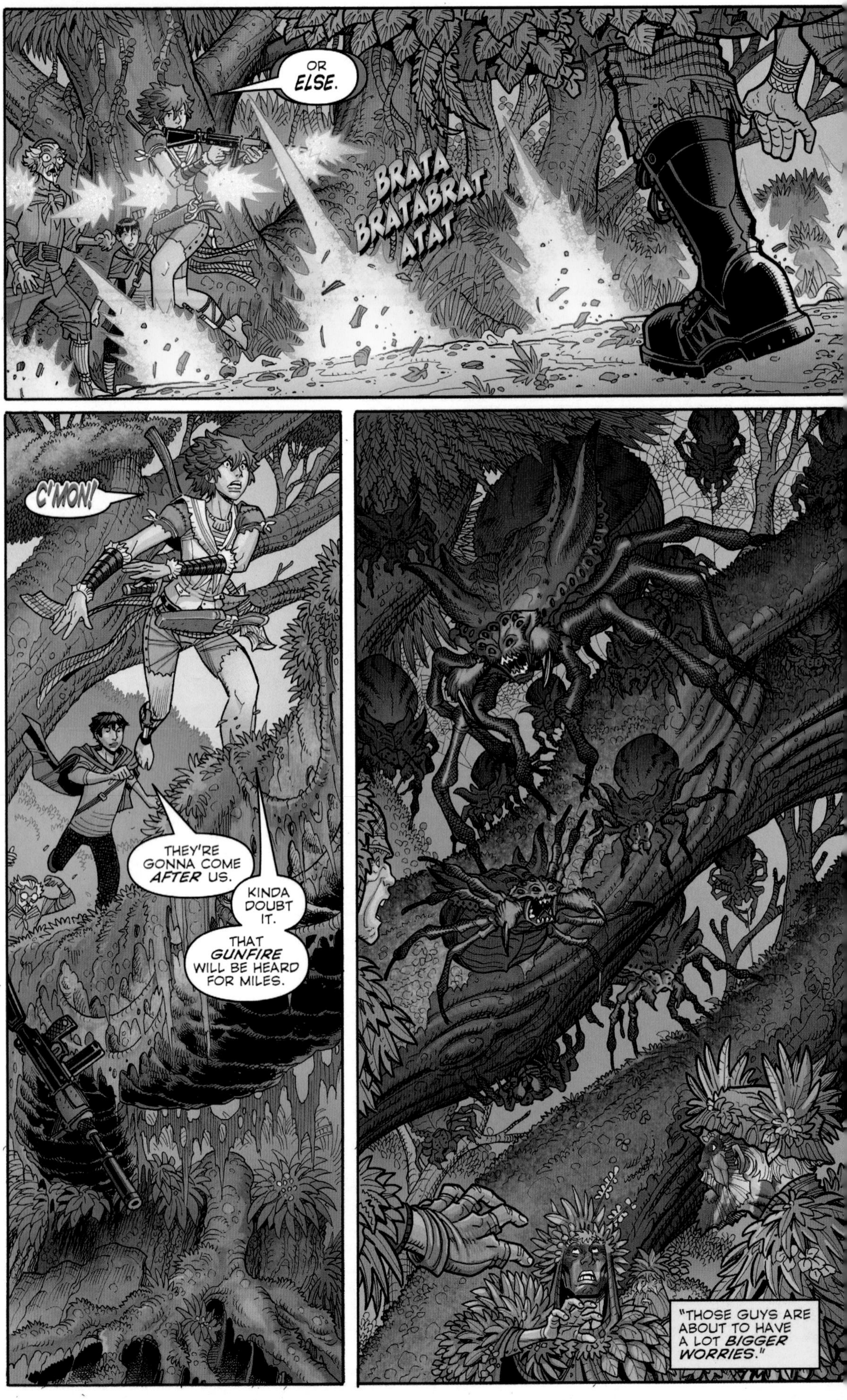
OR ELSE.
BRATA BRATABRAT ATAT
C'MON!
THEY'RE GONNA COME AFTER US.
KINDA DOUBT IT.
THAT GUNFIRE WILL BE HEARD FOR MILES.
"THOSE GUYS ARE ABOUT TO HAVE A LOT BIGGER WORRIES."

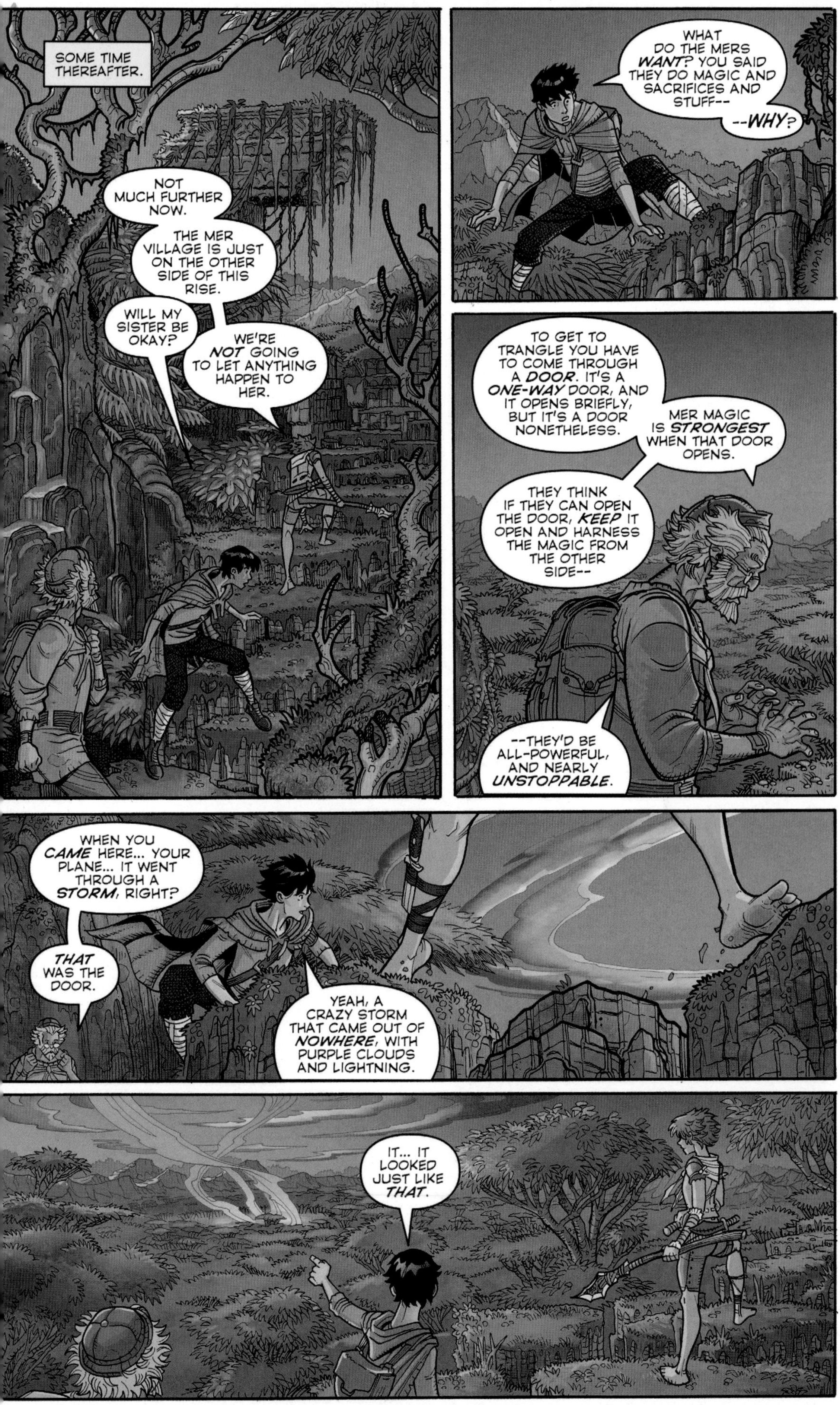
SOME TIME THEREAFTER.
NOT MUCH FURTHER NOW.
THE MER VILLAGE IS JUST ON THE OTHER SIDE OF THIS RISE.
WILL MY SISTER BE OKAY?
WE'RE *NOT* GOING TO LET ANYTHING HAPPEN TO HER.
WHAT DO THE MERS *WANT*? YOU SAID THEY DO MAGIC AND SACRIFICES AND STUFF--
--*WHY*?
TO GET TO TRANGLE YOU HAVE TO COME THROUGH A *DOOR*. IT'S A *ONE-WAY* DOOR, AND IT OPENS BRIEFLY, BUT IT'S A DOOR NONETHELESS.
MER MAGIC IS *STRONGEST* WHEN THAT DOOR OPENS.
THEY THINK IF THEY CAN OPEN THE DOOR, *KEEP* IT OPEN AND HARNESS THE MAGIC FROM THE OTHER SIDE--
--THEY'D BE ALL-POWERFUL, AND NEARLY *UNSTOPPABLE*.
WHEN YOU *CAME* HERE... YOUR PLANE... IT WENT THROUGH A *STORM*, RIGHT?
THAT WAS THE DOOR.
YEAH, A CRAZY STORM THAT CAME OUT OF *NOWHERE*, WITH PURPLE CLOUDS AND LIGHTNING.
IT... IT LOOKED JUST LIKE *THAT*.

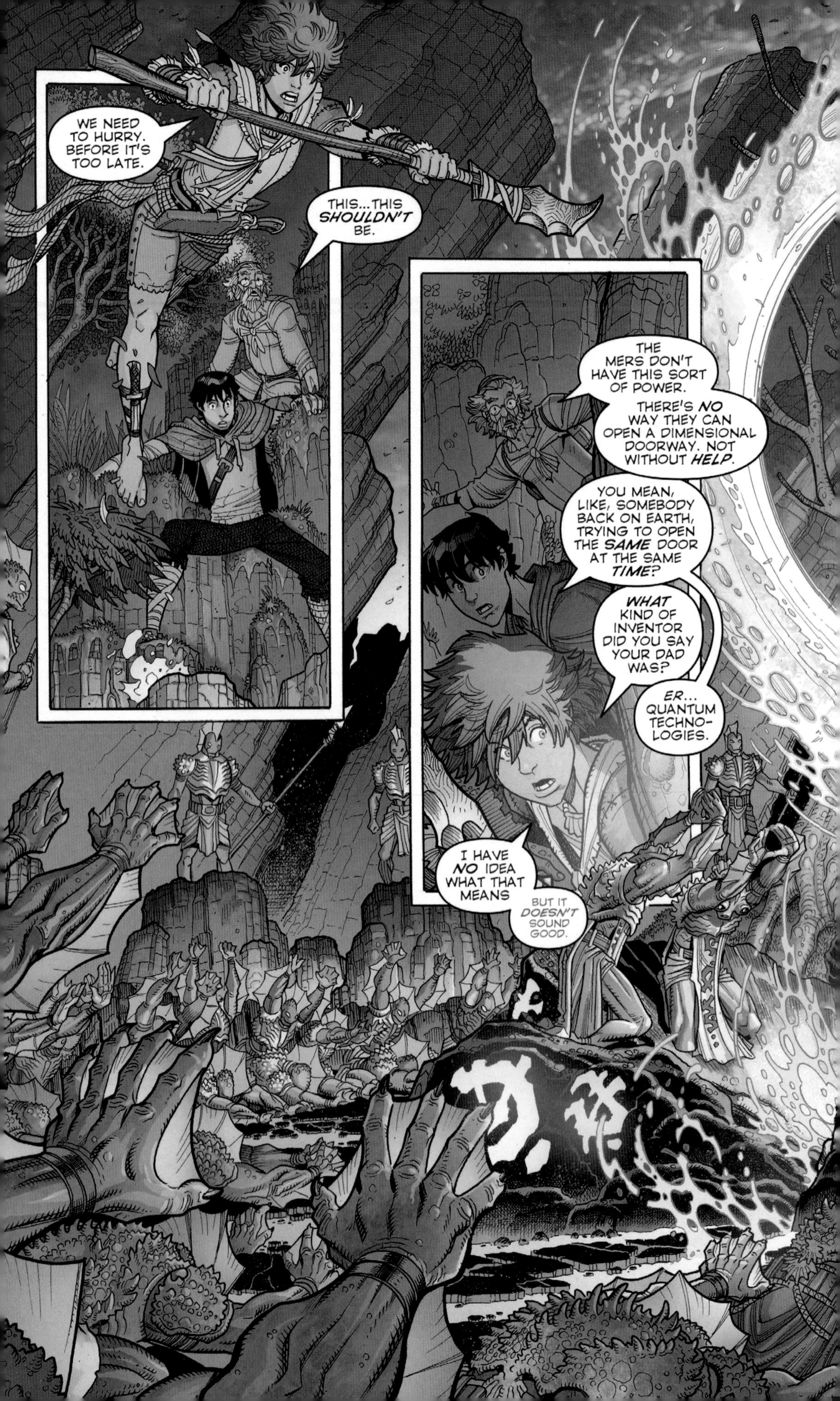
WE NEED TO HURRY. BEFORE IT'S TOO LATE.
THIS...THIS *SHOULDN'T* BE.
THE MERS DON'T HAVE THIS SORT OF POWER.
THERE'S *NO* WAY THEY CAN OPEN A DIMENSIONAL DOORWAY. NOT WITHOUT *HELP*.
YOU MEAN, LIKE, SOMEBODY BACK ON EARTH, TRYING TO OPEN THE *SAME* DOOR AT THE SAME *TIME*?
WHAT KIND OF INVENTOR DID YOU SAY YOUR DAD WAS?
ER... QUANTUM TECHNO-LOGIES.
I HAVE *NO* IDEA WHAT THAT MEANS
BUT IT *DOESN'T* SOUND GOOD.

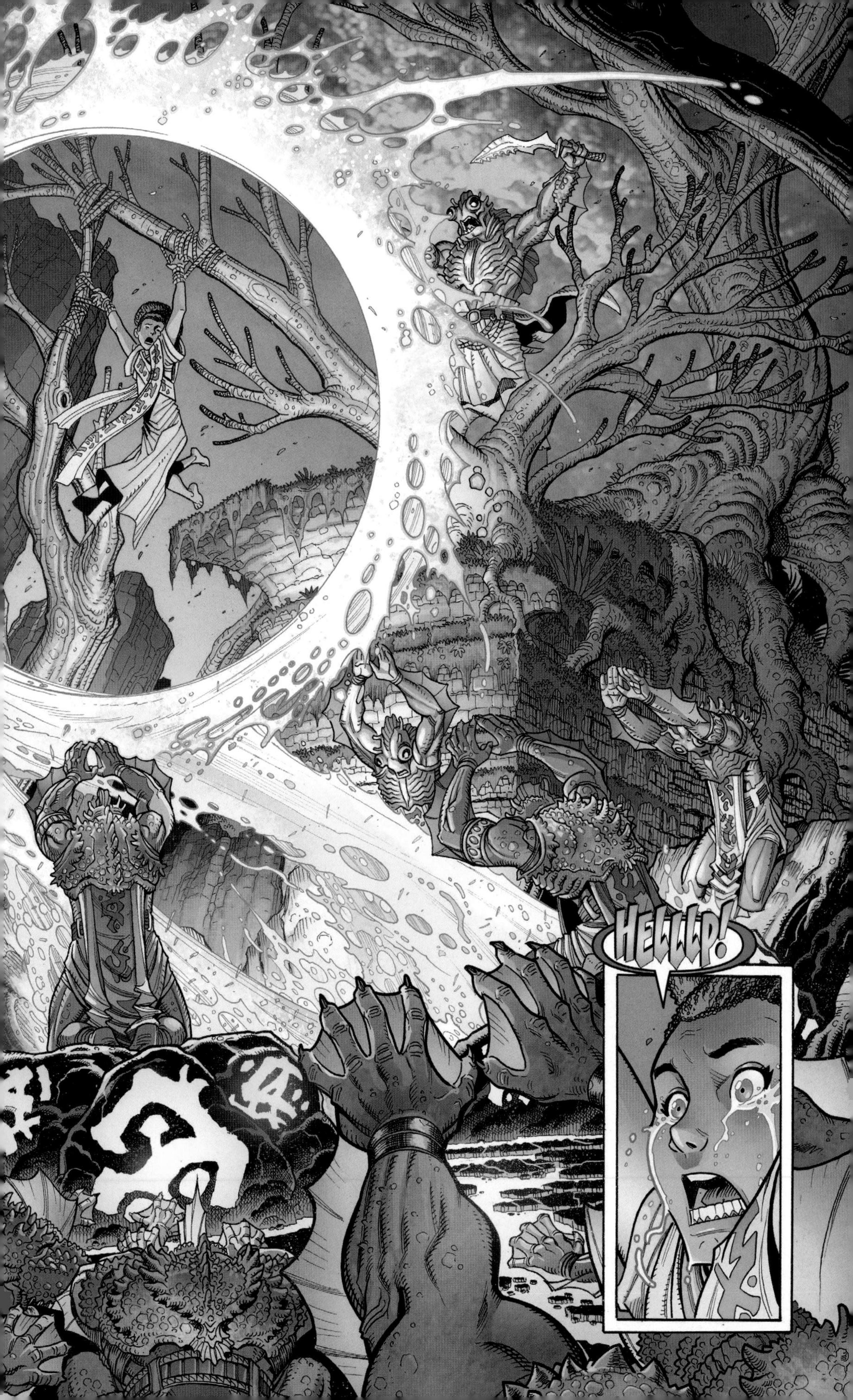
HELLLP!

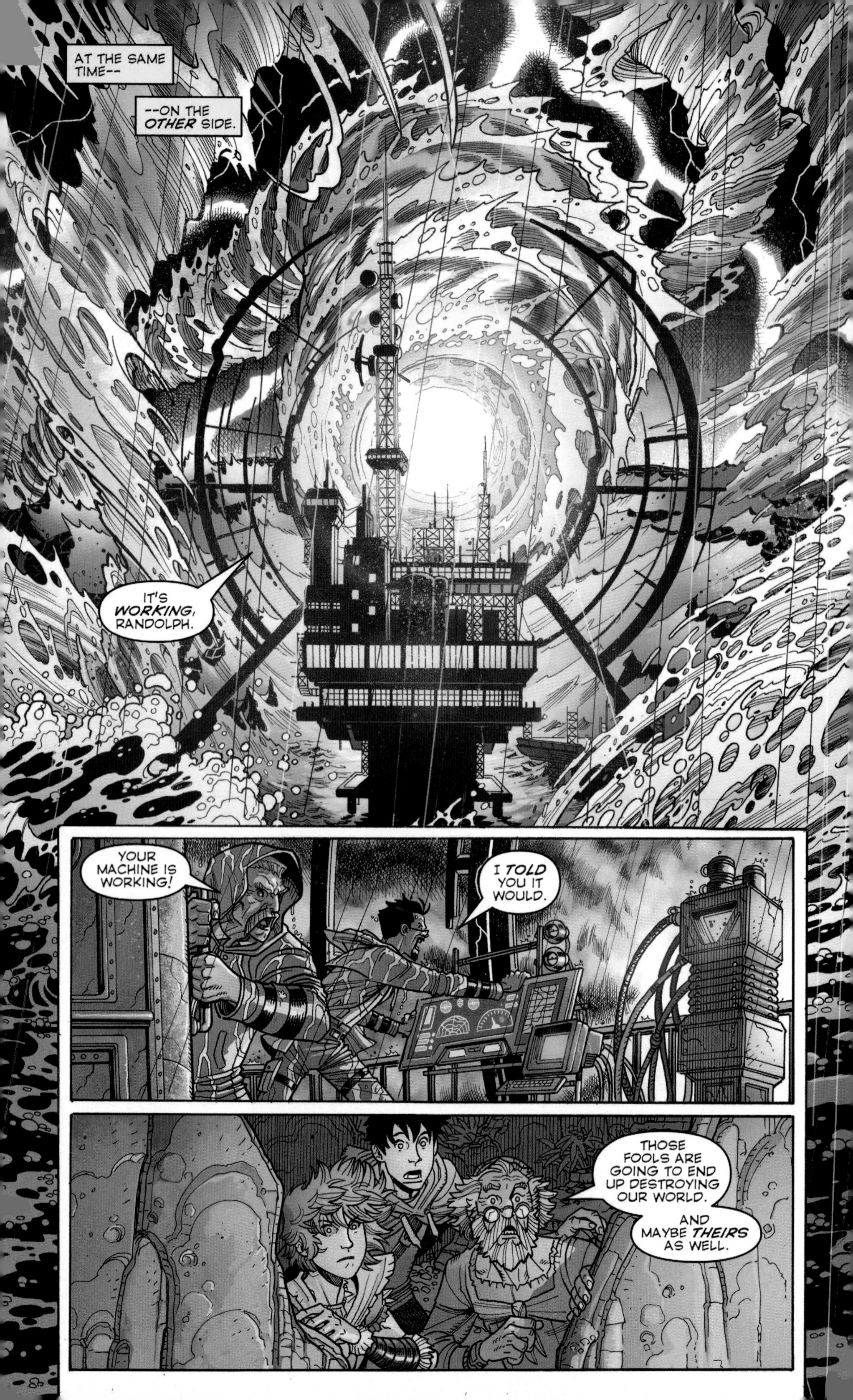
AT THE SAME TIME--
--ON THE OTHER SIDE.
IT'S WORKING, RANDOLPH.
YOUR MACHINE IS WORKING!
I TOLD YOU IT WOULD.
THOSE FOOLS ARE GOING TO END UP DESTROYING OUR WORLD.
AND MAYBE THEIRS AS WELL.

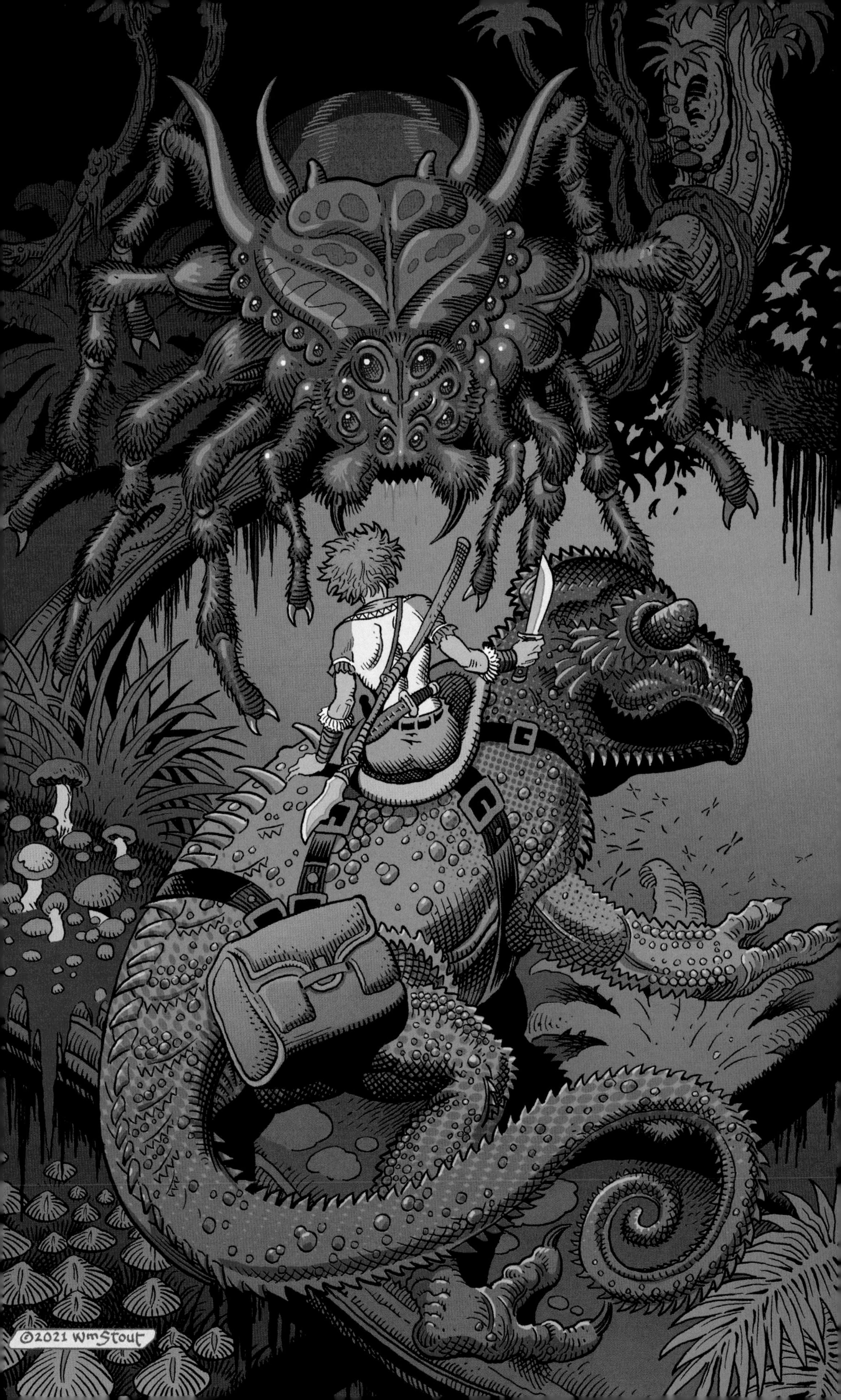
©2021 WmStout

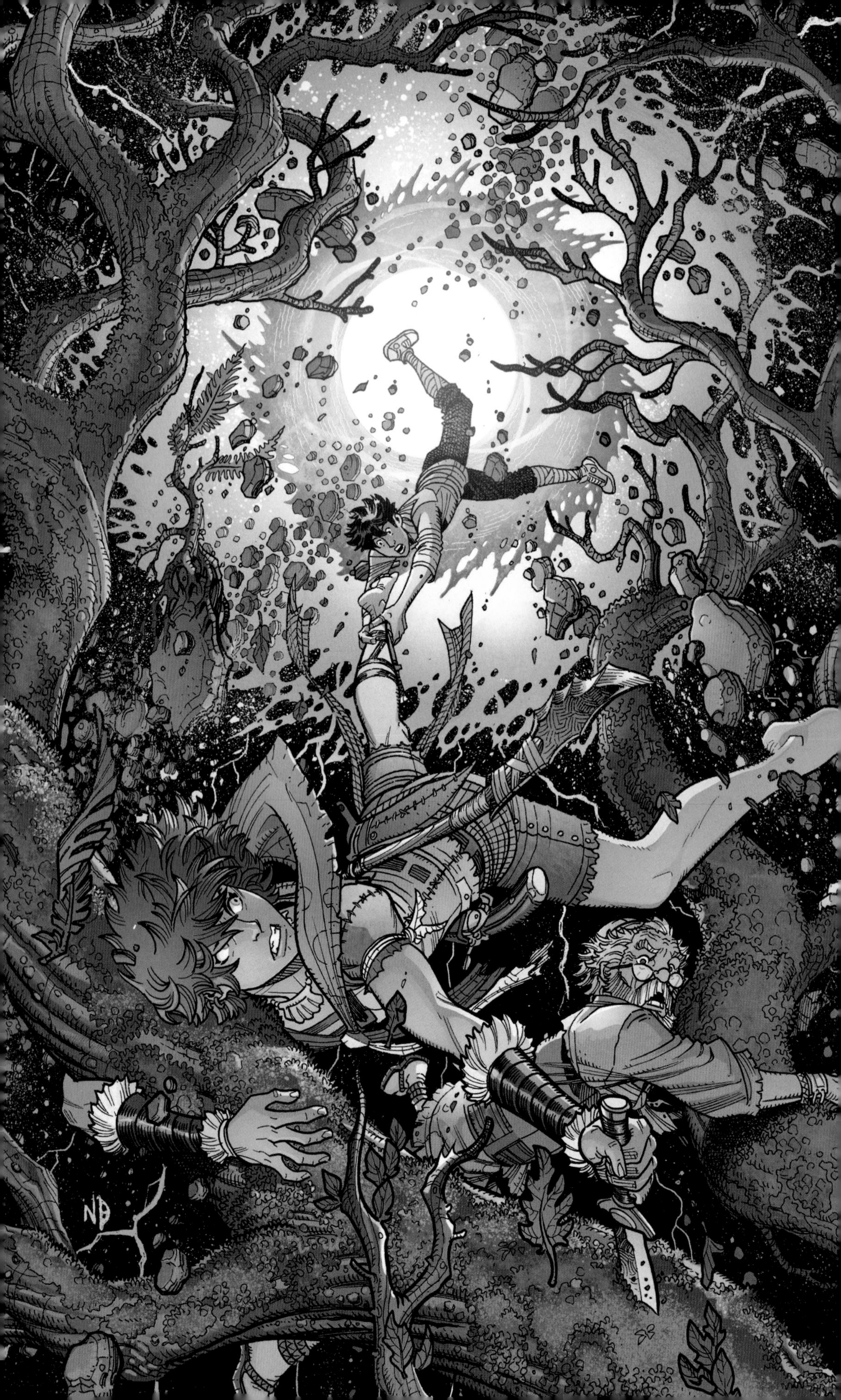

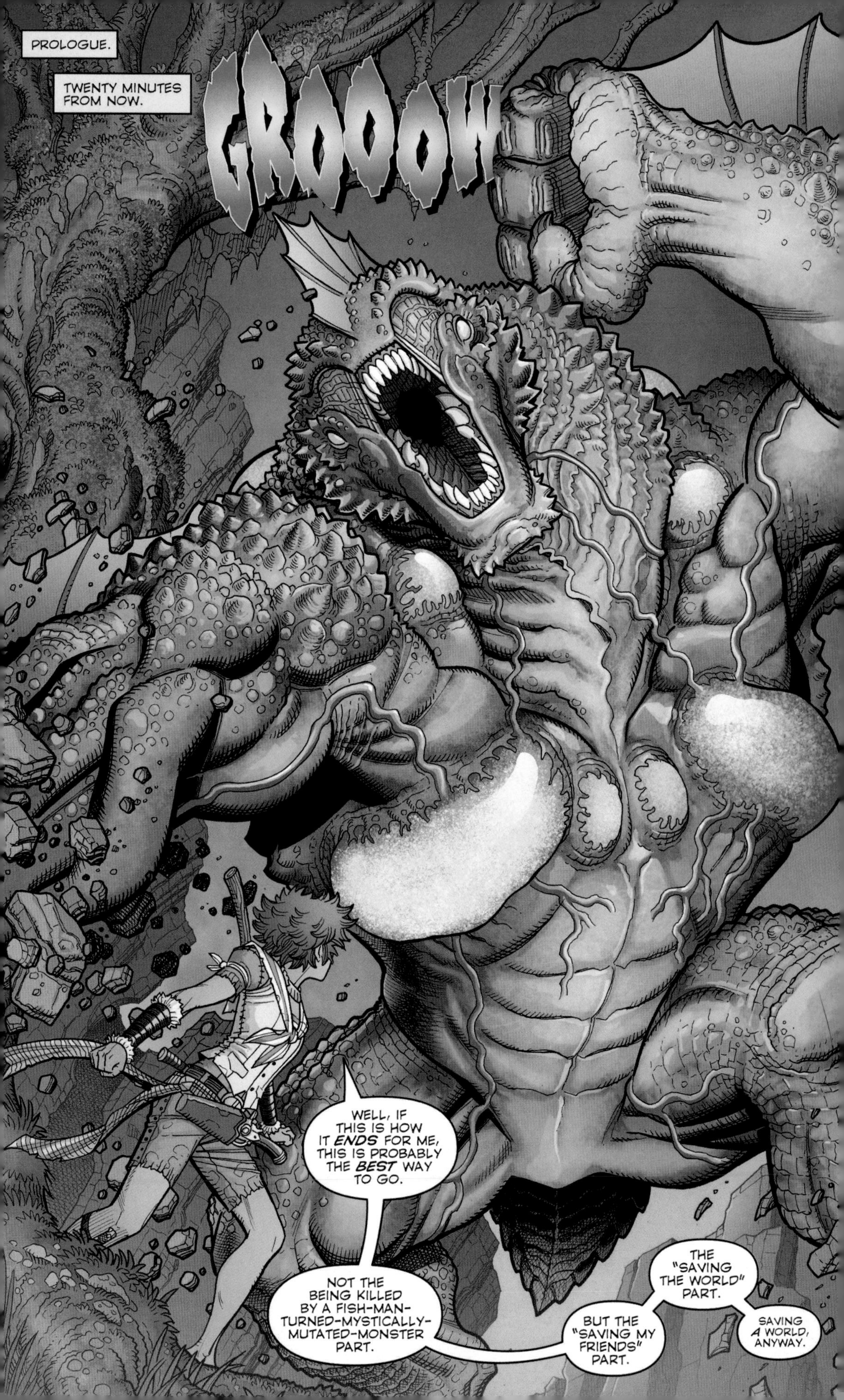
PROLOGUE.
TWENTY MINUTES FROM NOW.
GROOOW
WELL, IF THIS IS HOW IT ENDS FOR ME, THIS IS PROBABLY THE BEST WAY TO GO.
NOT THE BEING KILLED BY A FISH-MAN-TURNED-MYSTICALLY-MUTATED-MONSTER PART.
BUT THE "SAVING MY FRIENDS" PART.
THE "SAVING THE WORLD" PART.
SAVING A WORLD, ANYWAY.

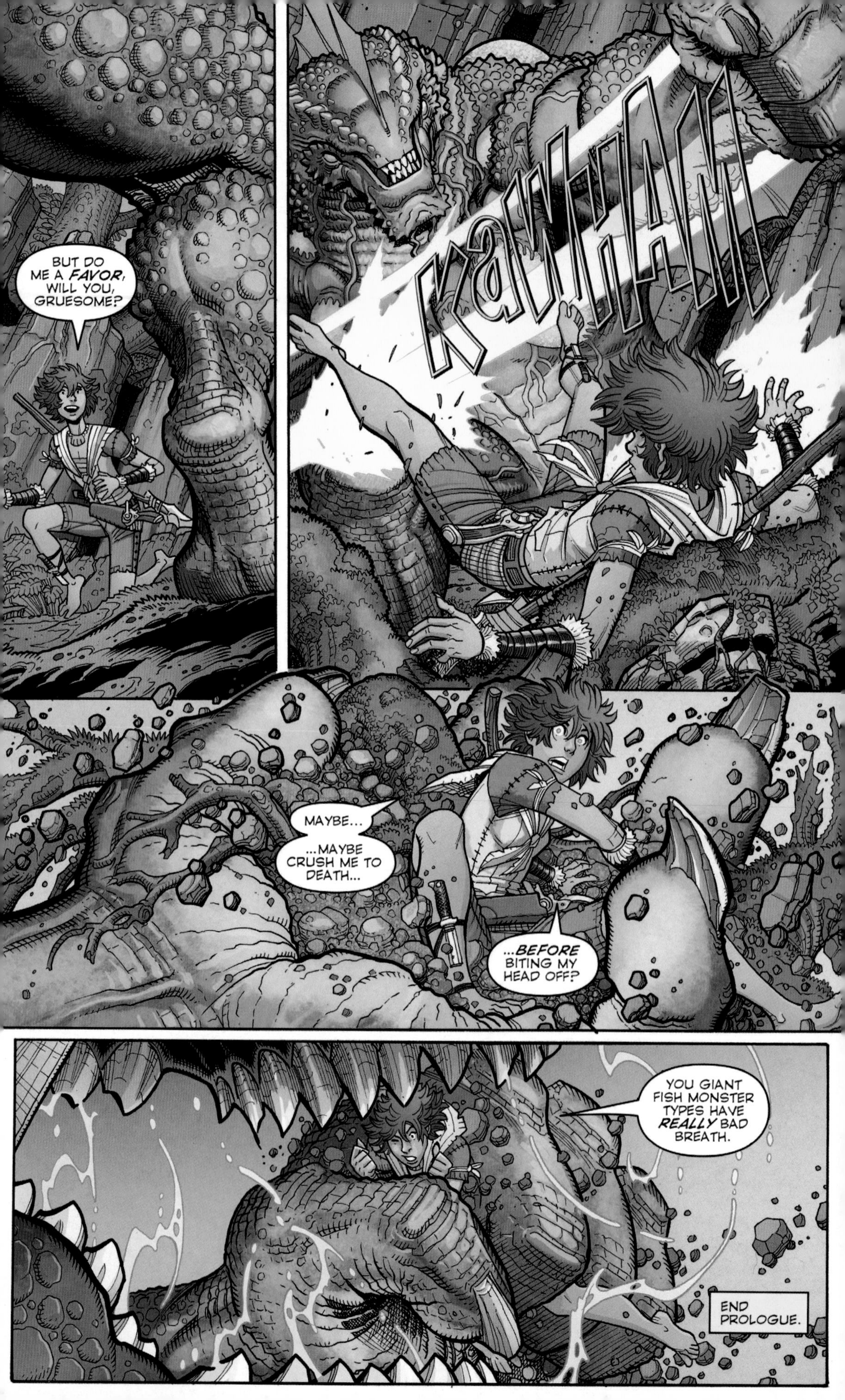
BUT DO ME A *FAVOR*, WILL YOU, GRUESOME?
KRAKTHAM
MAYBE...
...MAYBE CRUSH ME TO DEATH...
...*BEFORE* BITING MY HEAD OFF?
YOU GIANT FISH MONSTER TYPES HAVE *REALLY* BAD BREATH.
END PROLOGUE.

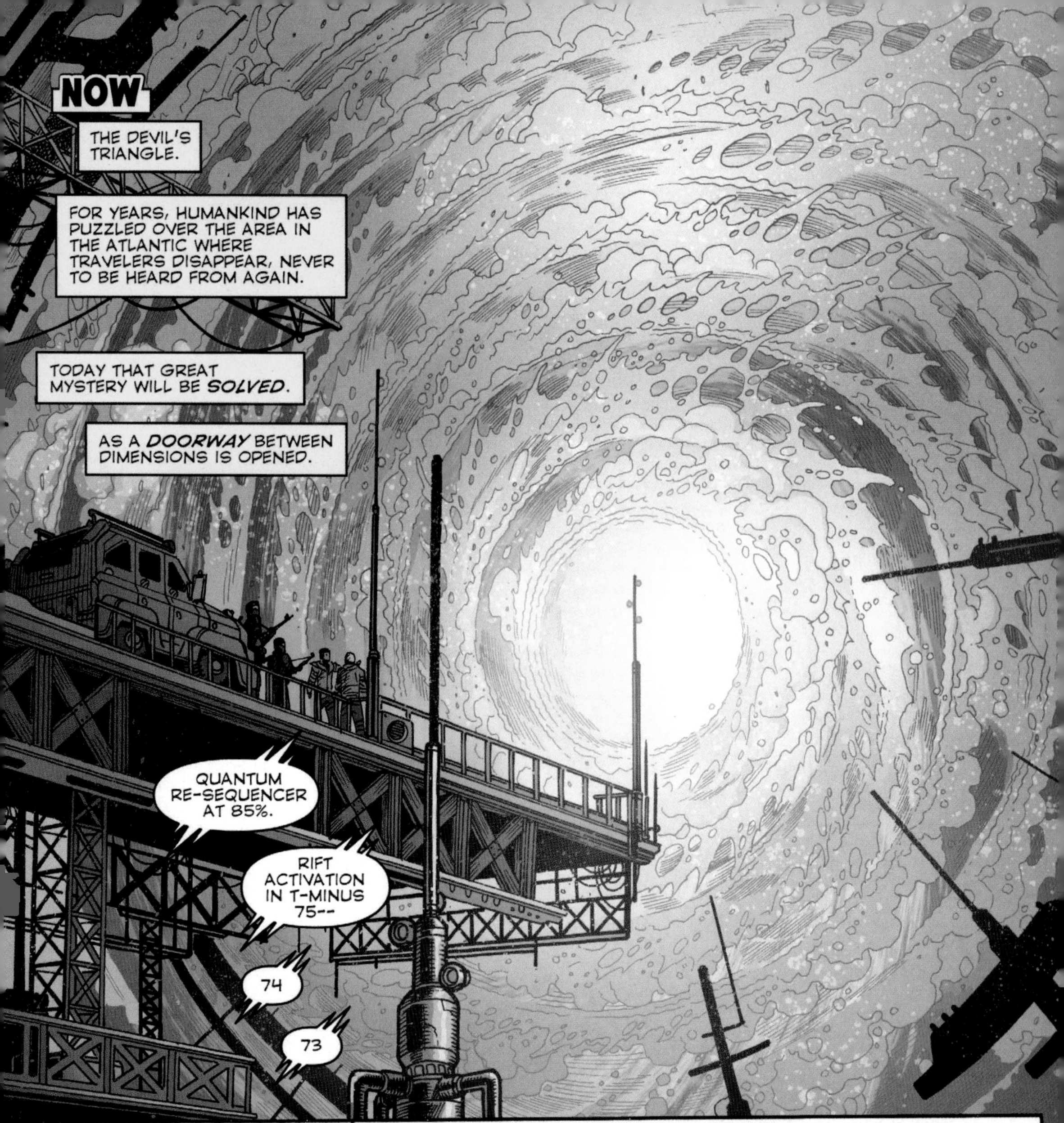
NOW
THE DEVIL'S TRIANGLE.
FOR YEARS, HUMANKIND HAS PUZZLED OVER THE AREA IN THE ATLANTIC WHERE TRAVELERS DISAPPEAR, NEVER TO BE HEARD FROM AGAIN.
TODAY THAT GREAT MYSTERY WILL BE SOLVED.
AS A DOORWAY BETWEEN DIMENSIONS IS OPENED.
QUANTUM RE-SEQUENCER AT 85%.
RIFT ACTIVATION IN T-MINUS 75--
74
73

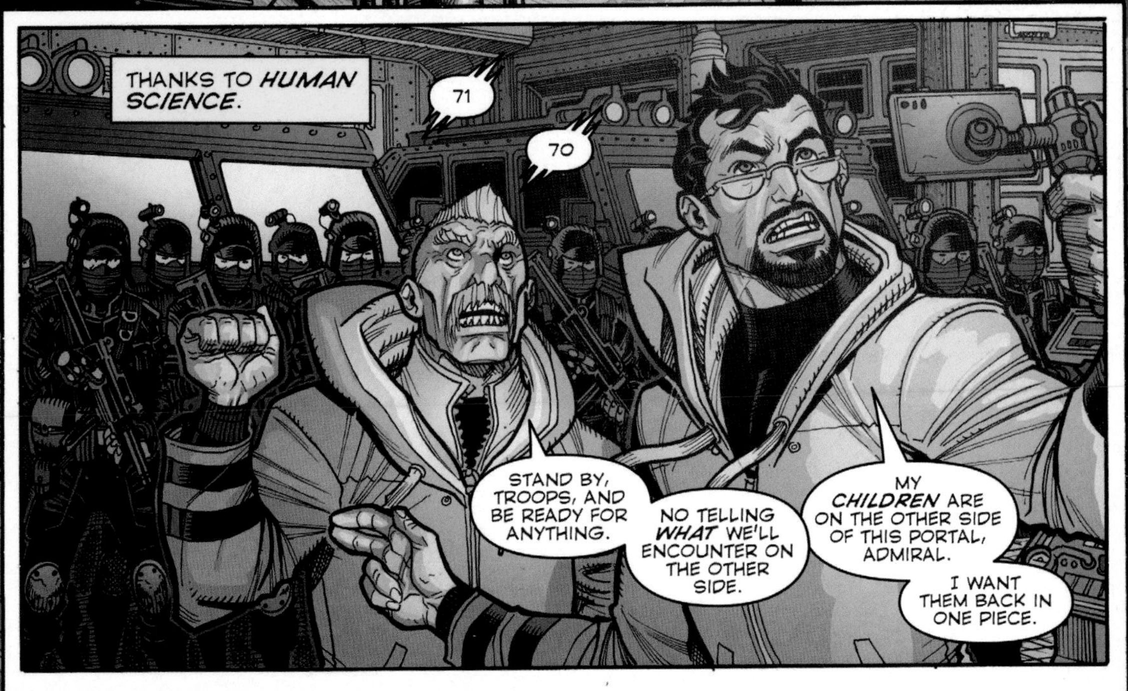
THANKS TO HUMAN SCIENCE.
71
70
STAND BY, TROOPS, AND BE READY FOR ANYTHING.
NO TELLING WHAT WE'LL ENCOUNTER ON THE OTHER SIDE.
MY CHILDREN ARE ON THE OTHER SIDE OF THIS PORTAL, ADMIRAL.
I WANT THEM BACK IN ONE PIECE.

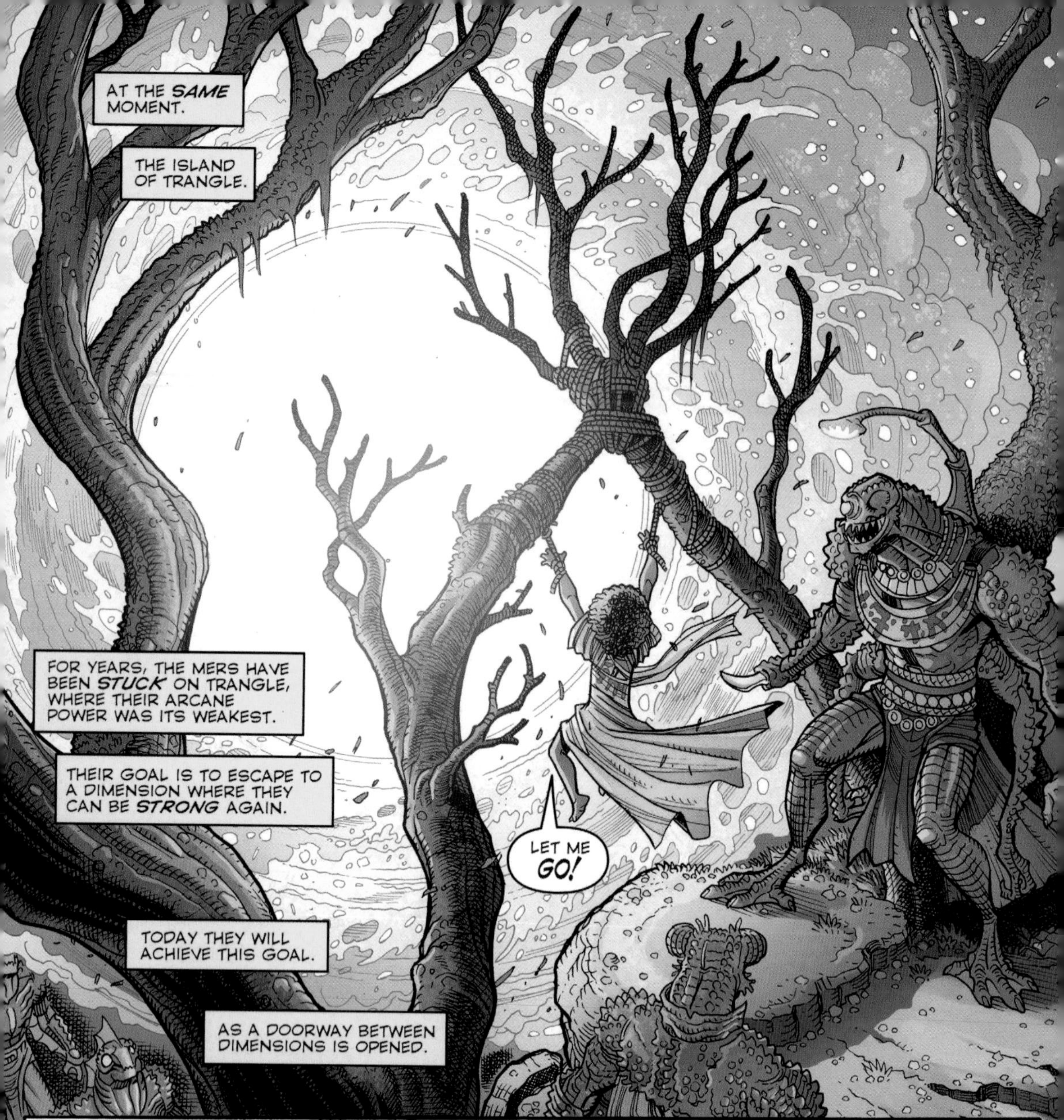
AT THE SAME MOMENT.
THE ISLAND OF TRANGLE.
FOR YEARS, THE MERS HAVE BEEN STUCK ON TRANGLE, WHERE THEIR ARCANE POWER WAS ITS WEAKEST.
THEIR GOAL IS TO ESCAPE TO A DIMENSION WHERE THEY CAN BE STRONG AGAIN.
LET ME GO!
TODAY THEY WILL ACHIEVE THIS GOAL.
AS A DOORWAY BETWEEN DIMENSIONS IS OPENED.
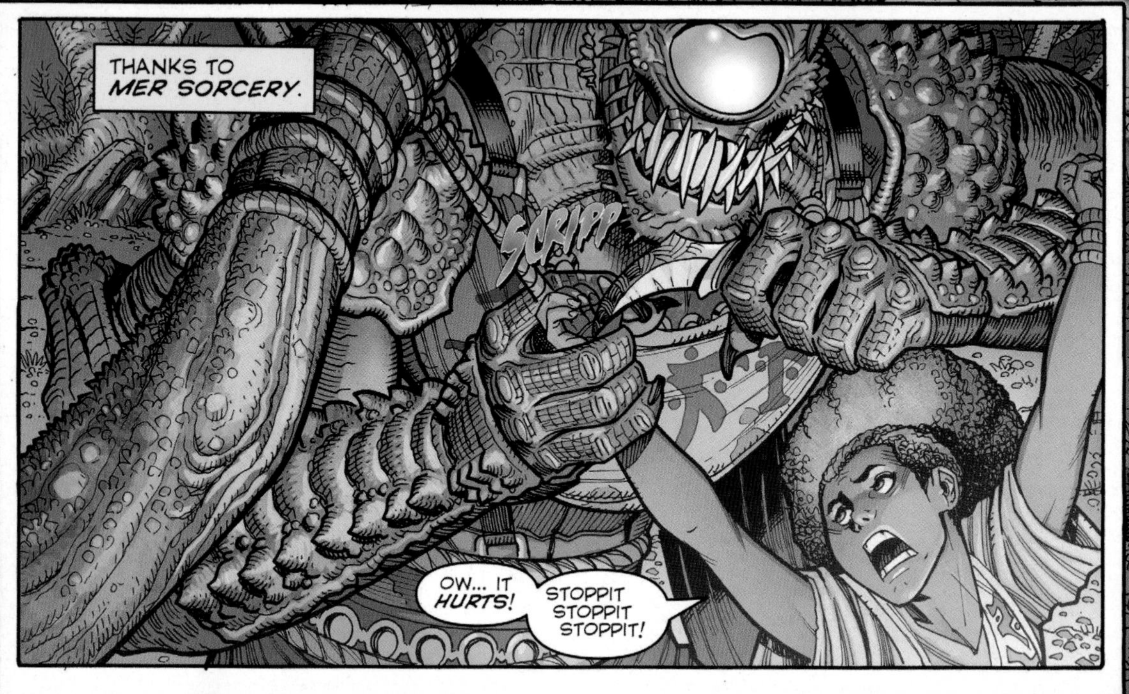
THANKS TO MER SORCERY.
SCRIPP
OW... IT HURTS!
STOPPIT STOPPIT STOPPIT!

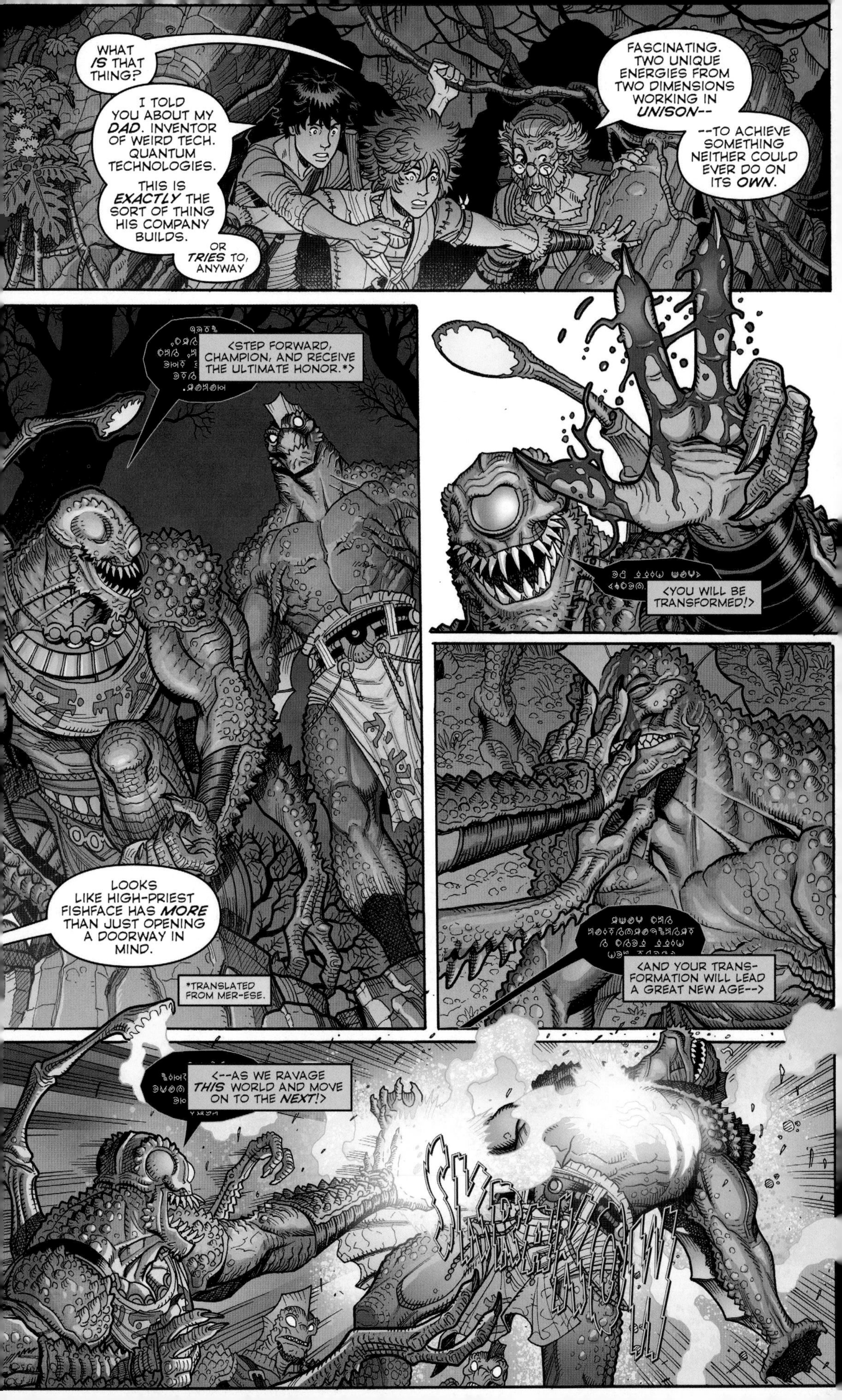

WHAT *IS* THAT THING?
I TOLD YOU ABOUT MY *DAD*. INVENTOR OF WEIRD TECH. QUANTUM TECHNOLOGIES.
THIS IS *EXACTLY* THE SORT OF THING HIS COMPANY BUILDS.
OR *TRIES* TO, ANYWAY
FASCINATING. TWO UNIQUE ENERGIES FROM TWO DIMENSIONS WORKING IN *UNISON*--
--TO ACHIEVE SOMETHING NEITHER COULD EVER DO ON ITS *OWN*.
<STEP FORWARD, CHAMPION, AND RECEIVE THE ULTIMATE HONOR.*>
LOOKS LIKE HIGH-PRIEST FISHFACE HAS *MORE* THAN JUST OPENING A DOORWAY IN MIND.
*TRANSLATED FROM MER-ESE.
<YOU WILL BE TRANSFORMED!>
<AND YOUR TRANS-FORMATION WILL LEAD A GREAT NEW AGE-->
<--AS WE RAVAGE *THIS* WORLD AND MOVE ON TO THE *NEXT*!>

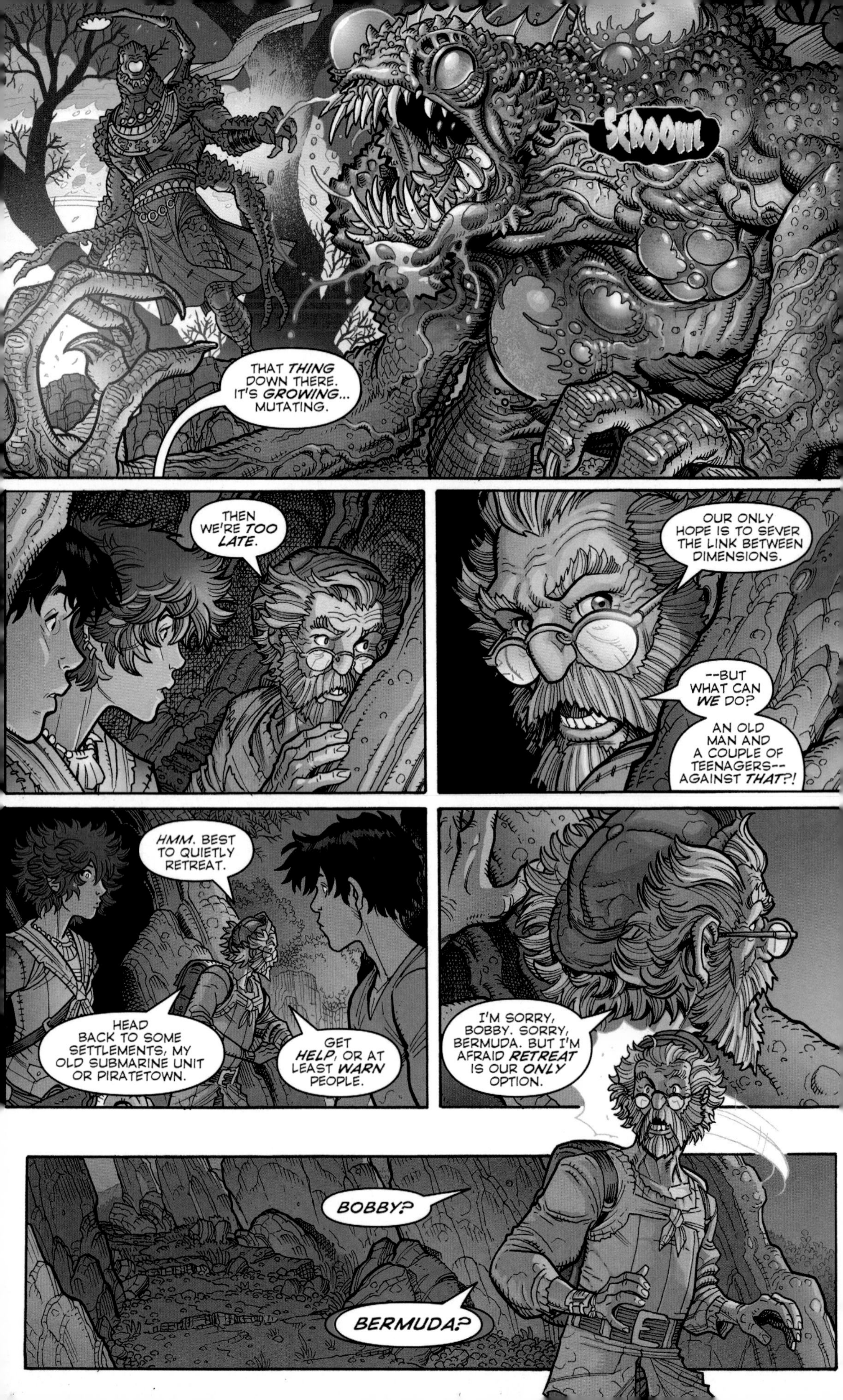
SCROOWL
THAT THING DOWN THERE. IT'S GROWING... MUTATING.
THEN WE'RE TOO LATE.
OUR ONLY HOPE IS TO SEVER THE LINK BETWEEN DIMENSIONS.
--BUT WHAT CAN WE DO?
AN OLD MAN AND A COUPLE OF TEENAGERS-- AGAINST THAT?!
HMM. BEST TO QUIETLY RETREAT.
HEAD BACK TO SOME SETTLEMENTS, MY OLD SUBMARINE UNIT OR PIRATETOWN.
GET HELP, OR AT LEAST WARN PEOPLE.
I'M SORRY, BOBBY. SORRY, BERMUDA. BUT I'M AFRAID RETREAT IS OUR ONLY OPTION.
BOBBY?
BERMUDA?

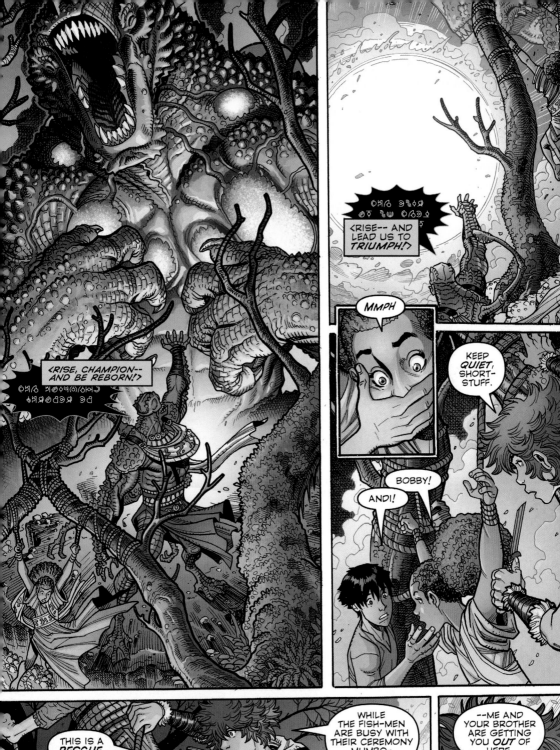

<RISE, CHAMPION-- AND BE REBORN!>

<RISE-- AND LEAD US TO *TRIUMPH!*>

MMPH

KEEP *QUIET,* SHORT-STUFF.

BOBBY!

ANDI!

THIS IS A *RESCUE.*

WHILE THE FISH-MEN ARE BUSY WITH THEIR CEREMONY MUMBO-JUMBO--

--ME AND YOUR BROTHER ARE GETTING YOU *OUT* OF HERE.

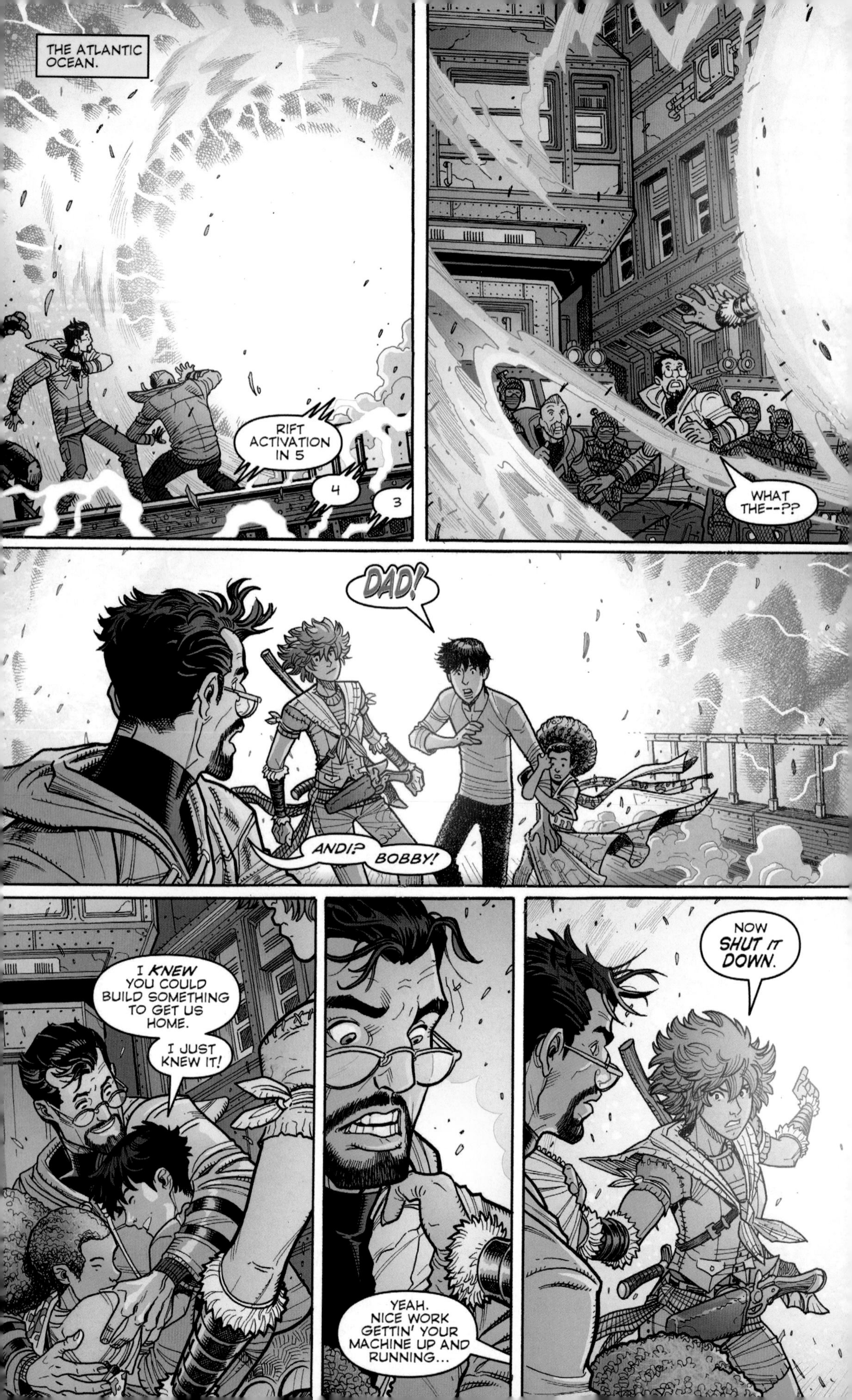
THE ATLANTIC OCEAN.
RIFT ACTIVATION IN 5
4
3
WHAT THE--??
DAD!
ANDI?
BOBBY!
I KNEW YOU COULD BUILD SOMETHING TO GET US HOME.
I JUST KNEW IT!
YEAH. NICE WORK GETTIN' YOUR MACHINE UP AND RUNNING...
NOW SHUT IT DOWN.

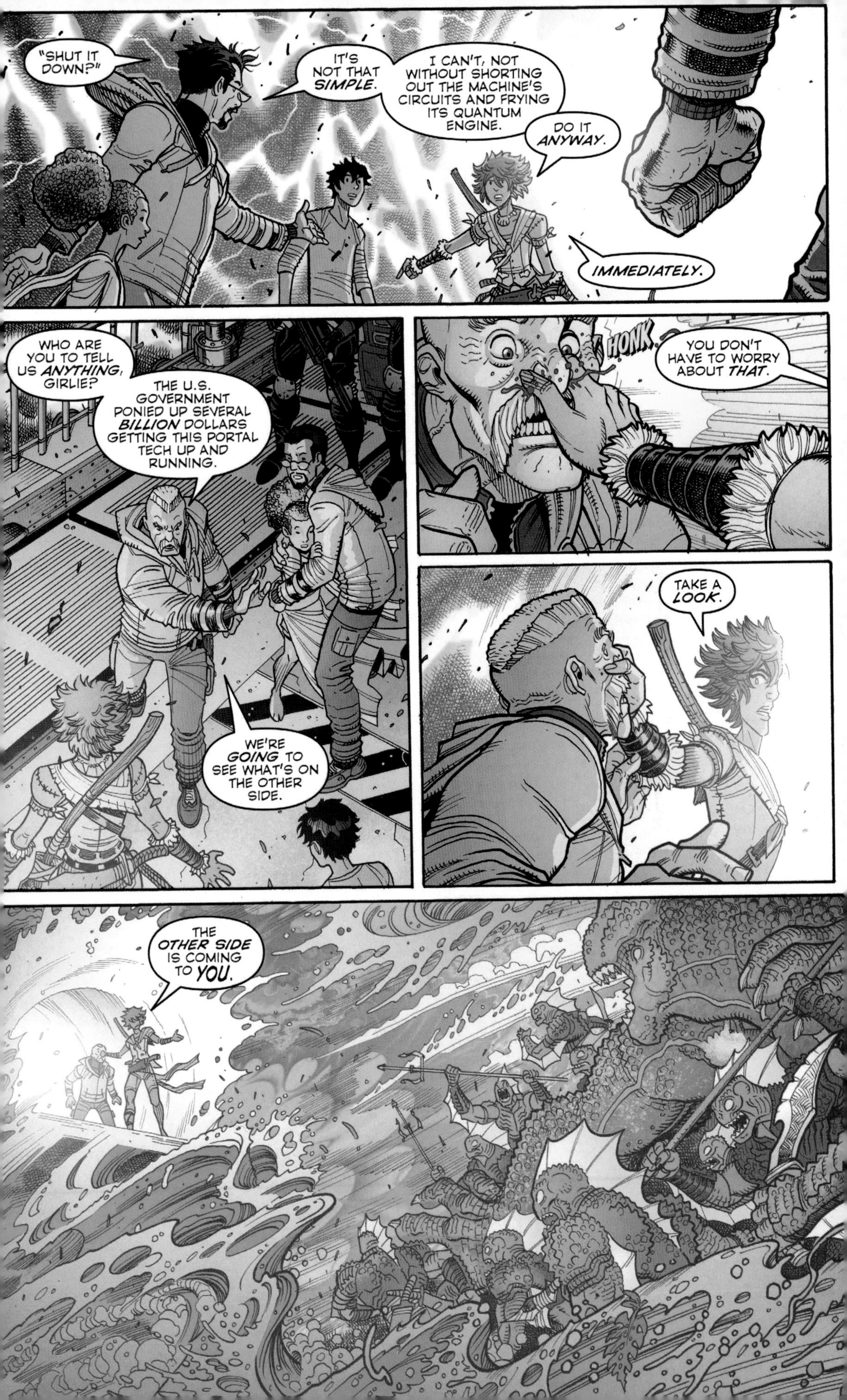
"SHUT IT DOWN?"
IT'S NOT THAT SIMPLE.
I CAN'T, NOT WITHOUT SHORTING OUT THE MACHINE'S CIRCUITS AND FRYING ITS QUANTUM ENGINE.
DO IT ANYWAY.
IMMEDIATELY.
WHO ARE YOU TO TELL US ANYTHING, GIRLIE?
THE U.S. GOVERNMENT PONIED UP SEVERAL BILLION DOLLARS GETTING THIS PORTAL TECH UP AND RUNNING.
WE'RE GOING TO SEE WHAT'S ON THE OTHER SIDE.
HONK
YOU DON'T HAVE TO WORRY ABOUT THAT.
TAKE A LOOK.
THE OTHER SIDE IS COMING TO YOU.

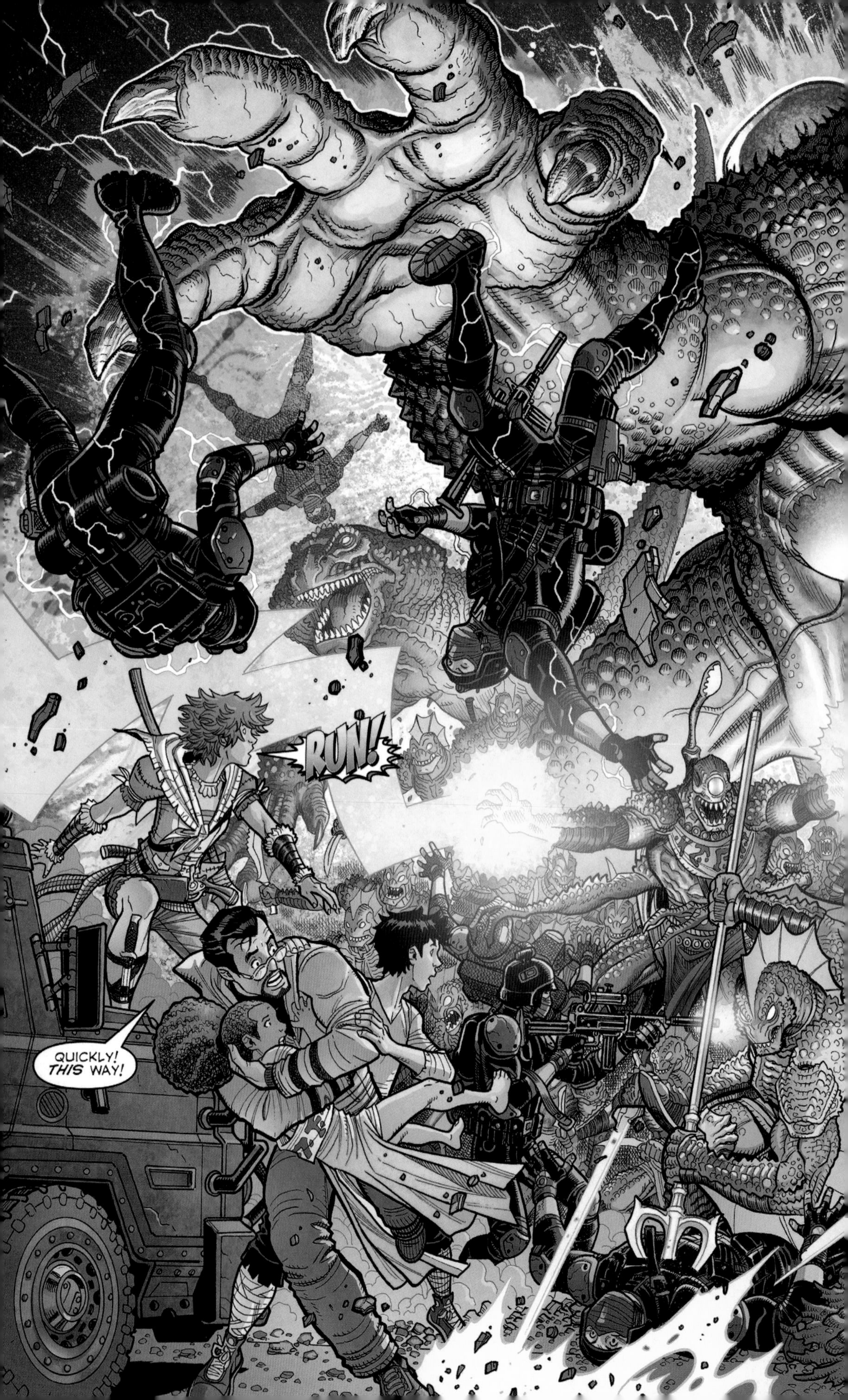
RUN!
QUICKLY! THIS WAY!

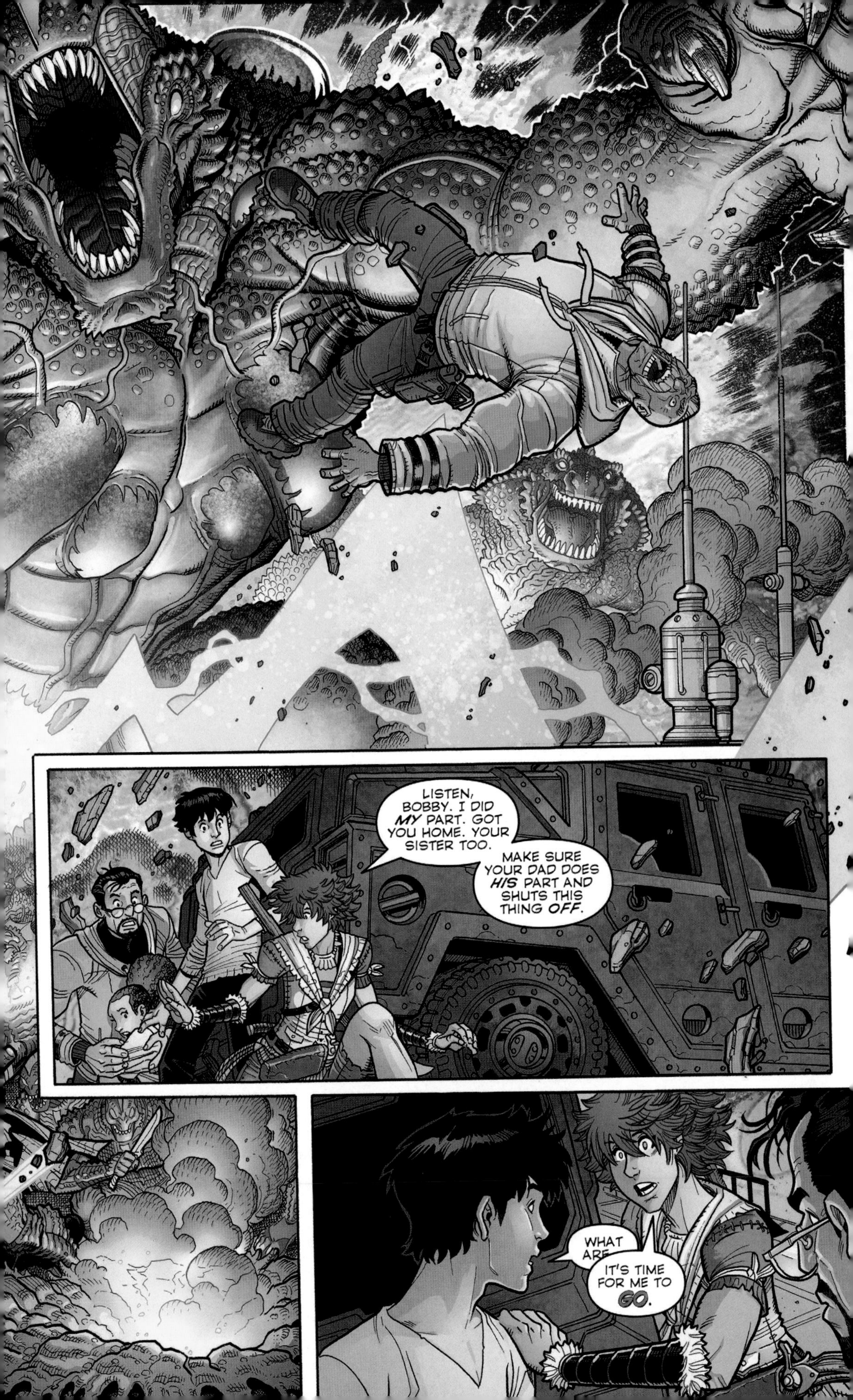
LISTEN, BOBBY. I DID MY PART. GOT YOU HOME. YOUR SISTER TOO.
MAKE SURE YOUR DAD DOES HIS PART AND SHUTS THIS THING OFF.
WHAT ARE
IT'S TIME FOR ME TO GO.

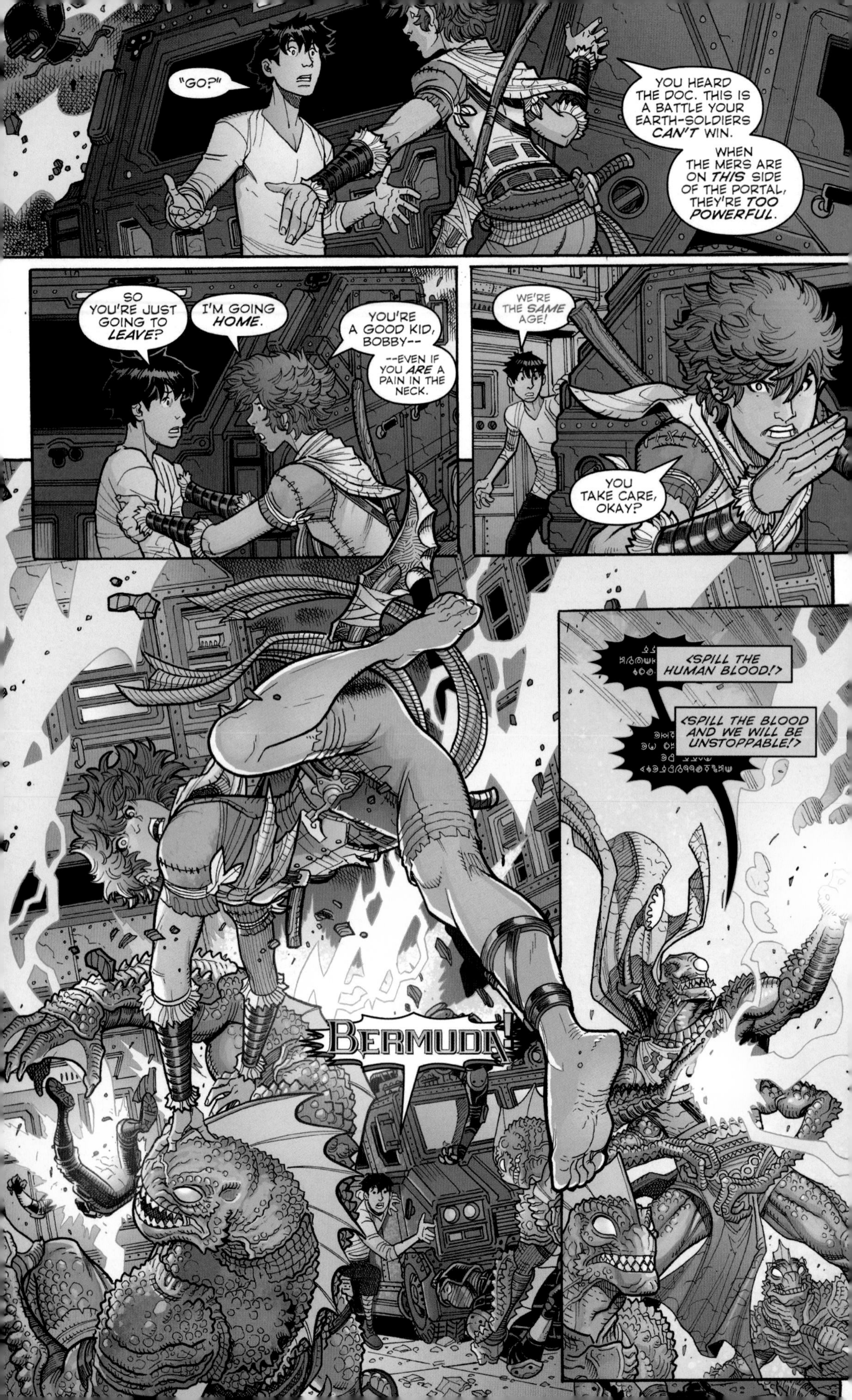
"GO?"
YOU HEARD THE DOC. THIS IS A BATTLE YOUR EARTH-SOLDIERS CAN'T WIN.
WHEN THE MERS ARE ON THIS SIDE OF THE PORTAL, THEY'RE TOO POWERFUL.
SO YOU'RE JUST GOING TO LEAVE?
I'M GOING HOME.
YOU'RE A GOOD KID, BOBBY--
--EVEN IF YOU ARE A PAIN IN THE NECK.
WE'RE THE SAME AGE!
YOU TAKE CARE, OKAY?
<SPILL THE HUMAN BLOOD!>
<SPILL THE BLOOD AND WE WILL BE UNSTOPPABLE!>
BERMUDA!

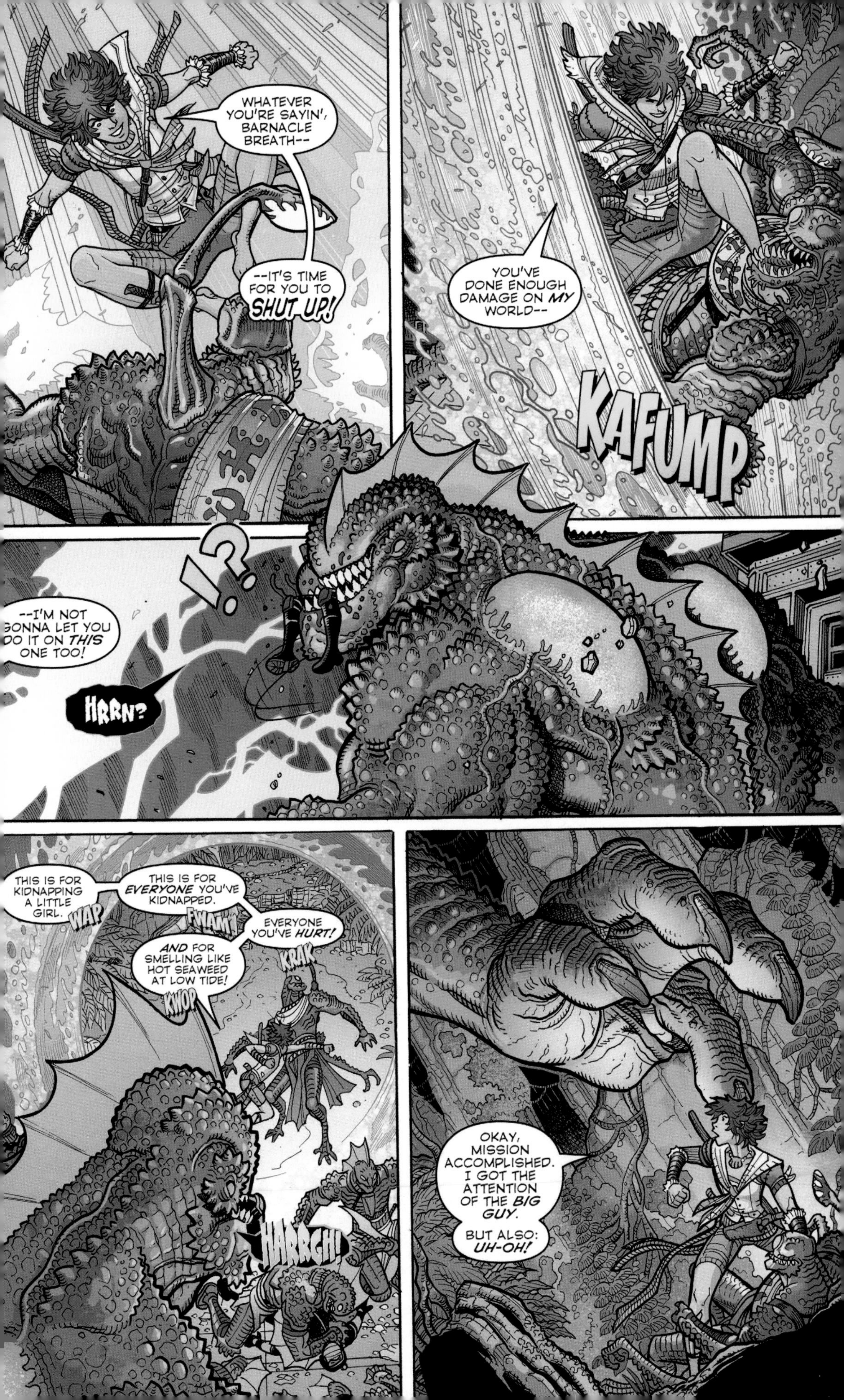
WHATEVER YOU'RE SAYIN', BARNACLE BREATH--
--IT'S TIME FOR YOU TO SHUT UP!
YOU'VE DONE ENOUGH DAMAGE ON *MY* WORLD--
KAFUMP
--I'M NOT GONNA LET YOU DO IT ON *THIS* ONE TOO!
!?
HRRN?
THIS IS FOR KIDNAPPING A LITTLE GIRL.
WAP
THIS IS FOR *EVERYONE* YOU'VE KIDNAPPED.
FWAM!
EVERYONE YOU'VE *HURT!*
KRAK
AND FOR SMELLING LIKE HOT SEAWEED AT LOW TIDE!
KWOP
HARRGH!
OKAY, MISSION ACCOMPLISHED. I GOT THE ATTENTION OF THE *BIG GUY*.
BUT ALSO: *UH-OH!*

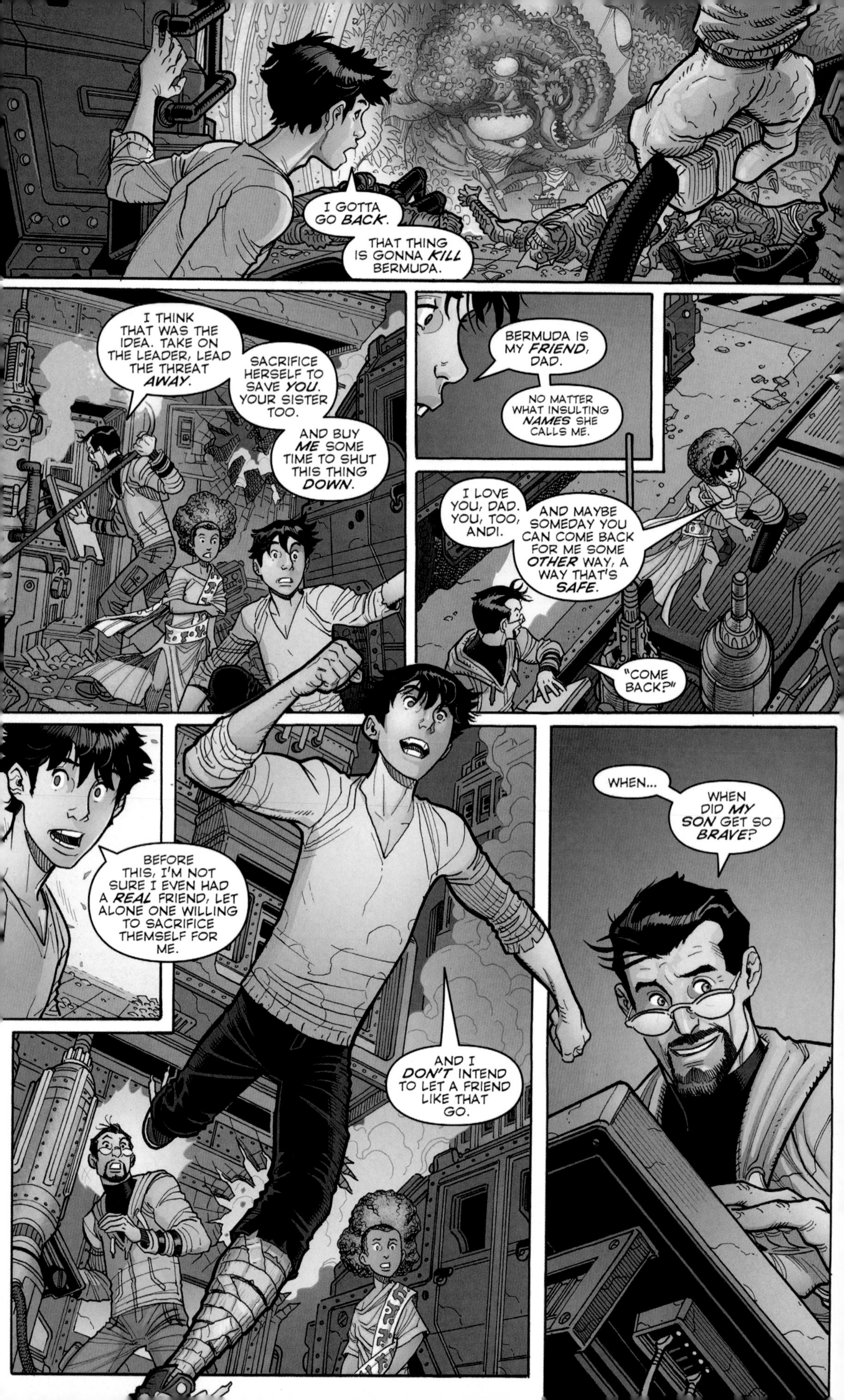
I GOTTA GO BACK.
THAT THING IS GONNA KILL BERMUDA.
I THINK THAT WAS THE IDEA. TAKE ON THE LEADER, LEAD THE THREAT AWAY.
SACRIFICE HERSELF TO SAVE YOU. YOUR SISTER TOO.
AND BUY ME SOME TIME TO SHUT THIS THING DOWN.
BERMUDA IS MY FRIEND, DAD.
NO MATTER WHAT INSULTING NAMES SHE CALLS ME.
I LOVE YOU, DAD. YOU, TOO, ANDI.
AND MAYBE SOMEDAY YOU CAN COME BACK FOR ME SOME OTHER WAY, A WAY THAT'S SAFE.
"COME BACK?"
BEFORE THIS, I'M NOT SURE I EVEN HAD A REAL FRIEND, LET ALONE ONE WILLING TO SACRIFICE THEMSELF FOR ME.
AND I DON'T INTEND TO LET A FRIEND LIKE THAT GO.
WHEN...
WHEN DID MY SON GET SO BRAVE?

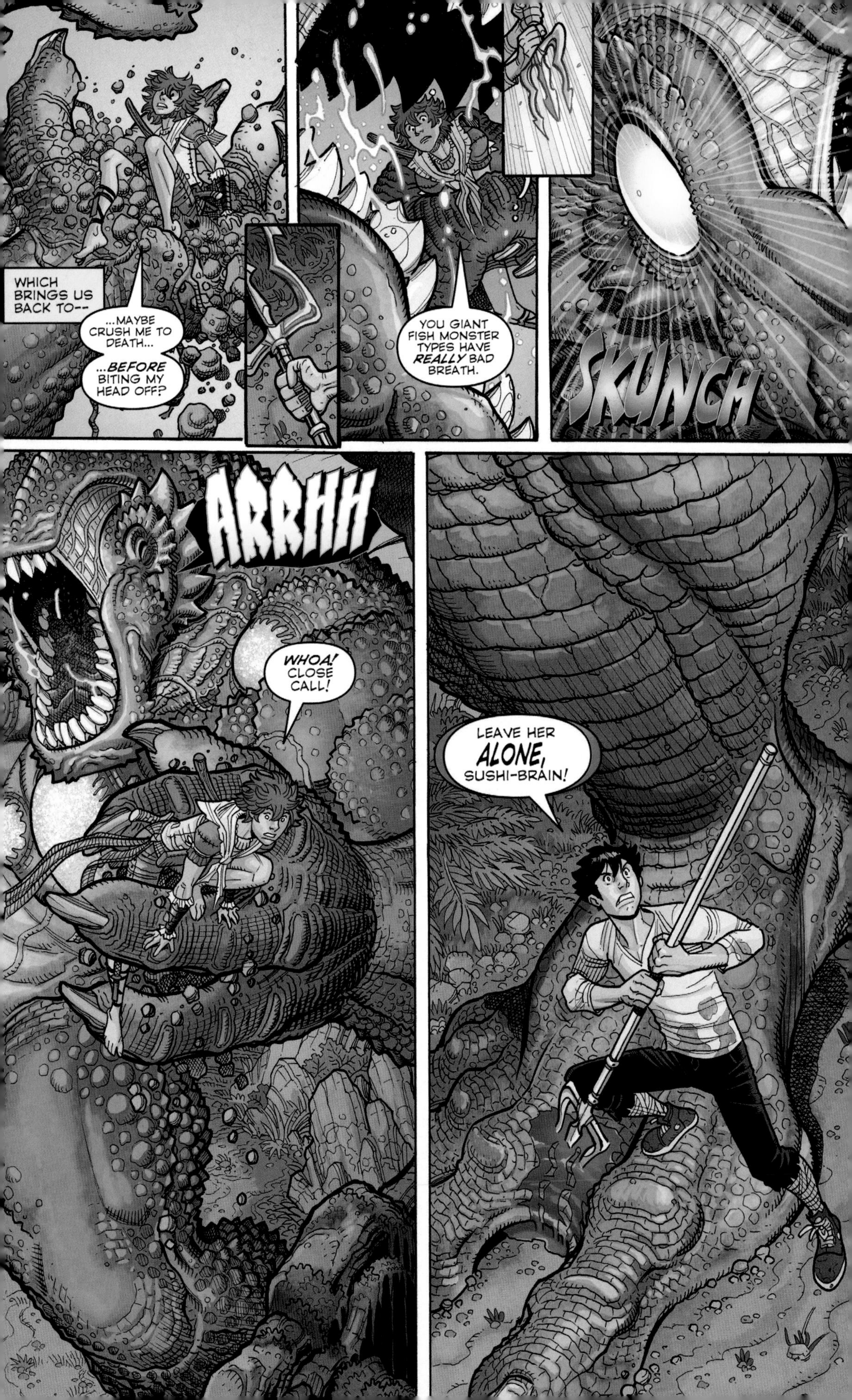
WHICH BRINGS US BACK TO--
...MAYBE CRUSH ME TO DEATH...
...BEFORE BITING MY HEAD OFF?
YOU GIANT FISH MONSTER TYPES HAVE REALLY BAD BREATH.
SKUNCH
ARRHH
WHOA! CLOSE CALL!
LEAVE HER ALONE, SUSHI-BRAIN!

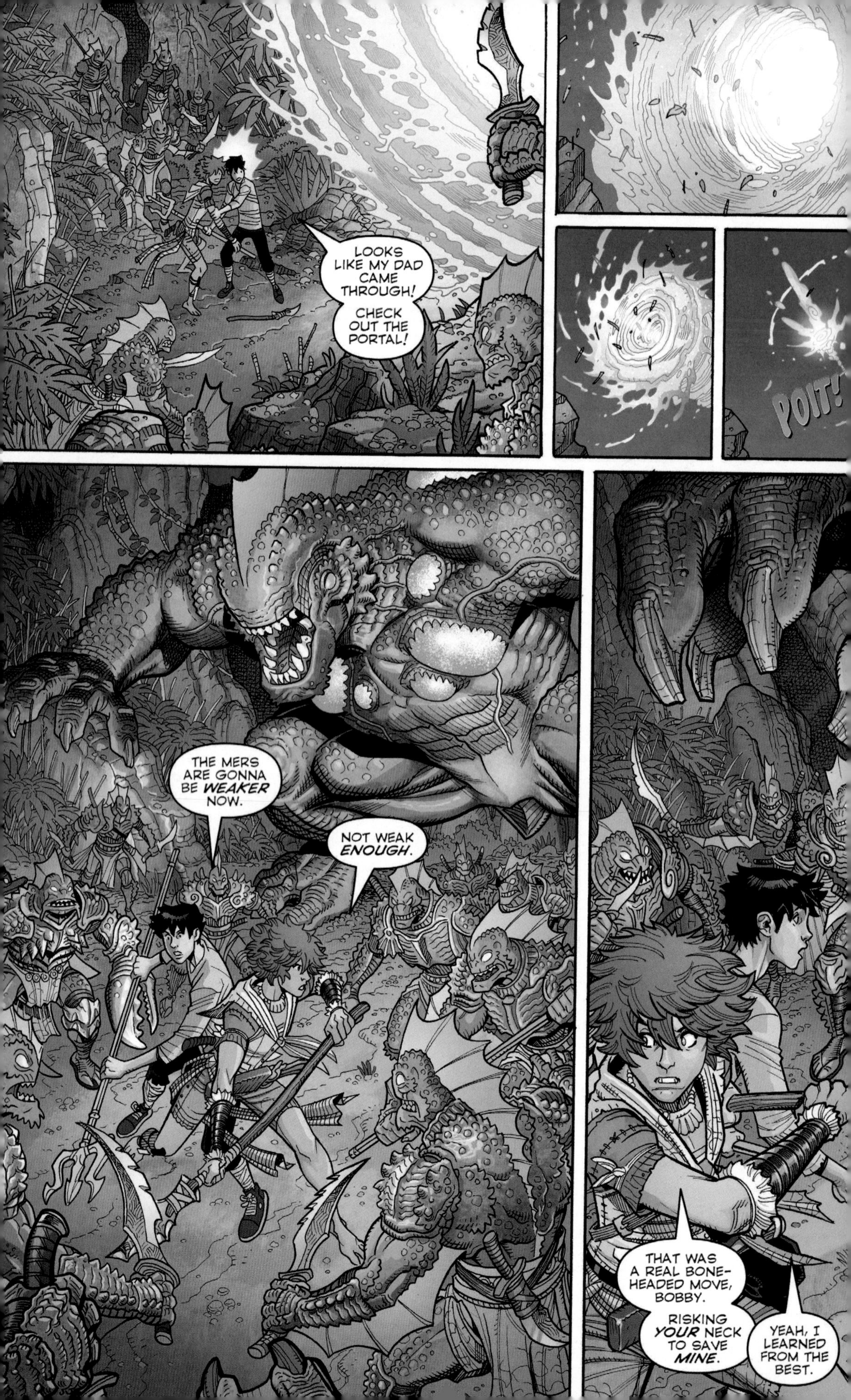
LOOKS LIKE MY DAD CAME THROUGH!
CHECK OUT THE PORTAL!
POIT!
THE MERS ARE GONNA BE *WEAKER* NOW.
NOT WEAK *ENOUGH*.
THAT WAS A REAL BONE-HEADED MOVE, BOBBY.
RISKING *YOUR* NECK TO SAVE *MINE*.
YEAH, I LEARNED FROM THE BEST.

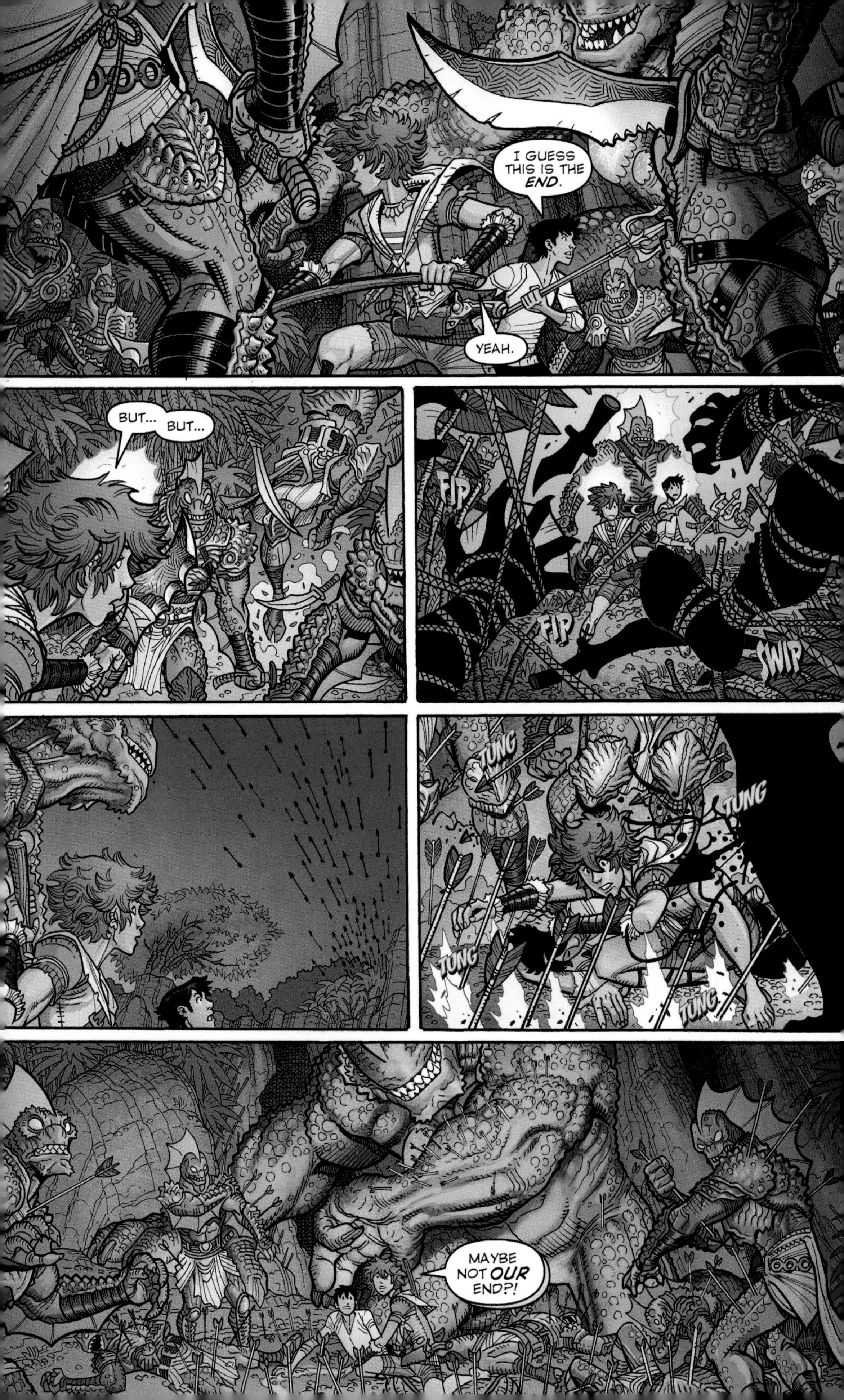
I GUESS THIS IS THE END.
YEAH.
BUT... BUT...
FIP
FIP
SWIP
TUNG
TUNG
TUNG
TUNG
MAYBE NOT OUR END?!

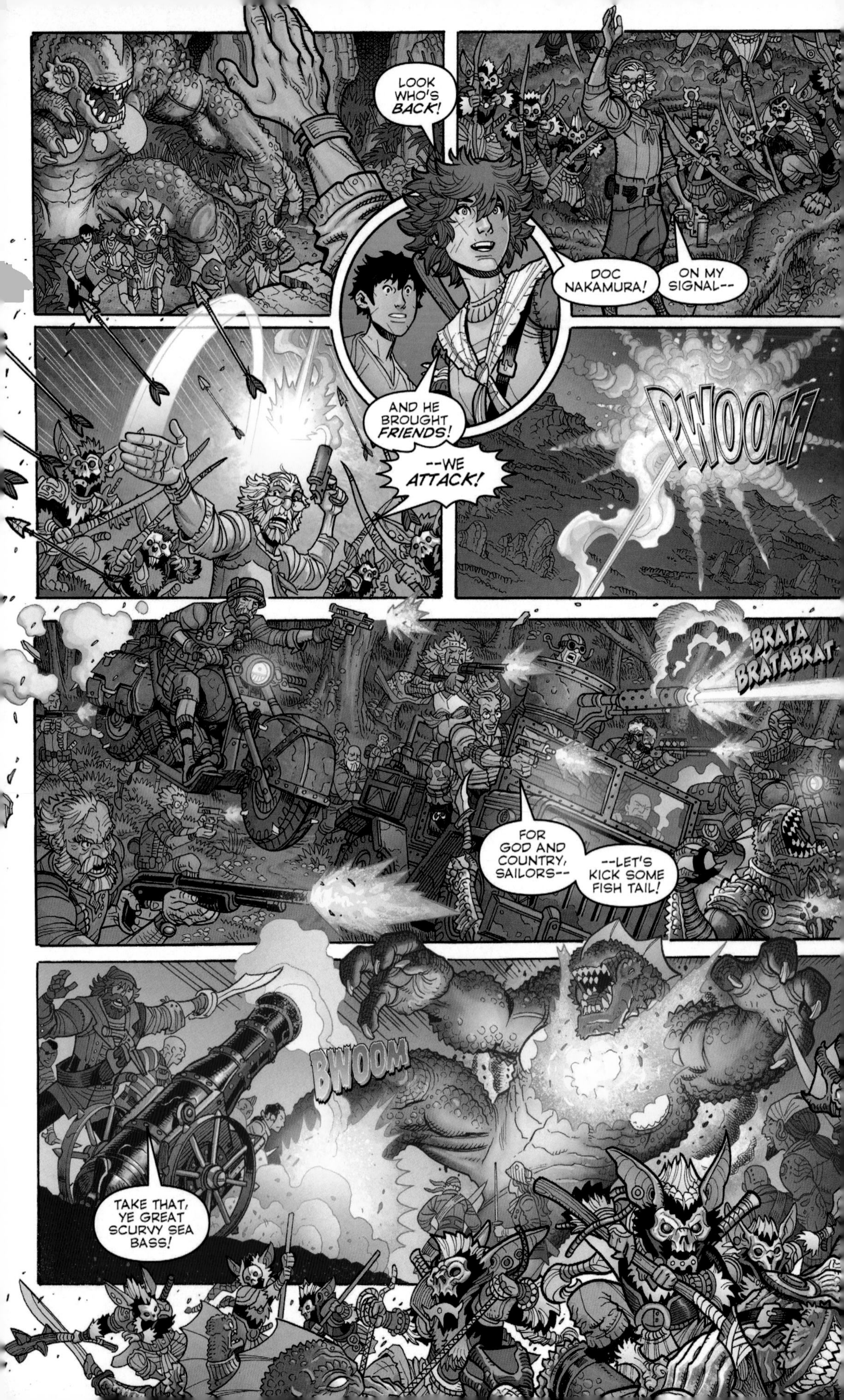
LOOK WHO'S BACK!
DOC NAKAMURA!
ON MY SIGNAL--
AND HE BROUGHT FRIENDS!
--WE ATTACK!
PWOOM
BRATA BRATABRAT
FOR GOD AND COUNTRY, SAILORS--
--LET'S KICK SOME FISH TAIL!
BWOOM
TAKE THAT, YE GREAT SCURVY SEA BASS!

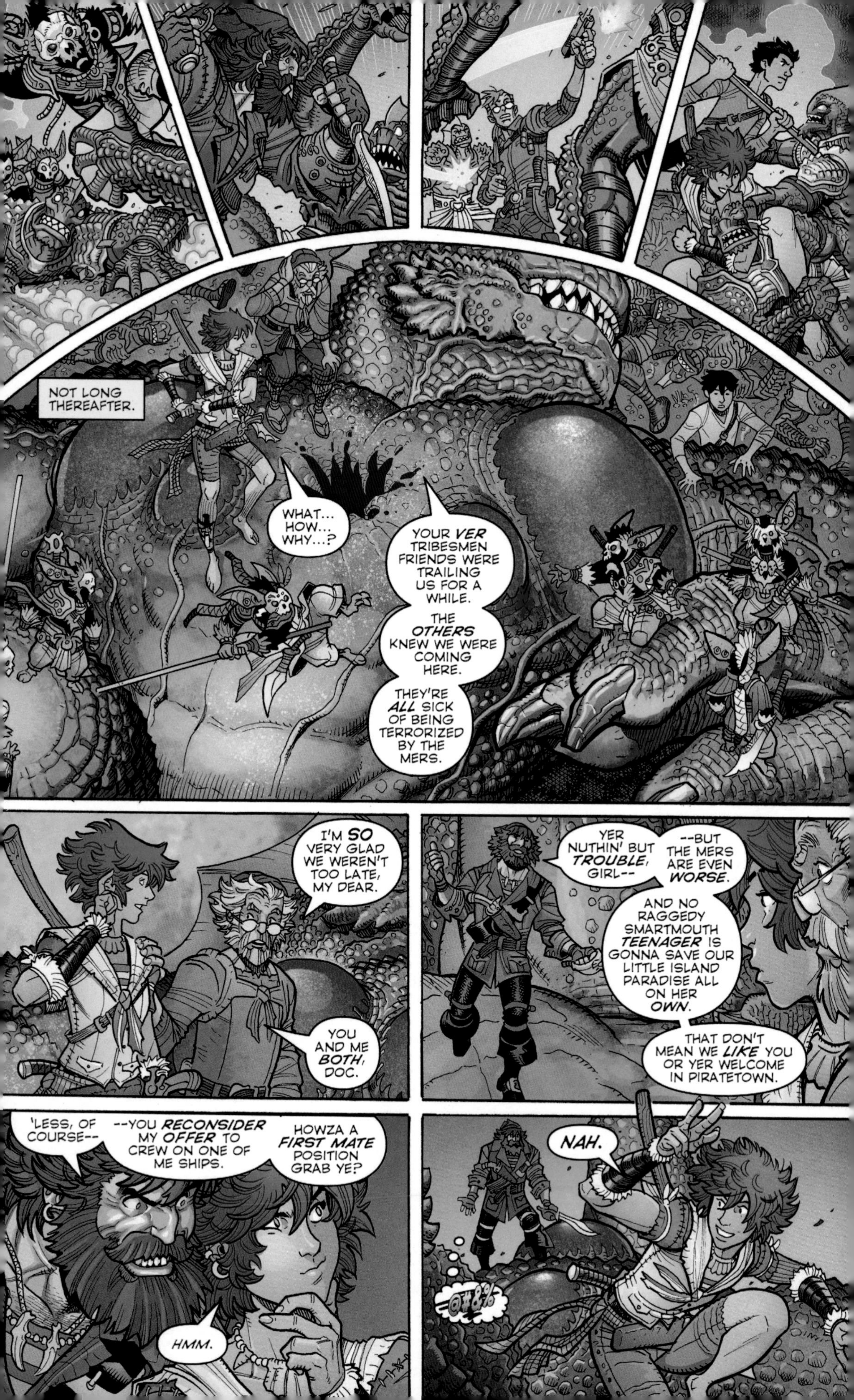
NOT LONG THEREAFTER.
WHAT... HOW... WHY...?
YOUR VER TRIBESMEN FRIENDS WERE TRAILING US FOR A WHILE.
THE OTHERS KNEW WE WERE COMING HERE.
THEY'RE ALL SICK OF BEING TERRORIZED BY THE MERS.
I'M SO VERY GLAD WE WEREN'T TOO LATE, MY DEAR.
YOU AND ME BOTH, DOC.
YER NUTHIN' BUT TROUBLE, GIRL--
--BUT THE MERS ARE EVEN WORSE.
AND NO RAGGEDY SMARTMOUTH TEENAGER IS GONNA SAVE OUR LITTLE ISLAND PARADISE ALL ON HER OWN.
THAT DON'T MEAN WE LIKE YOU OR YER WELCOME IN PIRATETOWN.
'LESS, OF COURSE--
--YOU RECONSIDER MY OFFER TO CREW ON ONE OF ME SHIPS.
HOWZA A FIRST MATE POSITION GRAB YE?
HMM.
NAH.
@#8%

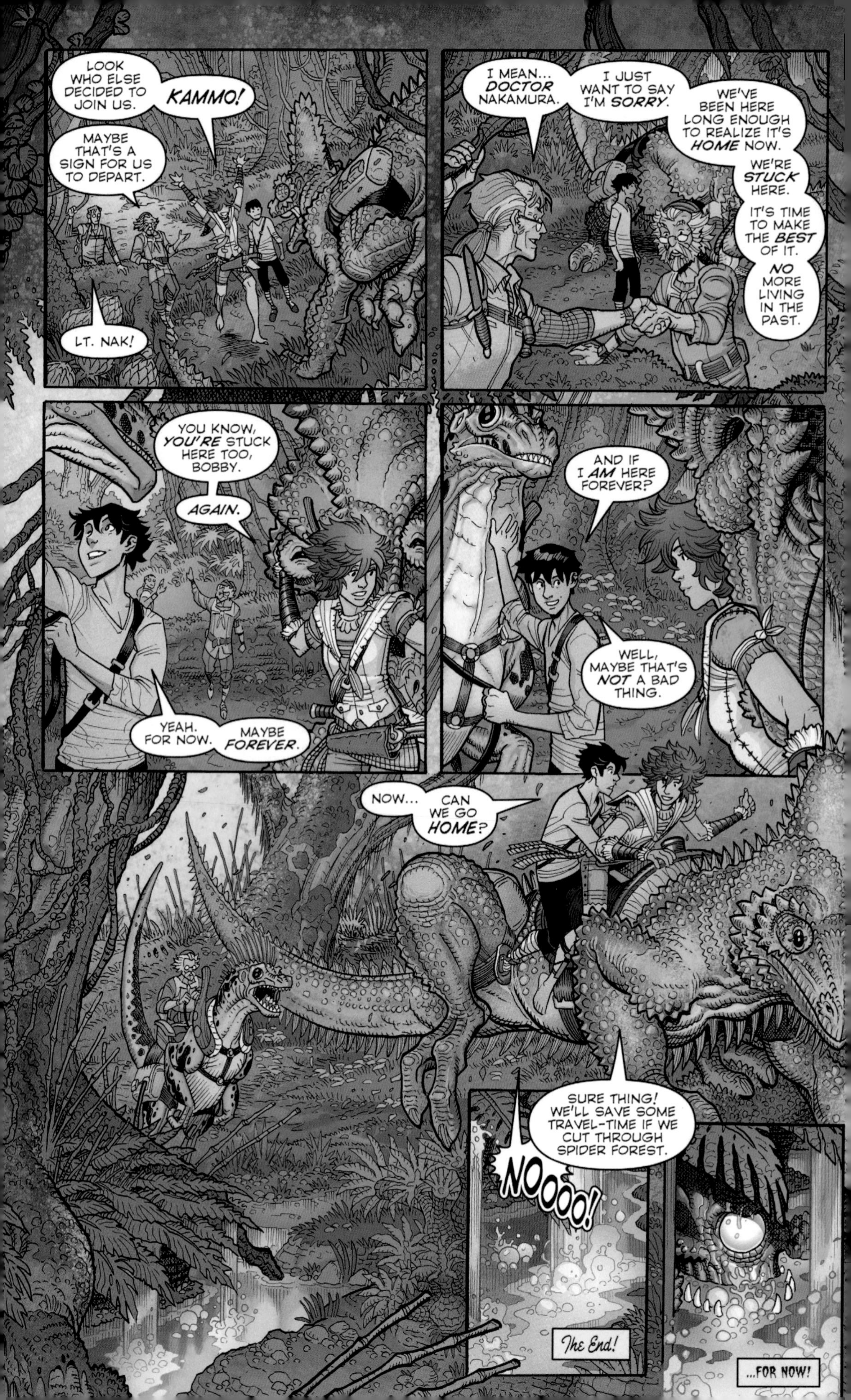
LOOK WHO ELSE DECIDED TO JOIN US.
KAMMO!
MAYBE THAT'S A SIGN FOR US TO DEPART.
LT. NAK!
I MEAN... DOCTOR NAKAMURA.
I JUST WANT TO SAY I'M SORRY.
WE'VE BEEN HERE LONG ENOUGH TO REALIZE IT'S HOME NOW.
WE'RE STUCK HERE.
IT'S TIME TO MAKE THE BEST OF IT.
NO MORE LIVING IN THE PAST.
YOU KNOW, YOU'RE STUCK HERE TOO, BOBBY.
AGAIN.
YEAH. FOR NOW.
MAYBE FOREVER.
AND IF I AM HERE FOREVER?
WELL, MAYBE THAT'S NOT A BAD THING.
NOW...
CAN WE GO HOME?
SURE THING! WE'LL SAVE SOME TRAVEL-TIME IF WE CUT THROUGH SPIDER FOREST.
NOOOO!
The End!
...FOR NOW!

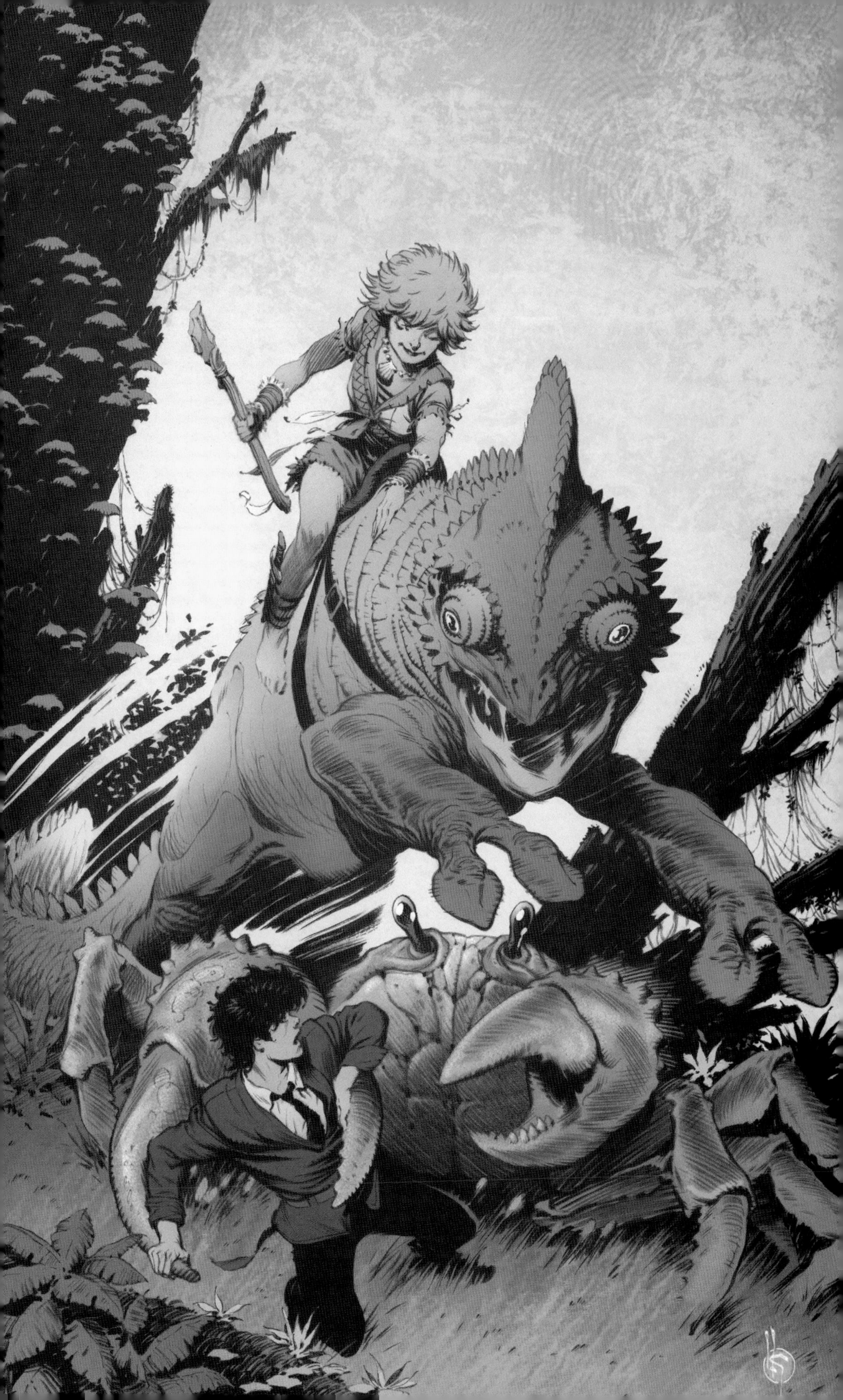

BERMUDA
GALLERY

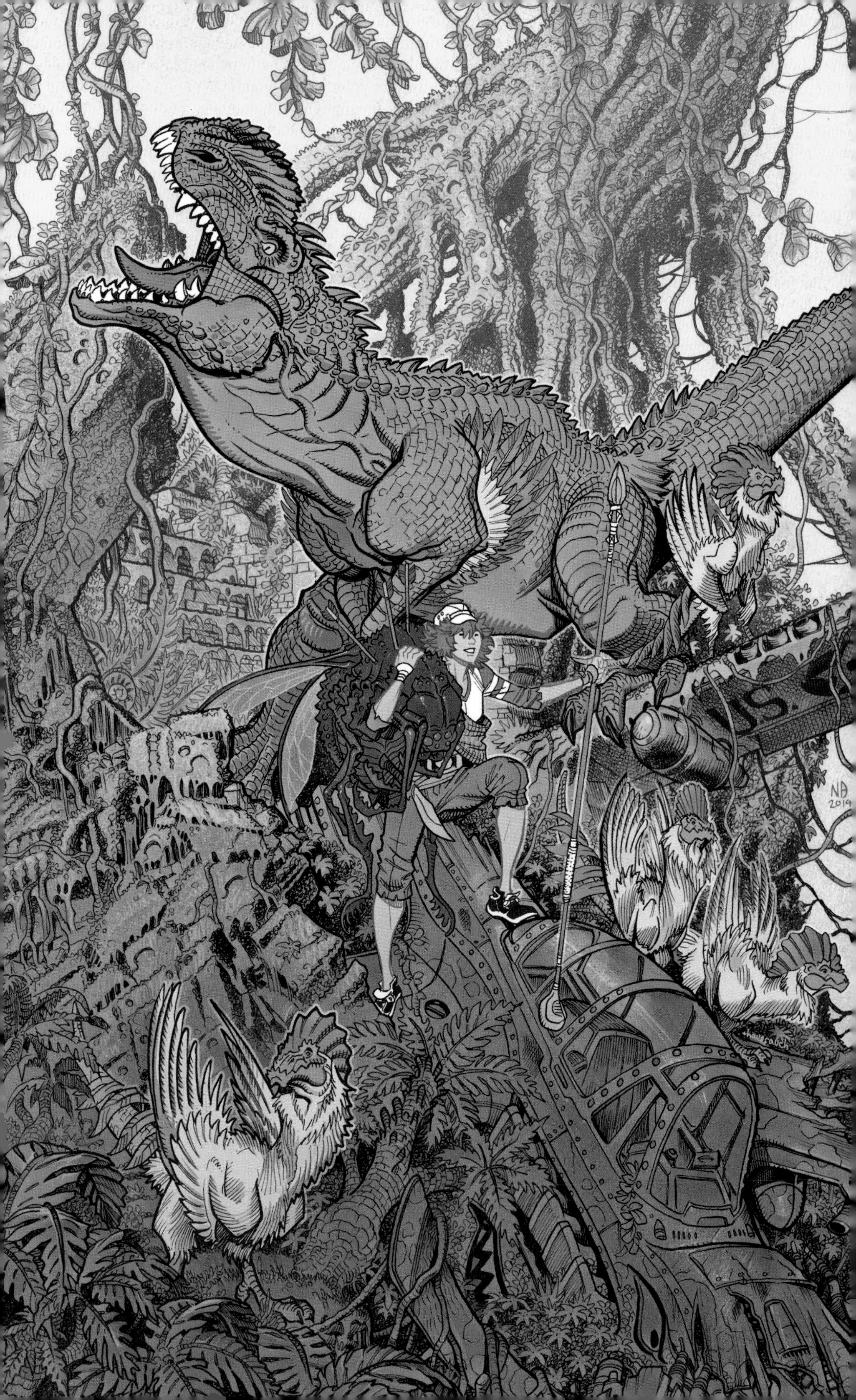

US
NA
2019

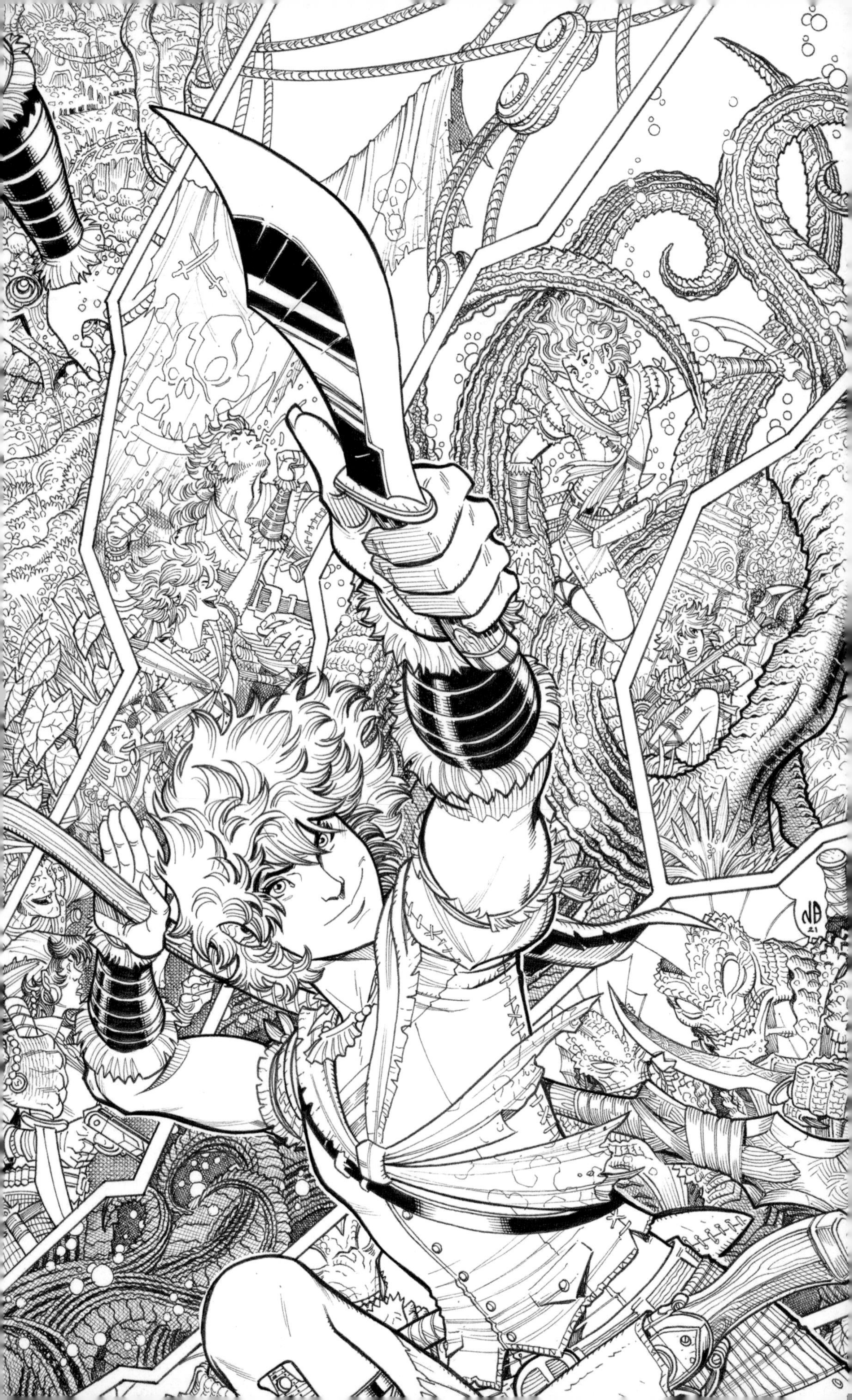

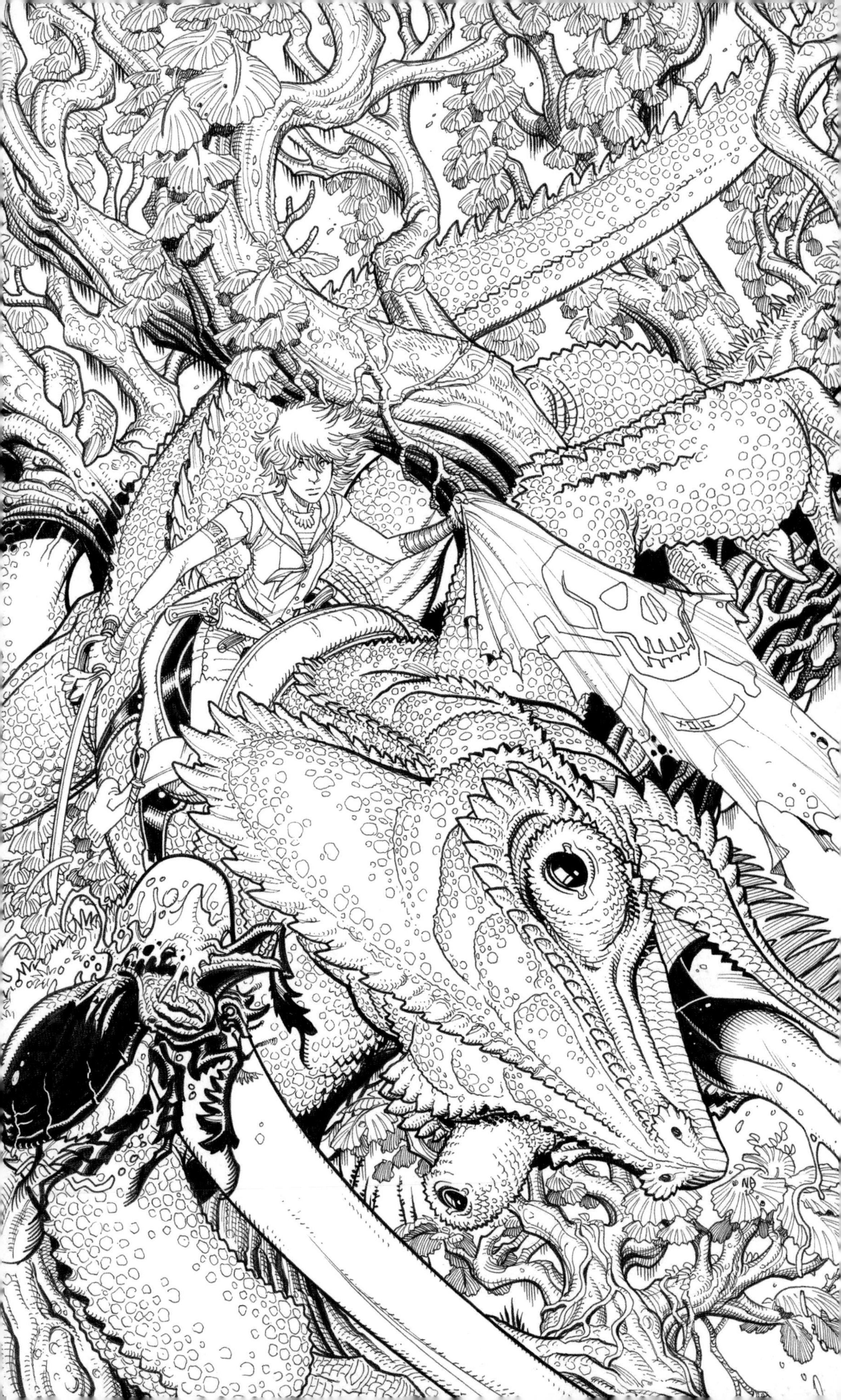

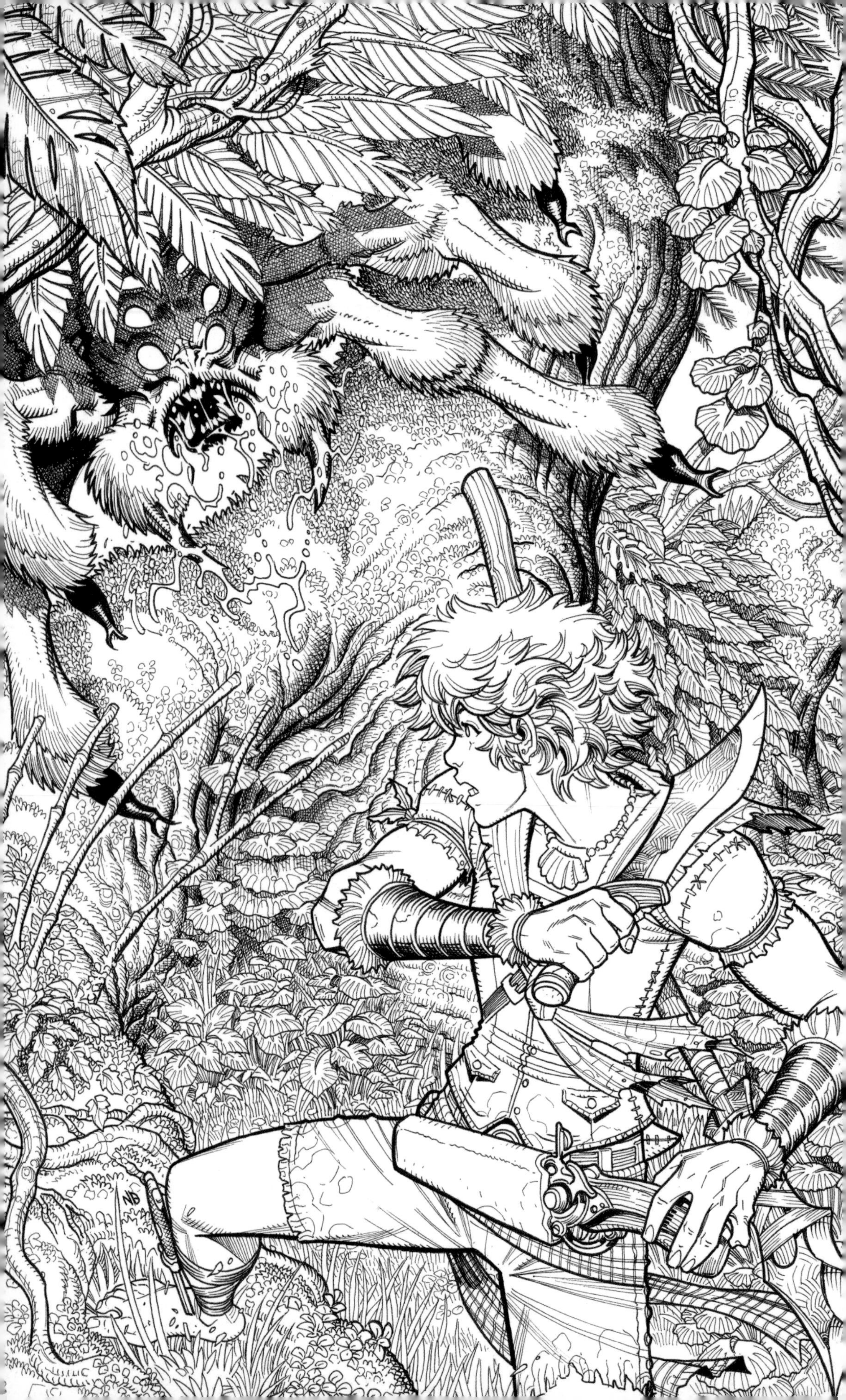

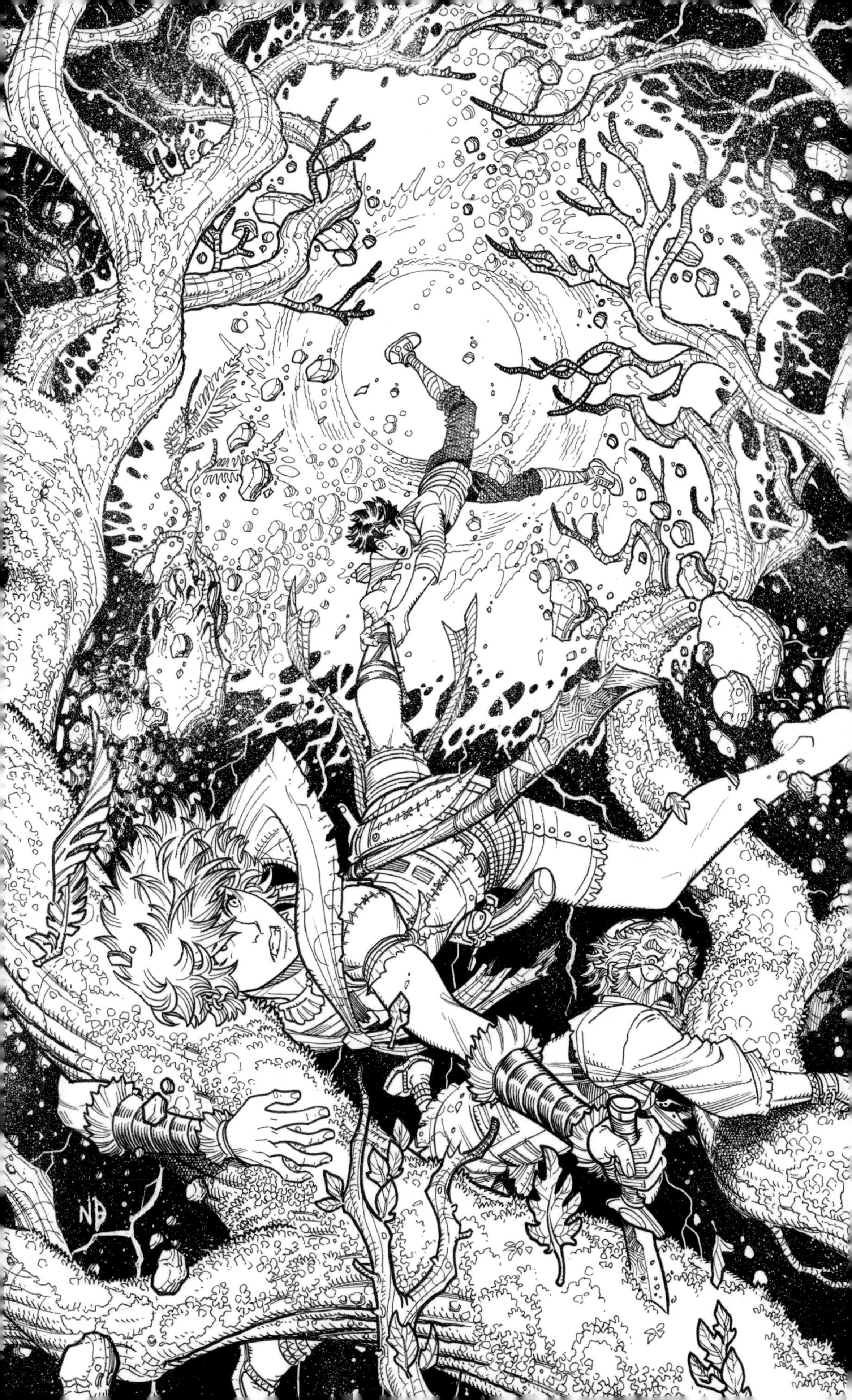

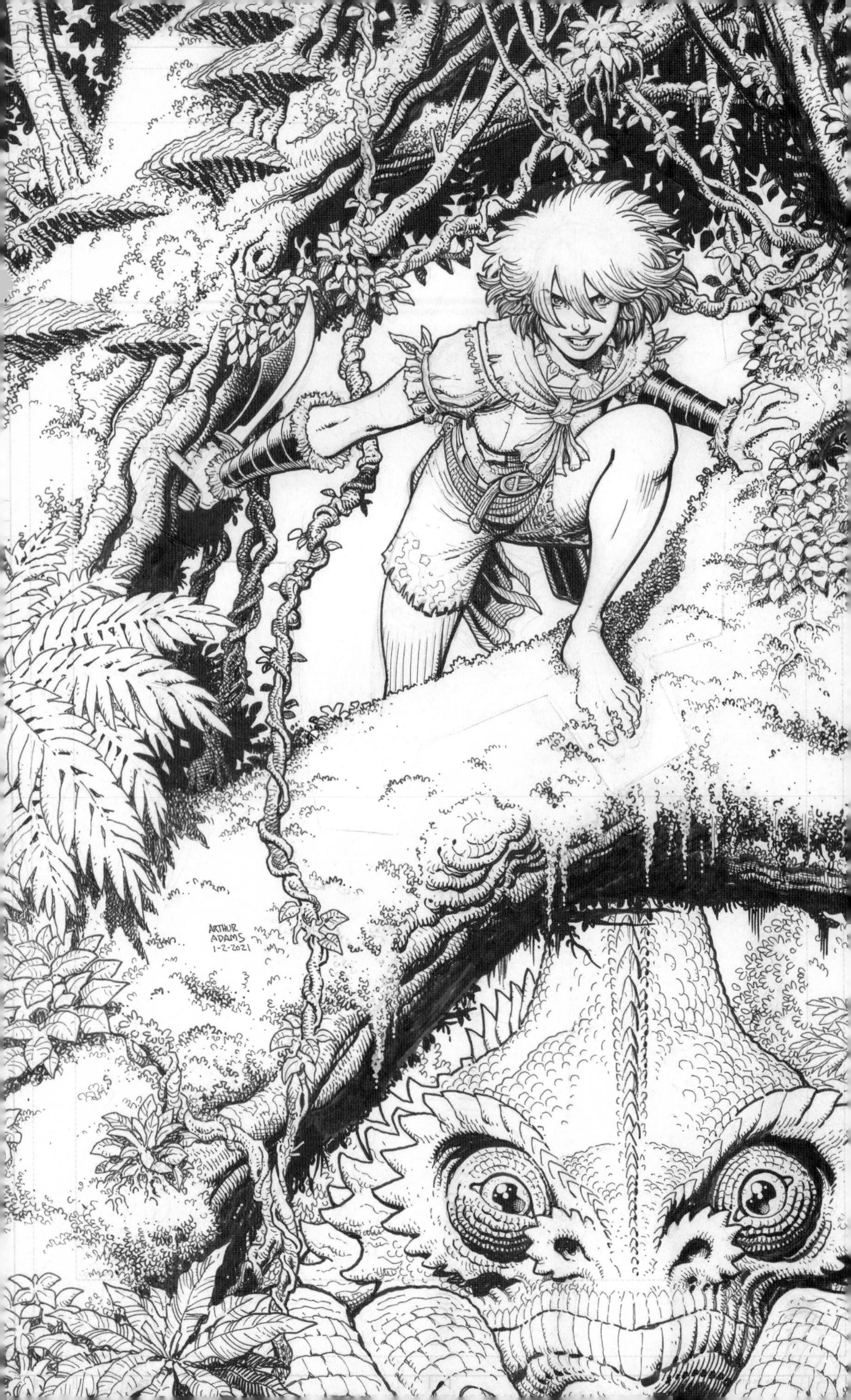
ARTHUR
ADAMS
1-2-2021

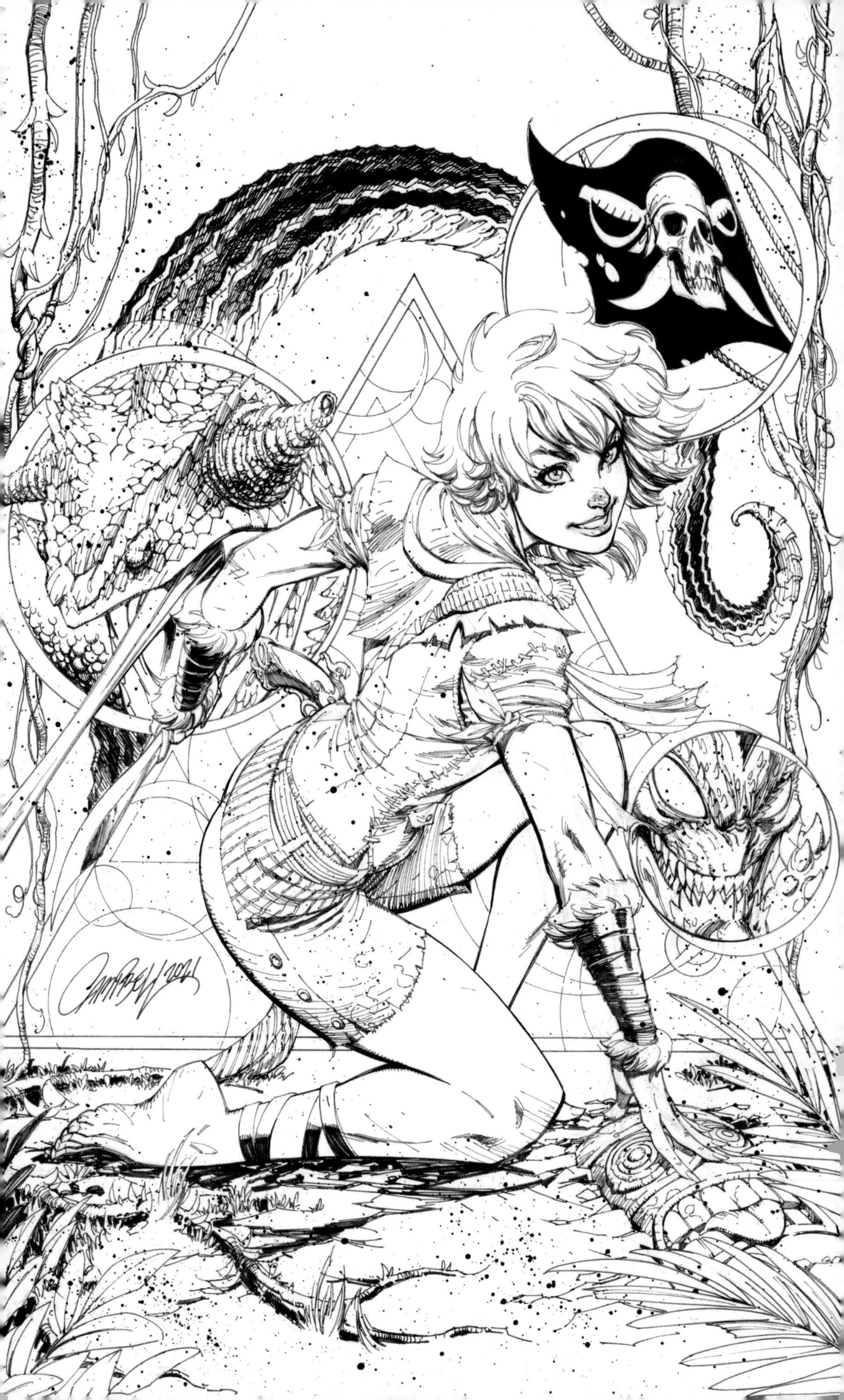

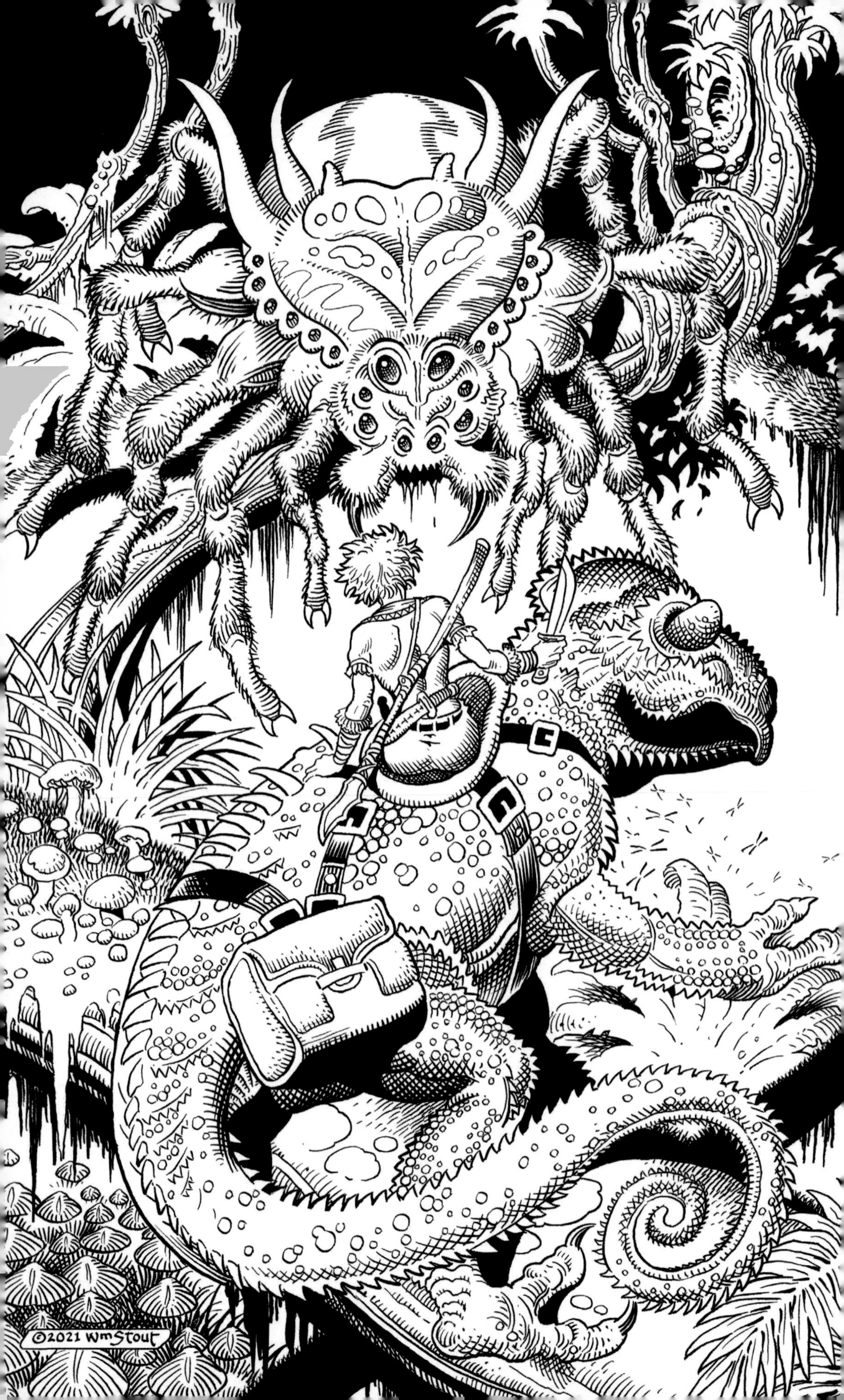
©2021 Wm Stout

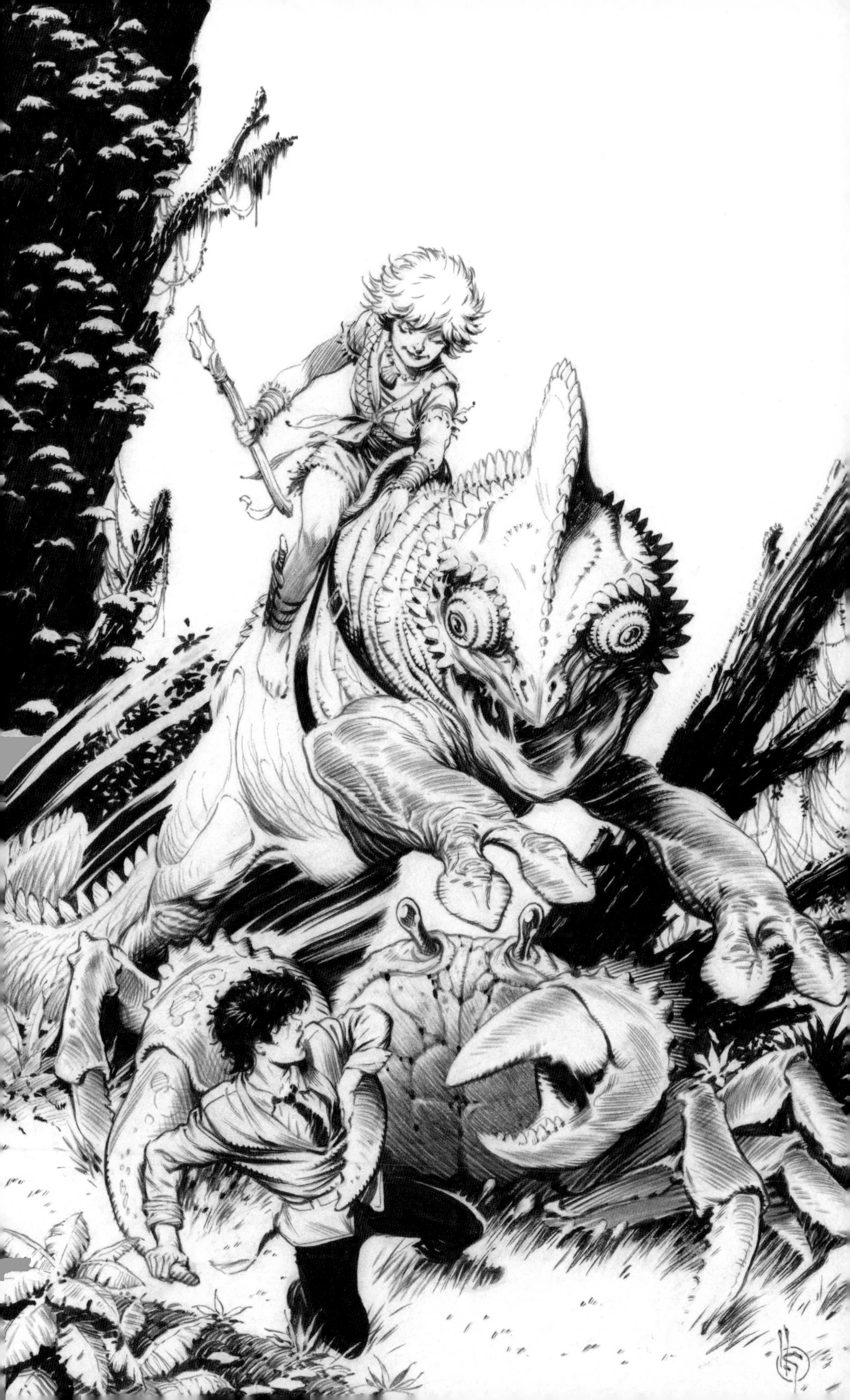

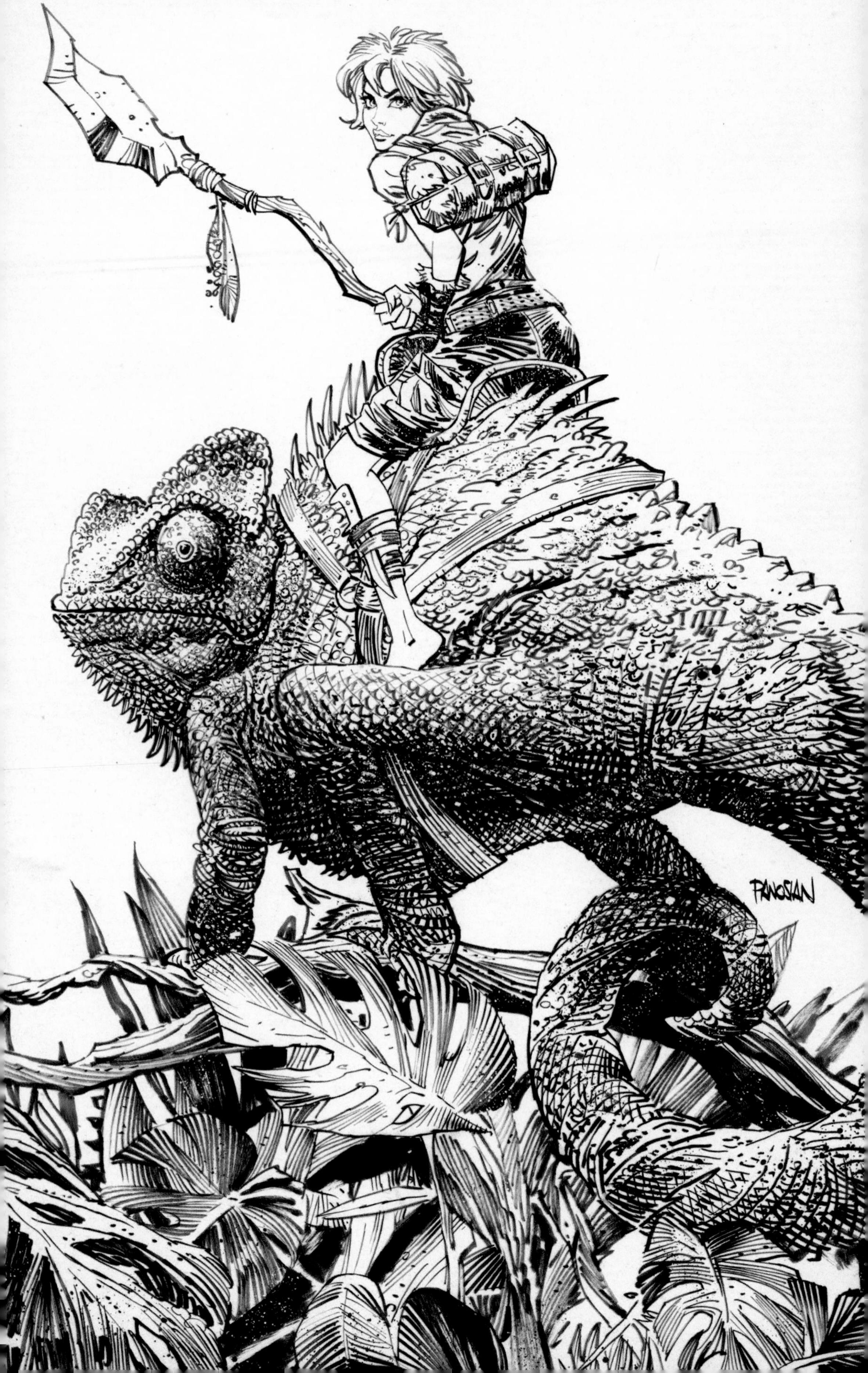
PANOSIAN

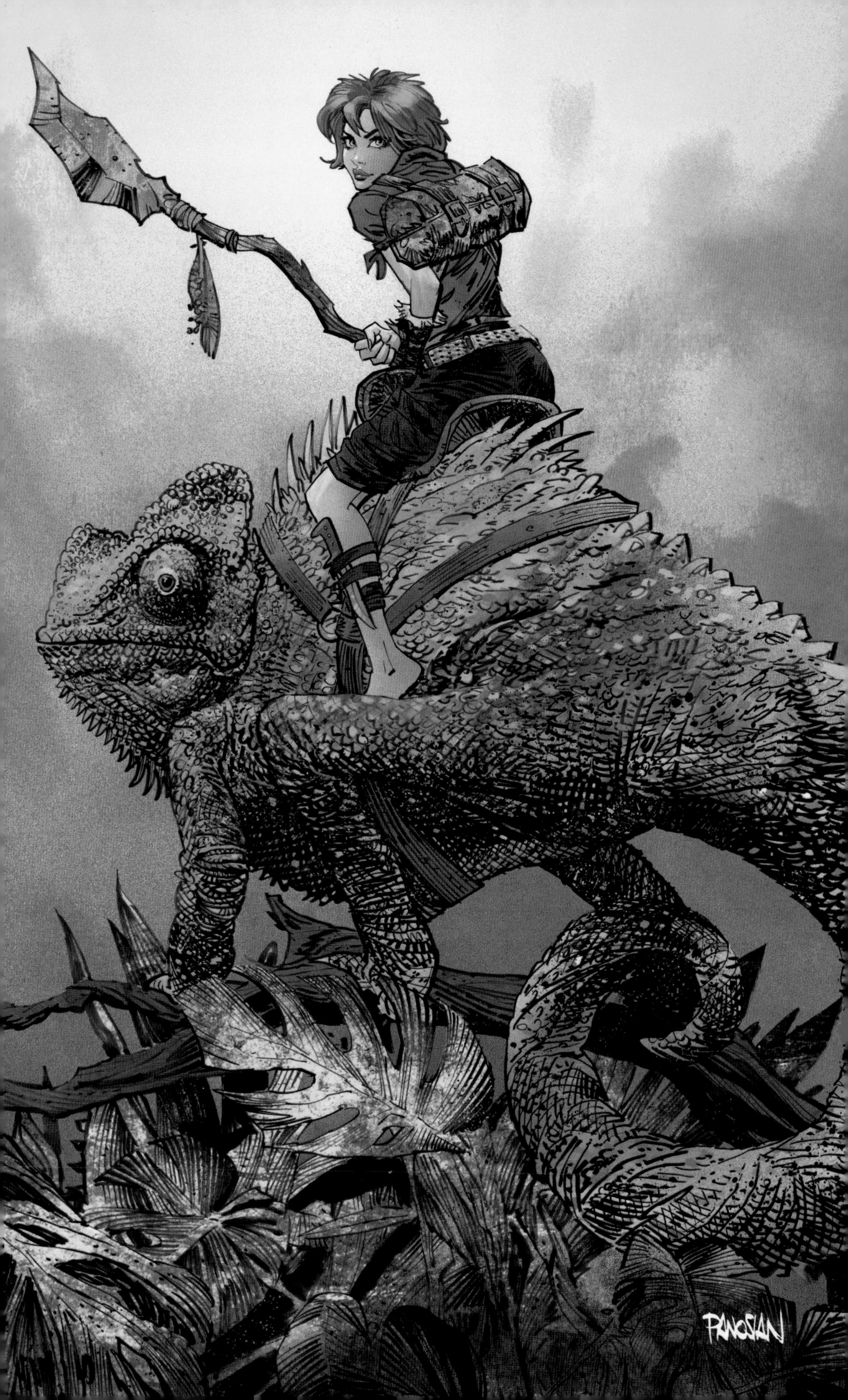
PANOSIAN

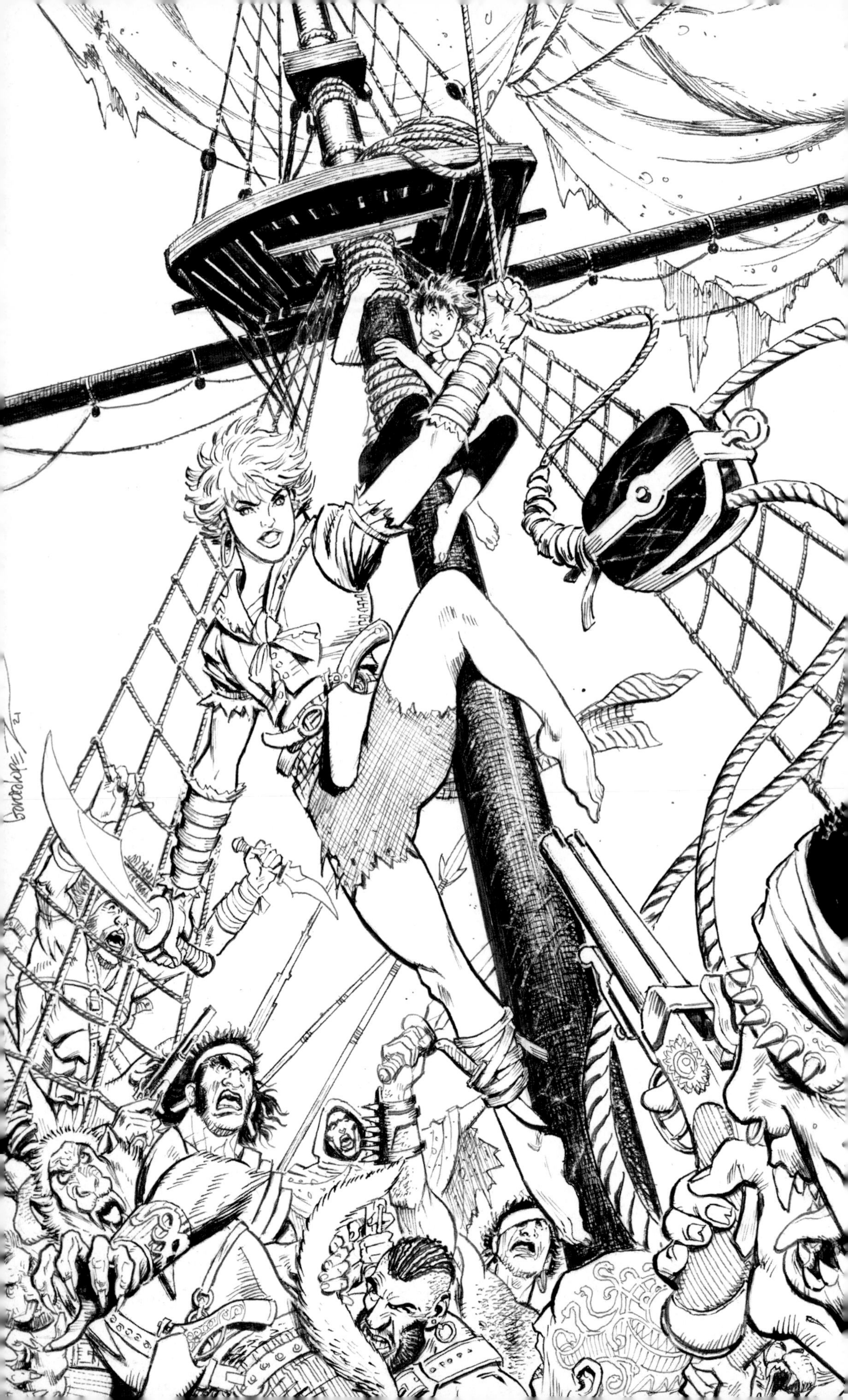

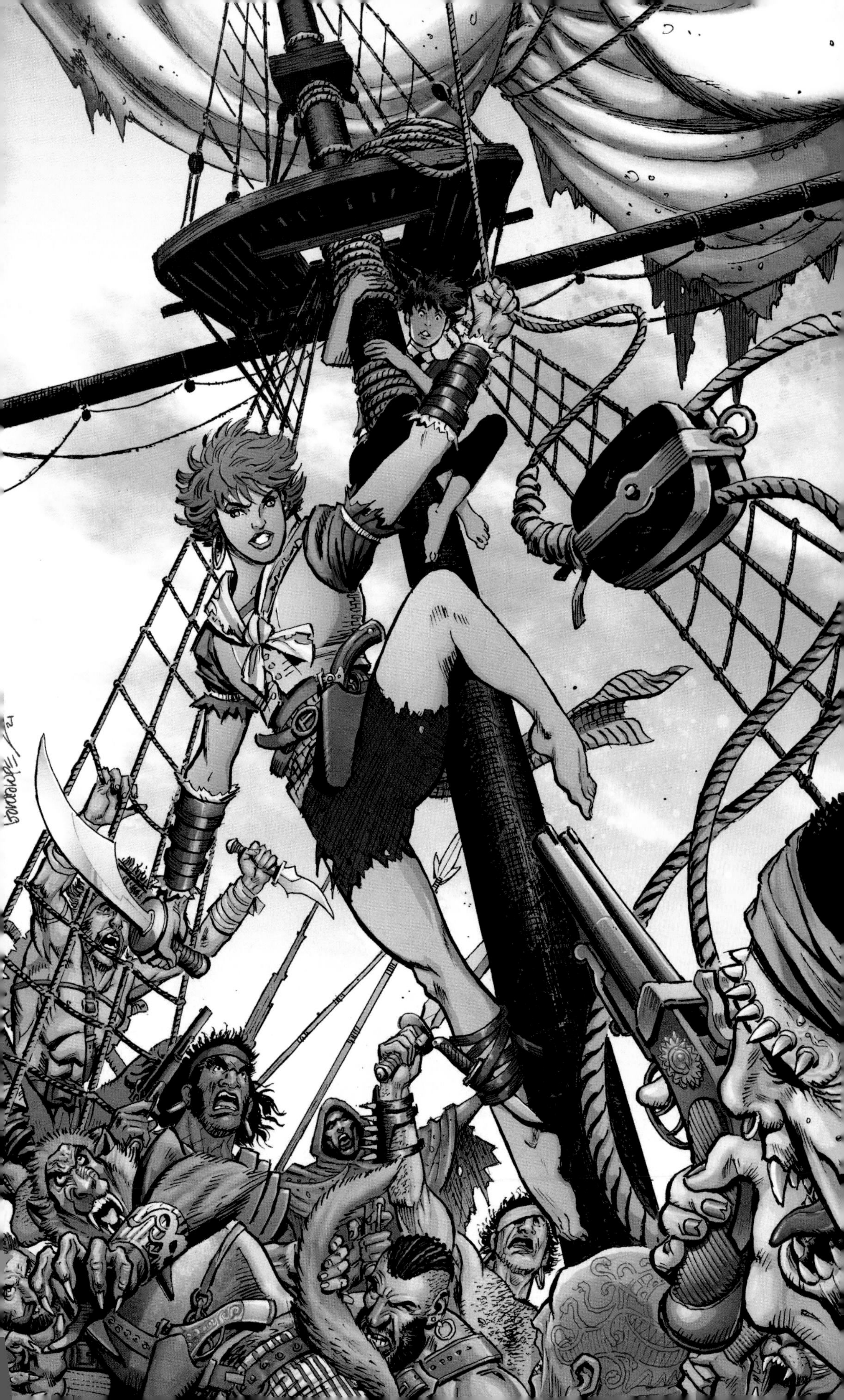

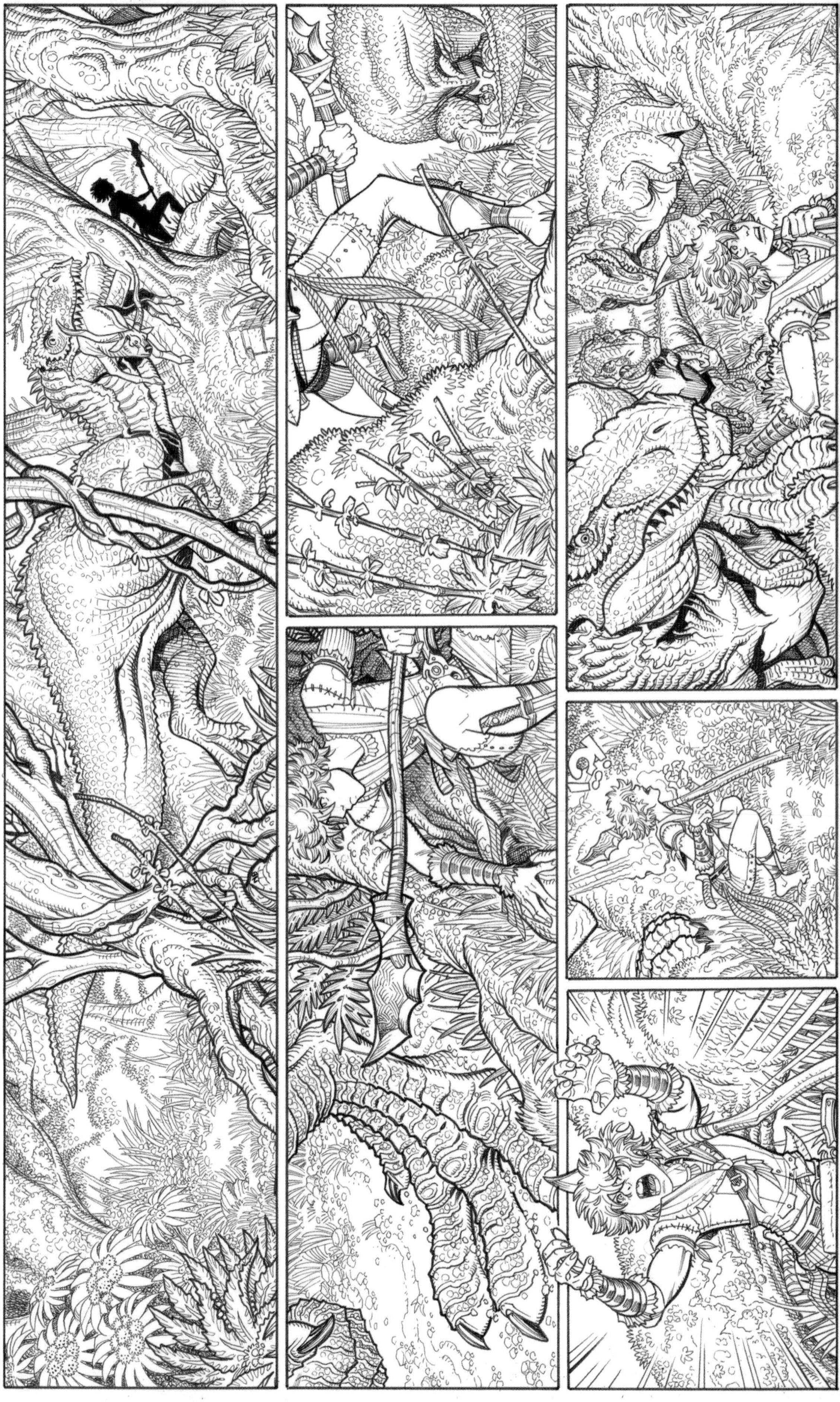

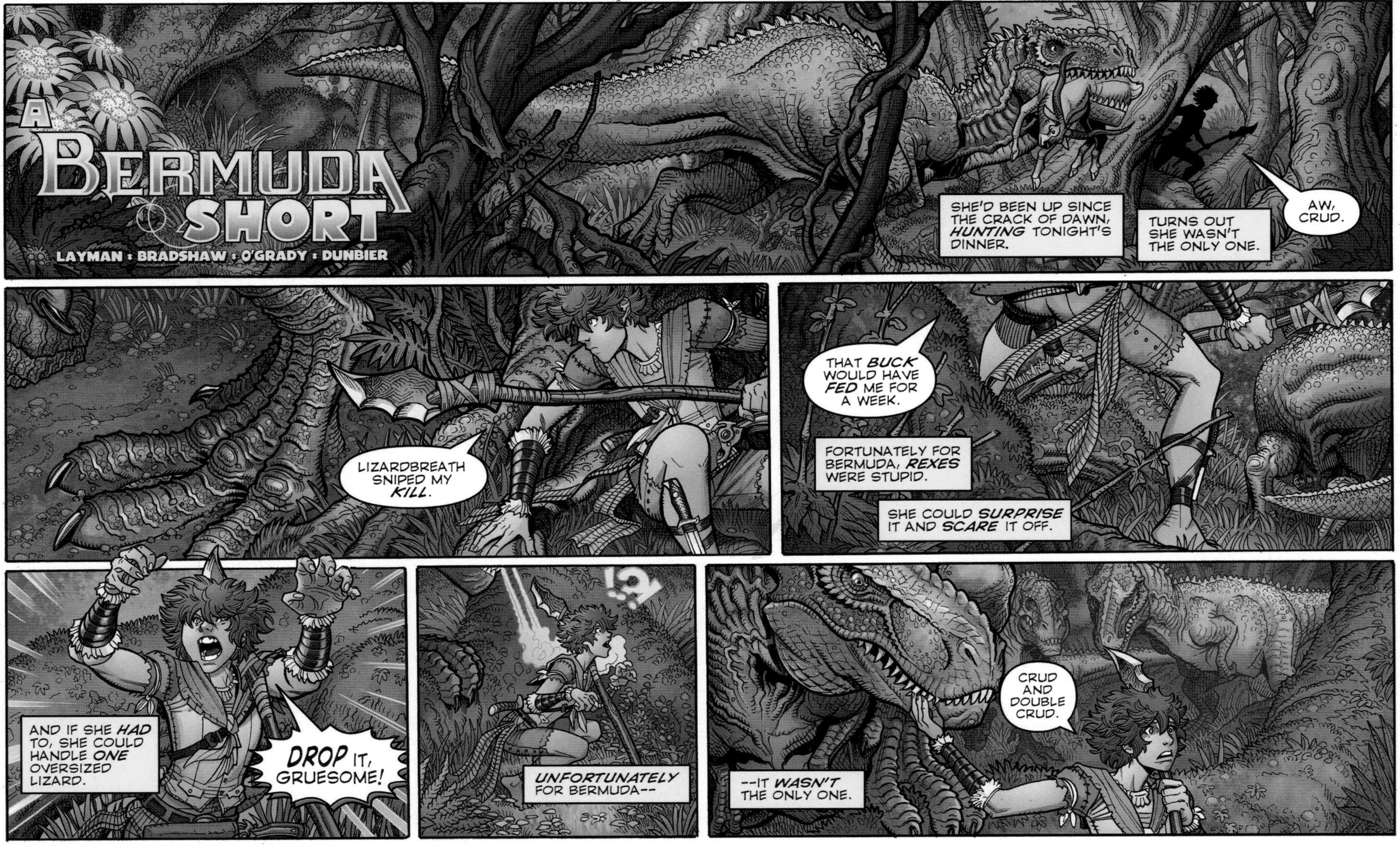

A BERMUDA SHORT
LAYMAN : BRADSHAW : O'GRADY : DUNBIER
SHE'D BEEN UP SINCE THE CRACK OF DAWN, HUNTING TONIGHT'S DINNER.
TURNS OUT SHE WASN'T THE ONLY ONE.
AW, CRUD.
LIZARDBREATH SNIPED MY KILL.
THAT BUCK WOULD HAVE FED ME FOR A WEEK.
FORTUNATELY FOR BERMUDA, REXES WERE STUPID.
SHE COULD SURPRISE IT AND SCARE IT OFF.
AND IF SHE HAD TO, SHE COULD HANDLE ONE OVERSIZED LIZARD.
DROP IT, GRUESOME!
!?
UNFORTUNATELY FOR BERMUDA--
--IT WASN'T THE ONLY ONE.
CRUD AND DOUBLE CRUD.

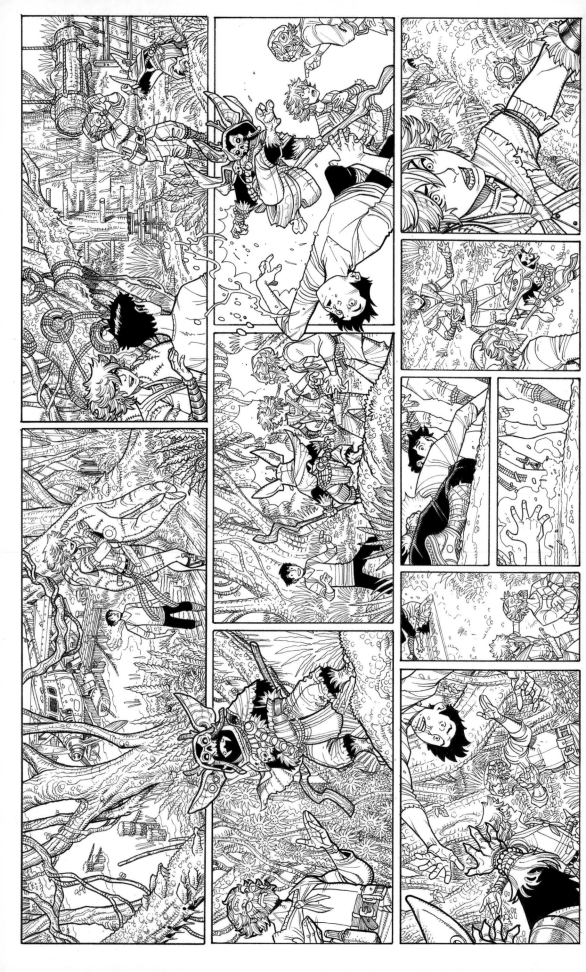

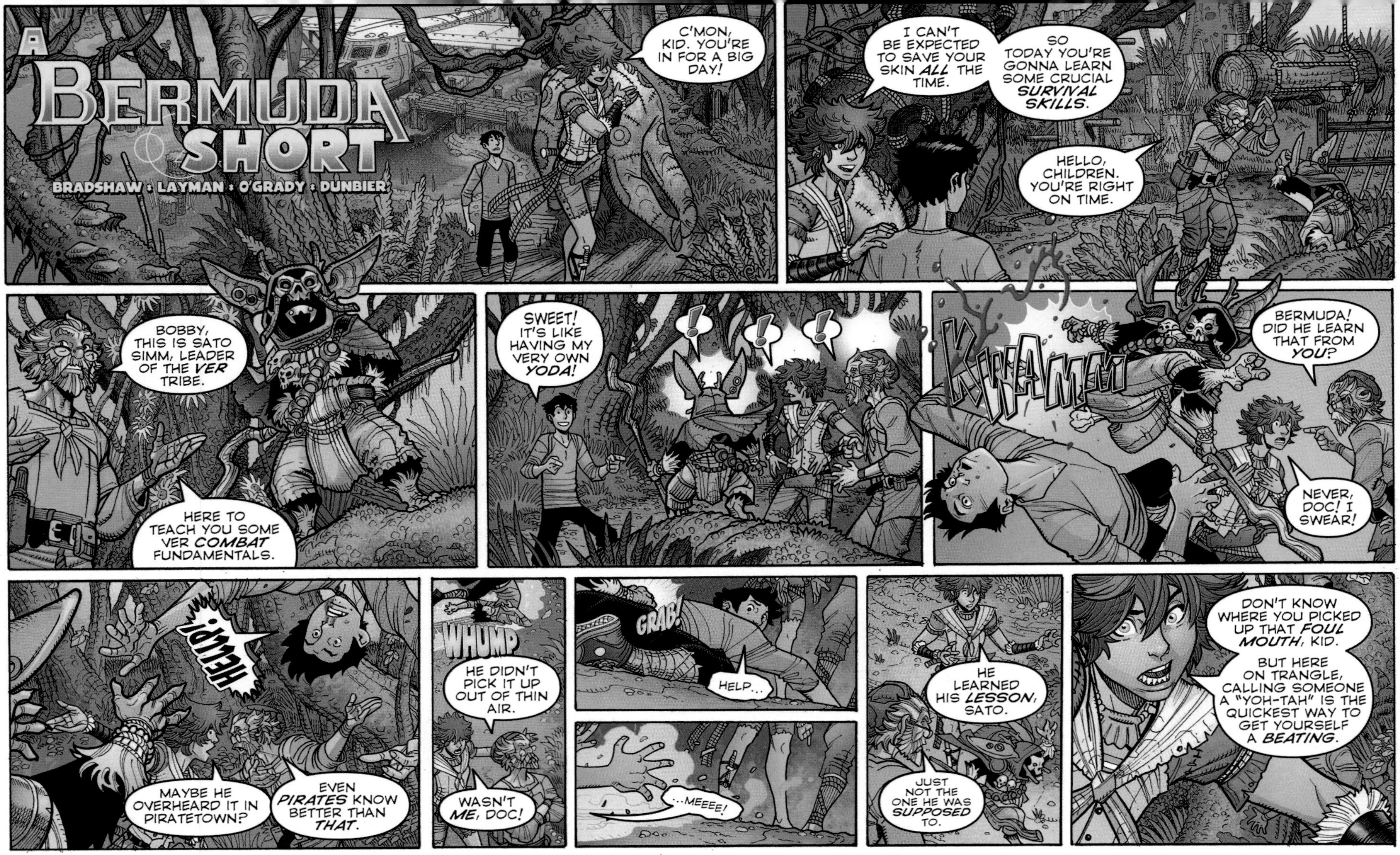
A BERMUDA SHORT
BRADSHAW : LAYMAN : O'GRADY : DUNBIER
C'MON, KID. YOU'RE IN FOR A BIG DAY!
I CAN'T BE EXPECTED TO SAVE YOUR SKIN ALL THE TIME.
SO TODAY YOU'RE GONNA LEARN SOME CRUCIAL SURVIVAL SKILLS.
HELLO, CHILDREN. YOU'RE RIGHT ON TIME.
BOBBY, THIS IS SATO SIMM, LEADER OF THE VER TRIBE.
HERE TO TEACH YOU SOME VER COMBAT FUNDAMENTALS.
SWEET! IT'S LIKE HAVING MY VERY OWN YODA!
!
!
!
KWAMM
BERMUDA! DID HE LEARN THAT FROM YOU?
NEVER, DOC! I SWEAR!
HELLP!
MAYBE HE OVERHEARD IT IN PIRATETOWN?
EVEN PIRATES KNOW BETTER THAN THAT.
WHUMP
HE DIDN'T PICK IT UP OUT OF THIN AIR.
WASN'T ME, DOC!
GRAB!
HELP...
...MEEEE!
HE LEARNED HIS LESSON, SATO.
JUST NOT THE ONE HE WAS SUPPOSED TO.
DON'T KNOW WHERE YOU PICKED UP THAT FOUL MOUTH, KID.
BUT HERE ON TRANGLE, CALLING SOMEONE A "YOH-TAH" IS THE QUICKEST WAY TO GET YOURSELF A BEATING.

Bermuda

I grew up on the coast where our Spring/Summer/Falls were spent exploring the beach, scavenging the surrounding woods, and having months-long adventures in the wild. Out of an army of cousins my age, all girls (whom I feel are like sisters really), my brother and I were the only boys. Bermuda was influenced in some small way by all of them. Her attitude, sense of adventure, bravery—there's a bit of love from each of them you'll find in her. I settled on a design that kinda reminded me of what they all looked like at the end of vacation before school— sporting whatever was salvaged, well worn, stitched together and comfortable, wild-haired and leathery barefoot, as our sneakers rotted off by mid-July.

- NB

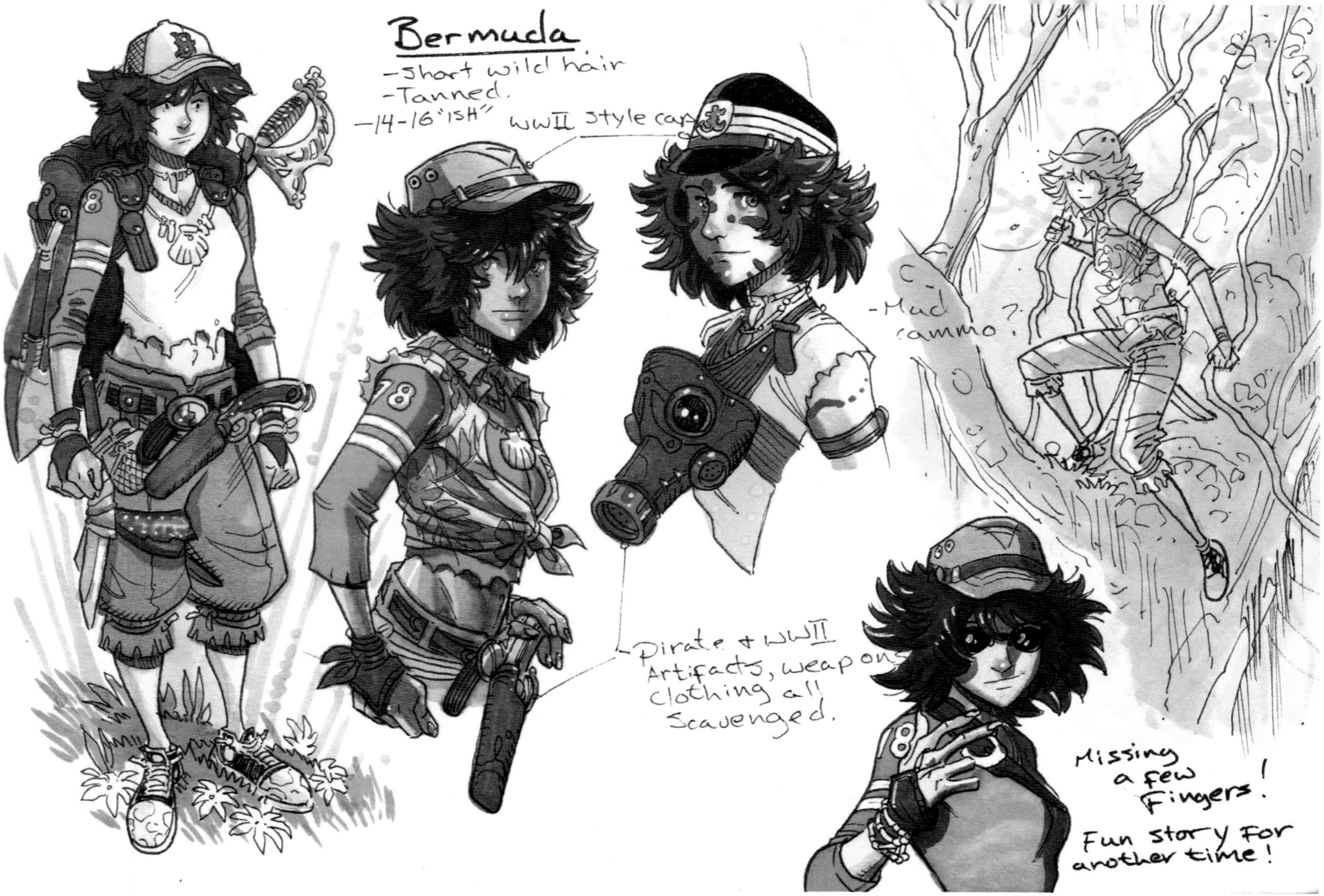
Bermuda
-Short wild hair
-Tanned.
-14-16"ISH"
WWII Style cap
-Mud cammo?
Pirate + WWII Artifacts, weapons clothing all Scavenged.
Missing a few Fingers!
Fun story for another time!

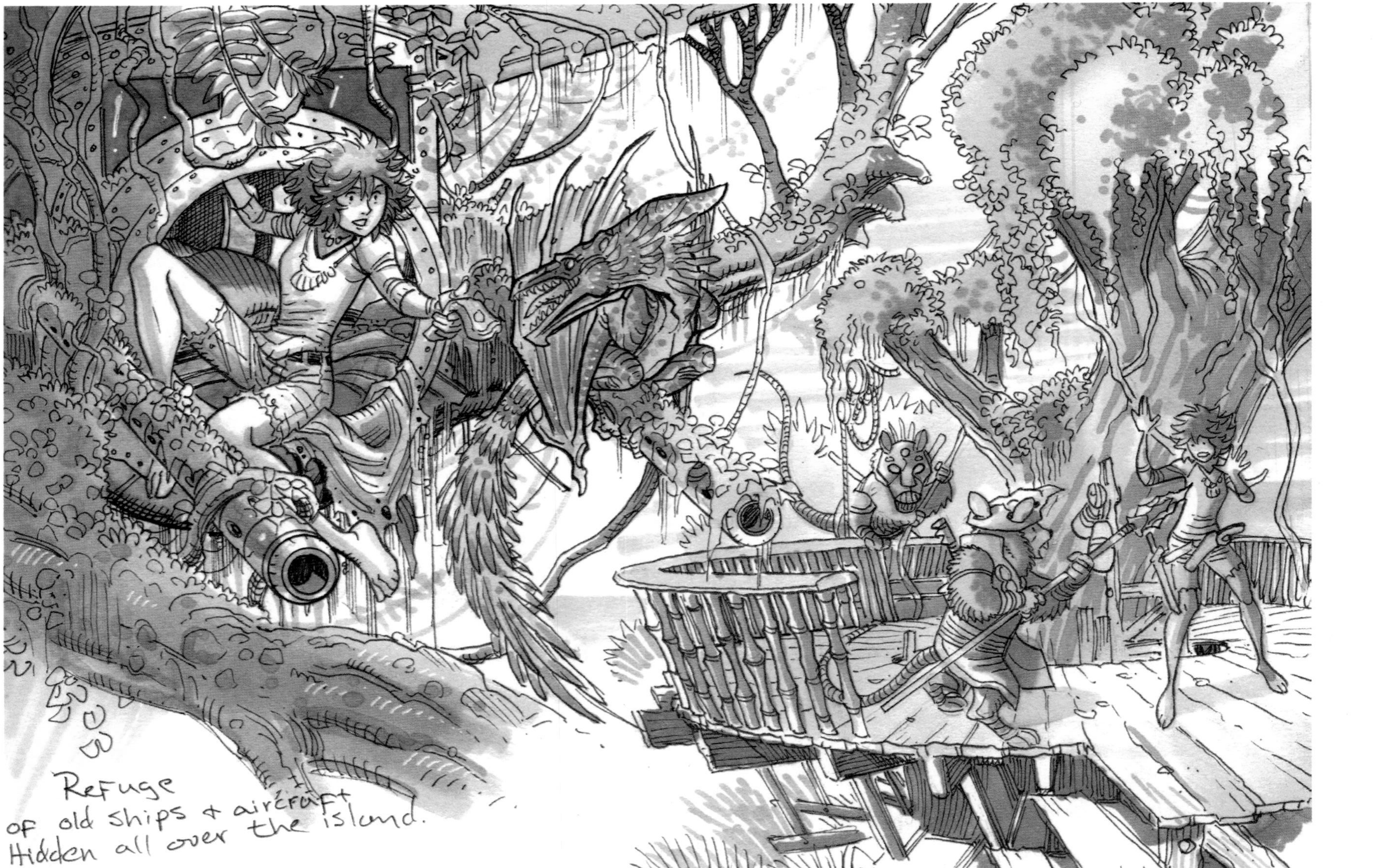
Refuge
of old ships & aircraft
Hidden all over the island.

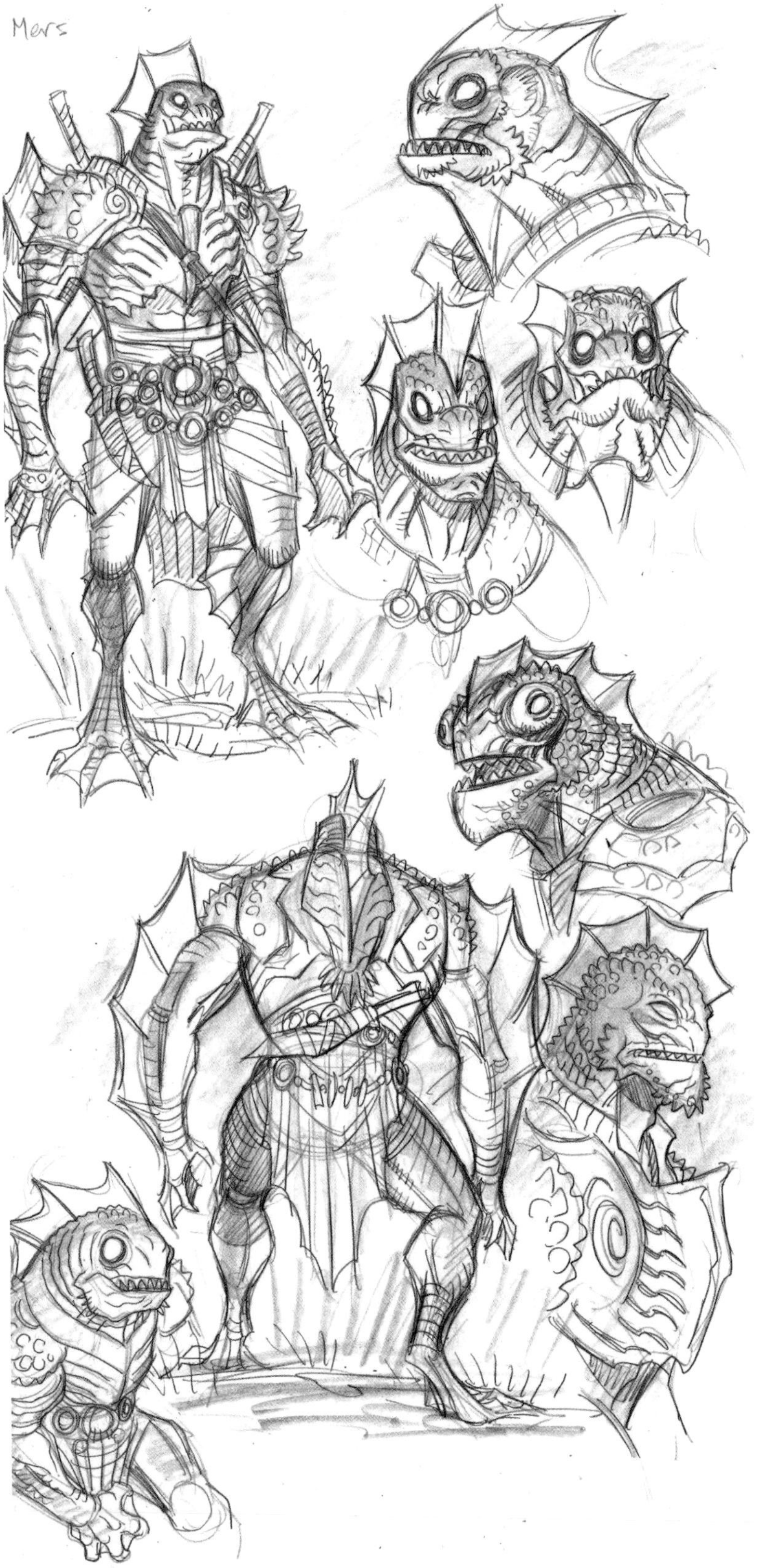
Mers

I didn't want to settle on one look for the "Mers." There are scout Mers In issue one that look more "un-evolved," soldier Mers you see more of in Issues 2-4 that are "leaner and meaner." They have a more intelligent look to them. Then there's the leader who I just wanted to look evil and deadly. I hope a few of them survive the story. I'd like to play around with their designs next arc.

The “Vers” were my favorites to design. They’re like little adept killer jungle vermin. I just wanted to have them be quick and agile. I was attempting to avoid cute and veered more for small but intimidating. They’re tree gliders, which make them fun jungle fighters. I can’t wait to tell an origin story with Bermuda just so we can introduce you more to the Ver tribes.

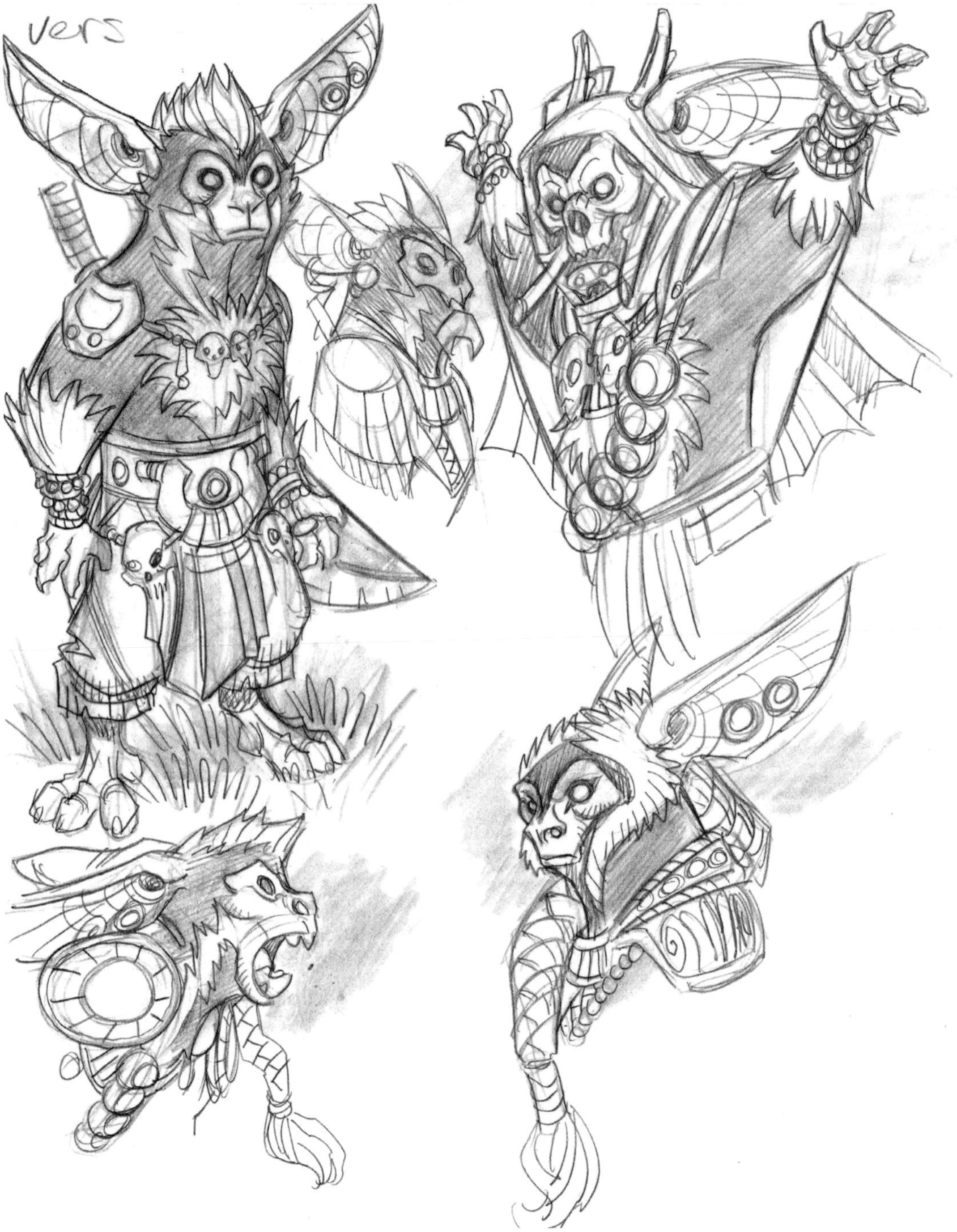
Vers

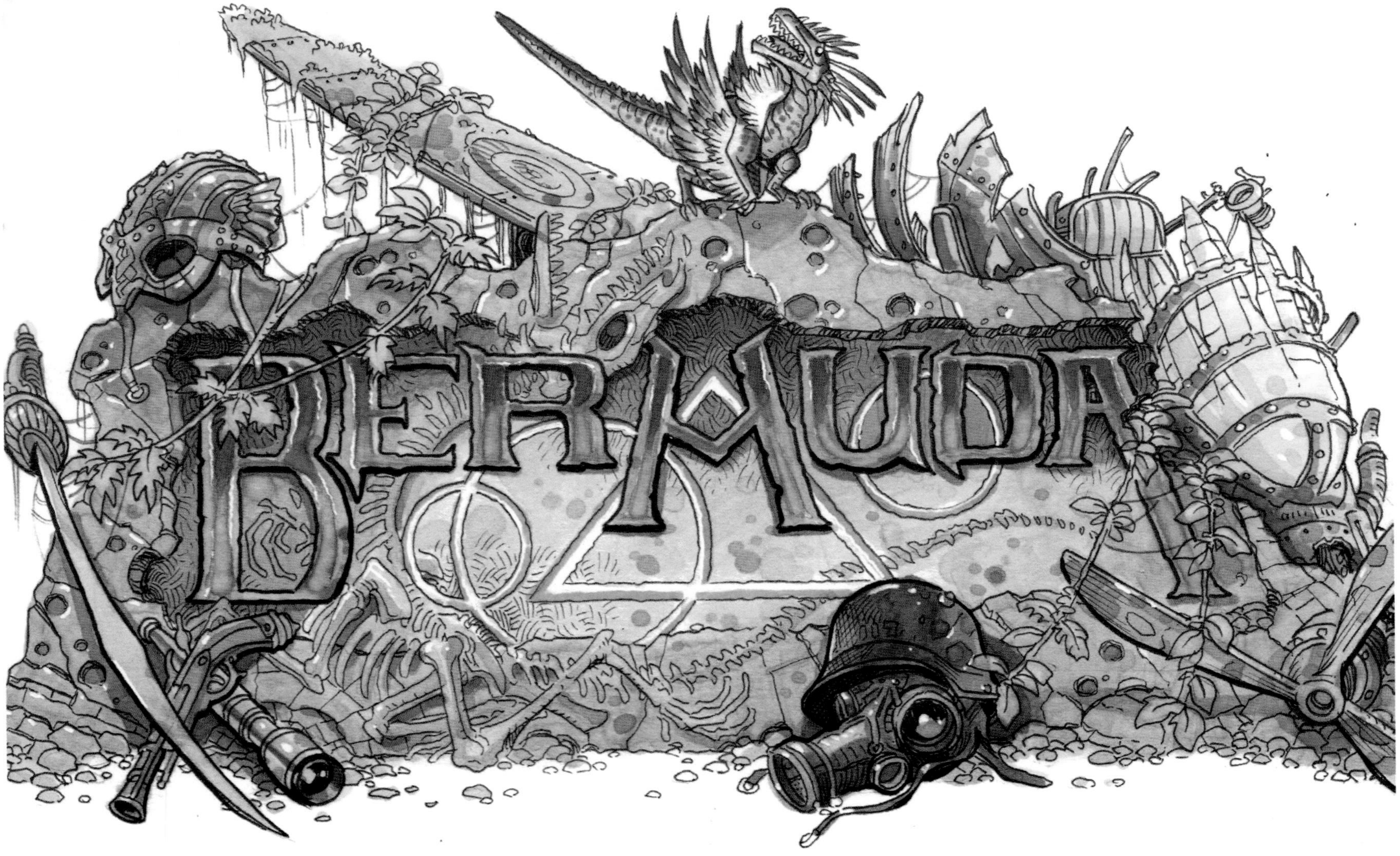
BERMUDA

ALL BLEED ART MUST EXTEND TO SOLID LINE

Book Bermuda Issue Story Page # 12 Artist(s)

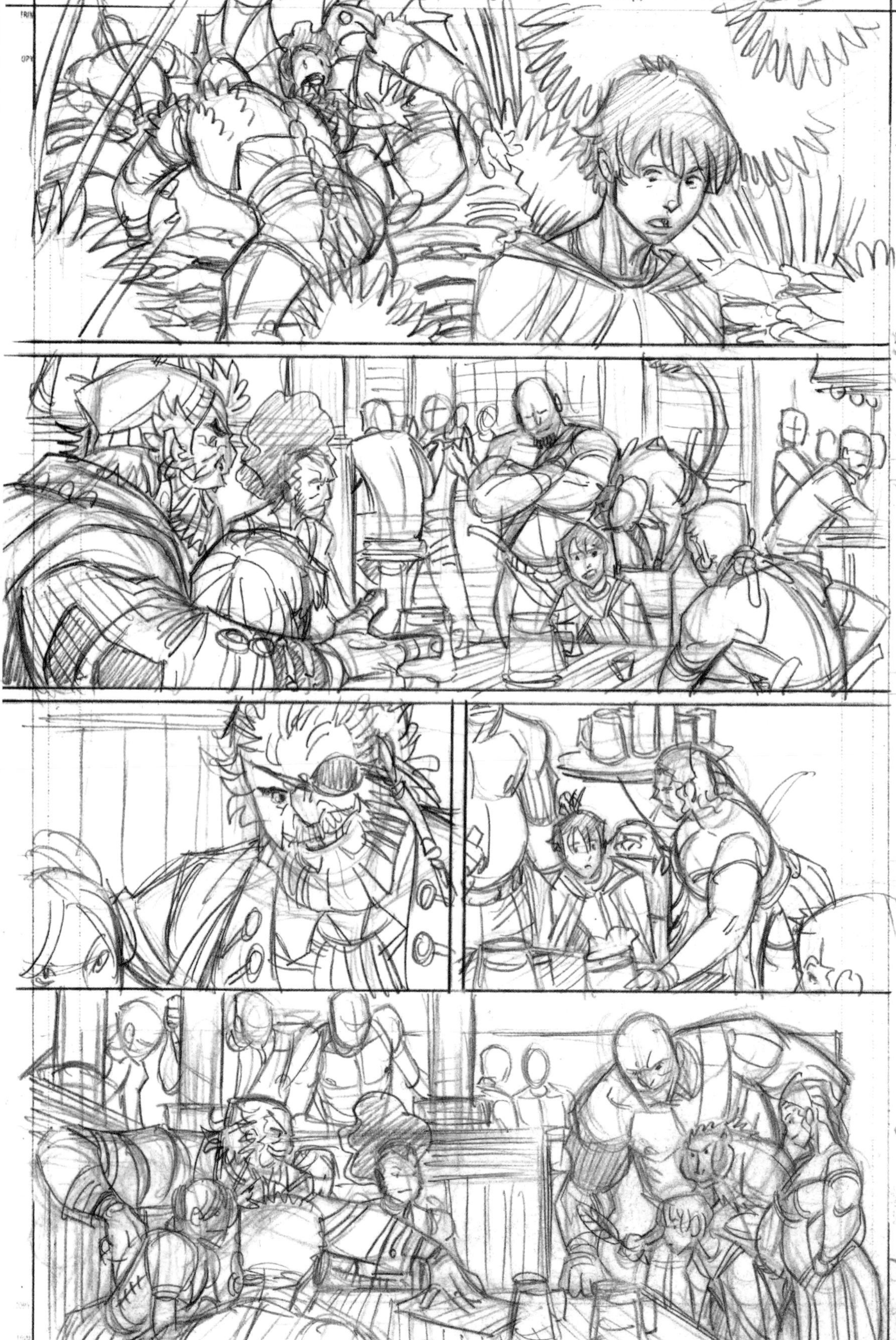

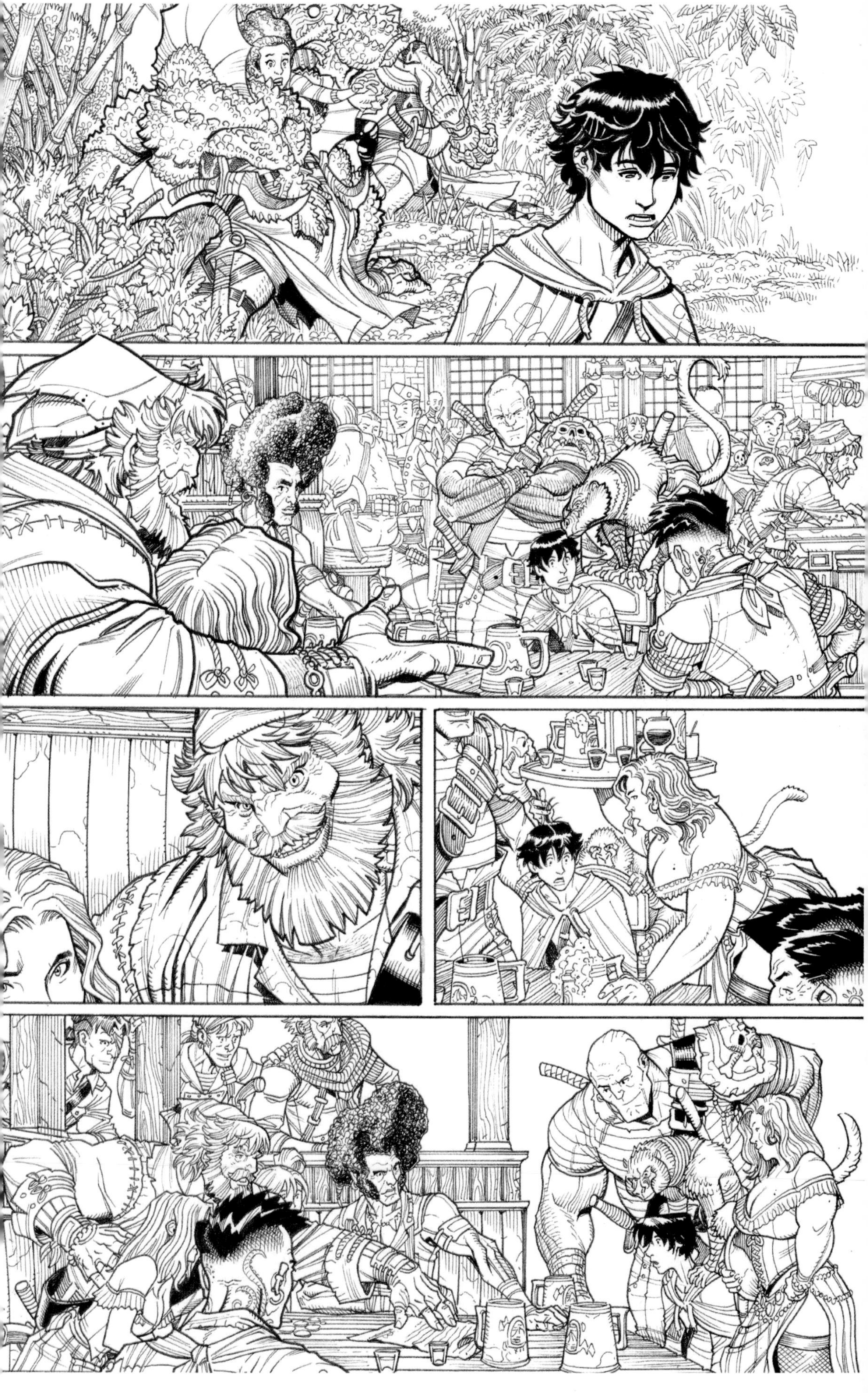

Book Bermuda Issue #2 Story Page # 13 Artist(s)

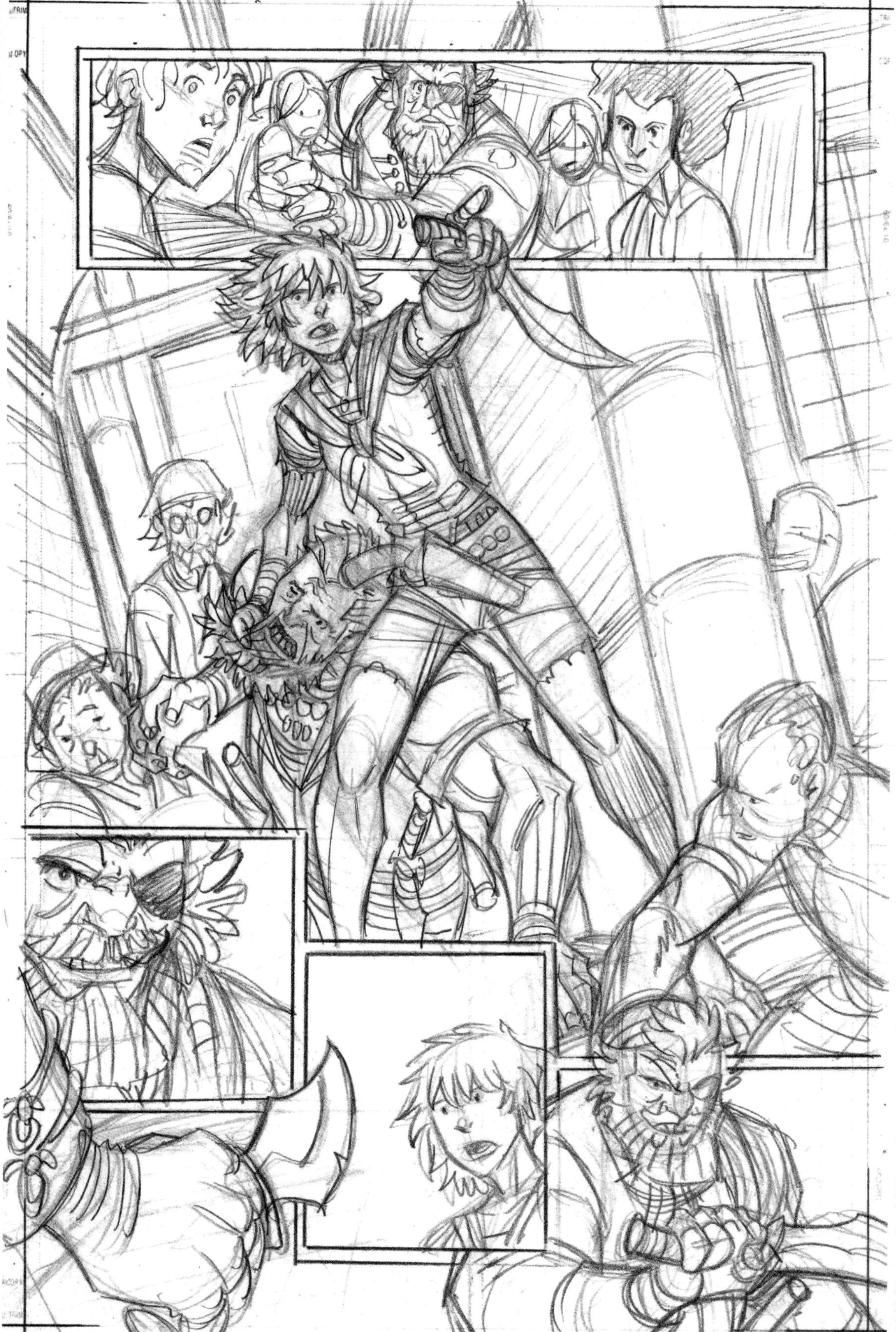

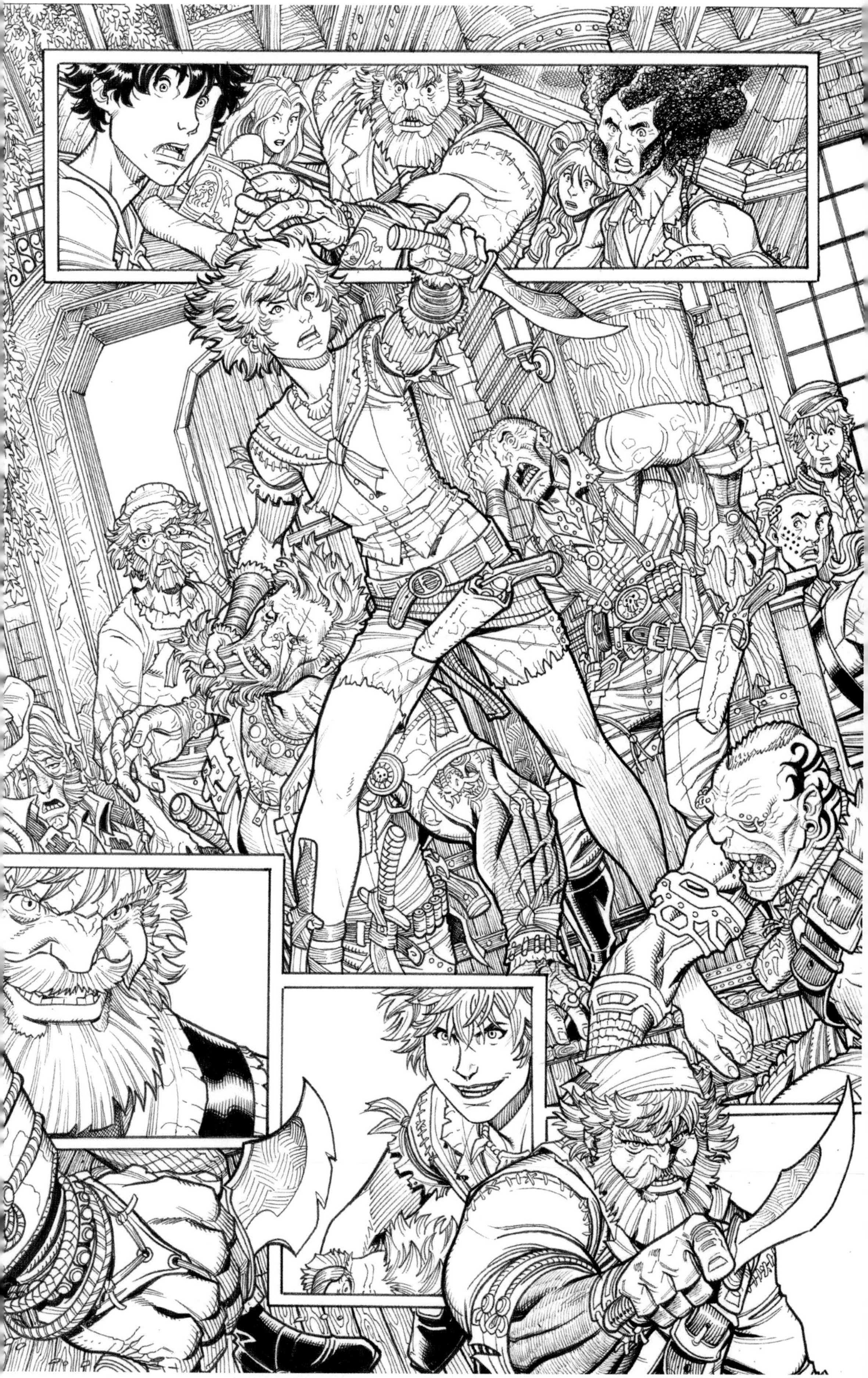

Book Bermuda Issue 3 Story Page # 1 Artist(s) Nick R

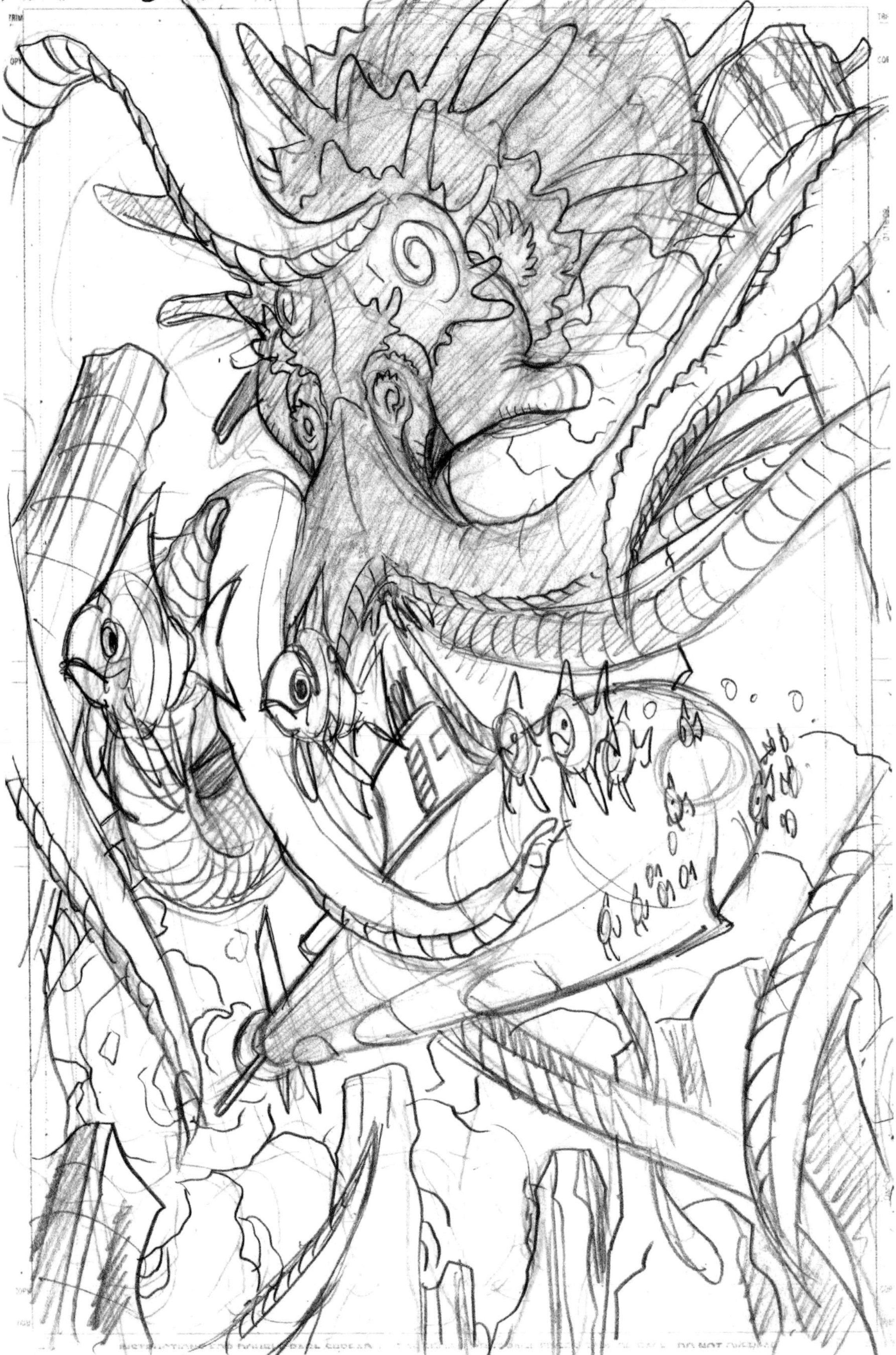

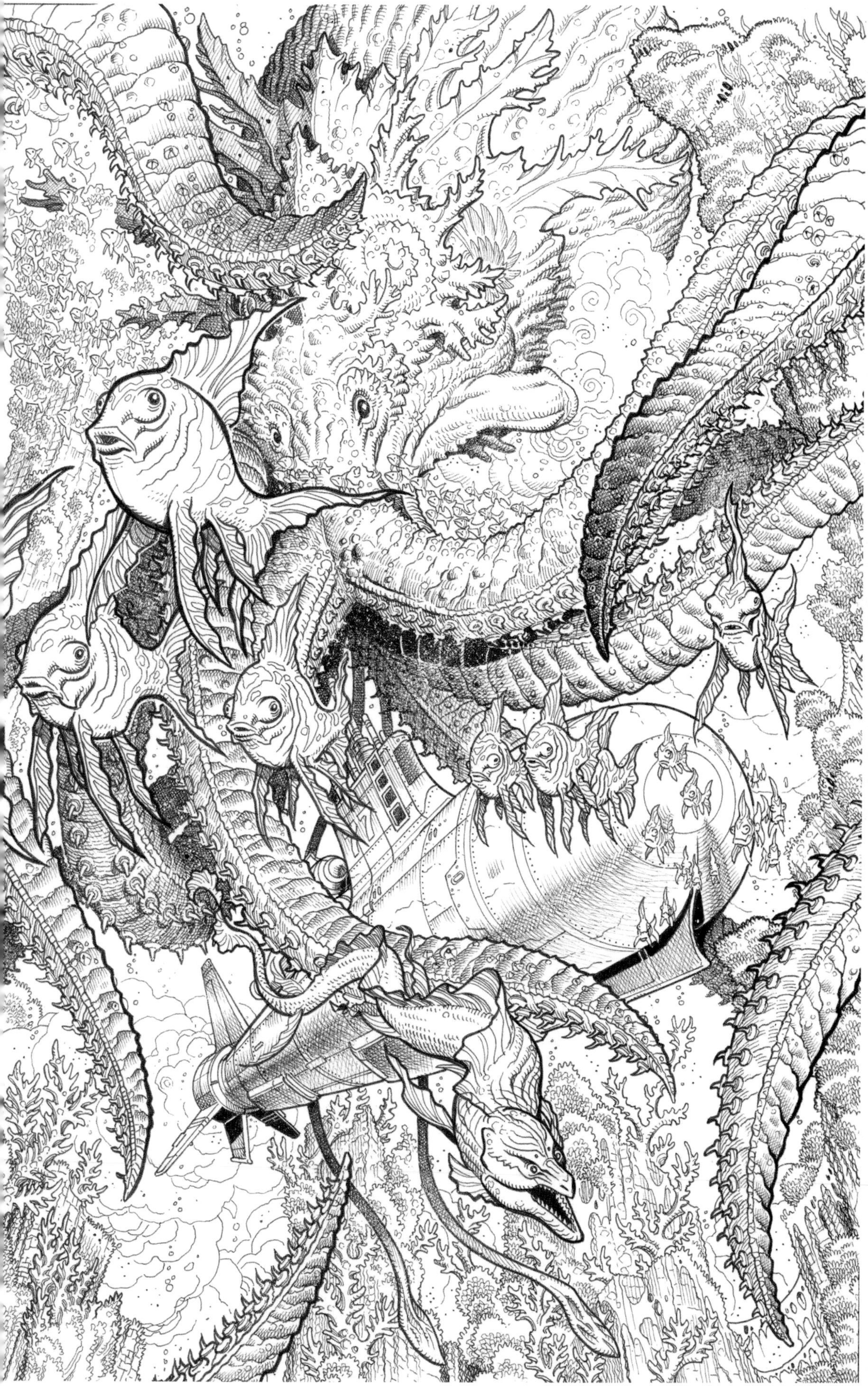

Book Bermuda Issue 4 Story Page # 10 Artist(s)

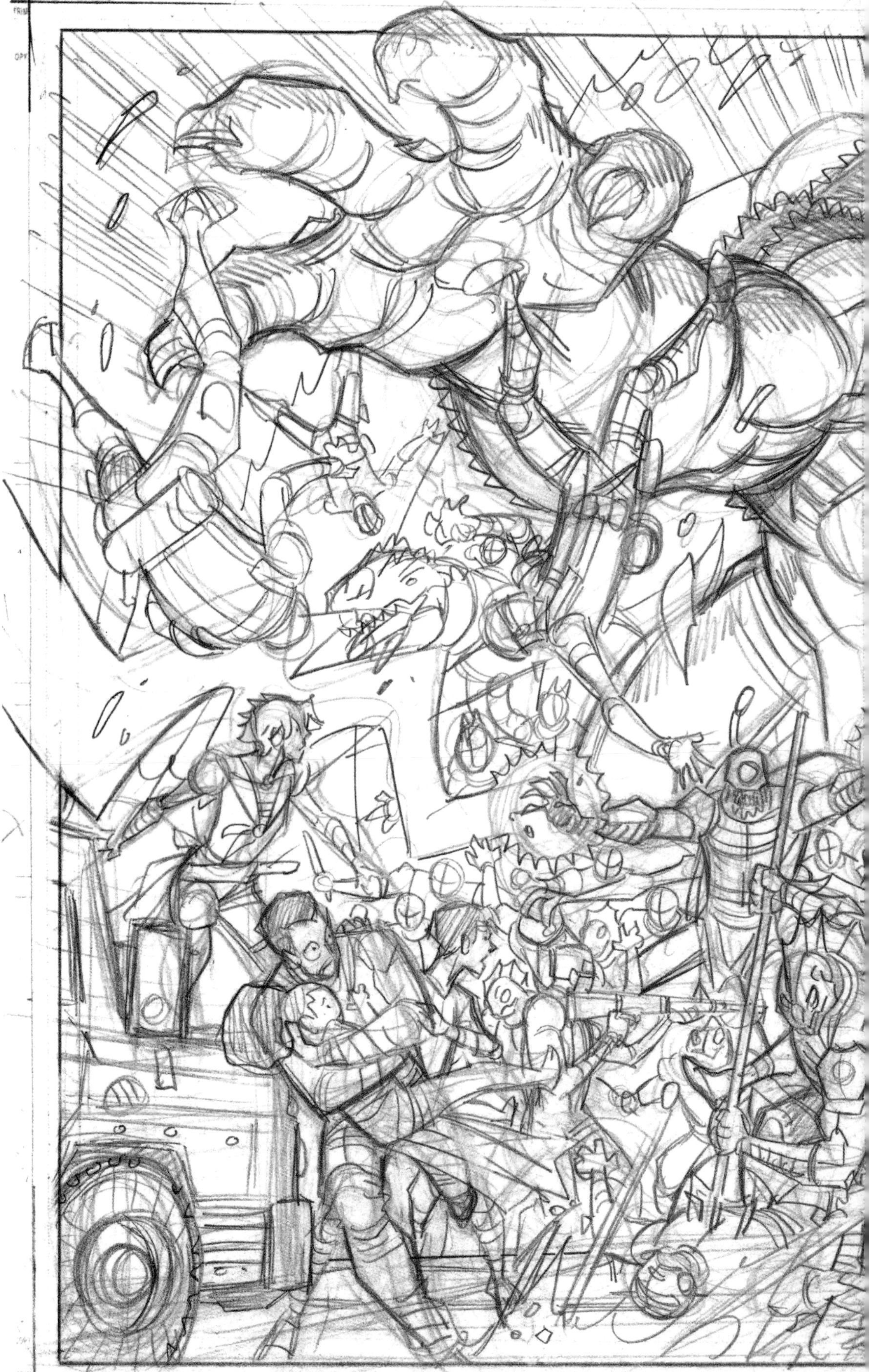

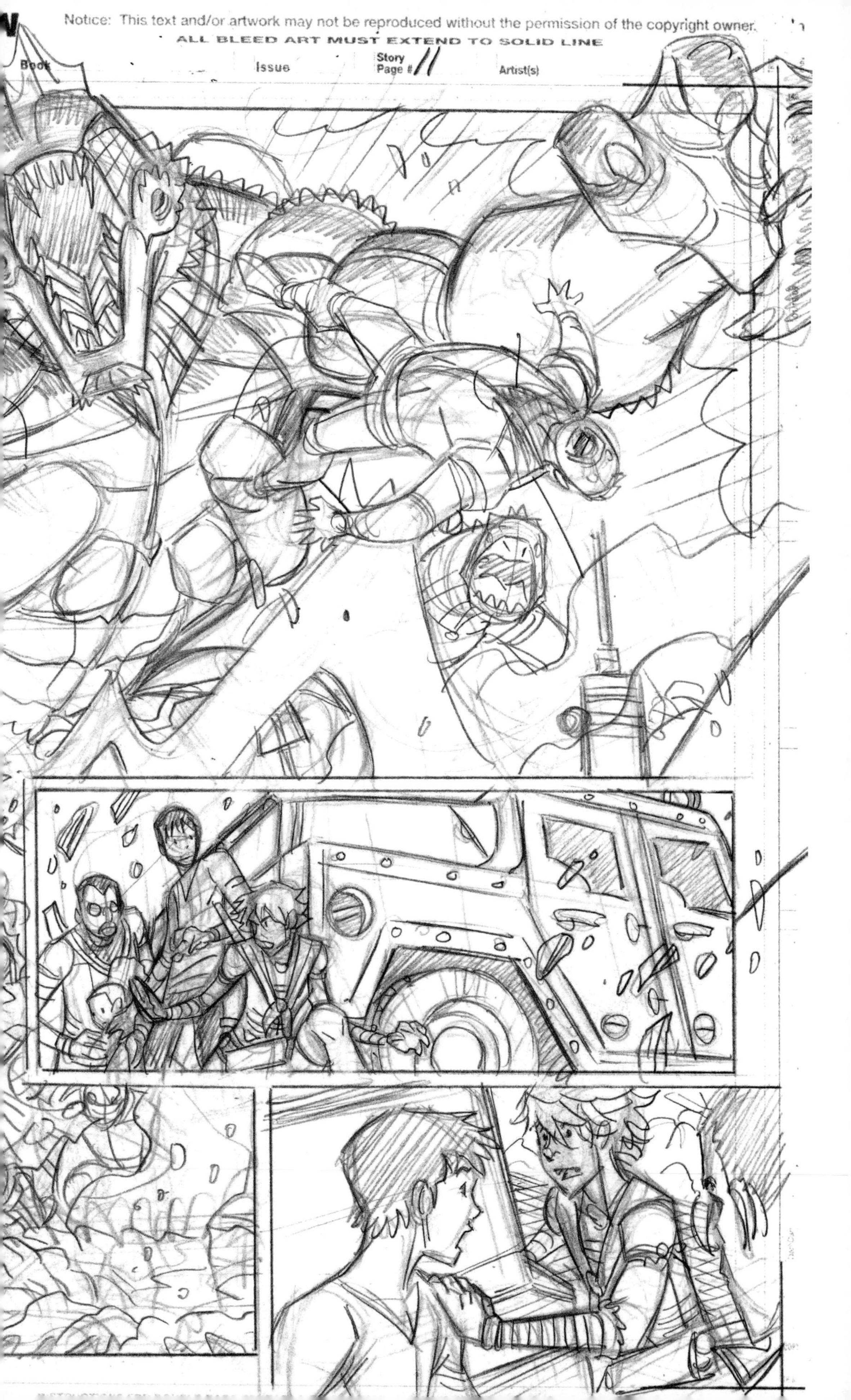

Notice: This text and/or artwork may not be reproduced without the permission of the copyright owner.
ALL BLEED ART MUST EXTEND TO SOLID LINE
Book
Issue
Story Page # 11
Artist(s)

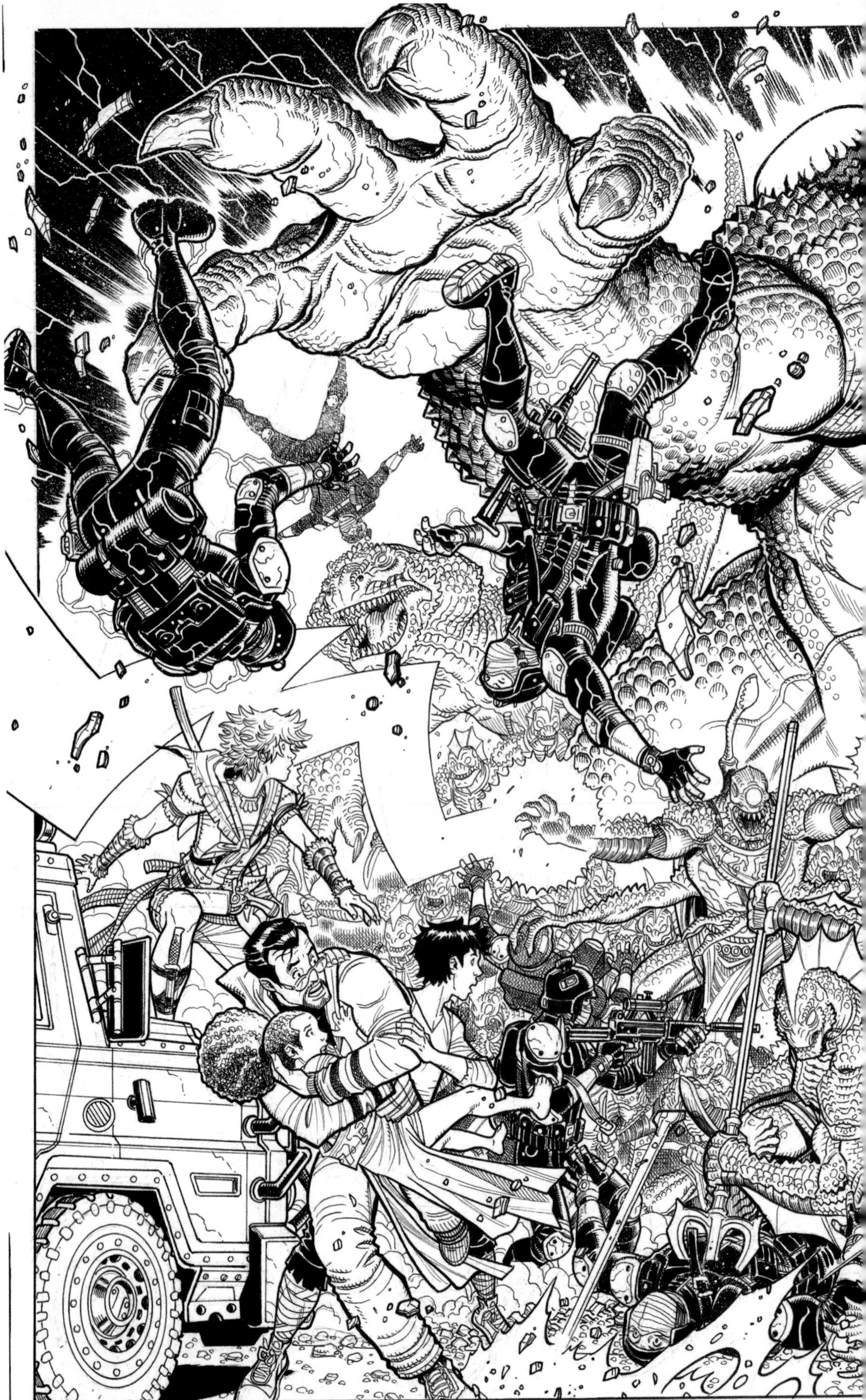

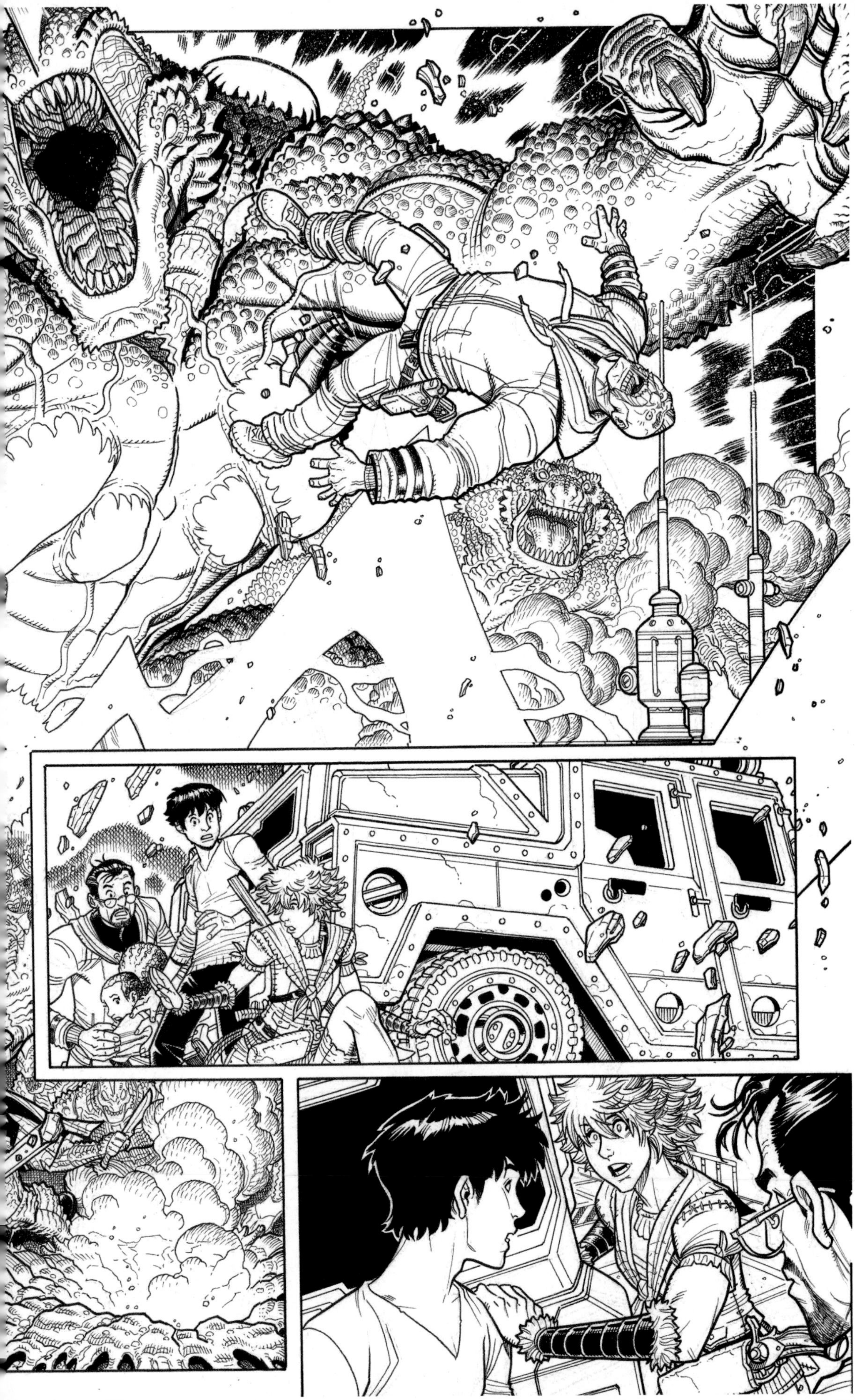

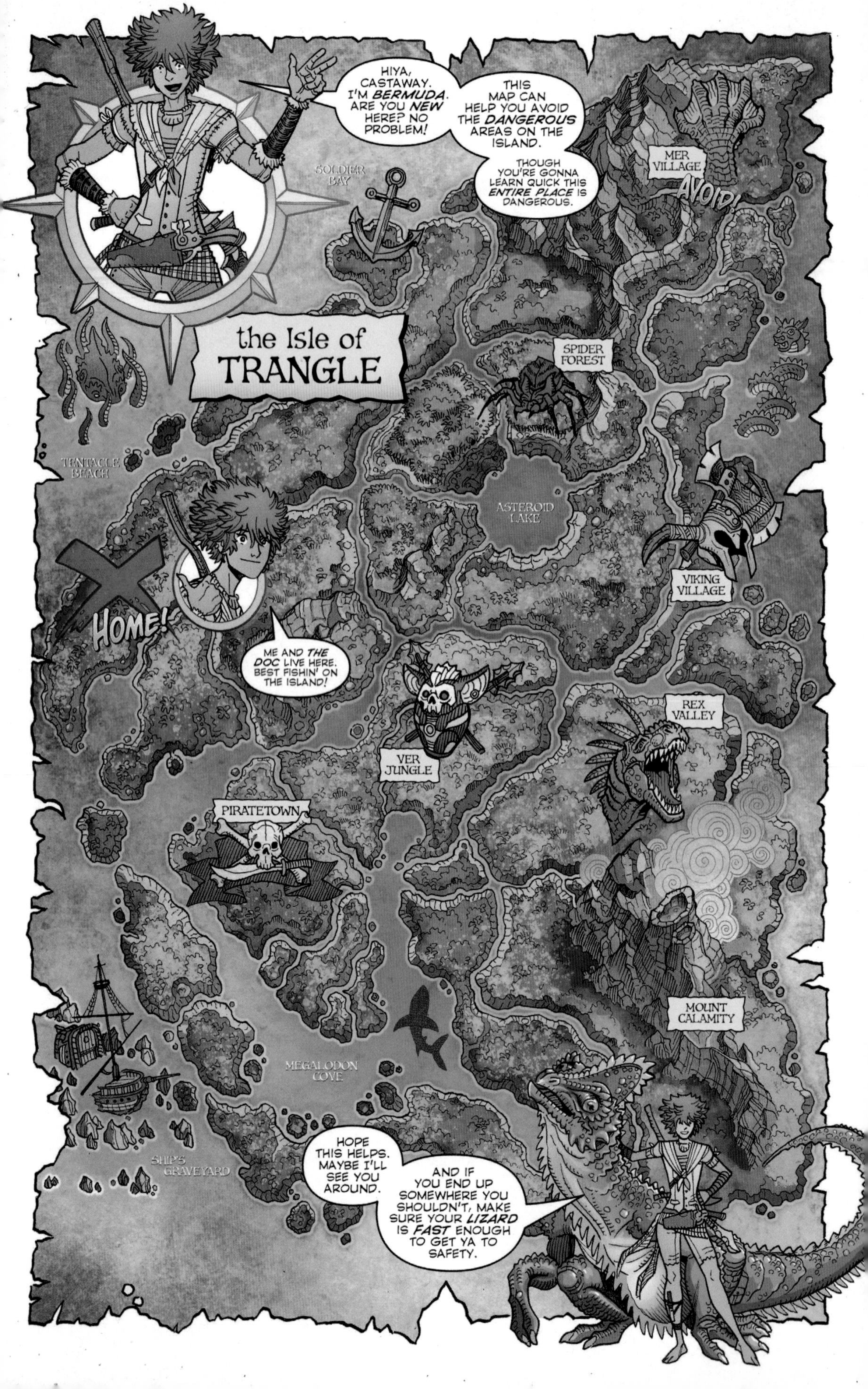

HIYA, CASTAWAY. I'M *BERMUDA*. ARE YOU *NEW* HERE? NO PROBLEM!
THIS MAP CAN HELP YOU AVOID THE *DANGEROUS* AREAS ON THE ISLAND.
THOUGH YOU'RE GONNA LEARN QUICK THIS *ENTIRE PLACE* IS DANGEROUS.
SOLDIER BAY
MER VILLAGE
AVOID!
the Isle of TRANGLE
SPIDER FOREST
TENTACLE BEACH
ASTEROID LAKE
VIKING VILLAGE
HOME!
ME AND *THE DOC* LIVE HERE. BEST FISHIN' ON THE ISLAND!
REX VALLEY
VER JUNGLE
PIRATETOWN
MOUNT CALAMITY
MEGALODON COVE
SHIPS GRAVEYARD
HOPE THIS HELPS. MAYBE I'LL SEE YOU AROUND.
AND IF YOU END UP SOMEWHERE YOU SHOULDN'T, MAKE SURE YOUR *LIZARD* IS *FAST* ENOUGH TO GET YA TO SAFETY.